The Interplanetary
Adventures of Dr Kinney

The Interplanetary Adventures of Dr Kinney

The Lord of Death • The Queen of Life
The Devolutionist • The Emancipatrix

Homer Eon Flint

LEONAUR

The Interplanetary Adventures of Dr Kinney: The Lord of Death,
The Queen of Life, The Devolutionist & The Emancipatrix
by Homer Eon Flint

Leonaur is an imprint of Oakpast Ltd

ISBN: 978-1-84677-558-1 (hardcover)
ISBN: 978-1-84677-557-4 (softcover)

http://www.leonaur.com

Publisher's Notes

The opinions expressed in this book are those of the author
and are not necessarily those of the publisher.

Contents

The Lord of Death

PART 1

The Discovery

1
THE SKY CUBE

The doctor, who was easily the most musical of the four men, sang in a cheerful baritone:

"The owl and the pussy-cat went to sea
In a beautiful, pea-green boat."

The geologist, who had held down the lower end of a quartet in his university days, growled an accompaniment under his breath as he blithely peeled the potatoes. Occasionally a high-pitched note or two came from the direction of the engineer; he could not spare much wind while clambering about the machinery, oil-can in hand. The architect, alone, ignored the famous tune.

"What I can't understand, Smith," he insisted, "is how you draw the electricity from the ether into this car without blasting us all to cinders."

The engineer squinted through an opal glass shutter into one of the tunnels, through which the anti-gravitation current was pouring. "If you didn't know any more about buildings than you do about machinery, Jackson," he grunted, because of his squatting position, "I'd hate to live in one of your houses!"

The architect smiled grimly. "You're living in one of 'em right now, Smith," said he; "that is, if you call this car a house."

Smith straightened up. He was an unimportant-looking man,

of medium height and build, and bearing a mild, good-humoured expression. Nobody would ever look at him twice, would ever guess that his skull concealed an unusually complete knowledge of electricity, mechanisms, and such practical matters.

"I told you yesterday, Jackson," he said, "that the air surrounding the earth is chock full of electricity. And—"

"And that the higher we go, the more juice," added the other, remembering. "As much as to say that it is the atmosphere, then, that protects the earth from the surrounding voltage."

The engineer nodded. "Occasionally it breaks through, anyhow, in the form of lightning. Now, in order to control that current, and prevent it from turning this machine, and us, into ashes, all we do is to pass the juice through a cylinder of highly compressed air, fixed in this wall. By varying the pressure and dampness within the cylinder, we can regulate the flow."

The builder nodded rapidly. "All right. But why doesn't the electricity affect the walls themselves? I thought they were made of steel."

The engineer glanced through the dead-light at the reddish disk of the Earth, hazy and indistinct at a distance of forty million miles. "It isn't steel; it's a non-magnetic alloy. Besides, there's a layer of crystalline sulphur between the alloy and the vacuum space."

"The vacuum is what keeps out the cold, isn't it?" Jackson knew, but he asked in order to learn more.

"Keeps out the sun's heat, too. The outer shell is pretty blamed hot on that side, just as hot as it is cold on the shady side." Smith seated himself beside a huge electrical machine, a rotary converter which he next indicated with a jerk of his thumb. "But you don't want to forget that the juice outside is no use to us, the way it is. We have to change it.

"It's neither positive nor negative; it's just neutral. So we separate it into two parts; and all we have to do, when we want to get away from the earth or any other magnetic-sphere, is to aim a bunch of positive current at the corresponding pole of the planet, or negative current at the other pole. Like poles repel, you know."

"Listens easy," commented Jackson. "Too easy."

"Well, it isn't exactly as simple as all that. Takes a lot of apparatus, all told," and the engineer looked about the room, his glance resting fondly on his beloved machinery.

The big room, fifty feet square, was almost filled with machines; some reached nearly to the ceiling, the same distance above. In fact, the interior of the "cube," as that form of sky-car was known, had very little waste space. The living quarters of the four men who occupied it had to be fitted in wherever there happened to be room. The architect's own berth was sandwiched in between two huge dynamos.

He was thinking hard. "I see now why you have such a lot of adjustments for those tunnels," meaning the six square tubes which opened into the ether through the six walls of the room. "You've got to point the juice pretty accurately."

"I should say so." Smith led the way to a window, and the two shaded their eyes from the lights within while they gazed at the ashy glow of Mercury, toward which they were travelling. "I've got to adjust the current so as to point exactly toward his northern half."

Smith might have added that a continual stream of repelling current was still directed toward the earth, and another toward the sun, away over to their right; both to prevent being drawn off their course.

"And how fast are we going?"

"Four or five times as fast as mother earth: between eighty and ninety miles per second. It's easy to get up speed out here, of course, where there's no air resistance."

Another voice broke in. The geologist had finished his potatoes, and a savoury smell was already issuing from the frying pan. Years spent in the wilderness had made the geologist a good cook, and doubly welcome as a member of the expedition.

"We ought to get there tomorrow, then," he said eagerly. Indoor life did not appeal to him, even under such exciting circumstances. He peered at Mercury through his binoculars. "Beginning to show up fine now."

The builder improved upon Van Emmon's example by setting up the car's biggest telescope, a four-inch tube of unusual excellence. All three pronounced the planet, which was three-fourths "full" as they viewed it, as having pretty much the appearance of the moon.

"Wonder why there's always been so much mystery about Mercury?" pondered the architect invitingly. "Looks as though the big five-foot telescope on Mt. Wilson would have shown everything."

"Ask doc," suggested Smith, diplomatically. Jackson turned and hailed the little man on the other side of the car. He looked up absently from the scientific apparatus with which he had been making a test of the room's chemically purified air, then he stepped to the oxygen tanks and closed the flow a trifle, referring to his figures in the severely exact manner of his craft. He crossed to the group.

"Mercury is so close to the sun," he answered the architect's question, "he's always been hard to observe. For a long time the astronomers couldn't even agree that he always keeps the same face toward the sun, like the moon toward the earth."

"Then his day is as long as his year?"

"Eighty-eight of our days; yes."

"Continual sunlight! He can't be inhabited, then?" The architect knew very little about the planets. He had been included in the party because, along with his professional knowledge, he possessed remarkable ability as an amateur antiquarian. He knew as much about the doings of the ancients as the average man knows of baseball.

Dr. Kinney shook his head. "Not at present, certainly."

Instantly Jackson was alert. "Then perhaps there were people there at one time!"

"Why not?" the doctor put it lightly. "There's little or no atmosphere there now, of course, but that's not saying there never has been. Even if he is such a little planet—less than three thousand, smaller than the moon—he must have had plenty of air and water at one time, the same as the Earth."

"What's become of the air?" Van Emmon wanted to know. Kinney eyed him in reproach. He said:

"You ought to know. Mercury has only two-fifths as much gravitation as the earth; a man weighing a hundred and fifty back home would be only a sixty-pounder there. And you can't expect stuff as light as air to stay forever on a planet with no more pull than that, when the sun is on the job only thirty-six millions miles away."

"About a third as far as from the Earth to the sun," commented the engineer. "By George, it must be hot!"

"On the sunlit side, yes," said Kinney. "On the dark side it is as cold as space itself—four hundred and sixty below, Fahrenheit."

They considered this in silence for some minutes. The builder went to another window and looked at Venus, at that time about sixty million miles distant, on the far side of the sun. They were intending to visit "Earth's twin sister" on their return. After a while he came back to the group, ready with another question:

"If Mercury ever was inhabited, then his day wasn't as long as it is now, was it?"

"No," said the doctor. "In all probability he once had a day the same length as ours. Mercury is a comparatively old planet, you know; being smaller, he cooled off earlier than the earth, and has been more affected by the pull of the sun. But it's been a mighty long time since he had a day like ours; before the earth was cool enough to live on, probably."

"But since Mercury was made out of the same batch of material—" prompted the geologist.

"No reason, then, why life shouldn't have existed there in the past!" exclaimed the architect, his eyes sparkling with the instinct of the born antiquarian. He glanced up eagerly as the doctor coughed apologetically and said:

"Don't forget that, even if Mercury is part baked and part frozen, there must be a region in between which is neither." He picked up a small globe from the table and ran a finger completely around it from pole to pole. "So. There must be a narrow

13

band of country where the sun is only partly above the horizon, and where the climate is temperate."

"Then—" the architect almost shouted in his excitement, an excitement only slightly greater than that of the other two— "then, if there were people on Mercury at one time—"

The doctor nodded gravely. "There may be some there now!"

2

A Dead City

From a height of a few thousand miles Mercury, at first glance, strongly reminded them of the moon. The general effect was the same—leaden disk, with slight prominences here and there on the circumference, and large, irregular splotches of a darkish shade relieved by a great many brilliantly lighted areas, lines, and spots.

A second glance, however, found a marked difference. Instead of the craters, which always distinguished the moon, Mercury showed ranges of bona fide mountains.

The doctor gave a sigh of regret, mixed with a generous amount of excitement. "Too bad those mountains weren't distinguishable from the earth," he complained. "We wouldn't have been so quick to brand Mercury a dead world."

The others were too engrossed to comment. The sky-car was rapidly sinking nearer and nearer the planet; already Smith had stopped the current with which he had attracted the cube toward the little world's northern hemisphere, and was now using negative voltage. This, in order to act as a brake, and prevent them from falling to destruction.

Suddenly Van Emmon, the geologist, whose eyes had been glued to his binoculars, gave an exclamation of wonder. "Look at those faults!" He pointed toward a region south of that for which they were bound; what might be called the planet's torrid zone.

At first it was hard to see; then, little by little, there unfolded before their eyes a giant, spiderlike system of chasms in the strange surface beneath them. From a point almost directly opposite the sun, these cracks radiated in a half-dozen different

14

directions; vast, irregular clefts, they ran through mountain and plain alike. In places they must have been hundreds of miles wide, while there was no guessing as to their depth. For all that the four in the cube could see, they were bottomless.

"Small likelihood of anybody being alive there now," commented the geologist sceptically. "If the sun has dried it out enough to produce faults like that, how could animal life exist?"

"Notice, however," prompted the doctor, "that the cracks do not extend all the way to the edge of the disk." This was true; all the great chasms ended far short of the "twilight band" which the doctor had declared might still contain life.

But as the sky-car rushed downward their attention became fixed upon the surface directly beneath them, a point whose latitude corresponded roughly with that of New York on the Earth. It was a region of low-lying mountains, decidedly different from various precipitous ranges to be seen to the north and east. On the west, or left-hand side of this district, a comparatively level stretch, with an occasional peak or two projecting, suggested the ancient bed of an ocean.

By this time they were within a thousand miles. Smith threw on a little more current; their speed diminished to a safer point, and they scanned the approaching surface with the greatest of care. The architect, who was a New Yorker, was strongly reminded of the fall aspect of the Appalachians; but Van Emmon, who was born and raised on the Pacific coast, declared that the spot was almost exactly like the region north of San Francisco. "If I didn't know where I was," he declared, "I'd be trying to locate Eureka right now."

The engineer smiled tolerantly. He had spent several years in Scotland, and he felt sure, he obligingly told the others, that this new locality was far more like the Ben Lomond country than any other spot on earth. He was so positive, he made the doctor, a New Zealander, smile quite broadly.

"It is just like the hills near my home," he stated, with an air of finality which made further discussion useless.

"There's a river!" the architect suddenly exclaimed, pointing;

15

then added, before the others could comment, "I mean, what was once a river." They saw that he was right; an irregular but well-defined streak of sandy hue trickled down the middle of their chosen destination—a long, L-shaped valley, surrounded by low hills.

"That's the most likely place, outside of the twilight zone, for life to be found," remarked the doctor. "Neither mountainous nor dead level."

He added: "The spectroscope has plainly shown that there's water vapour in what little air there is. Must be precious little. If the air was as humid as the earth's, we couldn't see the surface at all from this height."

The inviting-looking valley was now less than a hundred miles below. Inviting, however, only in outline; in colour it was a greyish buff, scorched and forbidding. The hills were yellower, and an alkali white on their summits.

"Do either of you fellows see anything *green?*" demanded the engineer, a little later. They were silent; each had noticed long before, that not even near the poles was there the slightest sign of vegetation.

"No chance unless there's foliage," muttered the doctor, half to himself. The builder asked what he meant. He explained: "So far as we know, all animal life depends upon vegetation for its oxygen. Not only the oxygen in the air, but that stored in the plants which animals eat. Unless there's greenery—"

He paused at a low exclamation from Smith. The engineer's eyes were fixed, in wonder and excitement, upon that part of the valley which lay at the joint of the "L" below them. It was perhaps six miles across; and all over the comparatively smooth surface jutted dark projections. Viewed through the glasses, they had a regular, uniform appearance.

"By Jove!" ejaculated the doctor, almost in awe. He leaned forward and scrubbed the dead-light for the tenth time. All four men strained their eyes to see.

It was the architect who broke the silence which followed. The other three were content to let the thrill of the thing have its way with them. Such a feeling had little weight with the expert in archaeology.

"Well," he declared jubilantly in his boyish voice, "either I eat my hat or that's a genuine, bona fide city!"

As swiftly as an elevator drops, and as safely, the cube shot straight downward. Every second the landscape narrowed and shrunk, leaving the remaining details larger, clearer, sharper. Bit by bit the amazing thing below them resolved itself into a real metropolis.

Within five minutes they were less than a mile above it. Smith threw on more current, so that the descent stopped; and the cube hung motionless in space.

For another five minutes the four men studied the scene in nervous silence. Each knew that the others were looking for the same thing—some sign of life. A little spot of green, or possibly something in motion—a single whiff of smoke would have been enough to cause a whoop of joy.

But nobody shouted. There was nothing to shout about. Nowhere in all that locality apparently was there the slightest indication that any save themselves were alive.

Instead, the most extraordinary city that man had ever laid eyes upon was stretched directly beneath. It was grouped about what seemed to be the meeting-point of three great roads, which led to this spot from as many passes through the surrounding hills. And the city seemed thus naturally divided into three segments, of equal size and shape, and each with its own street system.

For they undoubtedly were streets. No metropolis on earth ever had its blocks laid out with such unvarying exactness. This Mercurian city contained none but perfect equilateral triangles, and the streets themselves were of absolutely uniform width.

The buildings, however, showed no such uniformity. On the outskirts of this brilliantly tan mystery the blocks seemed to contain nothing save odd heaps of dingy, sun-baked mud. On the extreme north, however, lay five blocks grouped together, whose buildings, like those in the middle of the city, were rather tall, square-cut and of the same dusty, cream-white hue.

"Down-town" were several structures especially prominent for their height. They towered to such an extent, in fact, that their upper windows were easily made out. Apparently they were hundreds of stories high!

Here and there on the streets could be seen small spots, coloured a darker buff than the rest of that dazzling landscape. But not one of the spots was moving.

"We'll go down further," said the engineer tentatively, in a low tone. There was no comment. He gradually reduced the repelling current, so that the sky-car resumed its descent.

They sank down until they were on a level with the top of one of those extraordinary sky-scrapers. The roof seemed perfectly flat, except for a large, round, black opening in its centre. No one was in sight.

When opposite the upper row of windows, at a distance of perhaps twenty feet, Smith brought the car to a halt, and they peered in.

There were no panes; the windows opened directly into a vast room; but nothing was clearly visible in the blackness save the outlines of the opening in the opposite walls.

They went down further, keeping well to the middle of the space above the street. At every other yard they kept a sharp lookout for the inhabitants; but so far as they could see, their approach was entirely unobserved.

When within fifty yards of the surface, all four men made a search for cross-wires below. They saw none; there were no poles, even. Neither, to their astonishment, was there such a thing as a sidewalk. The street stretched, unbroken by curbing, from wall to wall and from corner to corner.

As the cube settled slowly to the ground, the adventurers left the deadlight to use the windows. For a moment the view was obscured by a swirl of dust, raised by the spurt of the current; then this cloud vanished, settling to the ground with astounding suddenness, as though jerked down by some invisible hand.

Directly ahead of them, distant perhaps a hundred yards, lay a yellowish-brown mass of unusual octagonal shape. One end contained a small oval opening, but the men from the Earth looked in vain for any creature to emerge from it.

The doctor silently set to work with his apparatus. From an air-tight double-doored compartment he obtained a sample of the ether outside the car; and with the aid of previously arranged chemicals, quickly learned the truth.

There was no air. Not only was there no oxygen, the element upon which all known life depends, but there was no nitrogen, no carbon dioxide; not the slightest trace of water vapour or of the other less known elements which can be found in small amounts in our own atmosphere. Clearly, as the doctor said, whatever air the astronomers had observed must exist on the circumference of the planet only, and not in this sun-blasted, north-central spot.

On the outer walls of the cube, so arranged as to be visible through the windows, were various instruments. The barometer showed no pressure. The thermometer, a specially devised one which used gas instead of mercury, showed a temperature of six hundred degrees, Fahrenheit.

No air, no water, and a baking heat; as the geologist remarked, how could life exist there? But the architect suggested that possibly there was some form of life, of which men knew nothing, which could exist under such circumstances.

They got out three of the suits. These were a good deal like those worn by divers, except that the outer layer was made of non-conducting aluminium cloth, flexible, air-tight, and strong. Between it and the inner lining was a layer of cells, into which the men now pumped several pints of liquid oxygen. The terrific cold of this chemical made the heavy flannel of the inner lining very welcome; while the oxygen itself, as fast as it evaporated, revitalized the air within the big, glass-faced helmet.

Once safely locked within the clumsy suits, Jackson, Van Emmon, and Smith took their places within the vestibule; while the doctor, who had volunteered to stay behind, watched them open the outer door. With a hiss all the air in the vestibule rushed out;

and the doctor earnestly thanked his stars that the inner door had been built very strongly.

The men stepped out on to the ground. At first they moved with great care, being uncertain that their feet were weighted heavily enough to counteract the reduced gravitation of the tiny planet. But they had been living in a very peculiar condition, gravitationally speaking, for the past three days; and they quickly adapted themselves. After a little shifting about, the three artificial monsters gave their telephone wires another scrutiny; then, keeping always within ten feet of each other, so as not to throw any strain on the connections, they strode in a matter-of-fact way toward the nearest doorway.

For a moment or two they stood outside the queer, peaked archway, their glimmering suits standing out oddly in the blinding sunlight. Then they advanced boldly into the opening; in a flash they vanished from the doctor's sight, and the ink-like blackness of the opening again stared at him from that dazzling wall.

3

THE HOUSE OF DUST

The geologist, strong man that he was, and by profession an investigator of the unknown—Van Emmon—took the lead. He stalked straight ahead into a vast space which, without any preliminary hallway, filled the entire triangular block.

Before their eyes were accustomed to the shadow—"Pretty cold," murmured the architect into the phone transmitter; it was fastened to the inside of the helmet, directly in front of his mouth, while the receiver was placed beside his ear. All three stopped short to adjust each other's electrical heating apparatus. To do this, they did not use their fingers directly; they manipulated ingenious non-magnetic pliers attached to the ends of fingerless, insulated mittens.

Before they had finished, the builder, who had been puzzling over the extraordinary suddenness with which that cloud of dust had settled, received an inspiration. He was carrying note-book and camera. With his pliers he tore out a sheet from the former, and holding book in one hand and the leaf in the other, he allowed them to drop at the same instant.

They reached the ground together.

"See?" The architect repeated the experiment. "Back home, where there's air, the paper would have floated down; it would have taken three times as long for it to fall as the book."

Smith nodded, but he had been thinking of something else. He said gravely: "Remember what I told you—it's air that insulates the earth from the ether. If there's no air here—" he glanced out into the pitiless sunlight—"then I hope there's no flaw in our insulation. We're walking in an electrical bath."

They looked around. Objects were pretty distinct now. They could easily see that the floor was covered with what appeared to be machines, laid out in orderly fashion. Here, however, as outside, everything was coated with that fine, cream-colored dust. It filled every nook and cranny; it stirred about their feet with every step.

The geologist led the way down a broad aisle, on either side of which towered immense machinery. Smith was for stopping to examine them one by one; but the others vetoed the engineer's passion, and strode on toward the end of the triangle. More than anything else, they looked for the absent population to show itself.

Suddenly Van Emmon stopped short. "Is it possible that they're all asleep?" He added that, even though the sun shone steadily the year around, the people must take time for rest.

But Smith stirred the dust with his foot and shook his head. "I've seen no tracks. This dust has been lying here for weeks, perhaps months. If the folks are away, then they must be taking a community vacation."

At the end of the aisle they reached a small, railed-in space, strongly resembling what might be seen in any office on the earth. In the middle of it stood a low, flat-topped desk, for all the world like that of a prosperous real-estate agent, except that it was about half a foot lower. There was no chair. For lack of a visible gate in the railing, the explorers stepped over, being careful not to touch it.

There was nothing on top of the desk save the usual coat of dust. Below, a very wide space had been left for the legs of whoever had used it; and flanking this space were two pedestals, containing what looked to be a multitude of exceedingly small drawers. Smith bent and examined them; apparently they had no locks; and he unhesitatingly reached out, gripped the knob of one and pulled.

Noiselessly, instantaneously, the whole desk crumbled to powder. Startled, Smith stumbled backwards, knocking against the railing. Next instant it lay on the floor, its fragments scarcely distinguishable from what had already covered the surface. Only a tiny cloud of dust arose, and in half a second this had settled.

The three looked at each other significantly. Clearly, the thing that had just happened argued a great lapse of time since the user of that desk officiated in that enclosure. It looked as though Smith's guess of "weeks, perhaps months," would have to be changed to years, perhaps centuries.

"Feel all right?" asked the geologist. Jackson and Smith made affirmative noises; and again they stepped out, this time walking in the aisle along the outer wall. They could see their sky-car plainly through the ovals.

Here the machinery could be examined more closely. They resembled automatic testing scales, said Smith; such as is used in weighing complicated metal products after finishing and assembling. Moreover, they seemed to be connected, the one to the other, with a series of endless belts, which Smith thought indicated automatic production. To all appearances, the dust-covered apparatus stood just as it had been left when operations ceased, an unguessable length of time before.

Smith showed no desire to touch the things now. Seeing this, the geologist deliberately reached out and scraped the dust from the nearest machine; and to the vast relief of all three, no damage was done. The dust fell straight to the floor, exposing a brilliantly polished streak of greenish-white metal.

Van Emmon made another tentative brush or so at other points, with the same result. Clean, untarnished metal lay beneath all that dust. Clearly it was some non-conducting alloy; whatever it was, it had successfully resisted the action of the elements all the while that such presumably wooden articles as the desk and railing had been steadily rotting.

Emboldened, Smith clambered up on the frame of one of the machines. He examined it closely as to its cams, clutches, gearing, and other details significant enough to his mechanical training. He noted their adjustments, scrutinized the conveying apparatus, and came back carrying a cylindrical object which he had removed from an automatic chuck.

"This is what they were making," he remarked, trying to conceal his excitement. The others brushed the dust from the thing, a huge piece of metal which would have been too much for their strength on the earth. Instantly they identified it.

It was a cannon shell.

Again Van Emmon led the way. They took a reassuring glance out the window at the familiar cube, then passed along the aisle toward the farther corner. As they neared it they saw that it contained a small enclosure of heavy metal scrollwork, within which stood a triangular elevator.

The men examined it as closely as possible, noting especially the extremely low stool which stood upon its platform. The same unerodable metal seemed to have been used throughout the whole affair.

After a careful scrutiny of the two levers which appeared to control the thing—"I'm going to try it out," announced Smith, well knowing that the others would have to go with him if they kept the telephones intact. They protested that the thing was not safe; Smith replied that they had seen no stairway, or anything corresponding to one. "If this lift is made of that alloy," admiringly, "then it's safe." But Jackson managed to talk him out of it.

When they returned to the heap of powdered wood which had been the desk, Smith spied a long work-bench under a nearby window. There they found a very ordinary vice, in which was clamped a piece of metal; but for the dust, it might have been placed there ten minutes before. On the bench lay several tools, some familiar to the engineer and some entirely strange. A set of screw-drivers of various sizes caught his eye. He picked them up, and again experienced the sensation of having wood turn to dust at his touch. The blades were whole.

Still searching, the engineer found a square metal chest of drawers, each of which he promptly opened. The contents were laden with dust, but he brushed this off and disclosed a quantity of exceedingly delicate instruments. They were more like dentists' tools than machinists', yet plainly were intended for mechanical use.

One drawer held what appeared to be a roll of drawings. Smith did not want to touch them; with infinite care he blew off the dust with the aid of his oxygen pipe. After a moment or two the surface was clear, but it offered no encouragement; it was the blank side of the paper.

There was no help for it. Smith grasped the roll firmly with his pliers —and next second gazed upon dust.

In the bottom drawer lay something that aroused the curiosity of all three. These were small reels, about two inches in diameter and a quarter of an inch thick, each encased in a tight-fitting box. They resembled measuring tapes to some extent, except that the ribbons were made of marvellously thin material. Van Emmon guessed that there were a hundred yards in a roll. Smith estimated it at three hundred. They seemed to be made of a metal similar to that composing the machines. Smith pocketed them all.

It was the builder who thought to look under the bench, but it was Smith who had brought a light. By its aid they discovered a very small machine, decidedly like a stock ticker, except that it had no glass dome, but possessed at one end a curious metal disk about a foot in diameter. Apparently it had been undergoing repairs; it was impossible to guess its purpose. Smith's pride was instantly aroused; he tucked it under his arm, and was impatient to get back to the cube, where he might more carefully examine his find with the tips of his fingers.

It was when they were about to leave the building that they thought to inspect walls and ceiling. Not that anything worthwhile was to be seen; the surfaces seemed perfectly plain and bare, except for the inevitable dust. Even the uppermost corners, ten feet above their heads, showed dust to the light of Smith's electric torch.

Van Emmon stopped and stared at the spot as though fascinated. The others were ready to go; they turned and looked at him curiously. For a moment or two he seemed struggling for breath.

"Good Heavens!" he gasped, almost in a whisper. His face was white; the other two leaped toward him, fearful that he was suffocating. But he pushed them away roughly.

"We're fools! Blind, blithering idiots—that's what we are!" He pointed toward the ceiling with a hand that trembled plainly, and went on in a voice which he tried to make fierce despite the awe which shook it.

"Look at that dust again! How'd it get there?" He paused while the others, the thought finally getting to them, felt a queer chill striking at the backs of their necks. "Men—there's only one way for the dust to settle on a wall! It's got to have air to carry it! It couldn't possibly get there without air!

"That dust settled long before life appeared on the Earth, even! It's been there ever since the air disappeared from Mercury!"

4

THE LIBRARY

"I thought you'd never get back," complained the doctor crossly, when the three entered. They had been gone just half an hour.

Next moment he was studying their faces, and at once he demanded the most important fact. They told him, and before they had finished he was half-way into another suit. He was all eagerness; but somehow the three were very glad to be inside the cube again, and firmly insisted upon moving to another spot before making further explorations.

Within a minute or two the cube was hovering opposite the

upper floor of the building the three had entered; and with only a foot of space separating the window of the sky-car and the dust-covered wall, the men from the earth inspected the interior at considerable length. They flashed a search-light all about the place, and concluded that it was the receiving-room, where the raw iron billets were brought via the elevator, and from there slid to the floor below. At one end, in exactly the same location as the desk Smith had destroyed, stood another, with a low and remarkably broad chair beside it.

So far as could be seen, there were neither doors, window-panes, nor shutters through the structure. "To get all the light and air they could," guessed the doctor. "Perhaps that's why the buildings are all triangular; most wall surface in proportion to floor area, that way."

A few hundred feet higher they began to look for prominent buildings. Only in forgetful moments did either of them scan the landscape for signs of life; they knew now that there could be none.

"We ought to learn something there," the doctor said after a while, pointing out a particularly large, squat, irregularly built affair on the edge of the "business district." The architect, however, was in favour of an exceptionally large, high building in the isolated group previously noted in the "suburbs." But because it was nearer, they manoeuvred first in the direction of the doctor's choice.

The sky-car came to rest in a large plaza opposite what appeared to be the structure's main entrance. From their window the explorers saw that the squat effect was due only to the space the edifice covered; for it was an edifice, a full five stories high.

The doctor was impatient to go. Smith was willing enough to stay behind; he was already joyously examining the strange machine he had found. Two minutes later Kinney, Van Emmon, and Jackson were standing before the portals of the great building.

There they halted, and no wonder. The entire face of the building could now be seen to be covered with a mass of carvings; for the most part they were statues in bas relief. All were fantastic in the extreme, but whether purposely so or not, there was no way to tell. Certainly any such work on the part of an earthly artist would have branded him either as insane or as an incomprehensible genius.

Directly above the entrance was a group which might have been labelled, "The Triumph of the Brute." An enormously powerful man, nearly as broad as he was tall, stood exulting over his victim, a less robust figure, prostrate under his feet. Both were clad in armour.

The victor's face was distorted into a savage snarl, startlingly hideous by reason of the prodigious size of his head, planted as it was directly upon his shoulders; for he had no neck. His eyes were set so close together that at first glance they seemed to be but one. His nose was flat and African in type, while his mouth, devoid of curves, was simply revolting in its huge, thick-lipped lack of proportion. His chin was square and aggressive; his forehead, strangely enough, extremely high and narrow, rather than low and broad.

His victim lay in an attitude that indicated the most agonizing torture; his head was bent completely back, and around behind his shoulders. On the ground lay two battle-axes, huge affairs almost as heavy as the massively muscled men who had used them.

But the eyes of the explorers kept coming back to the fearsome face of the conqueror. From the brows down, he was simply a huge, brutal giant; above his eyes, he was an intellectual. The combination was absolutely frightful; the beast looked capable of anything, of overcoming any obstacle, mental or physical, internal or external, in order to assert his apparently enormous will. He could control himself or dominate others with equal ease and assurance.

"It can't be that he was drawn from life," said the doctor, with an effort. It wasn't easy to criticize that figure, lifeless though it was. "On a planet like this, with such slight gravitation, there is no need for such huge strength. The typical Mercurian should be tall and flimsy in build, rather than short and compact."

But the geologist differed. "We want to remember that the earth has no standard type. Think what a difference there is between the mosquito and the elephant, the snake and the spider! One would suppose that they had been developed under totally different planetary conditions, instead of all right on the same globe.

"No; I think this monster may have been genuine." And with that the geologist turned to examine the other statuary.

Without exception, it resembled the central group; all the figures were neckless, and all much more heavily built than any people on earth. There were several female figures; they had the same general build, and in every case were so placed as to enhance the glory of the males. In one group the woman was offering up food and drink to a resting worker; in another she was being carried off, struggling, in the arms of a fairly good-looking warrior.

Dr. Kinney led the way into the building. As in the other structure, there was no door. The space seemed to be but one story in height, although that had the effect of a cathedral. The whole of the ceiling, irregularly arched in a curious, pointed manner, was ornamented with grotesque figures; while the walls were also partially formed of squat, semi-human statues, set upon huge, triangular shafts. In the spaces between these outlandish pilasters there had once been some sort of decorations, A great many photos were taken here.

As for the floor, it was divided in all directions by low walls. About five and a half feet in height, these walls separated the great room into perhaps a hundred triangular compartments, each about the size of an ordinary living room. Broad openings, about five feet square, provided free access from one compartment to any other. The men from the earth, by standing on tiptoes, could see over and beyond this system.

"Wonder if these walls were supposed to cut off the view?" speculated the doctor. "I mean, do you suppose that the Mercurians were such short people as that?" His question had to go unanswered.

They stepped into the nearest compartment, and were on the

28

point of pronouncing it bare, when Jackson, with an exclamation, excitedly brushed away some of the dust and showed that the presumably solid walls were really chests of drawers. Shallow things of that peculiar metal, these drawers numbered several hundred to the compartment. In the whole building there must have been millions.

Once more the dust was carefully removed, revealing a layer of those curious rolls or reels, exactly similar to what had been found in the tool chest in the shell works. A careful examination of the metallic tape showed nothing whatever to the naked eye, although the doctor fancied that he made out some strange characters on the little boxes themselves.

His view was shortly proved. Finding drawer after drawer to contain a similar display, varying from one to a dozen of the diminutive ribbons, Van Emmon adopted the plan of gently blowing away the dust from the faces of the drawers before opening them. This revealed the fact that each of the shallow things was neatly labelled!

Instantly the three were intent upon this fresh clue. The markings were very faint and delicate, the slightest touch being enough to destroy them. To the untrained eye, they resembled ancient Egyptian hieroglyphics; to the archaeologist, they meant that a brand-new system of ideographs had been found.

Suddenly Jackson straightened up and looked about with a new interest. He went to one of the square doorways and very carefully removed the dust from a small plate on the lintel. He need not have been so careful; engraved in the solid metal was a single character, plainly in the same language as the other ideographs.

The architect smiled triumphantly into the inquiring eyes of his friends. "I won't have to eat my hat," said he. "This is a sure-enough city, all right, and this is its library!"

Smith was still busy on the little machine when they returned to the cube. He said that one part of it had disappeared, and was busily engaged in filing a bit of steel to take its place. As soon as it was ready, he thought, they could see what the apparatus meant.

The three had brought a large number of the reels. They were confident that a microscopic search of the ribbons would disclose something to bear out Jackson's theory that the great structure was really a repository for books, or whatever corresponded with books on Mercury.

"But the main thing," said the doctor, enthusiastically, "is to get over to the 'twilight band.' I'm beginning to have all sorts of wild hopes."

Jackson urged that they first visit the big "mansion" on the outskirts of this place; he said he felt sure, somehow, that it would be worthwhile. But Van Emmon backed up the doctor, and the architect had to be content with an agreement to return in case their trip was futile.

Inside of a few minutes the cube was being drawn steadily over toward the left or western edge of the planet's sunlit face. As it moved, all except Smith kept close watch on the ground below. They made out town after town, as well as separate buildings; and on the roads were to be seen a great many of those octagonal structures, all motionless.

After several hundred miles of this, the surface abruptly sloped toward what had clearly been the bed of an ocean. No sign of habitations here, however; so apparently the water had disappeared *after* the humans had gone.

This ancient sea ended a short distance from the district they were seeking. A little more travel brought them to a point where the sun cast as much shadow as light on the surface. It was here they descended, coming to rest on a sunlit knoll which overlooked a small, building-filled valley.

According to Kinney's apparatus, there was about one-fortieth the amount of air that exists on the earth. Of water vapour there was a trace; but all their search revealed no human life. Not only that, but there was no trace of lower animals; there was not even a lizard, much less a bird. And even the most ancient-looking of the sculptures showed no creatures of the air; only huge, antediluvian monsters were ever depicted.

They took a great many photos as a matter of course. Also,

they investigated some of the big, octagonal machines in the streets, finding them to be similar to the great "tanks" that were used in the war, except that they did not have the characteristic caterpillar tread; their eight faces were so linked together that the entire affair could roll, after a jolting, slab-sided, flopping fashion. Inside were curious engines, and sturdy machines designed to throw the cannon-shells they had seen; no explosive was employed, apparently, but centrifugal force generated in whirling wheels. Apparently these cars, or chariots, were universally used.

The explorers returned to the cube, where they found that Smith, happening to look out a window, had spied a pond not far off. The three visited it and found, on its banks, the first green stuff they had seen; a tiny, flowerless salt grass, very scarce. It bordered a slimy, bluish pool of absolutely still fluid. Nobody would call it water. They took a few samples of it and went back.

And within a few minutes the doctor slid a small glass slide into his microscope, and examined the object with much satisfaction. What he saw was a tiny, gelatine-like globule; among scientists it is known as the amoeba. It is the simplest known form of life—the so-called "single cell." It had been the first thing to live on that planet, and apparently it was also the last.

5

The Closed Door

As they neared Jackson's pet "mansion" each man paid close attention to the intervening blocks. For the most part these were simply shapeless ruins; heaps of what had once been, perhaps, brick or stone. Once they allowed the cube to rest on the top of one of these mounds; but the sky-car's great weight merely sank it into the mass. There was nothing under it save that same sandy dust.

Apparently the locality they were approaching had been set aside as a very exclusive residence district for the elite of the country. Possibly it contained the homes of the royalty, assuming that there had been a royalty. At any rate the conspicuous structure Jackson had selected was certainly the home of the most important member of that colony.

When the three, once more in their helmets and suits, stood before the low, broad portico which protected the entrance to that edifice, the first thing they made out was an ornamental frieze running across the face. In the same bold, realistic style as the other sculpture, there was depicted a hand-to-hand battle between two groups of those half savage, half cultured monstrosities. And in the background was shown a glowing orb, obviously the sun.

"See that?" exclaimed the doctor. "The size of that sun, I mean! Compare it with the way old Sol looks now!"

They took a single glance at the great ball of fire over their heads; nine times the size it always seemed at home, it contrasted sharply with the rather small ball shown in the carvings.

"Understand?" the doctor went on. "When that sculpture was made, Mercury was little nearer the sun than the earth is now!"

The builder was hugely impressed. He asked, eagerly: "Then probably the people became as highly developed as we?"

Van Emmon nodded approvingly, but the doctor opposed. "No; I think not, Jackson. Mercury never did have as much air as the earth, and consequently had much less oxygen. And the struggle for existence," he went on, watching to see if the geologist approved each point as he made it, "the struggle for life is, in the last analysis, a struggle for oxygen.

"So I would say that life was a pretty strenuous proposition here, while it lasted. Perhaps they were—" He stopped, then added: "What I can't understand is, how did it happen that their affairs came to such an abrupt end? And why don't we see any—er—indications?"

"Skeletons?" The architect shuddered. Next second, though, his face lit up with a thought. "I remember reading that electricity will decompose bone, in time." And then he shuddered again as his foot stirred that lifeless, impalpable dust. Was it possible?

As they passed into the great house the first thing they noted was the floor, undivided, dust-covered, and bare, except for what had perhaps been rugs. The shape was the inevitable equilateral triangle; and here, with a certain magnificent disregard for precedent, the builders had done away with a ceiling entirely, and instead had sloped the three walls up till they met in a single point, a hundred feet overhead. The effect was massively simple.

In one corner a section of the floor was elevated perhaps three feet above the rest, and directly back of this was a broad doorway, set in a short wall. The three advanced at once toward it.

Here the electric torch came in very handy. It disclosed a poorly lighted stairway, very broad, unrailed, and preposterously steep. The steps were each over three feet high.

"Difference in gravitation," said the doctor, in response to Jackson's questioning look. "Easy enough for the old-timers, perhaps." They struggled up the flight as best they could, reaching the top after over five minutes of climbing.

Perhaps it was the reaction from this exertion; at all events each felt a distinct loss of confidence as, after regaining their wind, they again began to explore. Neither said anything about it to the others; but each noted a queer sense of foreboding, far more disquieting than either of them had felt when investigating anything else. It may have been due to the fact that, in their hurry, they had not stopped to eat.

The floor they were on was fairly well lighted with the usual oval windows. The space was open, except that it contained the same kind of dividing walls they had found in the library. Here, however, each compartment contained but one opening, and that not uniformly placed. In fact, as the three noted with a growing uneasiness, it was necessary to pass through every one of them in order to reach the corner farthest, from the ladder-like stairs. Why it should make them uneasy, neither could have said.

When they were almost through the labyrinth, Van Emmon, after standing on tiptoes for the tenth time, in order to locate himself, noted something that had escaped their attention before. "These compartments used to be covered over," he said, for some reason lowering his voice. He pointed out niches in the walls, such as undoubtedly once held the ends of heavy timbers. "What was this place, anyhow? A trap?"

Unconsciously they lightened their steps as they neared the last compartment. They found, as expected, that it was another stairwell. Van Emmon turned the light upon every corner of the place before going any further; but except for a formless heap of rubbish in one corner, which they did not investigate, the place was as bare as the rest of the floor.

Again they climbed, this time for a much shorter distance; but Jackson, slightly built chap that he was, needed a little help on the steep stairs. They were not sorry that they had reached the uppermost floor of the mansion. It was somewhat better lighted than the floor below, and they were relieved to find that the triangular compartments did not have the significant niches in their walls. Their spirits rose perceptibly.

At the corner farthest from the stairs one of the walls rose straight to the ceiling, completely cutting off a rather large triangle. The three paid no attention to the other compartments, but went straight to what they felt sure was the most vital spot in the place. And their feelings were justified with a vengeance when they saw that the usual doorway in this wall was protected by something that had, so far, been entirely missing everywhere else.

It was barred by a heavy door.

For several minutes the doctor, the geologist, and the architect stood before it. Neither would have liked to admit that he would just as soon leave that door unopened. All the former uneasiness came back. It was all the more inexplicable, with the brilliant sunlight only a few feet away, that each should have felt chilled by the place.

"Wonder if it's locked?" remarked Van Emmon. He pressed against the dust-covered barrier, half expecting it to turn to dust; but evidently it had been made of the time-defying alloy. It stood firm. And to all appearances it was nearly air-tight.

"Well!" said the doctor suddenly, so that the other two started nervously. "The door's got to come down; that's all!" They looked around; there was no furniture, no loose piece of material of any kind. Van Emmon straightway backed away from the door about six feet, and the others followed his example.

"All together!" grunted the geologist; and the three aluminium-armoured monsters charged the door. It shook under the impact; a shower of dust fell down; and they saw that they had loosened the thing.

"Once more!" This time a wide crack showed all around the edge of the door, and the third attempt finished the job. Noiselessly—for there was no air to carry the sound—but with a heavy jar which all three felt through their feet, the barrier went flat on the floor beyond.

At the same instant a curious, invisible wave, like a tiny puff of wind, floated out of the darkness and passed by the three men from the earth. Each noticed it, but neither mentioned it at the time. Van Emmon was already searching the darkness with the torch.

Apparently it was only an anteroom. A few feet beyond was another wall, and in it stood another door, larger and heavier than the first. The three did not stop; they immediately tried their strength on this one also.

After a half dozen attempts without so much as shaking the massive affair—"It's no use," panted the geologist, wishing that he could get a handkerchief to his forehead. "We can't loosen it without tools."

Jackson was for trying again, but the doctor agreed with Van Emmon. They reflected that they had been away from Smith long enough, anyhow. The cube was out of sight from where they were.

Van Emmon turned the light on the walls of the anteroom, and found, on a shelf at one end, a neat pile of those little reels, eleven in all. He pocketed the lot. There was nothing else.

Jackson and Kinney started to go. They retreated as far into the main room as their telephone wires would allow. Still the geologist held back.

"Come on," said the doctor uneasily. "It's getting cold."

Next second they stopped short, nerves on edge, at a strange exclamation from Van Emmon. They looked around to see him pointing his light directly at the floor. Even in that unnatural suit of mail, his attitude was one of horror.

"Look here," he said in a low, strained voice. They went to his side, and instinctively glanced behind them before looking at what lay in the dust.

It was the imprint of an enormous human foot.

The first thing that greeted the ears of the explorers upon taking off their suits in the sky-car, was the exultant voice of Smith. He was too excited to notice anything out of the way in their manner; he was almost dancing in front of his bench, where the unknown machine, now reconstructed, stood belted to a small electric-motor.

"It runs!" he was shouting. "You got here just in time!" He began to fumble with a switch.

"What of it?" remarked the doctor in the bland tone which he kept for occasions when Smith needed calming. "What will it do if it does run?"

The engineer looked blank. "Why—" Then he remembered, and picked up one of the reels at random. "There's a clamp here just the right size to hold one of these," he explained, fitting the ribbon into place and threading its free end into a loop on a spool which looked as though made for it. But his excitement had passed; he now cautiously set a small anvil between himself and the apparatus, and then, with the aid of a long stick, he threw on the current.

For a moment nothing happened, save the hum of the motor. Then a strange, leafy rustling sounded from the mechanism, and next, without any warning, a high-pitched voice, nasal and plaintive but distinctly human, spoke from the big metal disk.

The words were unintelligible. The language was totally unlike anything ever heard on the earth. And yet, deliberately if somewhat cringingly, the voice proceeded with what was apparently a recitation. There were modulations, pauses, sentences; but seemingly the paragraphs were all short and to the point.

As the thing went on the four men came closer and watched the operation of the machine. The ribbon unrolled slowly; it was plain that, if the one topic occupied the whole reel, then it must have the length of an ordinary chapter. And as the voice continued, certain dramatic qualities came out and governed the words, utterly incomprehensible though they were. There was a real thrill to it.

After a while they stopped the thing. "No use listening to this now," as the doctor said. "We've got to learn a good deal more about these people before we can guess what it all means."

And yet, although all were very hungry, on Jackson's suggestion they tried out one of the "records" that was brought from that baffling anteroom. Smith was very much interested in that unopened door, and Van Emmon was in the midst of it when Jackson started the motor.

The geologist's words stuck in his throat. The disk was actually shaking with the vibrations of a most terrific voice. Prodigiously loud and powerful, its booming, resonant bass smote the ears like the roll of thunder. It was irresistible in its force, compelling in its assurance, masterful and strong to an overpowering degree. Involuntarily the men from the earth stepped back.

On it roared and rumbled, speaking the same language as that of the other record; but whereas the first speaker merely *used* the words, the last speaker demolished them. One felt that he had extracted every ounce of power in the language, leaving it weak and flabby, unfit for further use. He threw out his sentences as though done with them; not boldly, not defiantly, least of all, tentatively, he spoke with a certainty and force that came from a knowledge that he could compel, rather than induce his hearers to believe.

It took a little nerve to shut him off; Van Emmon was the one who did it. Somehow they all felt immensely relieved when the gigantic voice was silenced; and at once began discussing the thing with great earnestness. Jackson was for assuming that the first record was worn and old, the last one, fresh and new; but after examining both tapes under a glass, and seeing how equally clear cut and sharp the impressions all were, they agreed that the extraordinary voice they had heard was practically true to life.

They tried out the rest of the records in that batch, finding that they were all by the same speaker. Nowhere among the ribbons brought from the library was another of his making, although a great number of different voices was included; neither was there another talker with a fifth the volume, the resonance, the absolute power of conviction that this unknown colossus possessed.

Of course this is no place to describe the laborious process of interpreting these documents, records of a past which was gone before earth's mankind had even begun. The work involved the study of countless photos, covering everything from inscriptions to parts of machinery, and other details which furnished clue after clue to that super-ancient language. It was not deciphered, in fact, until several years after the explorers had submitted their finds to the world's foremost lexicographers, antiquarians and palaeontologists. Even today some of it is disputed.

But right here is, most emphatically, the place to insert the tale told by that unparalleled voice. And incredible though it may seem, as judged by the standards of the peoples of this earth, the account is fairly proved by the facts uncovered by the expedition. It would be but begging the question to doubt the genuineness of the thing; and if, understanding the language, one were to hear the original as it fell, word for word from the iron mouth of Strokor[1] the Great-hearing, one would believe; none could doubt, nor would.

And so it does not do him justice to set it down in ordinary print. One must imagine the story being related by Stentor himself; must conceive of each word falling like the blow of a mammoth sledge. The tale was not told—it was *bellowed*; and this is how it ran:

---

1. Translator's note—In the Mercurian language, stroke means iron, or heart.

PART 2

The Story

1

THE MAN

I am Strokor, son of Strok, the armourer. I am Strokor, a maker of tools of war; Strokor, the mightiest man in the world; Strokor, whose wisdom outwitted the hordes of Klow; Strokor, who has never feared, and never failed. Let him who dares, dispute it. I—I am Strokor!

In my youth I was, as now, the marvel of all who saw. I was ever robust and daring, and naught but much older, bigger lads could outdo me. I balked at nothing, be it a game or a battle; it was, and forever shall be, my chief delight to best all others.

'Twas from my mother that I gained my huge frame and sound heart. In truth, I am very like her, now that I think upon it. She, too, was indomitable in battle, and famed for her liking for strife. No doubt 'twas her stalwart figure that caught my father's fancy.

Aye, my mother was a very likely woman, but she boasted no brains. "I need no cunning," I remember she said; and he who was so unlucky in battle as to fall into her hands could vouch for the truth of it—as long as he lived, which would not be long. She was a grand woman, slow to anger and a match for many a good pair of men. Often, as a lad, have I carried the marks of her punishment for the most of a year.

And thus it seems that I owe my head to my father. He was

a marvellously clever man, dexterous with hand and brain alike. Moreover, he was no weakling; perchance I should credit him with some of my agility, for he was famed as a gymnast, though not a powerful one. 'Twas he who taught me how to disable my enemy with a mere clutch of the neck at a certain spot.

But Strok, the armourer, was feared most because of his brain, and his knack of using his mind to the undoing of others. And he taught me all that he knew; taught me all that he had learned in a lifetime of fighting for the emperor, of mending the complicated machines in the armoury, of contact with the chemists who wrought the secret alloy, and the chiefs who led the army.

Some of this he taught me when I was not yet a man. Why he should have done so, I know not, save that he seemed to value my affection, and liked not my mother's demands that I heed her call, not his. At all events, I oft found his shop a place of refuge from her wrath; and I early came to value his teachings.

When I became a man he abruptly ended the practice. I think he saw that I was become as dexterous as he with the tools of the craft, and he feared lest I know more than he. Well he might; the day I realized this I laughed long and loud. And from that time forth he taught me, not because he chose to, but because I bent a chisel in my bare hands, before his eyes, and told him his place.

Many times he strove to trick me, and more than once he all but caught me in some trap. He was a crafty man, and relied not upon brawn, but upon wits. Yet I was ever on the watch, and I but learned the more from him.

"Ye are very kind," I mocked him one morning. When I had taken my seat a huge weight had dropped from above and crushed my stool to splinters, much as it would have crushed my skull had I not leaped instantly aside. "Ye are kinder than most fathers, who teach their sons nothing at all."

He foamed at his mouth in his rage and discomfiture. "Insolent whelp!" he snarled. "Thou art quick as a cat on thy feet!"

But I was not to be appeased by words. I smote him on the chest with my bare hand, so that he fell on the far side of the room. "Let that be a warning," I told him, when he had recovered, some time later. "If ye have any more tricks, try them for, not on, me." Which I claim to be a neat twist of words.

It was not long after that when I saw a change in my father. He no longer tried to snare me; instead, he began, of his own free will, to train my mind to other than warlike things. At first, I was suspicious enough. I looked for new traps, and watched all the closer. I told him that his next try would surely be his last, and I meant it.

But the time came when I saw that my father was reconciled to his master. I saw that he genuinely admitted my prowess; and where he formerly envied me, he now took great pride in all I accomplished, and claimed that it was but his own brains acting through my body.

I let him indulge in the conceit. I grudged it not to him, so long as he taught me. In truth, he was so eager to add to my store of facts, so intent upon filling my head with what filled his, that at times I was fairly compelled to stop him, lest I tire.

My mother opposed all this. "The lad needs none of thy wiles," she gibed. "He is no stripling; he is a man's man, and a fit son of his mother."

"Aye," quoth my father slyly. "He has thy muscle and thy courage. Thank Jon, he hath not thy empty head!"

Whereat she flew at him. Had she caught him, she would have destroyed him, such was her rage; and afterwards she would have mourned her folly and mayhap have injured herself; for she loved him greatly. But he stepped aside just in the nick of time, and she crashed into the wall behind him with such force that she was senseless for a time. I remember it well.

And yet, to give credit where credit is due, I must admit that I owe a great deal to that gray-beard, Maka, the star-gazer. But for him, perchance, the name of Strokor would mean but little, for 'twas he who gave me ambition.

Truly it was an uncommon affair, my first meeting with him. Now that I shake my memory for it, it seems that something else of like consequence came to pass on the same occasion. Curious; but I have not thought on it for many days.

Yes, it is true; I met Maka on the very morn that I first laid eyes on the girl Ave.

I was returning from the northland at the time. A rumour had come down to Vlama that one of the people in the snow country had seen a lone specimen of the *mulikka*. Now these were but a myth.

No man living remembers when the carvings on the House of Learning were made, and all the wise men say that it hath been ages since any being other than man roamed the world. Yet, I was young. I determined to search for the thing anyhow; and 'twas only after wasting many days in the snow that I cursed my luck, and turned back.

I was afoot, for the going was too rough for my chariot. I had not yet quit the wilderness before, from a height, I spied a group of people ascending from the valley. Knowing not whether they be friends or foes, I hid beside the path up which they must come; for I was weary and wanting no strife.

Yet I became alert enough when the three—they were two ditch-tenders, one old, one young, and a girl—came within ear-shot. For they were quarrelling. It seemed that the young man, who was plainly eager to gain the girl, had fouled in a try to force her favour. The older man chided him hotly.

And just when they came opposite my rock, the younger man, whose passion had got the better of him, suddenly tripped the older, so that he fell upon the ledge and would have fallen to his death on the rocks below had not the girl, crying out in her terror, leaped forward and caught his hand.

At once the ditch-tender took the lass about the waist, and strove to pull her away. For a moment she held fast, and in that moment I, Strokor, stood forth from behind the rock.

Now, be it known that I am no champion of weaklings. I have no liking for the troubles of others; enough of my own, say I. I was but angered that the ditch-tender should have done the trick so clumsily, and upon an old man, at that. I cared not for the gray beard, nor what became of the chit. I clapped the trickster upon the shoulder and spun him about.

"Ye clumsy coward!" I jeered. "Have ye had no practice that ye should trip the old one no better than that?"

"Who are ye?" he stuttered, like the coward he was. I laughed and helped the chit drag Maka—for it was he—up to safety.

"I am a far better man than ye," I said, not caring to give my name. "And I can show ye how the thing should be done. Come; at me, if ye are a man!"

At that he dashed upon me; and such was his fear of ridicule—for the girl was laughing him to scorn now—he put up a fair, stiff fight. But I forgot my weariness when he foully clotted me on the head with a stone. I drove at him with all the speed and suddenness my father had taught me, caught the fellow by the ankle, and brought him down atop me.

The rest was easy. I bent my knee under his middle, and tossed him high. In a flash I was upon my feet, and caught him from behind. And in another second I had rushed him to the cliff; and when he turned to save himself, I tripped him as neatly as father himself could have done it, so that the fellow will guard the ditch no more, save in the caverns of Hofe.

I laughed and picked up my pack. My head hurt a bit from the fellow's blow, but a little water would do for that. I started to go.

"Ye are a brave man!" cried the girl. I turned carelessly, and then, quite for the first time, I had a real look at her.

She was in no way like any woman I had seen. All of them had been much like the men: brawny and close-knit, as well fitted for their work as are men for war. But this chit was all but slender; not skinny, but prettily rounded out, and soft like. I cannot say that I admired her at first glance; she seemed fit only to look at, not to live. I was minded of some of the ancient carvings, which show delicate, lightly built animals that have long since been killed off; graceful trifles that rested the eye.

As for the old man: "Aye, thou art brave, and wondrous strong, my lad," said he, still a bit shaky from his close call. I was pleased with the acknowledgment, and turned back.

"It was nothing," I told them; and I recounted some of my

exploits, notably one in which I routed a raiding party of men from Klow, six in all, carrying in two alive on my shoulders. "I am the son of Strok, the armourer."

"Ye are Strokor!" marvelled the girl, staring at me as though I were a god. Then she threw back her head and stepped close.

"I am Ave. This is Maka; he is my uncle, but best known as a star-gazer. My father was Durok, the engine-maker." She watched my face.

"Durok?" I knew him well. My father had said that he was quite as brainy as himself. "He were a fine man, Ave."

"Aye," said she proudly. She stepped closer; I could not but see how like him she was, though a woman. And next second she laid a hand on my arm.

"I am yet a free woman, Strokor. Hast thou picked thy mate?" And her cheeks flamed.

Now, 'twas not my first experience of the kind. Many women had looked like that at me before. But I had always been a man's man, and had ever heeded my father's warning to have naught whatever to do with women. "They are the worst trick of all," he told me; and I had never forgot. Belike I owe much of my power to just this.

But Ave had acted too quickly for me to get away. I laughed again, and shook her off.

"I will have naught to do with ye," I told her, civilly enough. "When I am ready to take a woman, I shall take her; not before."

At that the blood left her face; she stood very straight, and her eyes flashed dangerously. Were she a man I should have stood on my guard. But she made no move; only the softness in her eyes gave way to such a savage look that I was filled with amaze. And thus I left them; the old man calling down the blessing of Jon upon me for having saved his life, and the chit glaring after me as though no curses would suffice.

A right queer matter, I thought at the time. I guessed not what would come of it; not then.

2
The Vision

'Twas a fortnight later, more or less, when next I saw Maka. I was lumbering along in my chariot, feeling most uncomfortable under the eyes of my friends; for one foot of my machine had a loose link, and 'twas flapping absurdly. And I liked it none too well when Maka stopped his own rattletrap in front of mine, and came running to my window. Next moment I forgot his impertinence.

"Strokor," he whispered, his face alive with excitement, "thou art a brave lad, and didst save my life. Now, know you that a party of the men of Klow have secreted themselves under the stairway behind the emperor's throne. They have killed the guards, and will of a certainty kill the emperor, too!"

"'Twould serve the dolt right," I replied, for I really cared but little. "But why have ye come to me, old man? I am but a lieutenant in the armoury; I am not the captain of the palace guard."

"Because," he answered, gazing at me very pleasingly, "thou couldst dispose of the whole party single handed—there are but four—and gain much glory for thyself."

"By Jon!" I swore, vastly delighted; and without stopping to ask Maka whence he had got his knowledge, I went at once to the spot. However, when I got back, I sought the star-gazer—I ought to mention that I had no trouble with the louts, and that the emperor himself saw me finishing off the last of them—I sought the star-gazer and demanded how he had known.

"Hast ever heard of Edam?" he inquired in return.

"Edam?" I had not; the name was strange to me. "Who is he?"

"A man as young as thyself, but a mere stripling," quoth Maka. "He was a pupil of mine when I taught in the House of Learning. Of late he has turned to prophecy; and it is fair remarkable how well the lad doth guess. At all events, 'twas he, Strokor, who told me of the plot. He saw it in a dream."

"Then Edam must yet be in Vlama," said I, "if he were able to tell ye. Canst bring him to me? I would know him."

And so it came about that, on the eve of that same day, Maka brought Edam to my house. I remember it well; for 'twas the

45

same day that the emperor, in gratitude of my little service in the anteroom, had relieved me from my post in the armoury and made me captain of the palace guard. I was thus become the youngest captain, also the biggest and strongest; and, as will soon appear, by far the longest-headed.

I was in high good humour, and had decided to celebrate with a feast. So when my two callers arrived, I sat them down before a meal such as cost a tenth of my year's salary.[1]

I served not only the usual products of the field, variously prepared, but as a special gift from the emperor's own stock, a piece of *mulikka* meat, frozen, which had been found in the northland by some geologists a few years aback. It had been kept in the palace icing-room all this time, and was in prime condition. Maka and I enjoyed it overmuch, but Edam would touch it not.

He was a slightly built lad, not at all the sturdy man that I am, but of less than half the weight. His head, too, was unlike mine; his forehead was wide as well as tall, and his eyes were mild as a slave's.

"Ye are very young to be a prophet," I said to him, after we were filled, and the slaves had cleared away our litter. "Tell me: hast foretold anything else that has come to pass?"

"Aye," he replied, not at all boldly, but what some call modestly. "I prophesied the armistice which now stands between our empire and Klow's."

"Is this true?" I demanded of Maka. The old man bowed his head gravely and looked upon the young man with far more respect than I felt. He added:

"Tell Strokor the dream thou hadst two nights ago, Edam. It were a right strange thing, whether true or no."

The stripling shifted his weight on his stool, and moved the bowl closer. Then he thrust his pipe deep into it, and let the liquid flow slowly out his nostrils.[2]

---

1. Since Mercury had no moon, its people never coined a word to correspond with our "month," and for the same reason they never had a week. Their time was reckoned only in days, years, and fractions of the two.
2. A curious custom among the Mercurians, who had no tobacco. There is no other way to explain some of the carvings. Doubtless the liquid was sweet-smelling, and perhaps slightly narcotic.

"I saw this," he began, "immediately before rising, and after a very light supper; so I know that it was a vision from Jon, and not of my own making.

"I was standing upon the summit of a mountain, and gazing down upon a very large, fertile valley. It was heavily wooded, dark green and inviting. But what first drew my attention was a great number of animals moving about *in the air*. They were passing strange affairs, some large, some small, variously coloured, and all covered with the same sort of fur, quite unlike any hair I have ever seen."

"In the air?" I echoed, recovering from my astonishment. Then I laughed mightily. "Man, ye must be crazy! There is no animal can live in the air! Ye must mean in the water or on land."

"Nay," interposed the star-gazer. "Thou hast never studied the stars, Strokor, or thou wouldst know that there be a number of them which, through the enlarging tube, show themselves to be round worlds, like unto our own.

"And it doth further appear that these other worlds also have air like this we breathe, and that some have less, while others have even more. From what Edam has told me," finished the old man, "I judge that his vision took place on Jeos,[3] a world much larger than ours according to my calculations, and doubtless having enough air to permit very light creatures to move about in it."

"Go on," said I to Edam, good-humouredly. "I be ever willing to believe anything strange when my stomach is full."

The dreamer had taken no offense. "Then I bent my gaze closer, as I am always able, in visions. And I saw that the greenery was most remarkably dense, tangled and luxuriant to a degree not ever seen here. And moving about in it was the most extraordinary collection of beings that I have ever laid these eyes upon.

"There were some huge creatures, quite as tall as thy house, Strokor, with legs as big around as that huge chest of thine. They

---

3. The Mercurian word for earth.

47

had tails, as had our ancient *mulikka*,[4] save that these were terrific things, as long and as big as the trunk of a large tree. I know not their names.

"And then, at the other extreme, was a tiny creature of the air, which moved with a musical hum. It could have hid under thy finger-nail, Strokor, yet it had a tiny sharp-pointed bill, with which it stung most aggravatingly. And between these two there were any number of creatures of varying size and shape.

"But nowhere was there a sign of a man. True, there was one hairy, grotesque creature which hung by its hands and feet from the tree-tops, very like thee in some way, Strokor; but its face and head were those of a brainless beast, not of a man. Nowhere was a creature like me or thee.

"And the most curious thing was this: Although there were ten times as many of these creatures, big and little, to the same space as on our world, yet there was no great amount of strife. In truth, there is far more combat and destruction among we men than among the beasts.

"And," he spoke most earnestly, as though he would not care to be disbelieved, "I saw fathers fight to protect their young!"

I near fell from my stool in my amaze. Never in all my life had I heard a thing so far from the fact. "What!" I shouted. "Ye sit there like a sane man, and tell me ye saw fathers fight for their young?"

He nodded his head, still very gravely. I fell silent for want of words, but Maka put in a thought. "It would appear, Strokor, that it be not so much of an effort for beings to live, there on Jeos, as here. Perchance 'tis the greater amount of vegetation; at all accounts, the animals need not prey upon one another so generally; and that, then, would explain why some have energy enough to waste in the care of their young."

"I can understand," I said, very slowly. "I can understand why a mother will fight for her babes; 'tis reasonable enough, no doubt. But as for fathers doing the same—Edam, dost mean to say that *all* creatures on Jeos do this?"

---

4. Probably the dinosaur.

48

"Nay; only some. It may be that fewer than half of the varieties have the custom. Howbeit, 'tis a beautiful one. When the vision ended I was right loath to go."

"Faugh!" I spat upon the ground. "Such softness makes me ill! I be glad I were born in a man's world, where I can take a man's chances. I want no favouring. If I am strong enough to live, I live; if not, I die. What more can I ask?"

"Aye, my lad!" said Maka approvingly. "This be a world for the strong. There is no room here for others; there is scarce enough food for those who, thanks to their strength, do survive." He slipped the gold band from off his wrist, and held it up for Jon to see. "Here, Strokor, a pledge! A pledge to—the survival of the fittest!"

"A neat, neat wording!" I roared, as I took the pledge with him. Then we both stopped short. Edam had not joined us. "Edam, my lad," spake the old man, "ye will take the pledge with us?"

The stripling's eyes were troubled. Well he knew that, once he refused such an act, he were no longer welcome in my house, nor in Maka's. But when he looked around it were bravely enough.

"Men, I have neither the strength of the one nor the brains of the other of ye. I am but a watchmaker; I live because of my skill with the little wheels.

"I have no quarrel with either of ye." He got to his feet, and started to the door. "But I cannot take the pledge with ye.

"I have seen a wondrous thing, and I love it. And, though I know not why—I feel that Jon has willed it for Jeos to see a new race of men, a race even better than ours."

I leaped to my feet. "Better than ours! Mean ye to say, stripling, that there can be a better man than Strokor?"

I full expected him to shrink from me in fear; I was able to crush him with one blow. But he stood his ground; nay, stepped forward and laid a hand easily upon my shoulder.

"Strokor—ye are more than a man; ye are two men in one. There is no finer—I say it fair. And yet, I doubt not that there can be, and will be, a better!"

And with that such a curious expression came into his face, such a glow of some strange land of warmth, that I let my hand drop and suffered him to depart in peace—such was my wonder.

Besides, any miserable lout could have destroyed the lad.

Maka sat deep in thought for a time, and when he did speak he made no mention of the lad who had just quit us. Instead, he looked me over, long and earnestly, and at the end he shook his head sorrowfully and sighed:

"Thou art the sort of a son I would have had, Strokor, given the wits of thy father to hold a woman like thy mother. And thou didst save my life."

He mused a little longer, then roused himself and spake sharply: "Thou art a vain man, Strokor!"

"Aye," I agreed, willingly enough. "And none has better cause than I!"

He would not acknowledge the quip. "Thou hast everything needful to tickle thy vanity. Thou hast the envy of those who note thy strength, the praise of them who love thy courage, and the respect of they who value thy brains. All these thou hast—and yet ye have not that which is best!"

I thought swiftly and turned on him with a frown: "Mean ye that I am not handsome enough?"

"Nay, Strokor," quoth the star-gazer. "There be none handsomer in this world, no matter what the standard of any other, such as Edam's Jeos.

"It is not that. It is, that thou hast no ambition."

I considered this deeply. At first thought it was not true; had I not always made it a point to best my opponent? From my youth it had been ever my custom to succeed where bigger bodies and older minds had failed. Was not this ambition?

But before I disputed the point with Maka, I saw what he meant. I had no *final* ambition, no ultimate goal for which to strive. I had been content from year to year to outdo each rival as he came before me; and now, with mind and body alike in the pink of condition, I was come to the place where none durst stand before me.

"Ye are right, Maka," I admitted, not because I cared to gratify his conceit, but because it were always for my own good to own up when wrong, that I might learn the better. "Ye are right; I need to decide upon a life-purpose. What have ye thought?"

The old man was greatly pleased. "Our talk with Edam brought it all before me. Know you, Strokor, that the survival of the fittest is a rule which governs man as well as men. It applies to the entire population, Strokor, just as truly as to me or thee.

"In fine, we men who are now the sole inhabitants of this world, are descended from a race of people who survived solely because they were fitter than the *mulikka*, fitter than the reptiles, the fittest, by far, of all the creatures.

"That being the case, it is plain that in time either our empire, or that of Klow's, must triumph over the other. And that which remains shall be the fittest!"

"Hold!" I cried. "Why cannot matters remain just as they now are—and forever?"

"That" he said rapidly, "is because thou knowest so little about the future of this world. But I am famed as a student of the heavens; and I tell thee it is possible, by means of certain delicate measuring instruments, together with the highest mathematics, to keep a very close watch upon the course of our world. And we now know that our year is much shorter than it was in the days of the *mulikka*."

I nodded my head. "Rightly enough, since our days are become steadily longer, for some mysterious reason."

"A reason no longer a mystery," quoth Maka. "It is now known that the sun is a very powerful magnet, and that it is constantly pulling upon our world and bringing it nearer and nearer to himself. That is why it hath become slightly warmer during the past hundred years; the records show it plain. And the same influence has caused the lengthening of our day."

He stopped and let me think. Soon I saw it clearly enough; a time must come when the increasing warmth of the sun would stifle all forms of vegetable life, and that would mean the choking of mankind. It might take untold centuries; yet, plainly enough, the world must someday become too small for even those who now remained upon it.

Suddenly I leaped to my feet and strode the room in my excitement. "Ye are right, Maka!" I shouted, thoroughly aroused. "There cannot always be the two empires. In time one or the other must prevail; Jon has willed it. And—" I stopped short and stared at him—"I need not tell ye which it shall be!"

"I knew thou wouldst see the light, Strokor! Thou hast thy father's brains."

I sat me down, but instantly leaped up again, such was my enthusiasm. "Maka," I cried, "our emperor is not the man for the place! It is true that he were a brave warrior in his youth; he won the throne fairly. And we have suffered him to keep it because he is a wise man, and because we have had little trouble with the men of Klow since their defeat two generations agone.

"But he, today, is content to sit at his ease and quote platitudes about live and let live. Faugh! I am ashamed that I should even have given ear to him!"

I stopped short and glared at the old man. "Maka—hark ye well! If it be the will of Jon to decide between the men of Klow and the men of Vlamaland, then it is my intent to take a hand in this decision!"

"Aye, my lad," he said tranquilly; and then added, quite as though he knew what my answer must be: "How do ye intend to go about it?"

"Like a man! I, Strokor, shall become the emperor!"

3

THE THRONE

A small storm had come up while Maka and I were talking. Now, as he was about to quit me, the clouds were clearing away and an occasional stroke of lightning came down. One of these, however, hit the ground such a short distance away that both of us could smell the smoke.

My mind was more alive than it had ever been before. "Now, what caused that, Maka? The lightning, I mean; we have it nearly every day, yet I have never thought to question it before."

"It is no mystery, my lad," quoth Maka, dodging into his chariot, so that he was not wet. "I myself have watched the thing from the top of high mountains, where the air is so light that a man can scarce get enough to fill his lungs; and I say unto you that, were it not for what air we have, we should have naught save the lightning. The space about the air is full of it."

He started his engine, then leaned out into the rain and said softly: "Hold fast to what thy father has taught thee, Strokor. Have nothing to do with the women. 'Tis a man's job ahead of thee, and the future of the empire is in thy hands.

"And," as he clattered off, "fill not thy head with wonderings about the lightning."

"Aye," said I right earnestly, and immediately turned my thoughts to my new ambition. And yet the thing Maka had just told me kept coming back to my mind, and so it does to this very day. I know not why I should mention it at all save that each time I think upon Maka, I also think upon the lightning, whether I will or no.

I slept not at all that night, but sat[1] till the dawn came, thinking out a plan of action. By that time I was fair convinced that there was naught to be gained by waiting; waiting makes me impatient as well. I determined to act at once; and since one day is quite as good as the next, I decided that this day was to see the thing begun.

I came before the emperor at noon and received my decorations. Within the hour I had made myself known to the four and ninety men who were to be my command; a picked company, all of a height and weight, with bodies that lacked little of my own perfection. Never was there a finer guard about the palace.

My first care was to pick a quarrel with the outgoing com-

---

1. It seems to have been the custom among the soldiers never to lie down, but to take their sleep sitting or standing; a habit not hard to form where the gravitation was so slight. No doubt this also explains their stunted legs.

mander. 'Twere easy enough; he was green with envy, anyhow. And so it came about that we met about mid afternoon, with seconds, in a well-frequented field in the outskirts.

Before supper was eaten my entire troop knew that their new captain had tossed his ball-slinger away without using it, had taken twenty balls from their former commander's weapon, and while thus wounded had charged the man and despatched him with bare hands! Needless to say, this exploit quite won their hearts; none but a blind man could have missed the respect they showed me when, all bandaged and sore, I lined them up next morning. Afterward I learned that they had all taken a pledge to "follow Strokor through the gates of Hofe itself!"

'Twere but a week later that, fully recovered and in perfect fettle, I called my men together one morn as the sun rose. By that time I had given them a sample of my brains through ordering a rearrangement of their quarters such as made the same much more comfortable. Also, I had dealt with one slight infraction of the rules in such a drastic fashion that they knew I would brook no trifling. All told, 'tis hard to say whether they thought the most of me or of Jon.

"Men," said I, as bluntly as I knew, "the emperor is an old man. And, as ye know, he is disposed to be lenient toward the men of Klow; whereas, ye and I well know that the louts are blackguards.

"Now, I will tell ye more. It has come to me lately that Klow is plotting to attack us with strange weapons." I thought best, considering their ignorance, not to give them my own reasons. "Of course I have told the emperor of it; yet he will not act. He says to wait till we are attacked."

I stopped and watched their faces. Sure enough; the idea fair made them ache. Each and every one of these men was spoiling for a fight.

"Now, tell me; how would ye like to become the emperor's body-guard?" I did not have to wait long; the light that flared in their faces told me plainly. "And—how would ye like to have me for your emperor?"

At that their tongues were loosed, and I hindered them not. They yelled for pure joy, and pressed about me like a pack of children. I saw that the time was ripe for action.

"Up, then!" I roared, and, of course, led the way. We met the emperor's guard on the lower stairs; and from that point on we fair hacked our way through.

Well, no need to describe the fight. For a time I thought we were gone; the guards had a cunningly devised labyrinth on the second floor, and attacked us from holes in a false ceiling, so that we suffered heavily at first. But I saw what was amiss, and shouted to my men to clear away the timbers; and after that it was clear work. I lost forty men before the guard was disposed of. The emperor I finished myself; he dodged right spryly for a time, but at last I caught him and tossed him to the foot of the upper stairs. And there he still lies for none of my men would touch him, nor would I. We covered him with quicklime and some earth.

As soon as we had taken care of those who were not too far gone, I called the men together and caused a round of spirits to be served. Then we all feasted on the emperor's store, and soon were feeling like ourselves.

"Men," I said impressively, "I am proud of ye. Never did an emperor have such a dangerous gang of bullies!"

At that they all grinned happily, and I added: "And 'tis a fine staff of generals that ye'll make!"

Need I say more? Those men would have overturned the palace for me had I said the word. As it was, they obeyed my next orders in such a spirit that success was assured from the first.

First, using the dead emperor's name, I caused the various chiefs to be brought together at once to the court chamber. At the same time I contrived, by means I need not go into here, to prevent any word of our action from getting abroad. So, when the former staff faced me the next morning, they learned that they were to be executed. I could trust not one; they were all friends of the old man.

With the chiefs out of the way, and my own men taking

55

their commands, the whole army fell into my hands. True, there were some insurrections here and there; but my men handled them with such speed and harshness that any further stubbornness turned to admiration. By this time the fame of Strokor was spread throughout the empire.

And thus it came about that, within a week of the night that old Maka first put the idea into my head, Strokor, son of Strok, reigned throughout Vlamaland. And, to make it complete, the army celebrated my accession by taking a pledge before Jon:

"To Strokor, the fittest of the fit!"

4

THE ASSAULT

Now, out of a total population of perhaps three million, I had about a quarter-million first-class fighters in my half of the world. Klow, by comparison, had but two-thirds the number; his land was not a rich one.

But he had the advantage of knowing, some while in advance, of the new ruler in Vlama; and shortly my spies reported that his armouries were devising a new type of weapon. 'Twas a strange verification of my own fiction to my men. I could learn nothing, however, about it.

Meanwhile I caused a vast number of flat-boats to be built, all in secret. Each of them was intended for a single fighter and his supplies; and each was so arranged, with side paddle wheels, that it would be driven by the motor in the soldier's chariot, and thus give each his own boat.

Again discarding all precedent, I packed not all my forces together, as had been done in the past, but scattered them up and adown the coast fronting the land of Klow; and at a prearranged time my quarter-million men set out, a company in each tiny fleet. Some were slightly in advance of the rest, who had the shorter distance to travel. And, just as I had planned, we all arrived at a certain spot on Klow's coast at practically the same hour, although two nights later.

'Twas a brilliant stroke. The enemy looked not for a fleet of water-ants, ready to step right out of the sea into battle. Their fleet was looking for us, true, but not in that shape. And we were all safely ashore before they had ceased to scour the seas for us.

I immediately placed my heavy machines, and just as all former expeditions had done, opened the assault at once with a shower of the poison shells. I relied, it will be seen, upon the surprise of my attack to strike terror into the hearts of the louts.

But apparently they were prepared for anything, no matter how rapid the attack.

My bombardment had not proceeded many moments before, to my dismay, some of their own shells began to fall among us. Soon they were giving as good as we.

"Now, how knew they that we should come to this spot?" I demanded of Maka. I had placed him in my cabinet as soon as I had reached the throne.

The old man stroked his beard gravely. "Perchance it had been wrong to come to the old landing. They simply began shelling it as a matter of course."

"Ye are right again," I told him; and forthwith moved my pieces over into another triangle. (Previously, of course, all my charioteers had gone on toward the capital). However, I took care to move my machines, one at a time, so that there was no let-up in my bombardment.

But scarce had we taken up the new position before the enemy's shells likewise shifted, and began to strike once more in our midst. I swore a great oath and whirled upon Maka in wrath.

"Think ye that there be a spy among us?" I demanded. "How else can ye explain this thing? My men have combed the land about us; there are none of the louts secreted here; and, even so, they could not have notified Klow so soon. Besides, 'tis pitch dark." I were sorely mystified.

All we could do was to fling our shells as fast as our machines would work and dodge the enemy's hail as best we could. Thus the time passed, and it were near dawn when the first messengers[1] returned.

"They have stopped us just outside the walls of the city," was the report. It pleased me that they should have pushed so far at first; I climbed at once into my chariot.

"Now is the time for Strokor to strike!" I gave orders for the staff to remain where it was. "I will send ye word when the city is mine."

But before I started my engine I glanced up at the sky, to see if the dawn were yet come; and as I gazed I thought I saw something come between me and a star. I brushed the hair away from my eyes, and looked again. To my boundless surprise I made out, not one, but three strange objects moving about swiftly in the air!

"Look!" I cried, and my whole staff craned their necks. In a moment all had seen, and great was their wonder. I blamed them not for their fears.

'Twas Maka who spoke first. "They are much too large to be creatures of Jon," he muttered. "They must be some trick of the enemy.

"Dost recall Edam's vision of the creatures in the air of Jeos?" he went on, knowing that I would not hinder him. "Now, as I remember it, he said they flew with great speed. Were it not possible, Strokor, for suitable engines to propel very light structures at such high speed as to remain suspended in the air, after the manner of leaves in a storm? I note these strangers move quite fast."

It was even so; and at that same instant one of them swung directly above our heads, so close that I could hear the hum of a powerful engine. So it was only a trick! I shook myself together.

"Attention!" My staff drew up at the word. "They are but

---

1. Messengers; no telegraph or telephone, much less wireless. In a civilization as strenuous as that of Mercury, there was never enough consideration for others to lead to such socially beneficial things as these, no more than railroads or printing presses. Civilization appears to be in exact proportion to the ease of getting a living, other conditions being equal.

few; fear them not! We waste no more time here! Pack up the machines, and follow!"

And thus we charged upon Klow.

I found that my men had entirely surrounded the city. Klow's men were putting up a plucky fight, and showing no signs of fearing us. Seeing this, I blew a blast on my engine's whistle, so that my bullies might know that I had come.

Immediately the word ran up and down the line, so that within a few minutes Klow was facing a roaring crowd of half-mad terrors. I myself set the example by charging the nearest group of the enemy, all of whom were mounted within the rather small and perfectly circular chariots which they preferred. They were quick, but slippery. Also, they could not stand before a determined rush, as several of them learned after vainly trying to slip some balls through my windows and, failing in that, striving to get away from me.

But I ran them down, and toppled them over, and dropped suffocation bombs into their little cages with such vigour and disregard of their volleys that my men could not resist the example. We charged all along that vast circular line, and we cheered mightily when the whole front broke, turned tail, and ran before us.

But scarce had they got away before a queer thing happened. A flock of those great air-creatures, some eight altogether, rose up from the middle of the city. It was now fairly light, and we could see well. One of them had some sort of engine trouble, so that it had to return at once; but the other seven came out to the battle-line and began to circle the city.

As they did so they dropped odd, misshapen parcels, totally unlike materials of war; but when they struck they gave off pro-digious puffs of a greenish smoke, of so terribly pungent a na-ture that my men dropped before it like apples from a shaken tree. 'Twas a fearful sight; lucky for us that the louts had had no practice, else few of us should be alive to tell the tale.

And so they swept around the great circle, many triangles in area; and everywhere the unthinkable things smote the hearts of my men with a fear they had never known. Only one of the devices suffered; it was brought down by a chance fling of a poison shell. The rest, after loosing their burdens, returned to the city for more.

I am no fool. I saw that we could do nothing against such weapons, but must use all our wits if we escaped even.

"Return!" I commanded, and instantly my staff whistled the code. The men obeyed with alacrity, making off at top speed with the men of Klow in hot pursuit, although able to do little damage.

Aye, it were a sorrowful thing, that retreat. The best I could do was to remain till the very last, having to deal with a number of persistent louts who all but suffocated me, at that. But I managed to empty my slinger into some of them and to topple the rest. I was mainly angry that Klow had not showed himself.

By the time I had reached the seashore, most of my men were in their boats. Again I stayed till the last, although I could see the enemy's fleet bearing down hard upon us from the north. In truth we would have all been lost, had we come in the manner of former campaigns, all together in big transports. But because we could scatter every which way, the fleet harmed us little; and four-fifths of us got safely back.

Happily, none of the air-machines had range enough to reach Vlamaland. As soon as I could get my staff together, I gave orders such as would insure discipline. Then, reminding my hearties that Klow, knowing our helplessness, would surely attack as soon as fully equipped, I made this offer:

"To the man who shall suggest the best way of meeting their attack, I shall give the third of my empire!"

So they knew that the case was desperate. As for myself, I slept not a bit, but paced my sleep-chamber and thought deeply.

Now, a bit of a shell, from an enemy slinger, had penetrated my arm. Till now, I had paid no attention to it. But it began to bother me, so I pulled the metal from my arm with my teeth. And quite by chance I placed the billet on the table within a few inches of the compass I had carried on my boat.

To my intense surprise the needle of the compass swung violently about, so that one end pointed directly at the fragment of metal. I moved them closer together; there was no doubt that they were strongly attracted. The enemy's shells were made of mere iron!

The moment I fully realized this, I saw clearly how we might baffle the men of Klow. I instantly summoned some men gave the orders much as though I had known for years what was to be done, and in a few moments had the satisfaction of seeing my messengers hurrying north and south.

And so it came about that, within three days of our shameful retreat, a tenth of my men were at work on the new project. As yet there was no word from my spies across the sea; but we worked with all possible haste. And this, very briefly, is what we did:

We laid a gigantic line of iron clear across the empire. From north to south, from snow to snow; one end was bedded in the island of Pathna, where the north magnetic-pole is found, while the other stopped on the opposite side of the world, in a hole dug through the ice into the solid earth of the South Polar Plain. And every foot of that enormous rod— 'twas as big around as my leg—was insulated from the ground with pieces of our secret non-magnetic alloy!

Not for nothing had our chemists sought the metal which would resist the lightning. And not for nothing did my bullies piece the rod together, all working at the same time, so that the whole thing were complete in seven days. That is, complete save for the final connecting link; and that lay, a log-like roll of iron, at the door of my palace, ready to be rolled into place when I were but ready.

And on the morrow the Klow reached our shores.

5

THE VICTORY

My first intent was to let them advance unhampered; but Maka pointed out that such a policy might give them suspicions, and so we disputed their course all the way. I gave orders to show no great amount of resistance; and thus, the louts reached Vlama in high feather, confident that the game was theirs.

I stood at the door of the palace as Klow himself rolled up to the edge of the parade-ground. My men, obeying orders, had given way to him; his crews swarmed the space behind and on all sides of him, while my own bullies were all about and behind the palace. Never did two such giant armies face one another in peace; for I had caused my banner to be floated wrong end to, in token of surrender.

First, a small body of subordinates waited upon me, demanding that I give up the throne. I answered that I would treat with none save Klow himself; and shortly the knave, surrounded by perhaps fifty underlings, stepped up before me.

"Hail, Strokor!" he growled, his voice shaking a bit with excitement; not with fear, for he were a brave man. "Hail to thee and to thine, and a pleasant stay in Hofe for ye all!"

"Hail, Klow!" replied I, glancing up meaningly at the air monsters wheeling there. "I take it that ye purpose to execute us."

"Aye," he growled savagely. "Thou didst attack without provocation. Thy life is forfeit, and as many more as may be found needful to guarantee peace."

"Then," I quoth, my manner changing, "then ye have saved me the trouble of deciding what shall be thy fate. Execution, say you? So be it!"

And I strode down to the great log of iron which lay ready to fill the gap. Klow looked at me with a peculiar expression, as though he thought me mad. True, it looked it; how could I do him harm without myself suffering?

But I kicked the props which held the iron, and gave it a start with my foot. The ends of the pole-to-pole rod lay concealed by brush, perchance fifty yards away. In ten seconds that last section had rolled completely between them; and only a fool would have missed seeing that, the last ten feet, the iron was fair jerked through the air.

As this happened we all heard a tremendous crackling, like

that of nearby lightning, while enormous clouds of dust arose from the two concealed ends, which were now become connections. And at the same time a loud, steely click, just one and no more, sounded from the intruding host.

For a moment Klow was vastly puzzled. Then he snarled angrily: "What means this foolery, Strokor? Advance, and give up thy axe!"

For answer I turned me about, so as to face my men, and held up my hand in signal. Instantly the whistles sounded, and my hearties came bounding into the field.

"Treachery!" shouted Klow; and his officers ran here and there, shouting: "To arms! Charge and destroy! No quarter!"

But I paid little attention to the hubbub. I were gazing up at those infernal creatures of the air; and my heart sang within me as I saw them, circling erratically but very surely down to the earth. And as they came nearer, my satisfaction was entire; for their engines were silent!

At the same time consternation was reigning among our visitors. Not a man of all Klow's thousands was able to move his car or lift a weapon. Every slinger was jammed, as though frozen by invisible ice; all their balls and shells were stuck together, like the work of a transparent glue. Even their side arms were locked in their scabbards; and all their tugging could budge them not!

But none of my men were so handicapped. Each man's chariot was running as though naught had happened; they thundered forward, discharging their balls and shells as freely as they had across the sea. Their charge was a murderous one; not a man of Klow's was able to resist, save with what force he could put into his bare hands.

Klow saw all this from the middle of his group of officers. None were able to more than place his body 'twixt us and their chief. In a very few moments they saw that the unknown magic had made them as children in our hands; they were utterly lost; and Klow turned away from the sight with a black face. Again he faced me.

"What means this, ye huge bundle of lies? What mean ye by

tricking us with yon badge of surrender, only to tie our hands with thy magic of Hofe? Is this the way to fight like a man?"

I had stood at ease in my door since rolling the iron. Now, I looked about me still more easily; my men were running down the louts, who had jumped from their useless chariots and taken to their heels.

'Twere but a matter of time before the army of Klow would be no more, at that rate.

"Klow," I answered him mildly; "ye are right; this is not the way to fight like a man. Neither," I pointed out one of the fallen air-cars; "neither is that the way, flitting over our heads like shadows, and destroying us with filthy smoke! Shame on ye, Klow, for stooping to such! And upon thy own head be the blame for the trick I have played upon ye!"

"You attacked us without provocation," he muttered, sourly.

"Aye, and for a very good reason," I replied. "Yet I see thy viewpoint, and shalt give thee the benefit of the doubt." I turned to my whistlers and gave an order; so that presently the great slaughter had stopped. My men and Klow's alike struggled back to see what were amiss.

I handed Klow an axe. "Throw away thine own, scabbard and all," I told him. "It is useless, for 'tis made of iron. Ours, and all our tools of war, are formed of an alloy which is immune from the magic."

He took the axe in wonderment. "What means it, Strokor?" asked he again, meanwhile stripping himself in a businesslike fashion that it were good to see.

"It means," said I, throwing off my robe, "that I have unchained the magnetism of this world. Know you, Klow, that all of the children of the sun are full of his power; it is like unto that of the tiny magnet which ye give children for to play; but it is mighty, even as our world is mighty."

"Good Jon!" he gasped; for his was not a daring mind. "What have ye done, ye trifler?"

"I have transformed this empire into one vast magnet," I answered coolly. Then I showed him a boulder on the summit of a distant hill; through the tube, Klow could see some of my men standing beside it.

"Place one of thy own men on the roof of the palace," I told Klow, "and give him orders to lower my banner should ye give him the word.

"For upon the outcome of this fight 'twixt me and thee, Klow, hinges the whole affair! If thou dost survive, down comes my banner; and my men on the hill shall topple the boulder which shall rush down the slope and burst the iron rod and break the spell. Stand, then, and defend thyself!"

And it did me good to see the spirit fly into his eyes. He saw that his empire lived or died as he lived or died, and he fought as he had never fought before. Small man that he was beside myself, he were wondrous quick and sure in his motions; before I knew it, he had bit his axe deep into my side.

And in another moment or two it was over. For, as soon as I felt the pain of that gash, I flung my own blade away; and with a roar such as would have shaken a stouter heart than his, I charged the man, took a second fearful blow full on my chest and heeding it not at all I snatched the axe from his hands. Then, as he turned to run, I dropped that tool also. And I ran him down, and felled him, and broke his head with my hands.

6
THE FITTEST

. . . . slaves; but the most were slain. Neither could we bother with their women and others left behind.[1]

Now, by this time the empire was as one man in its worship of me. I had been emperor but a year, and already I had made it certain that only the men of Vlamaland, and no others, should live in the sight of Jon. So well thought they of me, I might fair

---

1. This chapter was originally as long as the others, but an unfortunate accident of Mr. Smith's, before he was thoroughly familiar with the machine, mutilated a large portion of the tape so badly that it was made worthless. This explains why something appears to be missing from the account, and also why this chapter begins in the middle of a sentence.

have sat upon my reputation, and have spent my last days in feasting like the man before me.

But I was still too young and full of energy to take my ease. I found myself more and more restless; I had naught to do; it had all been done. At last I sent for old Maka.

"Ye put me up to this, ye old fraud," I told him, pretending to be wrathful. "Now set me another task, or I'll have thy head!"

He knew me too well to be affrighted. He said that he had been considering my case of late.

"Strokor, thy father was right when he told thee to have naught to do with women. That is to say, he were right at the time. Were he alive today"—I forgot to say that my father was killed in the battle across the sea—"he would of a certainty say that it were high time for thee to pick thy mate.

"Remember, Strokor; great though thou art, yet when death taketh thee thy greatness is become a memory. Methinks ye should leave something more substantial behind."

It took but little thought to convince me that Maka were right once more. Fact; as soon as I thought upon it, it were a woman that I was restless for. The mere notion instantly gave me something worthwhile to look forward to.

"Jon bless thee!" I told the old man. "Ye have named both the trouble and the remedy. I will attend to it at once."

He sat thinking for some time longer. "Has thought of any woman in special, Strokor?" said he.

I had not. The idea was too new to me. "The best in the world shall be mine, of course," I told him. "But as for which one—hast any notion thyself?"

"Aye," he quoth. "'Tis my own niece I have in mind. Perchance ye remember her; a pretty child, who was with me when thou didst save my life up there on the mountainside."

I recalled the chit fairly well. "But she were not a vigorous woman, Maka. Think you she is fit for me?"

"Aye, if any be," he replied earnestly. "Ave is not robust, true, but her muscles are as wires. It is because of what lies in her head, however, that I commend her. I have taught her all I know."

"So!" I exclaimed, much pleased. "Then she is indeed fit to be the empress. And as I recall her, she were exceedingly good to look at."

"Say no more. Ave shall be the wife of Strokor!" And so it was arranged.

Well, and there ye have the story of Strokor, the mightiest man in the world, and the wisest. More than this I shall not tell with my own lips; I shall have singers recite my deeds until half the compartments in the House of Words is filled with the records thereof. But it were well that I should tell this much in mine own way. My ambition is fulfilled. Let the hand of Jon descend upon our world, if it may; I care not if presently the sun come nearer, and the water dry up, and the days grow longer and longer, till the day and the year become of the same length. I care not; my people, such as be left of them, shall own what there is, and shall live as long as life is possible.

I shall leave behind no race of weaklings. Every man shall be fit to live, and the fittest of them all shall live the longer. And he, no matter how many cycles hence, shall look back to Strokor, and to Ave, his wife, and shall say:

"I am what I am, the last man on the world, because Strokor was the fittest man of his time!"

Aye; my fame shall live as long as there be life. Tonight, as I speak these things into the word machine, my heart is singing with the joy of it all. Thank Jon, I were born a man, not a woman!

Tomorrow I go to fetch Ave. I shall not send for her; I cannot trust her beauty to the hands of my crew. The more I think of her, the more I see that mine whole life hath been devised for this one moment. I see that, insignificant though she be, Ave is a needed link in the chain. I have come to want her more than food; I am become a lovesick fool!

Aye! I can afford to poke fun at myself. I can afford anything in this world; for I be its greatest man.

Its greatest man! Here is the place to stop. There is no more I can say, the story is done; the story of Strokor, the greatest man in the whole world!

7
The Going

'Tis several years since last I faced this machine, many and many a day since I said that my story was done, and placed the record on the shelf of my anteroom, my heart full of satisfaction. And today I must needs add another record, perhaps two, to the pile.

When I set out for the highlands on the morn following what I last related I took with me but two or three men; not that I had any need for guards, but because it looketh not well for the emperor to travel without retainers, however few. Practically, I was alone.

I reached the locality as the sun went down. The sky was a brilliant colour; I remember it well. Darkness would come soon, though not as quickly as farther south. Commonly, I think not upon such trifles; but I were nearing my love, and tender things came easily to my mind.

My chariot kept to the road which lay alongside the irrigating flume, a stone trough which runs from the snow-covered hills to the dry country below. I had already noted this flume where it emptied into the basin in the valley below; for it had had a new kind of a spillway affixed to it, a broad, smooth platform with a slightly upward curve, over which the water was shooting. I saw no sense in the arrangement, and made up my mind to ask Maka about it; for the empire prized this trough most highly. It ran straight and true, over expensive bridges where needed, with scarce a bend to hold back the flow.

When I stopped my car outside the house I was surprised that none should come out to greet me. Maka had sent word of my coming; all should have been in readiness. But I was forced to use my whistle. There was no stir. I became angry; I told my bullies to stay where they were, and myself burst in the door.

The house was a sturdy stone affair of one floor, set against the side of the mountain, a short distance above the flume. I looked about the interior in surprise; for not a soul was in sight in any of the compartments. There were signs that people had been there but a few moments before. I called it strange, for I had seen no one leave the house as I approached.

At last, as I was inspecting the eating place, I noted a small door let into the outer wall. It was open; and by squeezing I managed to get through. I found that it let into a long, dark passage.

I followed this, going steadily down a flight of stairs, and all of a sudden bumped into an iron grating. At the same moment I saw that the passageway made a turn just beyond; and by craning my neck and straining my eyes I could see a faintly lighted chamber just a few feet away.

And before my eyes could scarce make out the figures of some people in the middle of the place, a voice came to my ear.

"Hail, Strokor!" it said; and great was my astonishment as I recognized the tones of Edam, the young dreamer whom Maka had brought to my house.

"Edam!" I cried. "What do ye here? Come and open these bars!"

He made no reply, save to laugh in a way I did not like. I shook the grating savagely, so that I felt it give. "Edam!" I roared. "Open this grating at once; and tell me, where is Ave?"

"I am here," came another voice; and I stopped in sheer surprise, to peer closer and to see, for the first time, that it were really the dreamer and the chit, these two and no more, who sat there in the underground chamber. They seemed to be sitting in some sort of a box, with glass windows.

"Ave—come here!" I spoke much more gently than to Edam; for my heart was soft with thoughts of her. "It is thy lord, Strokor, the emperor, who calls thee. Come!"

"I stay here," said she in the same clear voice, entirely unshaken by my presence. "Edam hath claimed me, and I shall cleave to him. I want none of ye, ye giant!"

For a moment I was minded to throw my weight against the barrier, such was my rage. Then I thought better on it, and closely examined the bars. Two were loose.

"Ave," said I, contriving to keep my voice even, although

my hands were busy with the bars as I spake. "Ave—ye do wrong to spite me thus. Know ye not that I am the emperor, and that these bars cannot stand before me? I warn ye, if I must call my men to help me, and to witness my shame, it will go hard with ye! Better that ye should come willingly. Ye are not for such as Edam."

"No?" quoth the young man, speaking up for the chit. "Ye are wrong, Strokor. We defy thee to do thy worst; we are prepared to flee from ye at all costs!"

I had twisted one of the bars out of my way without their seeing it. I strove at the next as I answered, still controlling my voice: "'Twill do ye no good to flee, Edam; ye know that. And as for Ave—she shall wish she had never been born!"

"So I should," she replied with spirit, "if I were to become thy woman. But know you, Strokor, that Ave, the daughter of Durok, would rather die than take the name of one who had spurned her, as ye did me!"

So I had; it had slipped my mind. "But I want thee now, Ave," said I softly, preparing to slip through the opening I had made. "Surely ye would not take thine own life?"

"Nay," she answered, with a laugh in her voice. "Rather I would go with Edam here. I would go," she finished, her voice rising in her excitement, "away from this horrible man's world; away from it all, Strokor, and to Jeos! Hear ye? To Jeos! And—"

But at that instant I burst through the grating. Without a sound I charged straight for the pair of them. And without a sound they slipped away from before my grasp. Next second I was gazing stupidly at the rushing, swirling water of the flume.

And I saw that they had been sitting in the cabin of a tiny boat, and that they had got away!

There was an opening into the outer air; I rushed through, and stared in the growing twilight down the black furrow of the flume. Far in the distance, and going like a streak, I spied the glittering glass windows of the little craft. Once I made out the flutter of a saucy hand.

"We shall get them when they reach the valley!" I shouted

to the men. Then I reached for my tube, and sighted it on the lower end of the flume, far, far below, almost too far away to be clear to the naked eye.

In an incredibly short time the craft reached the end. It travelled at an extraordinary rate; perchance 'twas weighted; I marvelled that its windows could stand the force of the air. And I scarce had time to fear that the twain should be destroyed on that upturned spillway before it was there.

And then an awesome thing happened. As the boat struck the incline it shot upward into the air at a steep slant. Up, up it went; my heart jumped into my mouth; for surely they must be crushed when they came down.

But the craft did not come down. It went on and on, up and up; its speed scarcely slackened; 'twas like that of a shooting star. And in far less time than it takes to tell it, the little boat was high up among the stars, going higher every instant, and farther away from me. And suddenly the sweat broke cold on my forehead; for dead ahead, directly in line with their travel, lay the bluish white gleam of Jeos.

So great was my rage over the escape of the dreamer with my woman, at first I felt no sorrow. Later, after days and days of search in and about the basin, I came to grieve most terribly over my loss. When I came home to the palace, I was well-nigh ill.

In vain did I make the most generous of rewards. The whole empire turned out to search for the missing ones, but nothing came of it all. Yet I never ceased to hope, especially after my talk with Maka.

"Aye," he said, when I questioned him, "it were barely possible that they have left this world for all time. I have calculated the speed which their craft might have attained, had it the right proportions, and, in truth, it might have left the spillway at such a speed that it entirely overcame the draw of the ground.

"But I think it were a slim chance. It is more than likely, Strokor, that Ave shall return to thee."

Was I not the fitter man? Surely Edam's purpose could not succeed; Jon would not have it so. The woman was mine, because I had chosen her; and she must come back to me, and in safety, or I should tear Edam into bits.

But as time went on and naught transpired, I became more and more melancholy. Life became an empty thing; it had been empty enough before I had craved the girl, but now it was empty with hopelessness.

After a while I got to thinking of some of the things Maka had told me. The more I thought of the future, the blacker it seemed. True, there were many other women; but there had been only one Ave. No such beauty had ever graced this world before. And I knew I could be happy with no other.

Now I saw that all my fame had been in vain. I had lost the only woman that was fit for me, and when I died there would be naught left but my name. Even that the next emperor might blot out, if he chose. It had all been in vain!

"It shall not be!" I roared to myself, as I strode about my compartment, gnawing at my hands in my misery. And in just such a fit of helpless anger the great idea came to me.

No sooner conceived than put into practice. I will not go closely into details; I will relate just the outstanding facts. What I did was to select a very tall mountain, located almost on the equator, and proclaimed my intention to erect a monument to Jon upon its summit. I caused vast quantities of materials to be brought to the place; and for a year a hundred thousand men laboured to put the pieces together.

When they had finished, they had made a mammoth tower partly of wood and partly of alloy. It was made in sections so that it might be placed, piece upon piece, one above another high into the sky.

It was an enormous task. When it was complete, I had a tower as high as the mountain itself erected upon its summit.

And next I caused section after section of the long, iron, pole-to-pole rod, which had tricked Klow, to be hauled up into the tower. I was only careful to begin the process from the top and work downward. I gave word that the last three sections be inserted at midday at a given day.

And at that hour I was safe inside a non-magnetic room.

I know right well when the deed was done. There was a most terrific earthquake. All about me, though I could see nothing at all, I could hear buildings falling. The din was appalling.

At the same time the air was fairly shattered with the rattle of the lightning. Never have I heard the like before. The rod had loosed the wrath of the forces above our air!

And as suddenly the whole deafening storm ended. Perchance the rod was destroyed by the lightning; I never went to see. For I know, the electricity split the very ground apart. But I gazed out of a window in the top of my palace, and saw that I had succeeded.

Not a soul but myself remained alive.

None but buildings made of the alloy were standing. Not only man, but most of his works had perished in that awful blast. I, alone, remained!

I, Strokor, am the survivor! I, the greatest man; it were but fit that I should be the last! No man shall come after me, to honour me or not as he chooses. I, and no other, shall be, the last man!

And when Ave returns—as she must, though it be ages hence—when she comes, she shall find me waiting. I, Strokor, the mighty and wise, shall be here when she returns. I shall wait for her forever; here I shall always stay. The stars may move from their places, but I shall not go! For it is my intention to make use of another secret Maka taught me. In brief—[1]

---

1. The record ends here. It may be that Strokor left the machine for some trivial reason, and forgot to finish his story. At all events, it is necessary to refer to the further discoveries of the expedition in order to learn the outcome of it all.

PART 3

The Survivor

Provided with a sledge-hammer, a crowbar, and a hydraulic jack, and even with drills and explosives as a last resort, Jackson, Kinney, and Van Emmon returned the same day to the walled-in room in the top of that mystifying mansion. The materials they carried would have made considerable of a load had not Smith removed enough of the weights from their suits to offset their burden. They reached the unopened door without special exertion, and with no mishap.

They looked in vain for a crack big enough to hold the point of the crowbar; neither could the most vigorous jabbing loosen any of the material. They dropped that tool and tried the sledge. It got no results; even in the hands of the husky geologist, the most vigorous blows failed to budge the door. They did not even dent it.

So they propped the powerful hydraulic jack, a tool sturdy enough to lift a house, at an angle against the door. Then, using the crowbar as a lever, the architect steadily turned up the screw, the mechanism multiplying his very ordinary strength a hundredfold. In a moment it could be seen that he was getting results; the door began to stir. Van Emmon struck one edge with the sledge-hammer, and it gave slightly.

In another minute the whole door, weighing over a ton, had been pushed almost out of its opening. The jack overbalanced, toppled over; they did not readjust it, but threw their combined weight upon the barrier.

There was no need to try again. With a shiver the huge slab of metal slid, upright, into the space beyond, stood straight on end for a second or so, then toppled to the floor.

And this time they heard the crash.

For, as the door fell, a great gust of wind rushed out with a hissing shriek, almost overbalancing the men from the earth. They stood still for a while, breathing hard from their exertion, trying in vain to peer into the blackness before them. Under no circumstances would either of them have admitted that he was gathering courage.

In a minute the architect, his eyes sparkling with his enthusiasm for the antique, picked up the electric torch and turned it into the compartment. As he did so the other two stepped to his side, so that the three of them faced the unknown together. It was just as well. Outlined in that circle of light, and not six feet in front of them, stood a great chair upon a wide platform; and seated in it, erect and alert, his wide open eyes staring straight into those of the three, was the frightful mountainous form of Strokor, the giant, himself.

For an indeterminable length of time the men from the earth stood there, speechless, unbreathing, staring at that awful monster as though at a nightmare. He did not move; he was entirely at ease, and yet plainly on guard, glaring at them with an air of conscious superiority which held them powerless. Instinctively they knew that the all-dominating voice in the records had belonged to this Hercules. But their instinct could not tell them whether the man still lived.

It was the doctor's brain that worked first. Automatically, from a lifelong habit of diagnosis, he inspected that dreadful figure quite as though it were that of a patient. Bit by bit his subconscious mind pieced together the evidence; the man in the chair showed no signs of life. And after a while the doctor's conscious mind also knew.

"He is dead," he said positively, in his natural voice; and such was the vast relief of the other two that they were in no way startled by the sound. Instantly all three drew long breaths; the tension was relaxed; and Van Emmon's curiosity found a harsh and unsteady voice.

"How under heaven has he been preserved all this time? Especially," he added, remembering, "considering the air that we found in the room?"

The doctor answered after a moment, his reply taking the form of advancing a step or two and holding out a hand. It touched glass.

For the first time since the discovery, the builder shifted the light. He had held it as still as death for a full minute. Now he flashed it all about the place, and they saw that the huge figure was entirely encased in glass. The cabinet measured about six feet on each of its sides, and about five feet in height; but such were the squat proportions of the occupant that he filled the whole space.

A slight examination showed that the case was not fixed to the platform, but had a separate bottom, upon which the stump-like chair was set. Also, they found that, thanks to the reduced pull of the planet, it was not hard for the three of them to lift the cabinet bodily, despite its weight of almost a thousand pounds. They left the tools lie there, discarded as much weight as they could, and proceeded to carry that ages-old superman out into the light.

Here they could see that the great man was all but a negro in colour. It was equally clear, however, from an examination of his mammoth cranium and extraordinary expression, that he was as highly developed along most mental lines as the greatest men on earth. It was the back of his head, however, so flat that it was only a continuation of his neck, or, rather, shoulders, that told where the flaw lay. That, together with the hardness of his eye, the cruelty of his mouth, and the absolute lack of softness anywhere in the iron-like face or frame—all this condemned the monster for what he was; inhuman.

It was not easy to get him down the two flights of stairs. More than once they had to prop the case on a step while they rested; and at one time, just before they reached that curious heap of rubbish at the foot of the upper stairs, Jackson's strength gave way and it looked as though the whole thing would get away from them. Van Emmon saved it at the cost of a bruised shoulder.

Once at the bottom of the lower flight, the rest was easy. Within a very few minutes the astonished face of the engineer was peering into the vestibule; he could hardly wait until the air-tight door was locked before opening the inner valves. He stared at the mammoth figure in the case long and hard, and from then on showed a great deal of respect for his three friends.

Of course, at that time the members of the expedition did not understand the conditions of Mercury as they are now known. They had to depend upon the general impression they got from their first-hand investigations; and it is remarkable that the doctor should have guessed so close to the truth.

"He must have made up his mind to outlast everybody else," was the way he put it as he kicked off his suit. He stepped up to the cabinet and felt of the glass. "I wish it were possible, without breaking the case, to see how he was embalmed."

His fingers still rested on the glass. Suddenly his eyes narrowed; he ran his fingers over the entire surface of the pane, and then whirled to stare at a thermometer.

"That's mighty curious!" he ejaculated. "This thing was bitter cold when we brought it in! Now it's already as warm as this car!"

Smith's eyes lit up. "It may be," he offered, "that the case doesn't contain a vacuum, but some gas which has an electrical affinity for our atmosphere."

"Or," exclaimed the geologist suddenly, "the glass itself may be totally different from ours. It may be made of—"

"*God!*" shouted the doctor, jerking his hand from the cabinet and leaping straight backward. At the same instant, with a grinding crash, all three sides of the case collapsed and fell in splinters to the floor.

"Look out!" shrieked Jackson. He was staring straight into

the now unhooded eyes of the giant. He backed away, stumbled against a stool, and fell to the floor in a dead faint. Smith fumbled impotently with a hammer. The doctor was shaking like a leaf.

But Van Emmon stood still in his tracks, his eyes fixed on the Goliath; his fingernails gashed the palms of his hands but he would not budge. And as he stared he saw, from first to last, the whole ghastly change that came, after billions of years of waiting, to the sole survivor of Mercury.

A glaze swept over the huge figure. Next instant every line in that adamant frame lost its strength; the hardness left the eyes and mouth. The head seemed to sink lower into the massive shoulders, and the irresistible hands relaxed. In another second the thing that had once been as iron had become as rubber.

But only for an instant. Second by second that huge mountain of muscle slipped and jellied and actually melted before the eyes of the humans. At the same time a curious acrid odour arose; Smith fell to coughing. The doctor turned on more oxygen.

In less than half a minute the man who had once conquered a planet was reduced to a steaming mound of brownish paste. As it sank to the floor of the case, it touched a layer of coarse yellow powder sprinkled there; and it was this that caused the vapour. In a moment the room was filled with the haze of it; luckily, the doctor's apparatus worked well.

And thus it came about that, within five minutes from being exposed to the air of the sky-car, that whole immense bulk, chair and all, had vanished. The powder had turned it to vapour, and the purifying chemicals had sucked it up. Nothing was left save a heap of smoking, greyish ashes in the centre of the broken glass.

Van Emmon's fingers relaxed their grip. He stirred to action, and turned briskly to Smith.

"Here! Help me with this thing!"

Between them they got the remains of the cabinet, with its gruesome load, into the vestibule. As for the doctor, he was bending over Jackson's still unconscious form. When he saw what the others were doing, he gave a great sigh of relief.

"Good!" He helped them close the door. "Let's get away from this damned place!"

The outer door was opened. At the same time Smith started the machinery; and as the sky-car shot away from the ground he tilted it slightly, so that the contents of the vestibule was slid into space. Down it fell like so much lead.

The doctor glanced through a nearby window, and his face brightened as he made out the distant gleam of another planet. He watched the receding surface of Mercury with positive delight.

"Nice place to get away from," he commented. "And now, my friends, for Venus, and then—home!"

But the other's eyes were fixed upon a tiny sparkle in the dust outside the palace, where the vestibule had dropped its load. It was the sun shining upon some broken bits of glass; the glass which, for untold ages, had enclosed the throne of the Death-lord.

The Queen of Life

The Queen of Life

1
Next Stop, Venus!

When he first got the idea of the sky-car, the doctor never stopped to consider whether he was the right man for such an excursion. Personally, he hated travel. He was merely a general practitioner, with a great fondness for astronomy; and the sole reason why he wanted to visit the planets was that he couldn't see them well enough with his telescope. So he dabbled a little in magnetism and so forth, and stumbled upon the principle of the cube.

But he had no mechanical ability, and was on the point of giving up the scheme when he met Smith. He was instantly impressed by the engineer's highly commonplace face; he had had considerable experience with human contrariness, and felt sure that Smith must be an absolute wonder, since he looked so very ordinary.

Kinney's diagnosis proved correct. Smith knew his business; the machinery was finished in a hurry and done right. However, when it came to fitting the outfit into a suitable sky-car, Kinney was obliged to call in an architect. That accounts for E. Williams Jackson. At the same time, it occurred to the doctor that they would need a cook. Mrs. Kinney had refused to have anything whatever to do with the trip, and so Kinney put an ad in the paper. As luck would have it, Van Emmon, the geologist, who had learned how to cook when he first became a mountaineer, saw the ad and answered it in hope of adventure.

The doctor himself, besides his training in the mental and bodily frailties of human beings, had also an unusual command of the related sciences, such as biology. Smith's specialties have already been named; he could drive an airplane or a nail with equal ease. Van Emmon, as a part of his profession, was a skilled "fossilologist," and was well up in natural history.

As for E. Williams Jackson—the architect was also the sociologist of the four. Moreover, he had quite a reputation as an amateur antiquarian. Nevertheless, the most important thing about E. Williams Jackson was not learned until after the visit to Mercury, after the terrible end of that exploration, after the architect, falling in a faint, had been revived under the doctor's care.

"Gentlemen," said Kinney, coming from the secluded nook among the dynamos which had been the architect's bunk; "gentlemen, I must inform you that Jackson is not what we thought."

"He—I mean, she—is a woman!"

Which put an entirely new face upon matters. The three men, discussing it, marvelled that the architect had been able to keep her sex a secret all the time they were exploring at Mercury. They did not know that none of E. Williams Jackson's fellow architects had ever guessed the truth. Ambitious and ingenious, with a natural liking for house-planning, she had resolved that her sex should not stand in the way of success.

And when she finally came to herself, there in her bunk, and suspected that her secret was out—instead of shame or embarrassment she felt only chagrin. She walked, rather unsteadily, across the floor of the great cube-shaped car to the window where the three were standing; and as they quietly made a place for her, she took it entirely as a matter of course, and without a word.

The doctor had been speaking of the peculiar fitness of the four for what they were doing. "And if I'm not mistaken," he went on, "we're going to need all the brains we can pool, when we get to Venus.

"I never would have claimed, when we started out, that Mercury had ever been inhabited. But now that we've seen what we've seen, I feel dead sure that Venus once was peopled."

The four looked out the triple-glazed vacuum-insulated window at the steadily growing globe of "Earth's twin sister." Half in sunlight and half in shadow, this planet, for ages the synonym for beauty, was now but a million miles away. She looked as large as the moon; but instead of a silvery gleam, she showed a creamy radiance fully three times as bright.

"Let's see," reflected the geologist aloud. "As I recall it, the brightness of a planet depends upon the amount of its air. That would indicate, then, that Venus has about as much as the earth, wouldn't it?" remembering how the home planet had looked when they left it.

The doctor nodded. "There are other factors; but undoubtedly we are approaching a world which is a great deal like our own. Venus is nearly as large as the earth, has about nine-tenths the surface, and a gravity almost as strong. The main difference is that she's only two-thirds as far from the sun as we are."

"How long is her day?" Smith wanted to know.

"Can't say. Some observers claim to have seen her clearly enough to announce a day of the same length as ours. Others calculate that she's like Mercury; always the same face toward the sun. If so, her day is also her year—two hundred and twenty-five of our days."

Van Emmon looked disappointed. "In that case she would be blistering hot on one side and freezing cold on the other; except," remembering Mercury, "except for the 'twilight zone,' where the climate would be neither one nor the other, but temperate." He pointed to the line down the middle of the disk before them, the line which divided the lighted from the unlighted, the day from the night.

The four looked more intently. It should be remembered that the very brilliance of Venus has always hindered the astronomers; the planet as a whole is always very conspicuous but its very glare makes it impossible to see any details. The surface has always seemed to be covered by a veil of hazy, faintly streaked vapour.

Smith gave a queer exclamation. For a moment or two he stared hard at the planet; then looked up with an apologetic grin.

"I had a foolish idea. I thought—" He checked himself. "Say, doesn't Venus remind you of something?"

The doctor slowly shook his head. "Can't say that it does, Smith. I have always considered Venus as having an appearance peculiarly her own. Why?"

The engineer started to answer, stopped, thought better of it, and instead pointed out the half that was in shadow. "Why is it that we can make out the black portion so easily?"

Kinney could answer this. "The fact is, it isn't really black at all, but faintly lighted. Presumably it is star-shine."

"Star-shine!" echoed the architect, interested.

"Just that. You see," finished the doctor, "if that side is never turned toward the sun, then it must be covered with ice, which would reflect the star—"

"Ah!" exclaimed Smith with satisfaction. "I wasn't so crazy after all! My notion was that the whole blamed thing is covered with ice!"

It looked reasonable. Certainly the entire sphere had a somewhat watery appearance. It prompted the geologist to say:

"Kinney—if that reflection is really due to ice, then there must be plenty of water vapour in the air. And if that's the case—"

"Not only is life entirely possible," stated the doctor quietly, "but I'll bet you this sky-car against an abandoned soap-stone mine that we find humans, or near-human beings there when we land tomorrow!"

2

Speaking of Venus

The architect was still dressed in the fashionably cut suit of men's clothes she had worn while in the car. Van Emmon thought of this when he said, somewhat awkwardly:

"Well, I'm going to fix something to eat. It'll be ready in half an hour, Miss—er—Jackson."

She looked at him, slightly puzzled; then understood. "You mean to give me time to change my clothes? Thanks; but I'm used to these. And besides," with spirit, "I never could see why women couldn't wear what they choose, so long as it is decent."

There was no denying that hers were both becoming and "decent." Modelled after the usual riding costume, both coat and breeches were youthfully, rather than mannishly, tailored; and the narrow, vertical stripe of the dark gray material served to make her slenderness almost girlish. In short, what with her poet-style hair, her independent manner and direct speech, she was far more like a boy of twenty than a woman nearing thirty.

She walked with Van Emmon, dodging machinery all the way, across the big car to the little kitchenette over which he had presided.

There, to his dismay, the girl took off her coat, rolled up her sleeves, and announced her intention of helping.

"You're a good cook, Van—I mean, Mr.—"

"Let it go at Van, please," said he hastily. "My first name is Gustave, but nobody has ever used it since I was christened."

"Same with my 'Edna,' she declared. "Mother's name was Williams, and I was nicknamed 'Billie' before I can remember. So that's settled," with great firmness. The point is—Van—you're a good cook, but everything tastes of bacon. I wish you'd let me boss this meal."

He looked rebellious for an instant, then gave a sigh of relief. "I'm really tickled to death."

A little later the doctor and Smith, looking across, saw Van Emmon being initiated into the system which constructs scalloped potatoes. Next, he was discovering that there is more than one way to prepare dried beef.

"For once, we won't cream it," said E. Billie Jackson, dryly, as Van Emmon laid down the can-opener. "We'll make an omelette out of it, and see if anything happens."

She was already beating the eggs. He cut up the meat into small pieces, and when he was finished, took the egg-beater away from her. He turned it so energetically that a speck of foam flew into his face.

"Go slow," she advised, nonchalantly reaching up with a

dish-towel and wiping the fleck away. Whereupon he worked the machine more furiously than ever.

Soon he was wondering how on earth he had come to assume, all along, that she was not a woman. He now saw that what he had previously considered boyishness in her was, in fact, simply the vigour and freshness of an earnest, healthy, energetic girl.

It dawned upon him that her keen, gray eyes were not sharp, but alert; her mouth, not hard, but resolute; her whole expression, instead of mannish, just as womanly as that of any girl who has been thrown upon her own resources, and made good. He soon found that his eyesight did not suffer in any way because he looked at her.

"Now," she remarked, in her businesslike way, as she placed the brimming pan into the oven, "I suppose that I'll hear various hints to the effect that a woman has no business trying to do men's stunts. And I warn you right now that I'm prepared to put up a warm argument!"

"Of course," said the geologist, with such gravity that the girl knew he didn't mean it; "of course a woman's place is in the home. Surrounded by seventeen or eighteen children, and cooking for that many more hired men besides, she is simply ideal. We realize that."

"Then, admitting that much, why shouldn't a woman be as independent as she likes? Think what women did during the war; remember what a lot of women are doctors and lawyers! Is there any good reason why I couldn't design a library as well as a man could?"

"None at all," agreed Van Emmon, handing over the dish of chopped meat. The girl carefully folded the contents into the now sponge-like omelette as he went on: "By the way, a neighbour of mine told me, just before I left, that he was having trouble with a broken sewer. How'd you like to—"

"About as well as you'd like to darn socks!" she came back, evidently being primed for such comments. She took a look at the potatoes, and then permitted the geologist to open their sixth can of peaches. "I must say they're good," she admitted, as she noted the eagerness with which he obeyed.

Bread and butter, olives, coffee and cake completed that meal. The table was set with more care than usual, a clean cloth and napkins being unearthed for the occasion. When Smith and Kinney were called, both declared that they weren't hungry enough to do justice to it all.

"It's just as well you weren't very hungry," commented Billie, as she finished giving each of them a second helping of the potatoes. "There's barely enough left for me," and she took it.

"Say, I never thought of it before, Miss—er—Miss Billie," said Smith colouring; "but you eat just as much as a man!"

"Ye gods, how shocking!" she jeered. "Come to think of it, Smith, you eat *more* than a woman!"

The doctor's face grew red with some suppressed emotion. After a while he said soberly: "I'll tell you what's worrying Smith. He's afraid that women, having suddenly become very progressive, will forge entirely ahead of men. You understand—having started, they can't stop. And I must admit that I've thought seriously of it at times myself."

"Me too," added Van Emmon earnestly. "I have the same feeling about it that an elderly man must have when he sees a young one get on the job. Instead of being glad that the women are making good, I sort of resent it."

"I knew it!" exclaimed the girl delightedly. "But I never heard a man admit it before!"

"Perhaps it isn't as serious as we think," said the practical Smith, scraping the bottom of the potato pan. "I believe that the progress of women may have a fine effect upon men, making us less self-satisfied, and more alert. For one thing," glancing about the cube, "we've got to clean up a bit, now that we know you're a woman!"

The architect's eyes flashed. "Because you know mighty well I'll light in and do it myself, if you don't; that's what you mean! Please take notice that I'm to be respected, not because of what *I am*, but because of what I can *do!*"

"In behalf of myself and companions, I surrender!" said the doctor gallantly. Then he instantly added: "And yet, even when we are actually chivalrous, we are disregarding your desire to be appreciated for what you are worth. Pardon me, Miss Billie; I'll not forget again.

"At the same time, my dear," remembering that he had a daughter of his own, nearly the builder's age, "we men have come to think of women primarily as potential mothers, and secondarily as people of affairs. And considering that motherhood is something that is denied to us lords of the earth—"

"For which we can thank a merciful Providence," interjected the girl solemnly.

"Considering this—excuse my seriousness—really amazing fact, you can't blame us for expecting women to fulfil this vital function before taking up other matters."

"Yes?" remarked the girl, watching the peaches with anxious eye as Van Emmon helped himself. "Funny; but I always understood that the first function of man was to father the race; yet, invariably the young fellows try to make names for themselves before, not after, they marry!"

"Scalped!" chuckled Van Emmon, as the doctor hid his discomfiture behind a large piece of cake. "You may know a lot about Venus, doc, but you don't know much about women!"

"Speaking about Venus," Smith was reminded, "we may learn something bearing upon the very point we have been discussing if Kinney's right about the inhabitants."

The doctor nodded eagerly.

"You see, if there's people still alive on the planet, they're probably further advanced than we on the earth. Other things being equal, of course. Being a smaller planet than ours, she cooled off sooner, and thus became fit for life earlier.

"And having been made from the same 'batch,' to use Van's expression, that Mercury and all the rest were, why, in all likelihood evolution has taken place there much the same as with us, only sooner.

"I should expect," he elaborated largely, "that we shall find

90

the inhabitants much the same as we humans, only extremely civilized. It may be that they are as far above us as we are above monkeys."

Smith broke in by quoting an astronomer who contended that Venus kept only one face toward the sun. "Maybe she always did, Kinney."

The doctor shook his head. "See how perfectly round she is? No oblateness whatever. It proves that she once revolved, otherwise she'd be pear-shaped, from the sun's pull."

There was a short silence, during which Billie concluded that the only scraps left would be the coffee-grounds. Then Van Emmon pushed away from the table, got to his feet, stretched a little to relieve his nerves, and said:

"Well, whatever we find on Venus, I hope the women do the cooking!"

3
The First Venusian

When the sky-car was within a thousand miles of the surface, Smith adjusted the currents so that the floor was directed downward. The four changed from the window to the deadlight, and watched the approaching disk with every bit of the excitement and interest they had felt when nearing Mercury.

The doctor had warned them that the heavy atmosphere which Venus was known to possess would prevent seeing as clearly as in the case of the smaller planet. All were much disappointed, however, to find that they were still unable to make out a single definite detail. The great half-shining, half-black world showed nothing but that vaguely streaked, ice-like haze.

There was something very queer about it all. "Strange that we should see no movement in those clouds," mused the doctor aloud. "That is, if they really are clouds."

Van Emmon already doubted it. "Just what I was thinking. There ought to be terrific winds; yet, so far as I have seen, there's been nothing doing anywhere on the surface since we first began to observe it."

After a while the doctor put away his binoculars and rubbed his eyes. "We might as well descend faster, Smith. Can't see a thing from here."

Unhindered by air to impede its progress the sky-car had been hurtling through space at cometary speed. Now, however, Smith added the power of the apparatus to the pull of the planet, so that the disk began to rush toward them at a truly alarming rate. After a few seconds of it Billie found herself unconsciously moving to the side of the geologist.

He looked down at her, understood, and flushed with pleasure. "There's no danger," he confidently assured her, with the result that, her courage fortified, the girl moved back to her place again. Van Emmon inwardly kicked himself.

So deceptive was that peculiar fogginess Smith throttled their descent as soon as they had reached the point where the planet's appearance changed from round to flat. They were headed for the line which marked the boundary of the shadow. This gray "twilight zone" was three or four hundred miles in width; on the right of it—to the east—the dazzling surface of that sunlit vapour contrasted sharply with the all but black mistiness of the starward side. Clearly the zone ought to be temperate enough.

Down they sank. As they came nearer a curious pinkish tint began to show beneath them. Shortly it became more noticeable; the doctor gave a sudden grunt of satisfaction, and Smith stopped the car.

A minute later the doctor had taken a sample of the surrounding ether through his laboratory test-vestibule; and shortly announced that they were now floating in air instead of space.

"Good deal like ours back home, too"—exultingly. "Pretty thin, of course." He made a short calculation, referring to the aneroid barometer which was mounted on the outer frame of a window, and said he judged that their altitude was about five miles.

The descent continued, Smith using the utmost caution. The other three kept their eyes glued to the deadlight; and their mystification was only equalled by their uneasiness as that motionless, bleary glaze failed absolutely to show anything they had not seen a thousand miles higher. Not a single detail!

"It reminds me," said the girl in a low voice, "of something I once saw from the top of a hill. It was the reflection of the sun from the surface of a pond; not clear water, but covered with—"

"Good Heavens!" interrupted Van Emmon, struck with the thought. "Can it be that the whole planet is under water?"

Beyond a doubt his guess was justified. There was an oily smoothness about that dazzling haze which made it remarkably like a lake of still and rather dirty water under a bright sun.

But the doctor said no. "Any water I ever heard of would make clouds," said he; "and we know there's air enough to guarantee plenty of wind. Yet nothing seems to be in motion." He was frowning continually now.

It was Billie who first declared that she saw the surface. "Stop," she said to Smith evenly, and he instantly obeyed. All four gathered around the deadlight, and soon agreed that the peculiarly elusive skin of the planet was actually within sight. However, it was like deciding upon the distance of the moon—as easy to say that it were within arm's reach as a long ways off.

The doctor went to a window. There he could look out upon the sun, a painfully bright object much larger than it looks from the Earth. It was just "ascending," and half of it was below the horizon. A blinding streak of light was reflected from a point on the surface not far from the cube. Shading his eyes with his hand the doctor could see that the mysterious crust was absolutely smooth.

On the opposite side of the car the horizon ended in a sunrise glow of a slightly greenish radiance. From that side the pinkish tint of the surface was quite pronounced.

Before going any lower the doctor, struck with an idea, declared: "We always want to remember that this car is perfectly soundproof. Suppose we open the outer door of the vestibule. I imagine we'll learn something peculiar."

It was possible to open this door without touching the inner valves, using mechanism concealed within the walls. The moment it was done—the door faced the "north"—pandemonium itself broke loose. A most terrific shrieking and howling came from the outside; it was wind, passing at a rate such as would make a hurricane seem a mere zephyr. The doctor closed the door so that they could think.

"It's the draft," he concluded; "the draft from the sun-warmed side to the cold side."

As for Van Emmon, he was getting out a rope and a heavy leaden weight. On the rope he formed knots every five feet, about twenty of them; and after getting into one of the insulated, aluminium-armoured and oxygen-helmeted suits with which they had explored Mercury, he locked himself on the other side of the inner vestibule door and proceeded to "sound."

To the amazement of all except Billie "bottom" was reached in less than twenty feet. "I thought so," she said with satisfaction; but she was not at ease until Van Emmon had returned in safety from that booming, whistling turmoil.

His first remark upon removing his helmet almost took them off their feet. "The point is," said he, throttling his excitement—"the point is, the rope was nearly jerked out of my hands!

"Understand what I mean? The surface is *revolving!*"

This upset every idea they had had; it never occurred to any of them that the planet could revolve at such speed that it would appear stationary. Smith went at once to the eastern window and watched closely, for fear some irregularity in that apparently perfect sphere might catch them unawares. They did not learn till later that Venus's day is a little less than twenty-five hours, and therefore, since they had approached her near the equator, the wind they had encountered was moving at nearly nine hundred miles per hour!

Bit by bit, though, the cube answered to the wind-pressure. Soon they noted the sun rising slowly; and by the time it was two hours high the surface, which had been whizzing under them like some highly polished top, became entirely motionless: The cube had "stopped."

One minute later the car touched the level. Smith very slowly reduced the repelling current so that the immense weight of the cube was but gradually shifted to the unknown surface beneath. Ton after ton was added until—

"Stop!" came from the doctor. He had noted through the window a slight curvature in the material.

So the machinery was left in action. "At any rate," said Smith, "we know that the confounded stuff isn't antimagnetic, whatever it is." Of course this was true—even though the gelatine-like shell could not support the cube's weight, yet it did not insulate the planet from the repelling current.

The thermometer registered three hundred and thirty-five degrees Fahrenheit. "Two hundred and eighty degrees higher than it would be at home in the same latitude," remarked the doctor. "We'll have to use the suits." He took it for granted that exploration should begin at once.

No one stayed behind. The machines could be relied upon, as they knew from nearly two weeks of use, and certainly there was nothing in sight which could possibly interfere with the cube. Nevertheless, the matter-of-fact engineer took care to remove part of the door-operating apparatus when he left the vestibule, and nobody commented upon it. It seemed the sensible thing to do; that was all.

There was just about enough additional weight in their suits to balance the slightly reduced gravitation, so they moved about, four misshapen, metallic hulks, with as much freedom as though back home. Always they kept within a few feet of each other so as to throw no strain on their interconnecting telephone wires. The big, glass-faced helmets gave a remarkable sense of security.

They made a complete circuit of the cube, and at the end of it looked at each other in perplexity. Never, save in the middle of an ocean, in the doldrums, did any man ever see such a totally barren spot. Not a tree, much less a sign of human occupation; there was not even the slightest mound. The planet was, in actual fact, as smooth and as bare as a billiard ball!

Moreover, the surface itself remained as mysterious as before.

Of course they did not touch it with bare hands—all wore insulated mittens—but the dazzling stuff was certainly as hard as steel and as highly polished. It was neither transparent nor opaque, but translucent, "like pink mother-of-pearl," as Billie suggested.

She was the first to propose that they move to another spot. "We ought to try a place where it's not yet dawn," said she, shielding her eyes from the glare. (It will be remembered that the suits protected them from the heat itself.) "Can't see anything."

"Hush!" hissed the doctor. They turned and followed his gaze to a spot not thirty feet from where they stood.

At the same instant they felt a faint jar in the material under their feet. And next second they saw that a large section of the supposedly solid surface was in motion.

A portion about ten feet square was being lifted bodily in front of their eyes, and before another word was said this block of the unknown substance was raised until they could see that it was all of a yard thick. Up it went at the same deliberate rate; and the four involuntarily moved closer together as they saw that there was something underneath.

It was a cage, for all the world like that of an elevator except that it was made of clear glass. Another second and it had stopped, with its floor level with the surface; and the people from the earth saw that it contained a man.

He was quite tall, slenderly built, and dressed in a queer satiny material which fitted him like an acrobat's suit. He was extremely thin as to legs, narrow as to shoulders, deep in the chest and short in the waist. All this, however, they saw after their inspection of his head.

It was human! Marvellously refined in every detail, yet it was set upon a graceful neck, and modelled upon much the same lines as that of any man. It was not that of a brute, nor yet that of a bird; it was—human!

He stood at ease, resting slightly on one foot, and dispelled any notion that he might be unreal by shifting his weight occasionally. Meanwhile he watched the four with a grave, interested smile; and they, in turn, came closer.

His chin was small, even retreating; but his mouth was wide and curved into an exaggerated Cupid's bow. Even as he continued to smile the curves did not leave his lips; they, however, were thin rather than thick. His nose was quite small, with a decidedly Irish cast; but his eyes, set far apart above quite shallow cheekbones, were exceedingly large and of a brilliant blue. In fact, it was mainly his eyes that gave character to his face; although none could overlook his breadth of forehead, running back to a cranium that fairly bulged over the ears, and seemed ready to rise like a tightly inflated balloon. His skin was pure white.

And so they stood for uncounted minutes. At last the doctor noted that the stranger was eying them with far less interest than they showed in him; he stood as though he felt on display; and the doctor gave an exclamation of perplexity that broke the spell.

The four impulsively drew up to the glass; Van Emmon touched it with his mitten; and that is how the four explorers came to receive the vibrations that came next.

For the man in the cage, in turn, put out his hand and touched the glass opposite Van Emmon. Then he opened his mouth.

"I am very glad to see you," said he in a soft, pulsating voice— and in the best of English.

4

A Puzzled World

For a moment blank amazement gripped the four. Then amazement gave way to genuine apprehension. Were they insane to imagine that this man of another world had spoken to them in their own language? Each looked at the other, and was astounded to see that all had heard the same thing.

Presently the stranger spoke again; if anything, the kindly smile on his face became even broader. "Suppose we postpone explaining how I am able to use your tongue. It will be easier for you to understand after you have been with us a while." He spoke slowly and carefully, yet with a faint lisp, much as some infant prodigy might speak.

But there was no doubt that he had really done it. The doctor managed to clear his throat.

"You are right," said he, with vastly less assurance than the amazing stranger. "We will try to understand things in the order you think best to present them. You—should know best."

Kinney introduced himself by name and profession, also the other three. The stranger nodded affably to each. "You may call me Estra," said he, pronouncing it "Ethtra." "There is no occupation on the Earth corresponding with mine, but in my spare moments I am an astronomer like yourself."

The doctor silently marvelled. He had not told the stranger about his hobby. Meanwhile the architect attempted to break the ice even finer.

"We take it for granted," said she rather nervously, "that your people are somewhat further advanced than us on the earth. However, we expect to be given credit for having visited your planet before you visited ours!"

She said this with an engaging smile which won an instant response; the Venusian's lips almost lost their curves in his generous effort.

"You will find that we greatly respect all that you have accomplished," he declared earnestly. "As for your apparatus"— glancing at the cube— "you have the advantage on the earth of certain chemical elements which are entirely lacking here, otherwise we should have called upon you long ago."

He slipped a panel of glass to one side.

"Step in quickly!" he exclaimed, gasping; and the four obeyed him without thought. It was only when the panel was replaced that they noticed the floor of the cage; it was of clear glass, like the sides, and looked totally incapable of bearing their combined weight.

The Venusian smiled at Smith's worried look. "The material is amply strong enough," said he. "I am only concerned about your machine there. Is it safe to be left alone?"

"So far as we know, yes," answered Van Emmon, who did not feel quite as much confidence in the stranger as the rest.

"Then we can go down at once." With these words the man in satin turned to a small black box in one wall of the elevator and touched a button.[1]

Instantly the car began to descend, at first slowly and then with swiftly increasing velocity. By the time the explorers had accustomed their eyes to the sudden semi-darkness, the cage was dropping at such a speed that the air fairly sang past its sides.

Far overhead was a square, black shadow in the wax-like crust which they had left; it was the shadow of the cube. All about them was a dimly lit network of braces, arches and semitransparent columns; to all appearances the system seemed to support the crust. Billie whirled upon the Venusian:

"I've got it now! The whole globe is covered with glass!"

Estra smiled his approval. "For thousands upon thousands of centuries, my friend. The thing was done when our ancestors first suspected that our planet was doomed to come so near the sun. It was the only way we could protect ourselves from the heat."

"Great!" exploded the doctor, admiration overcoming regret that he had not thought of it himself. But Smith had other thoughts:

"How long did it take to finish the job? And what did it cost?"

"Two centuries; and about twice the cost of your last war. I need only suggest to you that we coloured the material so as to reflect most of the heat. That is why the material looks blue from below, although pink from above."

"Say"—from Billie—"how long are we to keep on dropping like this?"

"We will arrive in a moment or two," answered the smiling one. "The roof is raised several miles above the sea-level in order to cover all the mountains."

By this time the four were able to make out things pretty well. They saw that the dimness was only relative; the Venusian

---

1. For details of this and other matters of an electrical and mechanical nature, the technical reader is referred to Mr. Smith's reports to the A. S. M. E.

world was actually as well lighted as any part of the earth on a cloudy day. And they saw that they were descending in a locality of astonishing beauty.

The stranger halted the car so that they could inspect the scene as though from an airplane. In no way did the landscape resemble that of the earth. To begin with, pillars of huge dimensions were placed every quarter-mile or so; it was these that supported the intricate archwork above. They were made of the same translucent stuff as the crust, but had a light topaz tint. The Venusian said:

"You will not need to be told that the science of metallurgy has advanced quite far with us. All our metals can be made transparent, if we like; those pillars are coloured variously in different regions so as to be clearly distinguishable and prevent collisions of flying apparatus."

But Van Emmon and Billie were both more interested in what lay between the columns. They scarcely noticed that there were no people in sight at the time. The ground was covered with an indescribable wealth of colour; and it was only by a close examination that the buildings could be distinguished as such.

For they were all made of that semi-transparent stuff. Of every conceivable tint and shade, the structure showed an utter lack of uniformity in size, shape or arrangement. Moreover, the ground was absolutely packed with them; they spread as far as the eye could reach.

But if there was profusion, there also was confusion—apparently. Streets ran anywhere and everywhere; there was no visible system to anything. And where there was no space for a building, invariably there was a shrub, a bush or a small tree of some kind, all in full flower. The only sign of regularity to be seen was in the roofs—practically all of them were flat. Whether the building was some rambling, loosely gathered agglomeration of varicoloured wings, or a single, towering skyscraper of one tint, almost inevitably it was crowned with a perfectly level surface.

"I see," said Van Emmon, thoughtfully. "You have no rain."

"Precisely"—from Estra. "We have the air completely under our control. We give our vegetation artificial showers when we think it should have it, not when nature wills; and similarly we use electricity instead of sunlight that we may stimulate its growth."

"In short"—Van Emmon put it as the car slid slowly down the remaining distance—"in short, you have abolished the weather."

The Venusian nodded. "And I'll save you the trouble of suggesting," he added, "that we are nothing more nor less than hothouse people!"

5

The Human Conservatory

"But there is this difference," he cautioned as they stepped out of the elevator into a sort of a plaza, "that, whereas you people on the earth have only begun to use the hothouse principle, we here have perfected it.

"I suggest that you waste no time looking for faults."

Van Emmon stared at the doctor. "How does this idea fit your theory, Kinney—that Venus is simply the earth plus several thousand extra generations of civilization?"

"Fit?" echoed the doctor. "Fits like a glove. We humans are fast becoming a race of indoor-people despite all the various "back-to-nature" movements. Look at the popularity of enclosed automobiles, for example.

"The only thing that surprises me"—turning to their guide—"is that you use your legs for their original purpose."

Estra smiled, and pointed out something standing a few feet away. It was a small, shuttle-shaped air-craft, with clear glass sides which had actually made them overlook it at first. Peering closer they saw that the plaza and surrounding streets were nearly filled with these all but invisible cars.

The Venusian explained. "You marvel that I use my legs and walk the same as you do. I am glad you have brought up this point, because it is a fact that our people use mechanisms instead of bodily energy, almost altogether. These cars you see are uni-

101

versally used for transportation. I am one of the very few who appreciate the value of natural exercise."

"Do you mean to say," demanded Van Emmon, "that the average Venusian does no walking?"

"Not a mile a year," said Estra gravely.

"Just what he is obliged to do indoors from room to room." And he involuntarily glanced down at his own extremely thin legs.

The architect's eyes widened with a growing understanding. "I see now," she murmured. "That's why there was no one else to greet us."

The Venusian smiled gratefully. "We thought it best. You'd have been shocked outright, I am sure, had you been introduced to a representative Venusian without any explanation."

They fell silent. Still, without moving from the point where they had left the elevator, the four from the earth examined the surrounding buildings in a renewed effort to see some system in their arrangement. Directly in front of them was a particularly large structure. Like all the rest, it was of hopelessly irregular design, yet it had a large domed central portion which gave it the appearance of an auditorium; and the effect was further borne out by a subdued humming sound which seemed to come from it.

Smith asked Estra if it were a hall.

"Yes and no," was the answer. "It fills the purpose of a hall, but is not built on the hall plan." And Smith tried to stare through the translucent walls of the thing.

The other buildings within immediate reach were of every possible appearance. Some would have passed for cottages, others for stores, still others for the most fanciful of studios. And nowhere was there such a thing as a sign, even at the street corners, much less on a building.

"Not that we would be able to read your signs, if you had them," commented the doctor, "but I'd like to know how your people find their way without something of that kind to guide them."

Estra's smile did not change. "That is something you will understand better before long," said he, "provided you feel ready to explore a little further."

The four looked at each other in question, and suddenly it struck them all that they were a rather pugnacious-looking crew in their cumbersome suits of armour and formidable helmets. The doctor turned to Estra.

"You ought to know"—he appealed—"whether we can take off these suits now."

"It would be best," was the reply. "You will find the air and temperature decidedly more warm and moist than what you have been used to, but otherwise practically the same. There is a slightly larger proportion of oxygen; that is all. Just imagine you are in a hothouse."

Smith and the doctor were already discarding their suits. Van Emmon and Billie followed more slowly; the one, because he did not share the doctor's confidence in their guide; the other, because of a sudden shyness in his presence. The Venusian noted this.

"You need not feel any embarrassment," said he to Billie's vast astonishment. "There is no distinction here between the dress of the two sexes." And again all four marvelled that he should know so much about them.

Once out of the armour the visitors felt much more at ease. The slightly reduced gravitation gave them a sense of lightness and freedom which more than balanced the jungle-like oppressiveness of the air.

They found themselves guarding against a certain exuberance; perhaps it was the extra oxygen, too.

They strode toward the large structure directly ahead. At its entrance—a wide, square portal which opened into a fan-shaped lobby—Estra paused and smiled apologetically—as he mopped his forehead and upper lip with a paper handkerchief, which he immediately dropped into a small, trap-covered opening in the wall at his side.

These little doors, by the way, were to be seen at frequent

intervals wherever they went. Incidentally not a scrap of paper or other refuse was to be noted anywhere—streets and all were spotless.

As for Estra—"I am not accustomed to moving at such speed," he explained his discomfort. "If you do not mind, please walk a little more leisurely."

They took their time about passing through this lobby. For one thing, Estra said there would have to be a small delay; and for another, the walls and ceilings of the space were most remarkably ornamented. They were fairly covered with what appeared, at first glance, to be absolutely lifelike paintings and sculptures. They were so arranged as to strengthen the structural lines of the place, and, of course, they were of more interest to Billie than to the others.[1]

Desiring to examine some of the work far overhead, Billie clambered up on a convenient pedestal in order to look more closely. She took the strength of things for granted, and put her weight too heavily on a moulding on the edge of the pedestal; with the result that there was a sharp crack; and the girl struck the floor in a heap. She got to her feet before Van Emmon could reach her side, but her face was white with pain.

"Sprained—ankle," said she between set lips, and proceeded to stump up and down the lobby, "to limber up," as she said, although her three companions offered to do anything that might relieve her.

To the surprise of all, Estra leaned against a pillar and watched the whole affair with perfect composure. He made no offer of help, said nothing whatever in sympathy. In a moment he noticed the looks they gave him—their stares.

"I must beg your pardon," he said, still smiling. "I am sorry this happened; it will not be easy to explain.

"But you will find all Venusians very unsympathetic. Not that we are hard hearted, but because we simply lost the power of sympathy.

---

1. The specialist in architecture and related subjects is referred to E. Williams Jackson's report to the A.I.A., for details of these bas-relief photographs.

"We do not know what pity is. We have eliminated everything that is disagreeable, all that is painful, from our lives to such an extent that there is never any cause for pity."

The three young people could say nothing in answer. The doctor, however, spoke thoughtfully:

"Perhaps it is superfluous; but—tell me—have you done away with injustice, Estra?"

"That is just the point," agreed the Venusian. "Justice took the place of pity and mercy; it was so long ago I am barely able to appreciate your own views on the subject."

Billie, her ankle somewhat better, turned to examine other work; but at the moment another Venusian approached from the upper end of the lobby. Walking slowly, he carried four small parcels with a great deal of effort, and the explorers had time to scrutinize him closely.

He was built much like Estra, but shorter, and with a little more flesh about the torso. His forehead bulged directly over his eyes, instead of above his ears, as did Estra's; also his eyes were smaller and not as far apart. His whole expression was equally kind and affable, despite a curiously shrivelled appearance of his lips; they made the front of his mouth quite flat, and served to take attention away from his pitifully thin legs.

Estra greeted him with a cheery phrase, in a language decidedly different from any the explorers were familiar with. In a way, it was Spanish, or, rather, the pure Castilian tongue; but it seemed to be devoid of dental consonants. It was very agreeable to listen to.

Estra, however, had taken the four parcels from his comrade, and now presented him to the four, saying that his name was Kalara, and that he was a machinist. "He cannot use your tongue," said the Venusian. "Few of us have mastered it. There are difficulties.

"As for these machines"—unwrapping the parcels—"I must apologize in advance for certain defects in their design. I invented them under pressure, so to speak, having to perfect the whole idea in the rather short time that has elapsed since you, doctor, began the sky-car."

"And what is the purpose of the machines?" from Billie, as she was about to accept the first of the devices from the Venusian.

For some reason he appeared to be especially interested in the girl, and addressed half of his remarks to her; and it was while his smiling gaze was fixed upon her eyes that he gave the answer:

"They are to serve"—very carefully—"partly as lexicons and partly as grammars. In short, they are mechanical interpreters."

6

The Tr ansl at ing Mac hines

"First, let me remind you," said the Venusian, "of our lack of certain elements that you are familiar with on the Earth. We have never been able to improve on the common telephone. That is why we must still assemble in person whenever we have any collective activity; while on the Earth the time will come when your wireless principle will be developed to the point of transmitting both light and sound; and after that there will be little need of gatherings of any sort."

Then he explained the apparatus. It consisted of a miniature head-telephone, connected to a small, metallic case the size of a cigar-box, the cover of which was a transparent diaphragm. Estra did not open the case, but showed the mechanism through the cover.

"Essentially, this is a 'word-for-word' device," said he, pointing to a swiftly revolving dial within the box. "On one face of that dial are some ten thousand word-images, made by vibration, after the phonograph method. Directly opposite, on the other face, are the corresponding words in the other language. The disk is rotating at such an enormous speed that, for all practical purposes, any word which may chance to be spoken will be translated almost instantaneously."

He indicated two delicate, many-tentacled "feelers," as he called them, one on each face of the disk. One of these "felt" the proper word-image as it whirled beneath, while the other established an electrical contact with the corresponding waves beneath, at the same time exciting a complicated-looking talking machine.

"That," commented Estra, "is not so easy to explain. It transforms this literal translation into an idiomatic one. Perhaps you will understand its workings a little later when you learn how and why I am able to use your own language."

By this time the four had reached the point where nothing could surprise them. They were becoming accustomed to the unaccustomed. Had they been told that the Venusians had abolished speech altogether, they would have felt disappointed, but not incredulous. However, the doctor thought of something.

"Have you any extra 'records,' to be used in case we visit some other nations while we are here?"

For just a second the Venusian was puzzled; then his smile broadened. "The one record will do," said he, "wherever you go."

"A universal language!" Billie's eyes sparkled with interest.

"Long, long ago," Estra said. "It was established soon after our league of nations was formed."

"Does the league actually prevent war and promote peace?" demanded Van Emmon. This had been a disputed question when the four left the earth.

"We no longer have a league of nations," said their guide slowly. And instantly the four were eying him eagerly. This was really refreshing, to find that the Venusians were actually lacking in something.

"So it didn't work?" commented the doctor, disappointed.

But the Venusian's smile was still there. "It worked itself out," said he. "We have no further use for a league. We have no more nations. We are now—one."

And he helped them adjust the machines.

The cases were slung over their shoulders and the telephones clamped to their ears. When all ready, Estra began to talk, and his voice came nearly as sharp and clear through the apparatus as before. It was modified by a metallic flatness, together with a certain amount of mechanical noise in which a peculiar hissing was the most noticeable. Otherwise he said:

"I am now using my own language. If I make any mistakes, you must not blame the machine. It is as nearly perfect as I was able to make it."

He then asked them what blunders they noted. Billie, who was the most enthusiastic about the thing, declared that they would have no trouble in understanding; whereupon Estra quietly asked:

"Do you feel like going now to try them out?"

Once more an exchange of glances between the four from the earth. Clearly the Venusians were extremely considerate people, to leave their visitors in the care of the one man, apparently, who was able to make them feel at home. There seemed to be no reason for uneasiness.

But Van Emmon still had his old misgivings about Estra. There was something about the effeminate Venusian which irritated the big geologist; it always does make a strong man suspicious to see a weaker one show such self-confidence. Van Emmon drew the doctor and Billie aside, while Smith and Estra went on with the test. Said Van Emmon:

"It just occurred to me that the cube might look pretty good to these people. You remember what this chap said about their lack of some of our chemicals. What do you think—is it really safe to put ourselves entirely in their power?"

"You mean," said the doctor slowly, "that they might try to keep us here rather than lose the cube?"

Van Emmon nodded gravely, but Billie had strong objections. "Estra doesn't look like that sort," she declared vehemently.

"He's too good natured to be a crook; he needs a guardian rather than a warden."

It flashed into the doctor's mind that many a woman had fallen in love with a man merely because he seemed to be in need of someone to take care of him.

That is, the self-reliant kind of woman; and Billie certainly was self-reliant. Something of the same notion came vaguely to the geologist at the same time; and with a vigour that was quite uncalled for, he urged:

"I say, 'safety first.' We shouldn't have left the cube unguarded. I propose that one of us, at least, return to the surface while the others attend this meeting—or trap, for all we know."

"All right," said Billie promptly. "Get Estra to show you how to use the elevator, and wait for us in the vestibule."

Van Emmon's face flamed. "That isn't what I meant!" hotly. "If anybody goes to the cube, it should be you, Billie!"

If Billie did not notice the use of her nickname, at least the doctor did. The girl simply snorted.

"If you think for one second that I'm going to back out just because I'm a woman, let me tell you that you're very badly mistaken!"

Van Emmon turned to the doctor appealingly, but the doctor took the action personally. He shook his head. "I wouldn't miss this for anything, Van. Estra looks safe to me. Go and ask Smith; maybe he is willing to be the goat."

The geologist took one good look at the engineer's absorbed, unquestioning manner as he listened to the Venusian, and gave up the idea with a sigh. For a moment he was sour; then he smiled shyly.

"I'm more than anxious to meet the bunch myself," he admitted; and led the way back to Estra. The Venusian looked at him with no change of expression, although there was something very disconcerting in the precocious wisdom of his eyes. Their very kindliness and serenity gave him an appearance of superiority, such as only aggravated the geologist's suspicions.

But there was nothing to do but to trust him. They followed him through two sets of doors, which slid noiselessly open before them in response to some mechanism operated by the Venusian's steps. This brought them to another of the glass elevators, in which they descended perhaps ten feet, stepping out of it onto a moving platform; this, in turn, extended the length of a low dimly lighted passageway about a hundred yards long. When they got off, they were standing in a small anteroom.

The Venusian paused and smiled at the four again. "Do you feel like going on display now?" he asked; then added: "I should

have said: 'Do you feel like seeing Venus on display, for we all
know more or less about you already.'"

But the visitors were braced for the experience. Estra looked
at each approvingly, and then did something which made them
wonder. He stood stock still for perhaps a second, his eyes closed
as though listening; and then, without explanation, he led the
way through an opal-glass door into a brilliantly lighted space.

Next moment the explorers were standing in the midst of
the people of Venus.

7

The Ult imat e Race

The four were at the bottom of a huge, cone-like pit, such
as instantly reminded the doctor of a medical clinic. The space
where they stood was, perhaps, twenty feet in diameter, while
the walls enclosing the whole hall were many hundreds of feet
apart. And sloping up from the centre, on all sides, was tier upon
tier of the most extraordinary seats in all creation.

For each and every one of those thousands of Venusians was
separately enclosed in glass. Nowhere was there a figure to be
seen who was not installed in one of those small, transparent
boxes, just large enough for a single person. Moreover—and it
came somewhat as a shock to the four when they noted it—the
central platform itself was both covered and surrounded with
the same material.

"Make yourselves at home," Estra was saying. He pointed
to several microphones within easy reach. "These are provided
with my translators, so when you are ready to open up conversation, go right ahead as though you were among your own
people." And he made himself comfortable in a saddle-like chair,
as much as to say that there was no hurry.

For a long time the explorers stood taking it in.

The Venusians, without exception, stared back at them
with nearly equal curiosity. And despite the extraordinary
nature of the proceeding, this mutual scrutiny took place in
comparative silence; for while the glass gave a certain sense

of security to the newcomers, it also cut off all sound except that low humming.

The nearest row of the people got their closest attention. Without exception, they had the same general build as Estra; slim, delicate, and anaemic, they resembled a "ward full of convalescent consumptives," as the doctor commented under his breath. Not one of them would ever give a joke-smith material for a fat-man anecdote; at the same time there was nothing feverish, nervous, or broken down in their appearance. "A pretty lot of invalids," as Billie added to the doctor's remark.

Many observers would have been struck, first, by the extreme diversity in the matter of dress. All wore skin-tight clothing, and much of it was silky, like Estra's. But there was a bewildering assortment of colours, and the most extraordinary decorations, or, rather, ornaments. So far as dress went, there was no telling anything whatever about sex.

"Are they all men?" asked Billie, wondering, of Estra. The Venusian shook his head with his invariable smile. "Nor all women either," said he enigmatically.

But in many respects they were astonishingly alike. Almost to a soul their upper lips were withered and flat. One and all had short, emaciated-looking legs. Each and every one had a crop of really luxuriant hair; the shades varied between the usual blonde and brunette, with little of the reddishness so common on the earth; but there were no bald people at all. On the other hand, there were no beards or moustaches in the whole crowd; every face was bare!

"Like a lot of Chinamen," said Van Emmon in an undertone; "can't tell one from another." But Billie pointed out that this was not strictly true; a close inspection of the faces showed an extremely wide range of distinction. No two chins in the crowd were exactly alike, although not one of them showed any of the resolute firmness which is admired on the Earth. All were weak, yet different.

Neither were there any prominent noses, although there were none that could have been called insignificant. And while every

111

pair of eyes in the place was large, as large as Estra's, yet there was every desirable colour and expression.

To sum it all up, and to use the doctor's words: "They've developed a standard type, all right, just as the characteristic American face is the standard Earth type; but—did you ever see such variations?"

Nevertheless, the most striking thing about these people to the eyes of the visitors was their mutual resemblance. For one thing, there seemed to be no nervous people present. There were many children in the crowd, too; yet all sat very still, and only an occasional movement of the hands served to indicate consciousness. In this sense, they were all remarkably well bred.

In another, they were remarkably rude. At any given moment a good half of the people were eating, or, rather, sipping liquids of various sorts from small tumblers. Probably every person in the house, before the affair was over, had imbibed two or three ounces of fluid; but not once was the matter apologized for, nor the four invited to partake.

"So this may be the outcome of our outrageous habit of eating sweetmeats at theatres," muttered the doctor. And again noting the hairless faces: "Just what I said when men first began using those depilatories instead of shaving—no more beards!"

But it was Billie who explained the invariable crop of hair. "No use to look for baldness; they don't wear hats! Why should they, since there's neither sun nor rain to protect their heads from?"

Mainly, however, the architect was interested in the building itself. To her, the most striking feature was not the tremendously arched dome, nor yet the remarkable system of bracing which dispensed with any columns in all that vast space. It was something simpler—there were no aisles.

"Now, what do you make of that?" the girl asked Van Emmon. "How do they ever get to their places?" But he could not suggest anything more than to recall an individual elevator scheme once proposed.

To Smith, one object of interest was the telephone system. Remarkably like those used on the Earth, one was located in each of the tiny glass cages. He was likewise puzzled to account for the ventilation system; each cage was apparently air-tight, yet no Venusian showed any discomfort.

But the geologist, for want of anything strictly within his professional range, interested himself in trying to fathom the moral attitude of these people. He was still suspicious of them, notwithstanding a growing tendency to like every one of their pleasant, really agreeable faces. There was neither solemnity, sourness, nor bitterness to be seen anywhere; at the same time, there was no sign of levity. In every countenance was the same inexplicable mixture of wisdom and benevolence that distinguished Estra. Nowhere was there hostility, and nowhere was there crudity. Somehow, the big geologist would have felt more at home had he seen something antagonistic. Essentially, Van Emmon was a fighter.

At last the four felt their attention lagging. Novelties always pall quickly, no matter how striking. Estra sensed the feeling and inquired:

"Which of you will do the honours?"

Instinctively the three younger folk turned to the doctor. He made no protest, but stepped at once to one of the microphones, put on his most impressive professional face, and began:

"My friends"—and Van Emmon noted a pleased look come into every face about them—"my friends, I do not need to state how significant this meeting is to us all. From what Estra has said, I gather that you have informed yourselves regarding us, in some manner which he has promised to make clear. At all events, I am exceedingly anxious to see your astronomical apparatus."

At this a broad smile came to many of the faces before him; but he went on, unnoticing: "Certainly there is not much I could tell you which you do not already know; Estra's use of our language proves this. I only need to assure you that we will be glad to answer any questions that may occur to you. It goes without saying that we, of course, are filled with delight to find your planet so wondrously and happily populated, especially after our experience on Mercury, of which, I presume, you are informed."

Apparently they were. The doctor went on: "You may be sure that we are fairly bursting with questions. However, we are content to become informed as Estra sees fit to guide us.

"There is just one thing, more than any other, which I would like to know at this time. Why is it that, although you all show a great lack of exercise, and are continually eating, you never appear to be healthy?"

Instantly a Venusian in the fifth row, to the doctor's right, touched his phone and replied: "It is a matter of diet. We have nothing but 'absolute' foods; if you understand what that means."

And from that time on, despite the fact that the explorers asked questions which, at home, would have found hundreds ready and able to answer, on Venus only one person answered any given question, and always without any apparent prearrangement. For a long time they could not account for this.

The doctor motioned for Smith to take his place. The engineer looked a little embarrassed, but cleared his throat noisily and said:

"I am especially struck with the fact that each of you sits in a separate glass pew, or case. Why is this?"

The reply came from one of the few people present who showed any signs of age. He was, perhaps, sixty, and his hair was fast whitening. He said:

"For reasons of sanitation. It is not wise to breathe the breath of another."

"Also," supplemented someone from the other side of that vast pit— "also, each is thereby enabled to surround himself with the electrical influences which suit him best."

Smith stepped back, pondering. The doctor looked to the geologist to take his place, but Van Emmon made way for Billie. At any other time she would have resented his "woman-first" attitude; now she quickly found voice.

"How are you able to get along without aisles? It may seem a foolish question, to you; but on earth we would consider a hall without aisles about as convenient as a room without a door."

Immediately a Venusian directly in front of her, and on a level with her eyes, called out: "Watch me, madam." And quite without an effort beyond touching a button or two, the fellow rose straight into the air, glass and all, and then floated gently over toward the middle of the hall.

"It probably appears complicated to you," explained the Venusian whose side he had just left. "We make use of elements not found on your earth."

Billie's *sang froid* was not shaken. Instantly she came back energetically: "Apparently your method overcomes gravitation. Why haven't you tried to travel away from your planet?"

And she looked around with the air of one who has uttered a poser, only to have another of the satin-clad people reply, from a point which she was not able to locate:

"Because enough such power cannot be safely concentrated."

As Billie retired, Van Emmon noted with growing irritation that the continuously affable aspect of the Venusians had not altered in any way, unless it was to become even more genial and sure. The big man strode energetically to the microphone, and the other three noted a general movement of interest and admiration as the people inspected him.

"Why," demanded he, "do we see no signs of contention? If you are familiar with conditions on the earth, you surely know that rivalry, in one form or another, is the accepted basis of life. But all of you, here, appear to be perfectly happy, and at the same time entirely sure of yourselves.

"We have just come from a planet where we have seen the principle of combat, of competition, carried so far that it seems to have wrecked the race; so you will pardon my curiosity, I am sure. From your faces, one would conclude that you had abolished self-interest altogether. Just why are you so—well, extraordinarily self-complacent?" And he thrust out his aggressive jaw as though to make up for the lack of chins about him.

"Because there is nothing for us to combat, save within ourselves." This from a wide-faced chap in a bluish-white suit.

"But surely you have rivalry of some sort?"

"No." Another voice added: "Rivalry is the outgrowth of

getting a livelihood; on earth it is inevitable, because men do the work. Here, everything is done by machines." Still another put in: "Discontent is the mother of ambition, but we are all content, because each possesses all he desires."

But the geologist was far from satisfied. "Then," said he vigorously, "if you have eliminated all contention, you have nullified the great law of contrasts. You say you are all rich. How do you know, if you have no poverty to contrast it with?

"On earth, we appreciate warmth because we have experienced cold; pleasure, because we know pain; happiness, because we have always had misery with us. If we have not had the one, we cannot value the other.

"If you have never been discontented, how do you know that you are content?"

8

The Key-Note

For a minute or two it looked as though Van Emmon had raised an unanswerable question. There was no immediate reply. Even Estra looked around, as though in wonder at the silence, and seemed on the point of answering of his own accord when a voice came from a man far up on the left. He said:

"A little explanation may be wise. To begin with, you will agree that black is black because white is white; but it doesn't follow that blue is blue because green is green, or red is red. Blue is blue because it is neither green nor red nor any other colour. It is blue, not because it contrasts with these other colours, but because it merely differs from them.

"Now, we on Venus do not need poverty, in order to appreciate wealth. Instead, each of us is blessed with his own particular choice of wealth. Each is blessed in a different way; some with children, some with intellect, some with other matters; and the question of mere quantity never enters."

"We do not need pain or misery," spoke up someone else, "any more than you people on the earth require an additional colour, in order to appreciate the variety you already have."

And then, from a Venusian with an especially strong voice:

"That we are really content, we know absolutely. For each of us, in his own distinctive way, is wholly and peculiarly satisfied."

And it only added to the geologist's irritation to have these striking statements made in a good-humoured, impersonal fashion which totally disarmed all opposition. That the Venusians were perfectly sure of their ground, was undeniable; but they had such a cheerful way of looking at it, as though they didn't care a rap whether Van Emmon agreed or not, that—If they'd only have shown some spirit! Van Emmon would have liked it infinitely better if one of them had only become hot about it.

At this point Estra rose in his chair. "I think you had best approach us from a fresh viewpoint," said he in his unfailingly agreeable manner. The doctor nodded vigorously, and again Estra closed his eyes in that odd, hesitating way. Immediately everyone in the place, with the exception of a single person in the lowest row, took flight in his or her little glass pew. In a moment the great vault overhead was fairly swarming with people; and in less than a minute the last of them had floated out through one of the arches in the walls.

Estra opened a panel in the central cage, and admitted the Venusian who had stayed behind. She—for it appeared to be a young woman—walked with about the same facility as Estra; but as soon as she had entered the space, took the seat Estra had vacated, and waited.

The action rather disappointed the doctor. He removed the interpreting telephone from his head, and asked:

"I rather thought we were going to meet one of your officials, Estra. We'd hate to go back home without having met your president, or whatever you call your chief executive."

The two Venusians exchanged smiles, and to the surprise of the explorers the woman gave the reply, in language as good as Estra's, but an even sweeter expression: "There is no such thing as a chief executive on Venus, friends."

"I meant," explained the doctor, rattled, "the chairman of your cabinet, or council, or whatever it is that regulates your affairs. Perhaps," with an inspiration, "I should have said, the speaker of your congress."

The Venusian shook her head, still smiling. She hesitated while selecting the best words; and the four noted that, while her features were quite as delicate as Estra's, her face was proportionately larger, and her whole figure better filled out. No one would have said that she was pretty, much less beautiful; but none would deny that she was very good-looking, in a wholesome, intelligent, capable sort of a way. Her name, Estra told them later, was Myrin; and he explained that he and she were associated solely because of their mutual interest in the same planet—the Earth.

Said Myrin: "You are accustomed to the idea of government. We, however, have outgrown it.

"If you stop to think, you will agree that the purpose of government is to maintain peace, on the one hand, and to wage war, on the other. Now, as to war—we haven't even separate nations, any more. So we have no wars. And as for internal conflict—why should we ever quarrel, when each of us is assured all that he can possibly want?"

"So you have abolished government?"

"A very long time ago. You on the earth will do the same, as soon as your people have been educated up to the point of trusting each other."

"You haven't even a congress, then?"

Myrin shook her head. "All questions such as a congress would deal with, were settled ages ago. You must remember that the material features of our civilization have not changed for thousands of generations. The only questions that come up now are purely personal ones, which each must settle for himself."

Van Emmon, as before, was not at all satisfied. "You say that machinery does your work for you. I presume you do not mean that literally; there must be some duties which cannot be performed without human direction, at least. How do you get these duties accomplished, if you have no government to compel your people to do them?"

Myrin looked at a loss, either for the answer itself or for the most suitable words. Estra gave the reply: "Every device we possess is absolutely automatic. There is not one item in the materials we use but that was constructed, exactly as you see it now, many thousands of years ago."

Smith was incredulous. "Do you mean to say that those little glass pews have been in use all that time?"

Estra nodded, smiling gently at the engineer's amazement. "Like everything else, they were built to last. You must remember that we do not have anything like an 'investment,' here; we do not have to consider the question of 'getting our capital back.' So, if any further improvements were to be made, they also would be done in a permanent fashion."

Billie gave an exclamation of bewilderment. "I don't understand! You say that nothing new has been built, or even replaced, for centuries. How do you take care of your increase in population?" thinking of the great crowd that had just left.

Myrin was the one who answered this. As she did so, she got slowly to her feet; and speaking with the utmost care, watched to be sure that the four understood her:

"Ever since the roof was put on, our increase of population has been exactly balanced by our death rate!"

The four followed their guides in silence as they led the way into the plaza. Now, the space was alive with Venusians. The little cages were everywhere floating about in the air; some of the people were laboriously shifting themselves into their aircraft; others were guiding their "pews" direct to nearby houses. The visitors got plenty of curious stares from these quiet miracle-workers, who seemed vastly more at home in the air than on the ground. "As thick as flies," Van Emmon commented.

Estra and Myrin, walking very slowly, took them to a side street, where two of the cigar-shaped cars were standing. Billie and Smith got in with Estra, while Van Emmon and the doctor were given seats beside the Venusian woman. The two cars were connected by telephone, so that in effect the two parties were one.

By this time, the visitors had become so accustomed to the transparent material that they felt no uneasiness as the ground receded below them. Smith, especially, was tremendously impressed with Estra's declaration that the glass was, except for appearance, nothing more nor less than an extremely strong, steel alloy.

Propelled by the unexplained forces which the two drivers controlled by means of buttons in black cases, the two cars began to thread their way through the great roof-columns; and as they proceeded, the four grew more and more amazed at the great extent of the city. For miles upon miles that heterogeneous collection of buildings stretched, unbroken and without system, until the eye tired of trying to make out the limits of it.

"What is the name of this city?" asked Billie, secretly hoping that it might bear some resemblance to "New York." It struck her fancy to assume that this super-metropolis represented what Gotham, in time, might become.

Estra did not take his attention from what he was doing, but answered as readily as ever. "I do not blame you for mistaking this for a city. The fact is, however, that we have no such thing."

Billie stared at him helplessly. "You've abolished cities, too?"

"Not exactly. In the same sense that we have abolished nations, yes. Likewise we have abolished states, also counties. Neither have we such a thing as 'the country,' now.

"My friends, Venus is simply one immense city."

9

The Survival of All

Somehow all four were unwilling to press this question. It did not seem possible that Estra was right, or, if he was, that they could possibly understand his explanation, should he give it. The cars flew side by side for perhaps a hundred miles, while the visitors put in the time in examining the landscape with the never-ending interest of all aeronauts.

Here and there, in that closely-packed surface, a particularly large building was to be noted every half mile or so. "Factories?" asked Billie of Estra, but he shook his head.

"I'll show you factories later on," said he. "What you see are schools." But most observers would have considered the structures severely plain for their purpose.

After a long silence: "I'm still looking for streams," said Van Emmon to Myrin. "Are your rivers as large as ours?"

"We have no rivers," was the calm reply. "Rivers are entirely too wasteful of water. All our drainage is carried off through underground canals."

"You haven't done away with your oceans, too, have you?" the geologist asked, rather sarcastically. But he was scarcely prepared for the reply he got.

"No; we couldn't get along without them, I am afraid. However, we did the best we could in their case." And without signalling to Estra she dove the machine towards the ground. Smith looked for the telephone wires to snap, but Estra seemed to know, and instantly followed Myrin's lead. The doctor noticed, and wondered all the more.

And then came another surprise. As the machines neared the surface, a familiar odour floated in through the open windows of the air-craft; and the four found themselves looking at each other for signs of irrationality. A moment, and they saw that they were not mistaken.

For, although that kaleidoscopic expanse of buildings showed not the slightest break, yet they were now located on the sea. The houses were packed as closely together as anywhere; apparently all were floating, yet not ten square yards of open sea could be seen in any one spot.

Van Emmon almost forgot his resentment in his growing wonder. "That gets me, Myrin! Those houses seem to be merely floating, yet I see no motion whatever! Why are there no waves?"

The doctor snorted. "Shame on you, Van! Don't let our friends think that you're an absolute ignoramus." He added: "Venus has no moon, and no wind, at least under the roof. Therefore, no waves."

Smith put in: "That being the case, there is no chance to start a wave-motor industry here. Neither," as he thought further, "neither for water-power. Having no rain in your mountains, Estra, where do you get your power?"

But it was Myrin who answered. "I suppose you are all familiar with radium? It is nothing more or less than condensed sunlight, which in turn is simply electromagnetic waves; although it may take your scientists a good many centuries to reach that conclusion.

"Well, every particle of the material which composes this planet, contains radioactivity of some sort; and we long ago discovered a way to release it and use it. One pound of solid granite yields enough energy to—well, a great deal of power."

They had now been flying for two hours, and still no end to that thickly-housed, ever different appearance of the ground. Also, although they saw a great many birds, they noted no animals. Finally, Billie could hold in no longer.

"Are we to understand," she demanded of Estra, "that the whole of this planet is as densely populated as we see it?"

"Just that," replied the Venusian. "Why not? The roof makes our climate uniform from pole to pole, while our buildings are such that, whether on land or on sea, they are equally liveable."

"But—Estra!" expostulated the girl. "Venus is nearly as big as the earth. And it looks to be as thickly populated as—as Rhode Island! Why, you must have a colossal population; let me see." And she scribbled away in her memorandum book.

But both Smith and the doctor had already worked it out. They looked up, blinking dazedly.

"Over three hundred billion," murmured the doctor, as though dizzy.

The Venusian checked Smith's correction with, "You dropped one cipher, doctor. There are three and a half trillion of us!"

"Good lord!" whispered Van Emmon, all his antagonism gone for the moment. And again the explorers were silent for a long time.

By and by, however—"We have just seen what it meant, there

on Mercury," said the doctor, in a low voice, "for the principle of 'the survival of the fit' to be carried to its logical end; for who is to decide what is fitness, save the fittest? One man, apparently, outlived everyone else on the planet, and then he also died. "But here you have gone the limit in the other direction. Of course, we might have known that you long ago abolished poverty, unearned wealth, pestilence, drunkenness and the other causes of premature death; but as for three and a half trillion!"

"Nevertheless," remarked Myrin, "every last one of us, once born, lives to die of old age; and in most cases this means several hundred of your years."

Smith involuntarily rubbed his eyes; and they all laughed, a nervous sort of a laugh which left the visitors still in doubt as to their senses, and their guides' sanity. Van Emmon's suspicions came back with a rush, and he burst out:

"Say—you'll excuse me, but I can't swallow this! Here you've shown us houses as thick as leaves; not a sign of a farm, much less an orchard! No vegetation at all, except for a few flowers!

"Three and a half trillion! All right; let it go at that!" Out came his chin, and he brought one fist down upon the other as though he were cracking rocks with a hammer, and with every blow he uttered a word:

"How—do—you—feed—them—all?"

10
Loaves and Fishes

Without a word Myrin drove her machine toward the ground, and, as before, Estra followed despite the lack of any visible signal. Within a minute the two machines had come to rest, softly and without disturbance, on the roof of a handsome building, much like an apartment house. There was the usual transparent elevator, and a minute later the four were being introduced to the occupants of a typical Venusian house.

These two people, apparently man and wife, did not need to be told why the explorers had been brought there. They led the way from the dimly lighted hallway in which the elevator had stopped, into a group of brightly decorated rooms. Here the four were given seats in the usual saddle-like chairs, and then Myrin answered Van Emmon's question:

"I knew that this point would arise soon, and you will pardon me if I handle it in a prearranged fashion. I will admit that it is not an easy question Mr. Van Emmon has put; not because the answer is at all complicated but, on the contrary, extremely simple."

The four were listening unanimously. Despite himself, Van Emmon was highly impressed by the Venusian woman's serious manner. Perhaps it was because, in her earnestness, she was not quite so affable as before. She went on:

"From where you are sitting, you can see all the rooms in this house. You will look in vain for anything even remotely resembling a kitchen. There is not even a dining-room.

"And yet you must not jump to the conclusion that we all use restaurants. We have no such thing as a public eating place. Or rather," and here she spoke very carefully, "rather, every place is an eating place."

The doctor looked Myrin over as though she were a patient with a new kind of disease. "You do not mean that literally, of course," said he kindly.

But she nodded gravely. "You must not misunderstand. Remember, even on your own planet, the distribution of food is becoming more and more extensive, until you can now buy something to eat at every crossroads. We have merely carried the idea to its logical end, so that all Venusians can obtain food at any time, and at any spot."

She turned in her chair—all the chairs on Venus were pivoted, Estra said—and touched a button in the wall at her hand. A panel slid noiselessly aside, and revealed a tiny buffet. At least, Billie labelled it a buffet, for want of a more accurate term.

For it consisted of a silver bib, something like the nozzle of a soda-water fountain above which was a board containing a large number of tiny, numbered push buttons. Below the bib was a space in which a cup might be set, and projecting from a tube at one side was a solid block of telescoping, transparent cups.

"This," said Myrin, "is the Venusian Nutrition System. There is a station like this in every room on the planet." And she proceeded to take a cup from the tube, filling each from the silver faucet while she pressed a variety of the buttons.

The four watched in silence, and eagerly took what was given to them. It comprised liquids entirely; liquids of every degree of fluidity, from some as thin as water to others as thick as gruel. They varied even more as to colour, ranging from actual transparency to a deep chocolate.

"Now, I warn you not to be shocked," said Myrin, "although I fully expect that you will be. The fact is that we have no other kind of food than what you see; there are thousands upon thousands of different kinds and flavours, but they are all fluids. We have nothing whatever in solid form.

"You see," she explained, "we have no teeth."

All they could do was to stare at her as, with a return of her smile, she made a sudden gesture across the front of her mouth. Next instant a set of false teeth lay in her hand!

Estra spoke up. "We are both obliged to wear them in order that we might use your language." He removed his own, to show a mouth as free of teeth as a newborn baby's. Both Venusians replaced their sets, and smiled afresh at the explorers' astonishment.

"Teeth will soon be a thing of the past with you on the Earth, too," commented Myrin. "Dr. Kinney will surely testify to that. Your use of soft, cooked foods, instead of the coarse, hard articles provided by nature, is bound to have this effect in time. With us, it resulted in having teeth reduced to the standing of your appendix; and, like you, we resort to an operation rather than take chances on trouble. I may mention that the appendix is totally absent from all Venusians, while we are beginning to lose all traces of either the first or second molars; just as you are beginning to lose your wisdom teeth.

"However, suppose you try our diet while I explain."

The four once more looked at each other. The doctor was the first to take a sip of one of the cups handed to him, and Van Emmon was the last; the geologist waited to see the effects upon the others before gingerly tasting of the thickest, darkest liquid of them all. Another taste, and he discovered that it was very good, and that he was exceedingly hungry.

"Very delicately flavoured," commented Billie, after emptying her fourth glass, a golden fluid with a slightly oily appearance.

"Delicately is right," said the doctor. "This stuff is barely flavoured at all, Estra."

The Venusian was also "eating." "We much prefer them all that way," said he. "I suppose you would consider our tastes very finicky, on Earth; but the fact is we are able to distinguish between minute variations in flavouring such as would escape all on earth except a humming-bird."

"I suppose," remarked the doctor, smacking his lips over a reddish solution with a wine-like flavour, "I suppose we can expect something of that sort on the Earth, too, in time. Originally mankind was only able to distinguish fresh from stale, and animal from vegetable flavours."

After a while Myrin went on: "You know, the processes of nutrition, as they take place among your people, are extremely wasteful. You have probably heard it said that 'the average human is only fifty per cent efficient.' That simply means that digestion, assimilation and excretion require half the energy which they secure from the food.

"Now, the articles you have just swallowed require very little work on the part of your digestive apparatus, and none at all upon your eliminating tract. The food is almost instantly transformed into fresh blood; if I am not mistaken, you already feel much refreshed."

This was decidedly true. All four felt actually stimulated; Van Emmon instantly suspected the food of being alcoholic. As he continued to watch its effect, however, he saw that there was no harmful reaction as in the case of the notorious drug.

"I think I can now tell you how we produce enough food for the three and a half trillion of us, despite our lack of farms and orchards," said Myrin rising.

Returning to the air-craft, the four were taken a short distance in a new direction, and again descended, this time transferring to an elevator which dropped far below the surface. They came to a stop about ten floors down.

"Naturally," said Myrin, "we reserve all the surface for residence purposes; although, it is possible to live down here in comparative comfort, since we have plenty of electrical energy to spare." And she operated a switch, flooding the place with a brilliant glow. Thrown from concealed sources, this light was quite as strong as the subdued daylight which they had just left. "But unless we were free to fly about as much as we do, we should feel that life was a bore. Nobody stays below any longer than is necessary.

"Now, this is where our food comes from." Whereupon she showed them a series of automatic machines, all working away there in the solid rock of the planet; and of such an extraordinary nature that Smith, the engineer, moved about in an atmosphere of supreme bliss.

"You will understand," said Myrin, "that the usual processes of nutrition, on the Earth, depend entirely upon plant life. We, however, cannot spare room enough for any such system; so we had to devise substitutes for plants.

"In effect, that is what these machines are. They convert bedrock into loam, take the nitrates and other chemicals[1] directly from this artificial soil, and by a pseudo-osmotic process secure results similar to those produced by roots.

"Likewise we have developed artificial leaves," pointing out a huge apparatus which none but a highly trained expert in both botany and mechanics could half understood. "This machine first manufactures chlorophyll—yes, it does," as the doctor snorted incredulously; "not an imitation, but real chlorophyll—and then transforms the various elements into starch, sugar, and *proteids* through the agency of the sunlight recovered from the granite.

"In short, to answer your question, Mr. Van Emmon, as to

---

1. The geology of Venus is thoroughly described in Mr. Van Emmon's reports to the A. M. E. A.

how we are all fed—we do not grow our food at all; we go straight to the practically unlimited supply of raw materials under our feet, and manufacture our food, outright!"

11
The Super-Ambition

Billie was very quiet during their return to the surface. She said nothing until they had reached the two cars; and then pausing as she was about to step in, she said:

"Well, I never saw our old friend, the high cost of living, handled quite so easily!

"If that's the way you do things here, Estra," and the girl did not flinch at the gazes the others turned upon her, "if that's your way, it's good enough for me! I'm going to stay!"

For the first time, Estra looked astonished. He and Myrin exchanged lightning-like glances; then the Venusian's face warmed with the smile he gave the architect.

"It is very good of you to say that," he said impressively. "I was afraid some of our—peculiarities—might arouse very different feelings."

They stared at one another for a second or two, long enough for the doctor to notice, and to see how Van Emmon took it. The geologist, however, was smiling upon the girl in a big-brotherly fashion, which indicated that he thought she didn't mean what she had said. Had he been looking up at her, however, instead of down upon her, he would have seen that her chin was most resolute.

Just as they were about to start again, both Estra and Myrin stopped short in their tracks, with that odd hesitation that had mystified the four all along; and after perhaps five seconds of silence turned to one another with grave faces. It was Estra who explained.

"It is curious how things do pile up," said he, a little conscious of having employed an idiom. "Our planet has gone along for hundreds of generations without anything especially remarkable happening, so that recently many prophets have

128

foretold a number of startling events to take place on a single day. And this seems to have come true.

"You have been with us scarcely ten hours," and the visitors stared at each other in amazement that so much time had passed; "scarcely ten hours, and here comes an announcement which, for over a hundred years, has been looked forward to with—"

He stopped abruptly. The doctor gently took him up: "'Looked forward to with'—what, Estra?"

Estra and Myrin considered this for perhaps three seconds. It was the woman who replied: "The fact is, your approach to the planet has stimulated all sorts of research immensely. Matters that had been hanging fire indefinitely were revived; this is one of them. In that sense, you are to blame." But she smiled as reassuringly as she could, allowing for a certain anxiety which had now come to her face.

"Don't you think you could make it clear to us?" asked Billie encouragingly. At the same time all four noted that the air, which before had fairly thronged with machines, was now simply alive with them. People were flitting here and there like swarms of insects, and with as little apparent aim. Both Estra and Myrin were extra watchful; also, they displayed a certain eagerness to get away, setting their course in still another direction. In a minute or two the congestion seemed relieved, and Myrin began to talk slowly:

"You have doubtless guessed, by this time, that we Venusians have crossed what some call 'the animal divide.' We are predominantly intellectual, while you on the earth are, as a race, still predominantly animal. Excuse me for putting it so bluntly."

"It's all right," said the doctor, with an effort. "What you say is true—of most of us." He added: "Most thinking people realize that when our civilization reaches the point where the getting of a living becomes secondary, instead of primary as at present, a great change is bound to come to the race."

The Venusian nodded. "Under the conditions which now surround us, you can see, we have vastly more time for what you would call spiritual matters. Only, we label them psycho-logical experiences.

"In fact, the 'supernatural' is the Venusian's daily business!"

There was another pause, during which both Venusians, driv-ing at high speed though they were, once more closed their eyes for a second or so. Estra evidently thought it time to explain.

"For instance, 'telepathy.' With us it takes the place of wireless; for we have developed the power to such a point that any Venu-sian can 'call up' any other, no matter where either may be. That is why we need no signs or addresses. There are certain restric-tions; for instance, no one can read another's thoughts without his permission.

"Of course, we still have speech; speech and language are the ABC's of the Venusian; and we still keep the telephone, for the sake of checking up now and then. Just now, we are driving for my own house, where there is apparatus which will enable you to both hear and understand an announcement which is shortly to be made."

There was something decidedly satisfying, especially to Van Emmon, in being taken into the Venusian confidence to this extent.

When he put his question, it was with his former aggressive-ness much modified. He said:

"I should think that your people have pretty well exhausted the possibilities of the supernatural, by this time. Progress hav-ing come to an end, I don't see what you find to interest you, Myrin."

"The fact is," Billie put in, "we feel somewhat disappointed that your people have shown so little interest in us." And she gave a sidelong glance at Estra, who returned the look with a direct, smiling gaze which sent a flood of colour into the architect's face.

"Look out!" sharply, from Van Emmon; and with barely an inch to spare, Estra steered his car past another which he had nearly overlooked. For another minute or two there was silence; then Myrin said:

"You wonder what there is to interest us. And yet, every time you look up at the stars, the answer is before your eyes.

"You see, although we cannot read your thoughts without your permission, yet you on the earth cannot prevent us from 'overhearing' anything that may be said. Under proper conditions, our psychic senses are delicate enough to feel the slightest whisper on the earth.

"That is why Estra and I are able to use your language; we have learned it together with an understanding of your lives and customs, by simply 'listening in.' I may add that we are also able to use your eyes; we knew, directly, what you people looked like before you arrived.

"Well, it is our ambition to visit, in spirit, every planet in the universe!

"There are hundreds of millions of stars; every one is a sun; and each has planets. One in a hundred contains life; some very elementary, others much more advanced than we are.

"So far, we have been able to study nearly two thousand worlds besides those in this solar system. Do you still think, friend, we have nothing to interest us?"

She raised a hand in a gesture of emphasis; and it was then that Billie, her eyes on Myrin's fingers, saw another sign of the great advancement these people had made—direct proof, in fact, of what Myrin had just claimed.

For there must have been a tremendous gain in the intellect to have caused such a drain upon the body as Billie saw. In no other way could it be explained; the minds of the Venusians had grown at a fearful cost to flesh and blood.

Not only were the fingernails entirely lacking from Myrin's hand, but the lower joints of her four fingers, from the palm to the knuckles were grown smoothly together.

12
The Mental Limit

"Make yourselves at home," said Estra, as they stepped into his apartment. The cars just filled his balcony. "This is my 'workshop'; see if you can guess my occupation, from what you see. As for Myrin and myself, we must make certain preparations before the announcement is made."

They disappeared, and the four inspected the place. As in the other house they had entered, the room was provided with a double row of small windows; some being down near the floor and the others level with the eyes. These, in addition to two doors, all of which were of translucent material.

On low benches about the room were a number of instruments, some of which looked familiar to the doctor. He said he had seen something much like them in psychology class, during his college days. For the most part, their appearance defied ordinary description.[1]

But one piece of apparatus was given such prominence that it is worth detailing. It consisted of a hollow, cube-shaped metal framework; about a foot in either direction, upon which was mounted about forty long thumb-screws, all pointing toward the inside of the frame. The inner ends of the screws were provided with small silver pads; while the outer ends were so connected, each with a tiny dial, as to register the amount of motion of the screw. Smith turned one of them in and out, and said it reminded him of a micrometer gage.

Then Billie noted that the entire device was so placed upon the bench as to set directly over a hole, about ten inches in diameter. And under the bench was one of the saddle-like chairs. The architect's antiquarian lore came back to her with a rush, and she remembered something she had seen in a museum—a relic of the inquisition.

"Good Heavens!" she whispered. "What is this—an instrument of torture?"

It certainly looked mightily like one of the head-crushing devices Billie had seen. Thumb-screws and all, this appeared to be only a very elaborate "persuader," for use upon those who must be made to talk.

---

1. Physicians, biologists, and others interested in matters of this nature will find the above fully treated in Dr. Kinney's reports to the A. M. A.

But the doctor was thinking hard. A big light flashed into his eyes. "This," he declared, positively, "is something that will become a matter of course in our own educational system, as soon as the science of phrenology is better understood." And next second he had ducked under the bench, and thrust his head through the round hole, so that his skull was brought into contact with some of those padded thumb-screws.

"Get the idea?" he finished. "It's a cranium-meter!"

It did not take Smith long to reach the next conclusion. "Then," said he, "our friend Estra is connected with their school system. Can't say what he would be called, but I should say his function is to measure the capacity of students for various kinds of knowledge, in order that their education may be adapted accordingly.

"Might call him a brain-surveyor," he concluded.

"Or a noodle-smith," added the geologist, deprecatingly.

"Rather, a career-appraiser!" indignantly, from Billie. "People look to him to suggest what they should take up, and what they should leave alone. Why, he's one of the most important men on this whole planet!"

And again the doctor was a witness to a clash of eyes between the girl and the geologist. Van Emmon said nothing further, however, but turned to examine an immense book-case on the other side of the room.

This case had shelves scarcely two inches apart, and about half as deep, and held perhaps half a million extremely small books. Each comprised many hundreds of pages, made of a perfectly opaque, bluish-white material of such incredible thinness that ordinary India-paper resembled cardboard by comparison.

They were printed much the same as any other book, except that the characters were of microscopic size, and the lines extremely close together. Also, in some of the books these lines were black and red, alternating.

Billie eagerly examined one of the diminutive volumes under a strong glass, and pronounced the black-printed characters not unlike ancient Gothic type. She guessed that the language was synthetic, like Roman or Esperanto, and that the alphabet numbered sixty or seventy.

"The red lines," she added, not so confidently, "are in a different language. Looks wonderfully like Persian." By this time the others were doing the same as she, and marvelling to note that, wherever the red and black lines were employed, invariably the black were in the same language; while the red characters were totally different in each book.

Suddenly Smith gave a start, so vigorously that the other turned in alarm. He was holding one of the books as though it were white hot. "Look!" he stuttered excitedly. "Just look at it!"

And no wonder. In the book he had chanced to pick up, the red lines were printed in *English*.

"Talk about your finds!" exclaimed Billie, in an awe-struck tone. "Why, this library is a literal translation of the languages of—" she fairly gasped as she recalled Myrin's words—"thousands of planets!"

After that she fell silent. Plainly the discovery had profoundly affected and strengthened her notion of remaining on the planet. Van Emmon, watching her narrowly, saw her give the room an appraising glance which meant, plain as day, "I'd like to keep this place in spick and span condition!" And another, not so easy to interpret: "I'd like to show these people a thing or two about designing houses!" And the geologist's heart sank for an instant.

He turned resolutely to the bookcase, and shortly found something which he showed to the doctor. It was a book printed all in "Venusian." They carefully translated the title-page, using one of the interlinear English books as a guide; and saw that it was a complete text-book on astral development.

"With these instructions," the doctor declared, "anyone could do as the Venusians do—visit other worlds in spirit!"

Just then Estra and Myrin returned. They were moving at what was, for them, a rapid pace; and to all appearances they were rather excited.

"We were not able to make these records as perfect as we would like," said Estra, holding up four disks similar to the ones which still lay in the explorers' translating machines. He proceeded to open the little black cases and make the exchange. "There will be words used which I did not see fit to incorporate in the original vocabulary, but which you will have to understand perfectly if this announcement is to mean anything to you."

"Thank you," said the doctor quietly. "And now, don't you think we had best know in advance, just what is to be the subject of—"

"Hush!" whispered Estra; and next second they were listening to the telephone in amazement.

13
The War of the Sexes

"In accordance with my promise," stated a high-pitched effeminate voice, "I am going to demonstrate a juvenation method upon which I have worked for the past one hundred and twenty-two years."

There was a brief pause, during which Estra hurriedly explained that the man who was making the speech was located far on the other side of the planet, in a hall like the one the four had first visited; and that he was making the demonstration before a great gathering of scientists. "Too bad you cannot see as we do," commented the Venusian. "However, Savarona may go into the details of—"

"If the committeemen are entirely finished with their measurements," stated the unseen experimenter, "I would like to have the results compared with the recorded figures of Pario Camenol, who was born on the two hundred and fifteenth day of the year twenty-one thousand seven hundred and four."

Another rest, and Estra said: "They are examining a boy who appears to be about twelve years of age."

Then came other voices:

"As we all know, the craniums of us all are absolutely distinct; as much so as our finger-prints."

"The measurements correspond identically with those of Pario Camenol, beyond a doubt."

"This boy can be none other than Pario."

"Then," the high-pitched voice went on, "then notice the formula I have written on this blackboard. Using this solution, I have supplied nourishment to this lad from the hour of his birth. Until a few days ago, I was not satisfied with the results; the patient showed a tiny variation from the allowable subconscious maximum, together with only nine-tenths the required motor reaction.

"But I have corrected this. Briefly, I have incorporated in Pario Camenol's standard diet certain elements which have hitherto been unsafe to combine. These elements are derivatives of the potash group, for the most part, together with phosphates which need a new classification. Their effect," impressively, "has been to postpone age indefinitely!"

There must have been a tremendous sensation in that hall. The speaker's voice shook with excitement as he went on:

"We have sought in vain, friends, for a way to cheat death of his due. We have succeeded in postponing his advent until our average longevity is several times greater than on our neighbouring planet. But so far, it has been a mere reprieve.

"What I have done is to prevent age itself. This lad is a hundred and twenty-two years old, mentally, and still only twelve years old, as to body!

"In short, I offer you the fountain of youth itself!"

The speaker paused. There was no comment. Evidently all had been as greatly impressed as the explorers. Then the voice of the man Savarona finished, very deliberately:

"I regret to say that my treatment, despite all that I have been able to do, cannot be adapted to the female constitution. It would be fatal to any but males. I repeat—I can offer eternal youth, absolutely, but only to new-born males!"

This time there was a definite response. From the telephone came a confused murmuring, at which Van Emmon's face lighted up with delight.

The murmuring had an angry sound!

"This is outrageous!" a loud contralto voice was raised above the rest. "You are unethical, Savarona, to announce such a thing before adapting it to both sexes!"

The high-pitched voice replied shortly, and with more than a hint of malice: "If a woman had discovered this, instead of me, I dare say you would have no objections!"

The murmuring grew louder, angrier, more confused. The four from the earth looked at each other in some slight uneasiness. At the same time they noted that Estra, his eyes tightly closed and his fists clenched in the intensity of his concentration, suddenly gave a sigh of relief. Next second he began to speak into the telephone, in a voice so loud as to silence all the clamour.

"Savarona, and the people of Venus! Listen!

"The prophets were right when they said today would witness many great things! I have just learned of another experiment which transcends even that of Savarona!"

An instant's pause; then: "First let me remind you that we have been doing all we could to elevate our spiritual selves. We are daily trying to eliminate all that is animal, all that is gross and demeaning in us, even to the extent of reducing the flavours of our foods to the lowest tolerable point. And despite all this, we have not been able to get rid of sex jealousy!

"We still have the beast within us! No matter how pure our love may be, it is always tainted with rivalry! Always the husband and wife are held down by this mutual envy, forever dragging at their heels, constantly holding them back from the lofty heights of spiritual power to which they aspire!"

He paused, and Savarona's voice broke in, triumphantly: "You are right, Estra! You are right, except you did not mention that this jealousy becomes less and less as one grows older!

"Now, my discovery will put an end to your beast, Estra! My experiments took this lad before he had become a man, and allowed his brain to develop, while his body stopped growing! He is a man in mentality, and an innocent boy in body!

"Estra, I have done the thing you wish! This boy will never know jealousy, because he will never know love!"

The man in the room with the four answered in a flash: "So you have, Savarona, but only for *men*! No female can benefit by what you have done!"

"But I tell you that, within the past few minutes, a child has been born under circumstances which can be repeated at any time, and for any sex!"

"In this case," the Venusian's voice changed curiously; "in this case, however, it was a girl; for the mother controlled the sex in the customary manner." At this, the doctor's interest became acute. At the same time, the other three felt a tremendous, inexplicable thrill.

"Friends"—and Extra's face shone in his enthusiasm—"friends, for the first time in creation the human male germ has been dispensed with! The intellect has done what the laboratory could not do!

"I have the honour to announce that my sister, Amra, has just given birth"—his voice fairly rang—"has just given birth to a girl baby, whose only father was her mother's brain!"

14

Est r a

This time there was no drowning the confusion. The telephone fairly shook with innumerable cries, shouts, imprecations. The four gave up trying to hear, and watched the two Venusians.

Myrin was facing Estra now. Her expression had lost a great deal of its good humour, and there was a certain sharpness in her voice as she exclaimed:

"Estra—if your sister has done this, and I see no reason to doubt it, then she has made man superfluous! If women can produce children mechanically, and govern the sex at will, the coming race need be nothing but females!"

Estra nodded gravely. "That is what it amounts to, Myrin!"

For a moment the two stared at one another challengingly. On the earth, their attitude would have indicated some unimportant tiff. None would have dreamed that the most momentous question in their lives had come up, and had found them at outs.

Next instant Myrin turned, and without another word walked from the room. Estra followed slowly to the door, where he stood looking after her with an expression of the keenest concern on his sensitive, high-strung features. The three men from the earth, after a glance, studiously avoided looking at him; but Billie walked up and laid a hand on his arm.

"Are you really in favour of this—scheme?" she inquired, in a curiously tender voice. At the same time she gazed intently into Estra's eyes.

He turned, and the smile came back to his face. He took Billie's hand and laid it between both his own. His voice was even gentler than before.

"Most certainly I do favour my sister's method, Billie. It will be the greatest boon the race has ever known. We can look forward, now"—and his face shone again—"can look forward to generation upon generation of people whose spirituality will be absolute!"

The girl moved closer to him. She spoke with feverish earnestness.

"There may be some hitch in the idea, Estra. If God meant for man to become—to become obsolete, He would not have hidden the method all this time. Suppose some flaw should develop—later on?"

In the cube, Billie Jackson would not have stumbled over such a speech. She would have ignored the fact that Estra was holding her hand all this time, and gazing deep into her eyes; she would have been filled with what she was saying and not with what she was seeing.

On the other side of the room, Van Emmon watched and glowered; he could not hear.

The Venusian lifted his head suddenly. The voices from the telephone had subsided; only an occasional outburst came from the instrument. Estra closed his eyes again for a second, and when he opened them again, his manner was astonishingly alert, and his speech swift and to the point.

"So far as we know, Billie, the method has no flaws. It gives us the chance to throw off our lower selves; and if by so doing, we reduce the race to a single sex, only—"

He stopped short, as though at a sound; and with a word of apology stepped from the room. He opened another door, far down the corridor; and as he passed through, the wail of a new-born infant came faintly to the four.

"Wonder what's up?" said Smith. Van Emmon, who had gone to the window, whirled upon the engineer and motioned him to his side.

"Look at the people!"

Smith saw that the nearby houses were almost concealed by a throng which had gathered, silently and without confusion, during the past few minutes. Their numbers were increasing swiftly, fresh arrivals packing the background. People filled the streets; the space below Estra's balcony was already crowded as closely as it could be. Except for a low-voiced buzzing, there was no disturbance.

Billie came up. She seemed to divine the temper of the mob. She caught her breath sharply, and then said, very simply:

"It reminds me of—Bethlehem."

But the words had scarcely left her mouth before an uproar sounded from one end of the street below. A crowd of excited Venusians was pushing its way determinedly toward the house, their passage obstructed by shouting, protesting individuals. Van Emmon's breast began to heave; he fancied he saw blows struck.

"By George!" he exclaimed, next second. "They're fighting!"

It was true; a hand-to-hand battle was going on less than a block away. The people below the window surged in the direction of the fight; all were shouting, now; the clamour was deafening.

"Live and let live!" came one of the shouts. It was taken up by the group that was doing the attacking, and made into a cheer. Then came other cries from them. Smith made out something like "Down with sex monopoly!"

"Don't you see?" shouted Smith, above the din. "These people below are Estra's friends; those newcomers are backing Savarona! Get the idea?" he repeated. "If Estra wins out, the old boy with the fountain of youth will never get another boy baby to experiment on!"

"What!" The doctor leaped to their sides. He took it in at a glance; then whirled to the door. "We ought to warn Estra!"

"He knows it already!" reminded Billie swiftly. A great shout came from below; the attackers had forced their way through the crowd of Estra's friends.

"Well!" Van Emmon stood squarely in the middle of the room. "So far as I'm concerned, Estra and his sister can face that crowd alone! I don't approve of the scheme!"

The doctor eyed him thoughtfully. "I'm not so sure, Van. This is a tremendous thing; we ought to—"

"Van is—right!" exploded Billie. Her voice rose to a shriek as a crash shook the house.

Next instant Myrin, for once in a hurry, broke into the room. She glanced about, missed Estra, looked slightly puzzled, and then frowned angrily as the Venusian himself stepped in: "You fooled me!" she shot at him. But he smiled apologetically. He was carrying a large package of leaflets, closely printed in Venusian; there seemed to be several thousand in the lot. He said, by way of explanation:

"I had to get ready. Savarona's people will be here any moment; they have destroyed the elevator, and—"

A wave of clamour burst from below. "They've broken the barrier," remarked Estra calmly; he turned to the door, then whirled at a crash which sounded from above. "Through the roof," he added. He did not even glance at the balcony, where the two cars barred the way against any attack from that direction.

Next second he again quit the room. Myrin hesitated a moment, irresolute, and then followed him thoughtfully. They never saw her again. As for Estra, he came back in a moment carrying a small, white bundle, which stirred in his arms. He unhesitatingly handed the child to Billie. His mouth moved soundlessly as a muffled shriek arose from the other end of the corridor; there was a thud, a metallic crash, and a great roar of voices. The mob had broken in, and up, through the back of the house. The first of the attackers thrust his head and shoulders into sight not ten feet away.

Estra touched something with his foot, and a door shot across the corridor. There was an instant's silence; then, the thunder of the mob, hurling itself against the door. The people were fairly snarling now. Estra closed the inner door.

"Estra!" shrilly, from Billie. She laid the baby down, and strode to the Venusian. "Let's get out of here! The car's on the balcony; nobody's in the way to interfere! Why not—"

A grinding, ripping jar from above, and Estra shook his head. The smile was gone, and his mouth was set and grim. "They'd catch us before we went a mile," he said, glancing at the infant, who had begun to cry, in a stifled, gasping way that tore at the nerves.

"Estra!" Billie pleaded; but he turned away. The doctor strode up to him and gripped his shoulder.

"What's the good, Estra? What can you accomplish even if you—"

The Venusian tapped his forehead. "I can *tell!*" he exclaimed, with a return of that exalted flush. "Just give me a chance to offer my sister's discovery to the world, and I shall be satisfied!" He touched the package of leaflets. "These are not written as clearly as they should be; but if I cannot hold them back, then these"—fingering the papers—"these go to the friends down below!" He moved closer to the window, but his eyes were on the door.

A rending crash told that the corridor was now open to the mob. There was a rush, and then the storm of the people battering the last door.

"Van! Doc! Billie!" Smith had the window open, and was stepping into one of the cars. Kinney and the geologist were at his side in an instant. The girl held back.

"Estra!" she begged. She picked up the baby, and with her free hand tugged at the Venusian's arm. "Come on! Don't sacrifice yourself!"

142

The door bulged under the attack. The noise was ear-splitting. Nevertheless Estra heard, and shook his head without looking at the woman from the Earth. She dashed to the window, then came back. "Hurry! There's a chance!" He stood unmoved, watchful and ready. "Estra! I want you to come!" Her face flamed. "Can't you see? Can't you see that I—I want you?" She gasped as the door shrieked under the strain. "Come—if you're a man!"

The Venusian's face changed. He turned, and stared at the girl with eyes that held nothing but blank amazement. The grimness left his mouth, his lips partly opened. He took a step forward and threw an arm about her shoulders.

"Billie—I'm sorry! I never thought!" A crack showed at the edge of the door, and a roar smote their ears. Estra backed to the window. "Go!" he shouted. "Go quickly, while you can!"

Billie stood stock still, gazing at him. "I'm going to stay!" she screamed. "I'll take my chances with—"

He thrust her through the window. "You don't understand!" he shouted, and took the baby away from her, despite all her strength. Then a wonderfully tender light came into his eyes. He gripped Billie's hands, and spoke sorrowfully:

"Billie—I'm not what you thought! I'm not a man—I'm a woman!"

15
Back!

By the time Smith had driven the strange craft fifty yards, he had it under control. Billie glanced back; Estra was out on the balcony, now, and the mob was surging against the windows she had locked against them. She shifted the baby to the hollow of one arm while with the other she broke the cord of the packet.

At the sight, the crowd in the street gave voice. "Let us have it!" they were crying; they drowned out the uproar within the house. Estra did not even look at the other car.

Then the windows gave way. Like the breaking of a dam, a flood of Venusians poured and tumbled at Estra's feet. She raised her hand, and shouted something Billie could not hear; then, scarcely without pause, the crowd bore down upon her.

And even as she was crushed against the railing, with one hand she dropped the baby to eager, upstretched arms below; and with the other she tossed the package high in the air. There it broke apart, the air caught it, and the thousands of leaflets fluttered down upon that street full of sympathizers.

Leaflets, each of which described a discovery which was to give to women the power of abolishing the opposite sex, of making Venus a world not only one in country, one in industry and one in thought, but—one in sex!

The thunderous meaning of Estra's last action almost made Billie forget that it was, in truth, the woman's last act. For next moment her lifeless form was being crushed beneath the feet of that supremely cultured, marvellously civilized mob; for it was only a mob, despite its astounding advancement; a mob which had retained all the brute's fanaticism, and all the male jealousy of the female.

For they were all men.

The four had been on Venus almost twenty-four hours when Smith, knowing the condition of the machinery in the cube, warned the others that they must return. Secretly, he was tired of the Venusians' continual smiling; for they had fairly outdone each other to show the visitors all that could be shown. But it was Van Emmon who thought to ask for Estra's wonderful library.

"These chemicals and metals you are giving us," he said, making a regular speech of it, "are extremely welcome; they will enable us to perform experiments otherwise out of our reach.

"But Estra's books will mean still more to the people of the earth. If there is no one else with more need for them, who is going to put in a claim, then why not let us have them?"

Apparently the Venusians did not like the idea very well. "They must have thought it was like letting a monkey play with a rifle," the doctor afterward put it. But, for lack of a leader with any motive for objecting, and because Estra had no living relatives to claim the library, somehow that incredible collection of intellectual gems got into the possession of the four. Nothing was said about it during the quiet leave-taking, and when the cube finally rose away from the roof, Van Emmon's face beamed with happiness and a great sigh of satisfaction escaped him.

"Well"—looking at the books—"they kind of make up for the fact that the folks didn't ask us to call again!"

And he turned and went straight to the kitchenette, where he proceeded with great speed and efficiency to set out the following:

Canned Soup. Canned baked beans. Fried bacon and egg. Coffee. Peaches.

"Come and get it!" he shouted. The doctor tore himself away from the books; Smith crawled out from the beloved machines; Billie came out shortly from her cubby-hole, and slipped into her seat in a highly excited manner. There was a brightness in her cheeks, and a noticeable change in her usually assured manner. This timidity, so utterly new to the girl, seemed most pronounced whenever Van Emmon chanced to look at her; which was quite often.

All four were ravenous. They had been away from the cube a day and a night, and "all we had to eat was something to drink," as Smith complained. Nothing whatever was said except "Please pass that" and "Thanks," for fully fifteen minutes.

At last they were satisfied. The doctor went back to the books; Smith returned to his oil-can and wrench. But Billie stood by the table, and began helping Van Emmon to clear up. In a moment they were face to face.

"Van," she said softly, and looked up at him wistfully. "Van— do you like me better this way?" Her eyes were almost piteous.

Into the man's face there came a look of amazement followed by one of admiration, and another of genuine delight He gave a little laugh, and unconsciously threw out his hands.

"Much better, Billie." Neither of them cared a particle whether Smith or the doctor saw that Billie, very simply and naturally, walked right into Van Emmon's arms. "Much better. Besides, you're really too graceful to wear anything else."

The Devolutionist

The Devolutionist

1

Out of Their Minds

"Remember, now; don't make a sound, no matter what you see!"

Mrs. Kinney eyed her caller anxiously as they came to a pause in front of the door. His glance widened at her caution, but he nodded briefly. She turned the key in the lock.

Next second the two stepped softly into the room. Mrs. Kinney carefully closed and locked the door behind them; and meanwhile the man, peering closely into the shadows of the place, made out a scene of such strangeness that he nearly forgot the woman's injunction.

The room was the private study of Dr. William Kinney. In itself, it was not at all out of the ordinary. Shelves of books, cases of surgical and psychological instruments, star charts, maps and astronomical apparatus—these told at once both the man's vocation and avocation. With these contents and rather severe furnishings the room was merely interesting, not remarkable.

But its four chairs certainly were. Each of them was occupied by a human being; and as Mrs. Kinney and her caller entered, neither of the four so much as stirred. They were all asleep.

In the nearest chair was the doctor himself, half sitting and half reclining; in fact, all four of the sleepers were in attitudes of complete relaxation. The doctor's gray head was resting on one shoulder wearily.

On his left was a man of medium height and commonplace

countenance. "Mr. Smith," whispered Mrs. Kinney, placing her mouth close to the caller's ear, so that he might hear the better.

Opposite these two sat a man and a woman, their chairs placed close together. The one was a slender, well-dressed, boyishly good looking young woman of perhaps thirty; the other a large, aggressively handsome fellow possibly five years older. "Mr. and Mrs. Van Emmon," explained Mrs. Kinney, still in a whisper.

The four sat absolutely motionless; the caller, looking very closely, could hardly make out the rising and falling of their chests as they breathed. Also, he saw that they were all connected, the one with the other by means of insulated wires which ran to brass bracelets around their wrists. At one point in this curious circuit, a wire ran to a small group of electrical appliances placed on a pedestal at the doctor's side; while the caller was still further puzzled to note that each of the sleepers was resting his or her feet on a stool, the legs of which, like the legs of each chair, were tipped with glass.

After a minute of this the caller turned upon Mrs. Kinney in such complete bewilderment that she instantly unlocked the door, and again cautioning perfect silence, led the way into the corridor. Here she again locked the door. Upon leaving the spot, a quiet young man with keen gray eyes stepped from a room opposite, and at a nod from Mrs. Kinney proceeded to do sentry duty outside the study.

Once down-stairs and safely within the living-room—

"This is rather mean of you Mrs. Kinney!" protested the man. "Tell me all about it, quick!"

The lady complacently took a chair. "Well," she remarked innocently, "I knew you'd want to see him."

"Yes, but—"

"It serves you right," she went on blithely, "for staying away so long. Let's see—you left a year ago June, didn't you, Mr. Hill?"

He swallowed something and managed to reply, "Great guns, yes! I've been in the wilds of New Guinea for a year—without news of any kind! I saw my first newspaper on board the dirigible this morning!"

"Ah, well," commented Mrs. Kinney provokingly, "you'll have to be humoured, I suppose." She cogitated unnecessarily long, then left the room to get a folio of newspapers and magazines. One of these she selected with great deliberation, and opened it at the leading article. Even then she would not hand it over right away. "You remember that sky-car idea of the doctor's, don't you?"

"His machine to explore space? He couldn't talk of anything else when I—you don't mean to say"—incredulously—"that he made a success of that!"

"He certainly did. Took a three weeks' tour of the planets, month before last!"

Hill stared in amazement, then leaned forward suddenly and whisked the magazine out of Mrs. Kinney's fingers. He held the paper with hands that trembled in excitement; and this is what he read, in the matter-of-fact black-and-white of *The Scientific New Zealander*.

Star Explorers Return
Dr. Kinney and Party Visit
Venus and Mercury

Bringing proofs which will satisfy the most sceptical, Dr. William G. Kinney, G. Van Emmon, E. Williams Jackson, and John W. Smith, who left the earth on December 9 in a powerful sky-car of the doctor's design, returned on the 23rd, after having explored the two planets which lie between the earth and the sun.

They found Mercury to be a dead world, like the moon, except that it once supported a civilization nearly as advanced as our own. They tell of a giant human, a veritable colossus, who was the planet's last survivor.

But on Venus they discovered people still living! They are marvellously developed people, infinitely more advanced than the people of the earth, and enjoying a civilization that is well-nigh incredible. Among other things, they have learned how to visit other worlds without themselves leaving their planet. They do it by a kind of telepathy; they know all about us here on the earth; and they have accumulated data regarding the peoples of hundreds of thousands of other planets! The four explorers are able to prove their statements beyond the shadow of doubt. They possess photographs which speak for themselves; they have brought back relics from Mercury and materials from Venus, such as never existed on the earth. They submit a vast library of extraordinarily advanced scientific literature, which was given to them by the Venusians.

The article went on to detail, to the extent of some eight or ten pages, the main features of the exploration. Hill, however, did not stop to read it all just then. He looked up, his thoughts flying to the strange scene in the room up-stairs. "What are they doing—recuperating?"

"Not exactly." Mrs. Kinney was a little disappointed. "Here— let me point out the paragraph." And she ran a finger down the column until it indicated this line:

Among other things they have learned how to visit other worlds without themselves leaving their planet. They do this by a kind of telepathy.

"That's the explanation," Mrs. Kinney said quietly. Hill fairly blinked when he read the paragraph. "They are trying out one of the Venusian experiments?"

"Of course; you know the doctor. He couldn't resist the temptation. And I must say the others are just as bad.

"Mr. Smith is quite as much interested as Mr. Van Emmon. Mr. Smith is an electrical engineer; the other man is a geologist, and a very adventurous spirit. As for Mrs. Van Emmon—"

"But this account mentions"—Hill referred to the magazine—"'E. Williams Jackson.' Who was he?"

"She—not he. Mrs. Van Emmon now; she used to be an architect. She had the other three fooled for ten days; she passed herself off as a man!"

But Hill was too absorbed in the general strangeness of the affair to note this amazing item. He again glanced at the article, opened his mouth once or twice as though to ask a question, thought better of it each time, and finally got to his feet.

"Let me have this?" referring to the magazine.

Mrs. Kinney handed over the rest of the collection.

"I am sure the doctor would want you to read them. I remember he said, just before they started away, that he wished you could have gone with him."

"Did he?" much pleased. Hill made some affectionate remark, under his breath about "the star-gazing old fraud"; then, evidently in a hurry to get off by himself and read, he made his excuses and left the house.

Mrs. Kinney returned to the book she had been reading, glanced at the clock, and noted that it was almost at the hour, previously agreed upon, that she should arouse the four upstairs. She put the book down and started toward the stairs.

At that instant a large gong sounded in the hall. In the study up-stairs, the doctor's hand moved away from a pushbutton. He stirred in his chair; and as he did so, the other three awakened. First Van Emmon, then "Billie," his wife, and lastly the engineer.

Next second all four were sitting bolt upright, and looking at each other eagerly.

2

BACK ON EARTH

"Talk about results!" Billie was first to speak. "Why—where do you suppose I found myself? Out in mid-ocean, in a small boat, with the spray flying into my—that is, into the face of—" She broke off, confused.

"Your agent?" the doctor put in. All Billie could do was to nod; Van Emmon was bursting to talk.

"My agent was a Parisian apache, or I'm a bum guesser! I didn't catch all that was going on, but it certainly sounded like the plans and specifications of a garrotting!"

"No such excitement here," said Smith. But his eyes were sparkling. "I was going the rounds with a mail-carrier. How do you explain that, doc? I've never given mail-carrying a second thought."

"That would have nothing to do with it. As for myself, I was looking through the eyes of some member of the House of Representatives, in Washington. I recognized the building. They were calling the roll at the time."

He paused while he made a note of the incident, for the sake of checking up the hour with the newspaper accounts later on. Then he rubbed the knuckles of one hand in the palm of the other—a habit which indicated that a diagnosis was going on in his mind. The others waited expectantly.

"There's a big difference," commented he, thoughtfully, "between these experiences and our last experiments. Then, each of us knew exactly what to expect. Each had a definite image of a certain particular person in mind when he went into the teleconscious state. That made it comparatively easy for us to communicate the way we did, even when you"—indicating the bride and groom—"were still in Japan.

"But to-day neither of us had the slightest idea what was coming. That is, if we followed the rule. Did you"—addressing Smith—"take care to concentrate strictly upon the one idea of view-point?"

"Nothing else. I kept my attention fixed upon eyes and ears, only, just as the instructions read."

"Same here," answered Billie, for herself and the geologist.

"Then we know this much: So long as the four of us are connected up in this fashion"—holding up his braceleted wrists—"we combine our forces to such an extent that we do not need a definite object. It's simply the power of harmony."

Billie was anxious to get it down pat. "In other words, there's nothing to prevent me from locating someone—although unknown to me—so long as we four agree upon the same locality?"

"That's it exactly. If we agree to concentrate upon Greenland, even, we shall find four people there whose view-points resemble our own. The main thing is to find similar view-points."

There was some discussion along this line, in which the doctor made it clear that view-point was simply another name for perspective, and that it had nothing whatever to do with actual mental accomplishments. The view-point was really the soul.

"As yet," he went on, "we should make no attempt to 'put ourselves in the other fellow's place.' Such efforts require a violent exertion of the imagination, and we need practice before tackling the more advanced problems.

"Time enough, after a while, to get in touch with the Venusians. There's none of them that has a view-point like ours. And once we've done that—"

"What?" from Billie, breathlessly.

"Anything! The whole universe will be open to us! Why, I understand from reading these books"—indicating the Venusian manuscripts—"that there is such a thing as an intelligent creature, so utterly unlike ourselves that—" He stopped short.

"For the time being," said Smith quickly, "we'd better be content with something familiar. Is there some other planet in our solar system that would do, doc?"

"No. According to the Venusians, the only others that are habitable besides Venus and the earth, are Mars and Jupiter. And it seems that the people on these two are so totally different—"

"We couldn't get an answer?"

"Very unlikely. Besides, I am having the cube refitted for a two-months' cruise. Rather thought I'd like to visit Mars and Jupiter in person.

"But when it comes to leaving the solar system entirely the telepathic method is the only one that will work; even the nearest of the fixed stars is out of the question."

"How far is that?" Smith inquired.

"The nearest? About four and a half light-years."

"Yes, but what's a light-year?"

"It amounts to sixty-three thousand times the distance from here to the sun!"

Smith whistled. "Nothing doing in the cube, that's sure. Besides, could we expect to find any people like us in the neighbourhood of that star?"

"Not Alpha Centauri." The doctor reached for one of the Venusian books, and pointed out certain pages. "It seems that the Class IIa stars—that is, suns—are the only ones which have planets in the right condition for the development of humans. The astronomers already suspected as much, by the way. But the Venusians have definitely named a few systems whose evolution has reached points almost identical with that of the earth.

"Now, until we have acquired a certain amount of ability"— examining the books more closely—"our best chance will lie in the neighbourhood of a giant star known to us as Capella."

"Capella." Billie had drawn a star-chart to her side. "Where is that located?"

"In Auriga, about half-way from Orion to the Pole Star. She's a big yellow sun.

"At any rate, the Venusians say that this particular planet of Capella's has people almost exactly the same as those of the earth, except"—speaking very clearly—"except that they have had about one century more civilization!"

Billie exclaimed with delight. "Say—this is going to be the best yet! To think of seeing what the earth is going to be like, a hundred years from now!"

Instantly Van Emmon's interest became acute. "By George! Is that right, doc? Are we likely to learn what the next hundred years will do for us?"

"Don't know exactly." The doctor spoke cautiously. "That's merely what I infer from these books."

"If we do," ran on the geologist excitedly, "we'll see how a lot of our present day theories will be worked out! I'm curious to see what comes of them. Personally, I think most of them are plain nonsense!"

"That remains to be seen." The doctor glanced around. "Remember: what we want is the view-point only; and the place is Capella's planetary system. Ready?"

For answer the others leaned back in their chairs. The doctor touched the button at his side, as a signal to his wife; he settled himself in his chair; and in a minute his head was dropping over against his shoulder. In another second the minds of the four experimenters were out of their bodies; out, and in the twinkling of an eye, traversing space at absolute speed.

For thought, like gravitation, is instantaneous.

3

SMITH'S MIND WANDERS

Secretly Smith hoped he might find an agent who also was an engineer. He had this in mind all the while he was repeating the Venusian formula, the sequence of thought-images which was necessary to bring on the required state of mind. The formula had the effect of closing his mind to all save telepathic energy, and opening wide the channels through which it controlled the brain.

No sooner had he repeated the words, meanwhile concentrating with all the force of his newly trained will upon the single idea of seeing and hearing what was happening on the unknown, yet quite knowable planet—no sooner had his head sunk on his chest than he became aware of a strange sound.

On all sides unseen apparatus gave forth a medley of subdued jars and clankings. A variety of hissing sounds also were distinguishable. And meanwhile Smith was staring hard, with the eyes he had borrowed along with the ears, at a pair of human hands.

These hands were manipulating a group of highly polished levers and hand-wheels. So long as his borrowed sight was fixed upon that group Smith was entirely ignorant of the surroundings. All he could surmise was that his agents operated some sort of machinery.

Then the agent glanced up; and Smith got his first shock. For he now saw a cluster of indicating dials, such as one may see on the instrument board of any automobile; but the trained engineer found himself absolutely unable to interpret one of them. They were marked with unknown figures!

Nevertheless, the engineer received an unmistakable impression, quite as vivid as though something had been said aloud. "Progress; all safe," was the thought-image that came to him.

He listened closely in hope of hearing a spoken word. Also, he tried his best to make his agent look around the place. Other people might be within sight. However, for a couple of minutes the oddly familiar hands kept manipulating the unfamiliar instruments.

Then, somewhere quite close at hand, a deep-toned gong sounded a single stroke. Instantly the agent looked up; and Smith saw that he was inspecting the interior of a large engine-room. He had time to note the huge bulk of a horizontal cylinder, perhaps fifty feet in diameter, in the immediate background; also a variety of other mechanisms, more like immensely enlarged editions of laboratory apparatus than ordinary engines. Smith looked in vain for the compact form of a dynamo or motor, and listened in vain for the sound of either. Then, in swift succession, came two strokes on the unseen gong, followed by a shrill whistle.

Smith's borrowed eyes became fixed upon that group of dials again. Their indicators began to shift, some rapidly, some slowly. Once the agent gave a swift glance through a round window— the place seemed to be lighted by ordinary daylight—and Smith saw something unrecognizable flit by.

A little further progress, and then came three strokes on the gong, followed by a low thrumming. In response to these, the agent deliberately picked out two levers, and pulled them down. When his glance returned to the dials, one of them showed immense acceleration.

By and by came another triple clanging, another pair of levers was pulled down, and instantly the jarring and clanking gave way to a decided rumble, low and distinct, but so powerful that it shook the air. At the same time the agent quit his post and went over to the giant horizontal cylinder.

Now Smith could see that this vast structure was merely part of an engine whose dimensions were quite beyond any former experience. It was a simple affair, being merely a reciprocal machine like the most elementary form of steam engine. But, instead of being operated by steam, it was a chemical machine;

Smith's trained eyes told him that the cylinder was really an enormous retort. And he noted with further perplexity that the prodigious piston-rod not only moved with terrific speed, but in a strictly back-and-forth motion; its far end did not revolve.

The agent seemed satisfied with it all. He turned about and walked—so far as Smith could sense in the usual manner of earth's humans—back to the dials again. Just then a door opened a short distance away and another man entered.

Smith would have mistaken him for the employee of some garage. He was dressed in a suit of greasy blue overalls; and as he advanced toward the eyes Smith was using, he looked about the room with practiced glance. He merely nodded to Smith's man, who returned the nod just as silently; and such was the extreme brevity of it all, Smith was afterward unable to describe the man.

His agent, thus relieved of his duty temporarily, strolled out another door, which took him through a narrow corridor and another door, opening on to some sort of a balcony, or deck. Smith fully expected to look upon an ocean.

Instead, he found himself gazing into a sea of clouds. He was in some sort of aircraft!

Next moment, quite as though it had all been prearranged, a large sky-cruiser hove into sight perhaps a quarter of a mile away. It seemed to materialize out of the clouds, and rapidly bore down upon the craft in which the agent stood.

But the practical man of the earth was eying the air-ship in increasing amazement. For it was truly a ship; a huge vessel wonderfully like one of the old-fashioned freighters which used to sail the seas of the earth. What was more, it had four tall, sloping masts, each spread with something remarkably like canvas; and that whole incredible hulk was actually swinging in mid air!

Looking closer, Smith saw that the masts were exceedingly tall; they held enough canvas to propel ten ships. And each stick sloped back at so sharp an angle—much sharper than forty-five degrees—that the wind not only blew the craft along in its course, but actually supported it as well.

It meant a wind which would make a hurricane seem tame. Either that, or air with greater density than any Smith knew about.

Suddenly the cruiser came about into the wind, and at the same instant it began to take in sail, all the sheets furling in unison. Simultaneously great finlike wings shot out of slits in the sides of the hull; and immediately they began to beat the air, back and forth, back and forth, with the speed and motion of swallows.

So this was the meaning of the giant reciprocal engine! Instead of the screw propeller which characterized earth's aircraft, these vessels employed the true bird principle, combining it with the simple methods of primitive sailing craft.

As soon as the ship stopped its wind-driven rush and began to employ its wings, the speed straightway slackened; and the ships began to descend. About the same time the figures of several people appeared on what might be called the bridge; and assuming that these people were as large as the man whom Smith had seen enter the engine-room—a chap of average height—then that ship, in proportion, was all of a mile long!

But Smith's awe was not shared by his agent, who turned indifferently away and looked about the sky as though in search of other sights. In doing so, he leaned over the deck's railing; and Smith saw the sheer sides of the giant ship, extending fore and aft almost indefinitely; while far overhead billowed vast clouds of white cloth. The vessel was now under sail.

About a mile higher up, and almost that distance to one side, the agent's eyes made out two tiny specks. He watched them closely for a moment as they pitched and tossed queerly about; then darted into the engine-room, secured a pair of binoculars of an old, squat pattern, and swiftly focused upon the nearer of the two.

Smith instantly sensed a disaster. The object was a small aircraft, of a sort entirely strange to the engineer; yet he knew that it was disabled. One of its queer wings was broken and fluttering, as the little machine dropped, tumbling and twisting errati-

160

cally, in an inexplicably slow fashion toward the unseen ground. Smith glimpsed a single figure, presumably strapped in the seat.

Then the focus changed to cover the other machine. It was of the same type; and Smith saw that it was swooping in a steep spiral, its driver leaning over in his seat, looking down.

Next moment the two were in focus together. Every second they dropped closer and closer to Smith's borrowed eyes. And in less time than it takes to tell it, they had come so close that when the occupant of the disabled craft lurched heavily to one side, Smith could plainly make out the long, flying hair of a woman.

She was unconscious, and strapped in!

Her craft capsized. At the same time the other driver—a man—manoeuvred so as to spiral exactly around the wreck as it fell. When it came right side up again—now only a half a mile away—he drove down so close that his machine nearly grazed the woman's head. As he did so, he leaned over and tried to unfasten her. But the unsteadiness of her craft prevented this.

He made a second try. This time his own machine narrowly escaped injury; he steered it hastily away from that damaged wing. And then he made a supreme effort.

Bringing his machine directly across the top of the other as it once more righted itself, he touched one of his controls, so that his own flier's spiral increased in steepness. Straightening up, he poised himself while he coolly measured the distance; and then he calmly leaped a matter of ten or twelve feet, over and down to the top of the other craft.

The shock of his landing steadied it. Clinging fast with one hand, the man bent and unbuckled the woman's strap. Next instant he had lifted her, a dead weight, into his arms and then over his shoulders.

His own machine was still scooting downward, its speed even greater than that of the broken flier. When the man saw it swinging past and below him, he instantly clambered, burden and all, to the edge of the cockpit. For a second he stood, balancing precariously; and then, half jumping, half diving, he plunged once more.

Man and woman landed in a heap in the sound machine. In a flash the rescuer snatched his controls, and tried with all his might to "straighten out." But it began to skid; and Smith saw, despite the shakiness with which his excited agent held the binoculars, that the craft was hopelessly out of control. Next instant the man caught sight of the ship, not a hundred yards away; and steered straight for her.

Smith's agent rushed back to the engine-room, where he immediately located a new group of instruments. Smith recognized a telephone and some wireless apparatus; then found himself staring into some sort of a compound mirror system. Probably it was an illuminated tunnel affair, opening into a long white cabin. Seemingly the place was an emergency-ward.

A moment later the unconscious forms of the two aviators were brought within perhaps twenty feet. Smith could hear nothing; the apparatus seemed made for looking only. But he saw the doctors hurry in, saw restoratives administered, and saw both people revive.

The man was first to become conscious. He looked around, seemed to take in the situation at a glance, and swiftly got to his feet. The doctors laid restraining hands upon him, but he shook them off with a laugh.

He was a powerfully built man, considerably taller than normal and very deep in the chest. He was decidedly blond, and good looking in a cheerful, reckless sort of way.

His concern was for the woman. She regained her senses in half a minute, and shortly was sitting up and looking around. And Smith, ordinarily unobservant of the other sex, found himself staring with all his eyes.

She was young; for that matter, the man was under thirty, also. And the white bandage on her forehead only emphasized the dark eyes and vivid colouring of her face. Smith was half angry that he could not see her more distinctly. He decided that every feature was exquisitely modelled, that he had never seen such delicate lines, nor eyes as large, as appealing and as soft.

Then he was watching the man again. He approached the

162

woman and took her outstretched hand. He was laughing easily; she, smiling tremulously and gratefully. They looked into one another's eyes quite as though there were no one else in the cabin to be looked at. Next second one of the doctors stepped up brusquely, and Smith saw a swift blush come to the girl's cheeks. The man reddened, too, and turned away laughing to hide his confusion.

Smith's connection with his agent ended right there. When he reported to the other three, later on, he had to admit that, so far as he knew, the man and the girl were still holding hands.

4

New Hearts for Old

Billie's experience was totally different. She found herself transformed into a mental humming-bird.

Her mind seemed to be darting with infinite rapidity, here and there throughout the universe. She got only the most lightning-like glimpse of any one spot; flash after flash of unfamiliar, indescribable situations succeeded each other like the speeded-up scenes of a photoplay farce. For an unguessable length of time this helter-skelter process occupied her mind.

Then there came a scene which stayed. It was dim at first; she was more thoroughly aware of the sound of voices than anything else. Then she saw clearly.

She—that is, her agent—was in some sort of a room, giving instructions to a group of white-clad figures. Before Billie could concentrate upon what was being said the talk ceased; and next moment, amid perfect silence, the agent bent over something which lay on a high table.

Whereupon Billie got a severe jolt. For, unless she was most woefully mistaken, the thing she was now looking at was the unconscious form of a patient; the place was the operating-room of a hospital; and the eyes she was using belonged to a surgeon.

She watched breathlessly. The surgeon's nimble fingers proceeded with the utmost unconcern to open wide the patient's torso. Other pairs of hands, belonging to nurses, aided in this;

and Billie found the intricate process decidedly interesting rather than otherwise. Of course she was spared the odour of blood.

As soon as the ribs were entirely displaced, the lungs were carefully laid aside. Extraordinary delicacy seemed called for here. Billie shortly began to wonder if it were not high time to quit when her agent, assisted as before, calmly exposed the patient's heart to full view.

Billie could see it throbbing; more, she could hear it. She watched in wonder for the next step.

They consisted in forcibly untangling the mass of tubes and arteries all about the organ. Presently everything was clear; and then, without delay, the nurses brought forward a strange-looking device.

It was of silver, shaped like a flattened egg, and a trifle smaller than that labouring, human blood-pump; To it was attached a pair of long, flexible, silver pipes, which led to Billie knew not where. And near one extremity the egg was provided with eight curious nozzles.

At times the flying hands partly interfered with Billie's vision; yet she saw nearly all that amazing process, from beginning to end. To put it briefly, the eight nozzles were boldly introduced, almost at a single operation, into tiny incisions in the eight corresponding tubes of the heart. In they were forced, until they filled the arteries and veins; and once inserted, silver clamps were instantly tightened on the outsides of the tubes. All this was done in two or three seconds; and when all was complete, the heart itself had been entirely isolated and its place absolutely taken by that little silver egg.

The patient gave no sign that anything out of the ordinary had occurred. Not a drop of blood had been spilled except in the process of getting at the organ; but now, with a few deft motions of certain instruments, the heart was sliced away from the surrounding tissues, the tubes were severed, and the whole powerful pump, still beating faintly, was removed from the body altogether.

Next, the surgeon proceeded to stanch the bleeding of the

tubes; that is, of the stubs projecting below those tight silver nozzles. This done, the nimble fingers calmly replaced the lungs and other items, quite as though they were reassembling a piece of machinery. Lastly, the opening was sewed up in a manner which would have delighted any seamstress.

The two long silver pipes were left protruding. Now, for the first time, Billie saw where they led to.

On a stand alongside the operating-table stood an extremely small, flat box, with its lid open. The pipes ended there. And as the surgeon inspected the outfit Billie saw that it comprised, in effect, a pair of diminutive air-pumps. There were two tiny dials, a regulating device, some sort of an automatic electric switch, and what looked like a steel storage tank; all on a watch-like scale.

Looking more closely, Billie made out two pairs of electric wires running from this case to another of the same size. The surgeon lifted its lid, disclosing two electric storage batteries, each with its own circuit.

In short, the arrangement provided duplicate sources, in vest-pocket size, of power for operating a mechanical heart. The electricity worked the air-pumps, which in turn supplied the little silver egg—implanted in the patient—with both pressure and vacuum, while doubtless the artificial organ itself housed a valve system which did the rest. The regulating device kept the blood circulating at the proper rate.

The surgeon seemed satisfied with it all, and, after another critical examination of the patient, glanced about the room, straightened up, took a deep breath, and spoke:

"Quick work. Thanks very much, everybody."

And Billie did not know which to be the more astonished at: the fact that the voice was unmistakably a woman's, or that she, Billie, was able to understand all that was said. She did not fully appreciate until afterward that it was her own brain which did the translating; the surgeon's subconscious mind had merely furnished a thought-image which would have been exactly the same, regardless of language.

"Any special instructions, Surgeon Aldor?" inquired one of the white-clad, face-swathed figures.

"No. The usual handling. Simply keep the batteries charged in rotation."

The surgeon took off a mouth mask and a blood-soaked apron, and then swiftly washed her hands. Next she stepped briskly from the room; and the architect who was using her eyes rejoiced to see the door-knobs of the standard height of thirty-five inches, indicating that this agent of hers was of about her own height.

From the sound of her footsteps, however, Billie concluded that she was somewhat heavier than herself.

Reaching another room, the surgeon proceeded to don hat and coat. Next, she stepped in front of a long mirror; but the action was so quick, and it took Billie so completely by surprise, she was not able to inspect the image closely. To be frank, she looked first at the woman's clothes, finding that her suit was a very trim affair of blue leather, cut in a semi-military fashion. Slashes of dark-red material across the sleeves were repeated about the collar, while the cap, a jaunty affair with a bell crown, matched the suit. The lower ends of the breeches, much like ordinary riding trousers, were tucked into high lace-up boots of red leather.

Before Billie could see any more other than that the surgeon was small-featured in striking contrast to the robustness of her body, she stepped from the room. A moment later an automatic elevator took her to a lower floor, where she was greeted by a person whom Billie assumed to be a head nurse.

"Anything out of the ordinary, surgeon?"

"No," with a brusqueness which was startling by comparison with her cheeriness upstairs. "I understand that Dr. Norbith wishes to go home as soon as possible?"

"Yes."

"He may go as soon as the cast is hard. Make sure his machine is a smooth one."

The nurse simply nodded as the surgeon stepped on, through

a very ordinary pair of sliding doors, and so on out into an anteroom and thence to a porch, where she stood looking into the street for a moment.

It was exceedingly broad, and lined on both sides with imposing structures whose architecture was entirely strange to Billie. She would liked to have examined them all in detail; but she had no control over her agent, who straightway walked down a short flight of steps and thence to a sidewalk.

Here Billie became perfectly willing to neglect the architecture. People were coming and going; people apparently quite as human as herself. Except for a certain gorgeous voluminousness of dress, they seemed for the most part simply men and women of affairs.

For it was comparatively easy to distinguish the sexes. The women's garments, while not making any display of the strictly feminine lines, nevertheless did not attempt to disguise them. Billie saw that loose breeches had completely displaced the skirt with these women; while the men invariably wore either knickerbockers or some other form of short trousers; so that the general effect was very youthful. She saw no men with beards, although several wore their hair long, down to their shoulders, as though to compensate for those women who chose to wear theirs short.

The surgeon seemed to have more leisure than most doctors. She stood for some minutes, greeting perhaps a score of passers-by, all of whom seemed to be proud of the acquaintance. Presently, however, the sidewalk became temporarily clear of pedestrians; and then Billie heard the surgeon mutter something to herself, such as was past all understanding at the time:

"The fools! The poor, ignorant cattle!"

And she turned and stepped to the middle of the street, where Billie had already marked a large number of flying-machines. In fact, the space from curb to curb was practically filled with them, all neatly parked.

Without exception they were ornithopters; that is, machines built on the bird-wing principle, sustaining themselves by a flapping motion rather than by air-pressure due to a propeller. Their size varied from one-seater affairs of very small size to craft large enough to hold a score. Most were gaudily painted.

The surgeon's own machine was a two-seater, small but powerful in design. She stepped up a short ladder into a comfortable cockpit, provided with a folding top, which at that time was laid back out of the way. She proceeded to adjust various levers and hand-wheels, glanced at certain dials, touched a button, and immediately the craft took flight, its wings beating the air with a dull leathery rhythm which drowned out the faint clanking of the machinery.

A moment later the flier was high above the street. To Billie's disappointment, the surgeon did not glance down enough to tell the architect whether the street belonged to a city of any size. Instead, her agent drove carefully through the traffic, which Billie would have called dangerously dense. She remembered that she had seen nothing but aircraft in that street; no automobiles at all.

And then the flier was rushing through the air at a lively rate. Billie caught quick glimpses of innumerable machines, few of which were moving in the same direction as the surgeon's.

A few minutes more elapsed, and then Billie was experiencing a much higher level, with the machine flying at what must have been a tremendous velocity. Shortly it was all but alone in the sky.

After a while the surgeon's eyes made out something far below, which puzzled Billie exceedingly. It seemed to be a ship under full sail; only, so far as she could see the craft was resting upon clouds, not air. It was still a long way ahead.

And then Billie was given a glance aloft, where she saw another craft, a small flapping affair like the surgeon's. It was just rising on a long slant so as to cross above her course. And at that very instant there came a sharp crack, followed by a splintering crash. The surgeon's flier lurched heavily to one side.

Next second the woman was staring at her left wing. It was broken about the middle and thrashing wildly. Another instant, and a part of the thing came loose, flew off, and struck the surgeon on the top of her head. A muffled cry, and then blackness came.

And the next thing Billie saw was the emergency ward of Smith's great skycruiser, with the surgeon, blinking as she recovered, looking up into the smiling face of her big blond rescuer.

5

CAPELLA'S DAUGHTER

The first thing that met the doctor's gaze, when his mind entered that of his distant agent, was a clock. It was a very ordinary sort of an instrument, such as one sees in schools and offices; it had two hands, and a pendulum of the usual size and length.

However, this pendulum was swinging at a very rapid rate; nearly twice as fast, judged the doctor, as that of his own chronometer. And its dial was divided into twenty-five equal parts, instead of twelve, each of these parts being further divided into five equal portions. At the moment, these two hands indicated what would have been called, on the earth, about half past three.

Before the doctor could speculate on this, his unknown agent shifted his gaze to a newspaper on a desk before him. Apparently he was thinking of something entirely different; for he absently turned the pages, one by one, his subconscious mind taking it all in.

And the doctor saw that the paper was called simply The Hourly Journal; that it was of very nearly the size of most sheets; and that it consisted of about ten pages. The front and back pages, only, contained news items; the remainder were packed solid with advertisements. Not one of these were striking enough for the doctor to remember; he said they were exactly like large-size professional "cards," except that they applied to every business, from candy to bridges. As for the news items, each was short, unsensational, with the simplest kind of head-lines. More the doctor had no chance to observe.

Abruptly the agent stowed the paper away, and looked up. Presumably he was seated in some sort of a theatre. Directly ahead was the familiar white rectangle of a photoplay-house screen. And all about him were heads and shoulders, seemingly belonging to young folks, of about high-school age. Even to "low necks" for the girls and white collars for the boys, they were identically like people of the earth.

In fact, if it had not been for that clock the doctor would have concluded that there was some mistake, and have ended the experiment. For some time he learned little; the place was filled with a confused murmur. His agent, however, took no part in the conversation that produced this effect; once or twice he yawned.

Suddenly the buzz came to a stop; and next moment a tall figure stepped upon the platform in front of the screen.

"Class," began this person immediately, "to-day we will summarize what we have learned during the past week about the solar system of which our planet is one element."

And as he spoke the doctor saw that there had been no mistake. For, although the agent's subconscious mind had served to translate what was said into language understandable by the doctor, yet his eyes plainly told him that the professor's lips were saying something else.

There was no doubt about it. For all that the doctor could tell by watching the speaker's mouth, he might have been talking in Eskimo. But his meaning was quite as clear as though he had said it in English.

"We will begin with a picture of the sun herself." As the words were spoken, a motion-picture film was projected on the screen. The doctor instantly noted the natural colours, stereoscopic effect, and marvellous clearness, such as branded this exhibition as not of the earth. But the professor was saying:

"The sun controls, besides this world, no less than thirty others"—and the doctor knew, as well as other people know their A B C's, that the earth's planetary family consists of only eight— "no less than thirty others, of which eight are now without life." The speaker turned toward a student on the far left. "Tell us how many of the thirty are still too hot to support life, Miss Ballens."

The girl did not get to her feet. "Ten," was her answer.

"Which leaves, of course, twelve besides our own planet which now possess life in one form or another. Mr. Ernol, can you give us some idea of conditions on any one of these?"

To the doctor's immense satisfaction, the brain whose loan he was enjoying responded to the question. "On Saloni, the vertebrates have not yet appeared. None but the lowest forms of life have been found."

"Is this planet larger or smaller than ours, Mr. Ernol?"

"Larger. It will be a matter of millions of centuries before such beings as humans are evolved there."

"How do we know these facts?"

As though it were a signal, the entire class, with one accord, uttered a single word: "Runled!"

And the doctor found his agent's eyes turned, together with those of every other student in the room, toward the portrait of a highly intellectual-looking man; it hung in the most conspicuous spot on the wall.

"We must never forget," continued the man on the platform, "that, but for the explorations of this man and his space-boat, some eighty years ago, we should know very little. Can anyone tell me why his explorations have never been repeated?"

Two hands went up. The professor nodded to a girl seated next to the young fellow whom the doctor now knew as "Ernol." This girl spoke very clearly: "Because the expedition was extremely costly, and the commission has never been willing to appropriate enough to duplicate the work."

"The commission's judgment is, of course, sound," commented the professor calmly. Then he signalled for a change in the picture, which had been showing, in rapid succession, glimpses of world after world. The new picture was more leisurely.

"The planet Alma. Can anyone explain why it is of special interest to us?"

For a moment there was no comment, and the doctor found himself studying a "panorama" of some exceedingly striking people. There was quite a crowd; and the doctor was amazed to note how much like the Venusians they were. Without exception they were delicately built, with thin, shrivelled legs; all were seated, none standing, in cigar-shaped aircraft of a type entirely new to the doctor.

"The people of Alma," spoke up a boy out of sight of Ernol, "are especially interesting to us because they are, so far as is known, the most highly developed beings in existence."

"In what way are they like us?"

"They are vertebrates, mammals, primates, just as we are."

"And how do they differ from us?"

"They are 'cooperative democrats'; that is, they do not compete with each other for a living, but work together in all things, in complete equality. In this way they have become so wonderfully advanced that—"

The professor interrupted. "We will not go into that." The scene shifted from people to things: a large, complicated-looking column of some sort was being shown. "What does this tell us?"

"It tells us," spoke up some one, "that Alma is entirely surrounded and covered by a great roof, which stands several miles above the surface."[1]

"What is the purpose of this roof?"

"To keep in the air and moisture, which all other planets are steadily losing. Alma is a much older planet than ours, which is why her people are so far advanced."

Next came "close-ups" of some inhabitants. At once the doctor saw that these were not Venusians; they had facial expressions as sour and cynical as the typical Venusian's had been pleasant and wise.

"You will note," commented the professor very quietly, "that these people are far from happy."

The class seemed to take it for granted; but the doctor's trained ears instantly caught a false note in the speaker's voice. Was the man sure of his statement?

---

1. Compare with Venus. It would seem that, whenever a planet reached a certain age, its people will always take steps to preserve its atmosphere; that is, provided their civilization is high enough.

At the same time the doctor became aware of a certain dullness in the vision he was borrowing. Also, the speaking became much less distinct. It occurred to him that the boy might be drowsy; and an unmistakable nodding shortly made this certain.

"As we see from these photographs," droned the voice on the platform, "happiness does not exist on Alma. And if not there, where else can we expect to find it? Certainly not among the less developed planets.

"So we must conclude that ours is the only world where the people are truly happy. We must thank the commission for the peculiar distinction which we enjoy. Ours is the only civilization which guarantees happiness to all; these pictures prove it for us."

At that instant young Ernol lifted his head with a jerk. "How do we know," he demanded, "that these photographs were not very cunningly selected to give us a wrong idea? Perhaps they lie, professor!"

Instantly consternation reigned. The professor fairly froze in his tracks, while every eye in the room was turned in amazement upon the lad.

"What!" exclaimed the speaker sternly. "Where did you get such an extraordinary notion, Mr. Ernol?"

The boy had sat up straight, looking about uncertainly. He got unsteadily to his feet. "Why—" he stammered helplessly. "Why, I haven't any idea—What have I been saying, sir?"

The professor checked a hasty answer. He said quietly: "Do you mean to say you are unaware that you spoke just now?"

"Yes, sir. I mean—" The boy was badly puzzled. "To be frank, sir, I was almost asleep. I studied about Alma years ago. I know I said something, but as to what it was—"

"That will do." The professor made a sign, and Ernol sat down, tremendously embarrassed. "The class will understand that people, when talking in their sleep, usually say things which are the exact opposite of what they know to be true."

The man wet his lips, as though with satisfaction at the neatness of his wording. He added in a generous tone: "I will not reprimand Mr. Ernol, because his previous work indicates, as he says, that Alma is an old topic to him. I only wish that he stood as well in certain other studies!"

A ripple of laughter ran over the class, and again the puzzled youth was the target for the combined stares of the students. He slipped down deep into his seat.

"That will do for to-day," said the teacher, glancing at the clock. "Tomorrow we will begin the study of the other suns of the universe—what we commonly call stars.

"However, before you go"—his voice took on a certain ominousness—"let me remind you that it is the custom not to question the sources of our information. We take them for granted. In fact, it is more than a custom; the regulations require that any student who is not satisfied with the sincerity of our public school system shall be suspended for the first objection, and for the second shall forfeit all educational rights whatever.

"You will readily see for yourselves, then, that it will not be wise for any of you to repeat what Mr. Ernol unconsciously let slip. And of course none of you will be so unkind as to remind him of what he said."

The students rose thoughtfully to their feet, and Ernol passed out with the rest. He had no idea what it was all about, nor the slightest suspicion that his eyes and ears had been used.

But the doctor had learned something of enormous value. He had learned that, when his agent was in a semiconscious state, his—the doctor's—conscious mind could influence the agent.

It was not Ernol, but the doctor, who had made the slip!

6

THE WORLD'S BOSSES

Van Emmon was afterward unable to recall any experience between his entering the subliminal state and becoming teleconscious. That is, his only recollection was of a definite scene, experienced through the eyes and ears of his agent.

The place was a large high-ceilinged room, its architecture suggesting some public building. In the centre, and directly in front of Van Emmon's agent, stood a large, rectangular table, about which sat a number of men. Van Emmon counted nine of them.

The whole atmosphere was solemn and important. Van Emmon was reminded of old photographs of cabinet meetings in Washington, of strategy boards during the great war. He listened intently for something to be said.

Near the foot of the table—Van Emmon's agent sat at the head—a tall man with an imposing, square-cut beard rose to his feet. He gazed at each of the other eight in turn, significantly; and when he spoke the geologist was so impressed with the deadly seriousness of the scene that he forgot to be amazed at his ability to understand what was said, forgot to marvel that these men were, undeniably, human beings of exceptional character.

"Gentlemen," said the man who had risen, "I do not need to remind you of the seriousness of this occasion. I only wish to congratulate you, and myself, on the fact that we now have a chairman to whom we can look with confidence. I say this without meaning any reflection upon his predecessor."

He sat down, and immediately a white-haired man with a wide, complacent type of face arose and declared: "No reflection is felt, sir. On the contrary, I am exceedingly glad that Mr. Powart is to take my place. I only wish that the commission felt free to discard its rule of choosing by lots; I should like to present Mr. Powart with the chair for as long a period as he would care to fill it."

He took his seat amid a general murmur of approval, while nine pair of eyes were turned in unison upon the pair Van Emmon was sharing. His agent, then, was chairman of some sort of a council, known as "the commission."

Powart got to his feet. Even in this simple act his motions were swift and sure; they harmonized perfectly with the way he talked.

"Thanks, both you. To be frank, I am glad, for the sake of the association, that the youngest commissioner has come to its head at this time. If there were a younger than myself, I would say the same."

He paused and glanced at some memoranda in his hand. Van Emmon was struck, first, by the smooth skin and perfect formation of the hand and wrist; and, second, by the peculiar writing on the papers. He had no idea what it meant, although his agent certainly did. (Afterward the four concluded that, in the case of words written in code or otherwise requiring an effort of the agent's conscious mind, the people on the earth, being in touch only with the subconscious, were never informed. But they never had any trouble in understanding anything that was said aloud.)

"If there are any special matters which should be handled in general session, now is the time to bring them up," said Powart, and remained standing.

An undersized man with a remarkably large head of hair spoke up from the right-hand side of the table: "I want to suggest that it is high time we sent another expedition to Alma."

"I agree," from the man who had been Powart's predecessor. Apparently these ten men had nearly dispensed with parliamentary rules. "What are the prospects, Powart?"

"First rate. Runled's old space-boat has been renovated recently, and I understand that enough of the required materials have been mined to insure one round trip."

"It is very fortunate that we shall be able to visit Alma again, even though we use up our entire supply in the attempt. It seems that we shall soon need, and need badly, certain chemical secrets which they alone possess."

"When can the boat start?"

"Within a week. I shall keep in touch with the crew by wireless, and advise you of their progress from time to time. Alma is a sort of a hobby with me; I wouldn't mind taking the trip myself."

There was a long pause. Powart waited, as though in expectation of further remarks, then gave another glance at his memoranda and began:

"Of course, we are mainly concerned with the demonstration in Calastia. As to its cause, I may mention that Eklan Norbith was in a hospital at the time, having a substitution. Had he been on the spot, the uprising would have been checked before any one heard of it.

"But it now seems that Calastia, during the last few hours, has become a seething hotbed of rebellion. Of course, we have isolated the district, and a search for arms is now in progress.

"The head of the recalcitrants is a man named Ernol. He takes his confinement as a matter of course, and no amount of pressure will induce him to talk. Neither can we get anything from his companions, nor from his son.

"It is up to us to decide what measures to adopt."

A large, pugnacious-looking man on the left put in the first comment. "Would it not be a saving of time to provoke violence, in one way or another, and thus form a pretext for disposing of the entire lot?"

"I admire your bluntness," remarked the former chairman across the table, "although I can't say as much for your philosophy. It is our duty to keep everybody contented; we cannot do any public weeding-out until the others are satisfied that the malcontents are really weeds."

"That is clear enough," spoke the shock-headed man. "What are the conditions, Powart?"

"Nearly normal. The percentage of overhead is only slightly higher than average. Until Ernol moved into the locality everyone seemed contented with the regular arrangements."

"What is his contention?"

"The usual democratic nonsense. He claims that the commission is autocratic, down to its last deputy. Denies that we have the right to apportion one-half the earnings to the workers and the other half to the owners. States that our system is wasteful, unjust, and demoralizing."

"And what does he propose?"

"Democratic control of industry. You know—that old line of talk."

"Does he deny that the commission has abolished poverty and war?"

"No; but he points out that our present standard of living has not changed for generations, and argues that degeneration must result. Of course, he is right in his fact but wrong in his conclusion."

"Doesn't he admit the necessity of some sort of an international governing body?"

"Yes; but he claims that the commission should be elected by direct vote of the people!"

A general smile of derision greeted this. The only face that remained serious was that of the shock-headed man. He said:

"There must be a slip somewhere, Powart. Isn't there a heavy fine and imprisonment for teaching such stuff? How did Ernol ever get hold of the notion?"

"Probably through tradition. We can't keep people from talking to their own children; perhaps Ernol's great-grandparents told him of the days when everyone was allowed to vote."

The shock-headed man got another idea. "What has the man to say against our system of voting in proportion to property interests?"

"Says it's all right in principle; but he claims that the earth belongs to one and all, equally, and therefore each should have an equal voice in its disposition and government."

This time there was no smiling. The pugnacious-looking man spoke for the rest when he said:

"We cannot allow such ideas to gain headway, Powart! Have you a plan?"

"We must keep a close watch upon Calastia, and allow no one to leave its borders. As for Ernol, I have concluded that the best thing will be—turn him loose!"

They looked at him in consternation. He explained:

"I have been reading up the experience of the past few centuries in such cases; and if there is one thing that stands out clearer than any other it is this: the surest way to make the public sympathize with a radical is to persecute him. But disregard him and ridicule him, and his philosophy doesn't last long.

"Instead of trying to make an example of this chap, by severely punishing him, we shall let him go. It may be that he will object to this; he may have discovered the same truths I have been reading, and would like nothing better than to become a 'martyr.' But we shall force him out, if need be."

"But suppose he continues his talking?"

"In that case we must simply watch our chance, and take him secretly; if need be, arrest a thousand others at the same time. The main thing is secrecy; so that the people cannot know, no matter what they may suspect, what has become of him. His final disposition will be a question of mere expediency."

The former chairman approved heartily. "You've got the right idea, Powart. Is there anything further on tap?"

Powart put his notes away. "Every national report is the same as usual; all quiet, and people apparently well satisfied.

"If there is no further business, we may consider ourselves adjourned."

The men got to their feet with the usual accompanying noises. The tall man with the square-cut beard immediately came and offered Powart his hand. Van Emmon noticed that they shook hands almost exactly as Americans would.

"Things seem to be coming your way, my boy," said the bearded man, his keen eyes softening slightly. "I saw the paper this morning. Congratulations! She is one girl in millions. Has she fixed the date?"

"No. Mona was rather taken by surprise—to be frank with you, uncle."

As Powart spoke, he was eyeing the door and nodding permission for an attendant to enter. The man stepped obsequiously forward and presented a message, for all the world like any ordinary aerogram. Powart opened it while his uncle signed.

The chairman gave a low whistle of surprise. "Mona had an accident with her flier, a little while ago, and was rescued by

"—he looked closer at the aerogram—"a chap named Fort. She is now recuperating on board the Cobulus."

The tall man took the message and read it himself, while Powart glanced about the room. Van Emmon caught a glimpse of a clock, and he noted the pendulum especially. But before he could learn anything further, Dr. Kinney's hand jerked as before, and the gong rang. The four awakened.

They had been "visiting" over an hour.

7

A WORLD BECALMED

"I think we have learned enough to form some general conclusions," said the doctor, after the four had told what each had heard and seen. "Van Emmon's friend, Powart, seems to be anything but a democrat. He probably represents the most aristocratic element on the planet; while this man Fort, who rescued the girl, is also probably a member of the leisure class.

"On the other hand, we have Smith's agent, whose name we do not know; he seems to be one of the working class, which Powart despises. The two are at opposite ends of the social scale. Young Ernol, whose father is in trouble, appears to be a rising young revolutionist.

"But Mona—to use the name Powart gave his fiancée—Billie's surgeon—the girl whose life Fort saved—she is not so easy to classify. On the earth we would call her occupation a middle-class one; but that remark she made about people being cattle gives me the impression that she is an aristocrat at heart. I call her a mystery, for the time being.

"As for the planet itself—of course, the people simply refer to it as the earth, or some term which translates that way to us. We need a name for it. What shall we call her—this daughter of Capella's?"

"Capellette," from Billie promptly.

"Fine!" The other two looked their approval. "Now, we are ready to analyze things. What shall we say of her people in general?"

"Speaking for my surgeon," observed Billie, "doesn't she argue a rather high degree of development?"

The others were plainly willing for the doctor to take the lead. He rubbed his knuckles harder than ever as he considered Billie's suggestion.

"A higher degree of development? H-m! Not easy to say. Safer to assume that the development is higher in spots, not in general. Perhaps we'll do well to consider other things first.

"Take those two clocks, for instance. The one that I saw had a pendulum of ordinary length, which vibrated twice as fast as that"—indicating an astronomical clock at his side. "What about the time-piece you saw, Van?"

"Twenty-five-hour dial, and a pendulum of the usual length, same as yours. But—it vibrated no faster than any I ever saw before."

"You're sure?" At the emphatic nod the doctor frowned. "We are forced to conclude that Capellette is not as round as our earth. No other way to account for such a difference in gravitation as the two clocks indicate. Roughly, I should say that the planet's diameter, at the place where I saw the clock, is fifty per cent greater than at the point where Van's agent is located; maybe ten thousand miles in its greatest diameter, Capellette.

"Having greater gravitation would explain why that disabled aircraft which Smith saw fell so very slowly; the planet has much more air than the earth, which means far greater density near the surface. It also explains those big sailing cruisers; nothing else can.

"At any rate, we can guess why we have seen no surface travel. The people of Capellette never tried to work out such a thing as an automobile; why should they, with the birds to imitate, and extra dense air all about them?

"I think we have found the key." The doctor cogitated for a second or two.

"However, let's consider that schoolroom a bit. It was in no way different from what you will find on the earth right now. Why?"

Smith had a notion. "There is such a thing as perfection. Like some electrical apparatus; you simply can't improve them."

"Sounds reasonable," from Van Emmon.

"Yes. And that is undoubtedly how the Capellettes look at the matter.

"Why haven't they got talking-pictures? Because they've perfected the silent variety, of course. Why don't they reform their ways of living, instead of replacing a worn-out heart with a new one? They've perfected surgery, that's why! And why haven't they tried the screw-propeller? They've perfected the bird-wing principle!"

"But that doesn't explain," objected Billie, "why they've been content with an autocratic system of government."

Van Emmon considered this a dig at Powart. "Why, of course their government is autocratic, dear! How else can it be protective?"

"You seem to have a lot of admiration for your Mr. Powart," laying her hand on his.

"I have. He and the others seem to be highly capable fellows, who have undertaken to maintain happiness, and have made good."

"But without the direct consent of the people."

"What of that?" warmly. "Most folks don't care to burden their heads with law-making, anyhow. They'd rather leave it up to specialists."

"Who are only too willing, my dear, to handle the matter—at their own price!"

The doctor put in hastily: "From what you tell me, Van, this commission determines the living conditions for the majority, although it has no popular authority whatever. Moreover, conditions are no better than they were a hundred years ago. There's been no progress. Powart admits that.

"Now, placing that fact alongside the rest, I reach this conclusion: that the people of Capallette, no matter what may have been their experience in the past, do not now care for revolutionary ideas. They want standardization, not change.

"It all roots back in that extra dense air of theirs. See why?"

Apparently the three did not. The doctor explained: "Life is much easier for them than for us. It is no great struggle to gain a livelihood where transportation is so easy and simple. In consequence of this their advancement was much more rapid than ours here on the earth, up to a certain point; and they've reached that point already.

"Coming back to that commission again: instead of trying out a democratic form of government, in which every citizen would be equally responsible regardless of property—they've standardized the protective, paternalistic principle."

"Which is precisely the correct method!" insisted the geologist. "Radical changes of any kind are always dangerous. The only safe method is to improve what we already have."

"Suppose," remarked Billie—"suppose government becomes so thoroughly standardized that it can't be improved further?"

"Then it becomes permanent."

"If it isn't overthrown."

The doctor smilingly interposed.

"Let me finish and get this out of my system. By their own confession, the commission's chief function is to keep the majority in ignorance, which is said to be the same thing as bliss. This man Ernol and his pitiful rebellion only serve to prove the rule.

"In a word, the Capellans have carried the principle of improvement, as opposed to reform, to its logical conclusion. They can go no further."

"And why not?" challenged Van Emmon. "Because the fittest have survived, on Capellette as elsewhere. These commissioners are the fittest."

The doctor nodded gravely. "True enough, Van. But the point I want to make is, the commissioners have put an end to the processes of evolution. They won't allow progress. They stopped all that a century ago.

"Friend, Capellette is a world that has given up. It has quit!"

The Upper Crust

The next time Billie went into the teleconscious state, forty-eight hours later, she found that she had "arrived" in the midst of a conversation. It told her worlds.

"I answered the telephone," someone was saying, "and Mr. Powart clearly said that he would be here within the hour."[1]

"I suppose it is just as well," answered the surgeon whom Billie now knew as Mona. "Yes, I dare say it is quite as well."

"Is there any reason why he shouldn't, dear?" inquired the other party, a middle-aged woman, magnificently dressed, of decidedly distinguished appearance.

"No, mother," replied the girl; "not so far as he is concerned. But—Mr. Fort also is coming to-day."

The older woman saw nothing alarming about this. "I am glad to hear it. He impressed me as being a very nice boy, although rather impulsive."

"You don't understand. It's going to be very embarrassing for me. Mr. Fort warned me last night—laughingly, of course, but I think he meant it—that he intended to propose to-day."

Swift anxiety came to the mother's face. For a while she kept silence. And while Mona's conscious mind was occupied with thoughts which Billie could not fathom, her subconscious mind was faithfully taking in all that her roving eyes beheld.

The two Capellans were seated upon the terrace of a large, handsome house, whose architecture Billie tentatively classified as semi-Moorish. Mona next glanced into the grounds, telling Billie that the house was set upon a knoll, high up on the ridge of a tremendous range of mountains. Similar houses dotted what landscape was visible through a mass of foliage. It was just the sort of residence colony that Billie herself would have chosen.

Then the eyes came back to the mother, who was saying: "Perhaps, my dear, you would rather that I told Mr. Fort of your

---

1. The word hour is used advisedly. Of course, the Capellan hour may have an entirely different length from ours.

engagement." She watched the daughter as though expecting her to refuse the offer.

Which is just what the heart-specialist did, with a proud toss of the head. "Thank you; but I cannot have him think that I lack the nerve to tell him myself."

She excused herself and went into the house, passing through rooms so rapidly that Billie learned little, save that the place fairly swarmed with men in livery. Once in Mona's room, however, Billie discovered that metallic furniture was the rule; that the windows were without screens,[2] and that the bed was set down very close to the floor.

Otherwise, the room was much like any on the earth.

Mona's clothes interested Billie immensely. Without exception the garments were skirtless, and a large proportion of the suits were in one piece. Headgear was limited to caps, of which Mona owned an immense variety; while she wore nothing but high lace-up boots or pumps. Billie was sure that these were all of leather.

With the aid of no less than four maids, all of whom were very pretty girls, Mona changed to a garment of some lustrous brown material, like silk velvet but with a much longer nap, together with stockings of the golf pattern, and black pumps. Next she proceeded to inspect herself carefully in a mirror.

Billie saw that Smith's estimate of "not over thirty" was accurate enough. The girl was still young as to face, although her body was remarkably robust. And Billie found that her delicacy of feature did not suffer from the close-up.

Instead, her refinement was made only the more striking. Probably it was the high arching of her eyebrows that had made her face patrician; that, together with the sensitiveness of her nostrils. For there was nothing at all cold about her eyes; they were a very dark brown, large and full. And her lips were anything but haughty; they were a deep red and piquantly upturned at the corners. The whole carriage of her head, however, marked her as an aristocrat, but a lovable one.

---

2. The Capellans seem to have utterly stamped out all forms of insect life except those directly beneficial to man.

As she turned from the glass the sound of a laugh came from the front of the house. Billie instantly recognized Fort's voice. Mona gave her hair a final touch and went straight to the terrace.

"How do you do?" said the surgeon coolly, as she took Fort's eagerly outstretched hand. And again Billie was more interested in the man's gray-leather flying suit, so well becoming his fine muscular development, than in the conventional reply he made. Next moment Mona's mother was saying:

"I have been trying to thank Mr. Fort for what he did yesterday. It was a remarkably brave thing!"

"Indeed it was," declared Mona, with feeling. "And yet, try as I might last night, I was unable to make him see that it was anything out of the ordinary, mother."

"Why, of course," protested the athlete carelessly. "There was nothing brave about it. One is not brave unless one is afraid; and I wasn't afraid. I can take no credit for the thing."

"Do you mean," questioned Mona, "that you are never afraid?"

"Not when I am in the air."

There was silence for a minute, and again Billie used Mona's eyes to good advantage. Fort was certainly a good-looking chap, although slightly untidy in small items of his costume. He was the kind which looks best when somewhat dishevelled, anyhow. As to face—a large, handsomely curved mouth, a slightly Roman nose, eyes as big as Mona's and as blue as hers were brown. Decidedly, the man was worth looking at, again and again. Most daredevils are sharp-featured; Fort was kindly. There was something positively reassuring about his kind of audacity.

Presently the mother mentioned Ernol, the radical; seemingly these people had been privately informed of what Powart was keeping from the workers. Fort commented:

"I was really frightened when I heard of it. Why, if that fellow's philosophy is listened to, we all may have to work for a living!" His laughter rang above the rest; then he thought of Mona. "Oh, I say, I quite forgot, I assure you."

"Don't mention it," returned the surgeon humorously. "I don't mind telling you that this service of mine is largely camouflage. I belong to the Delusion Brigade."

Fort was greatly surprised. "You, a volunteer?"

"Quite so. There must always be some one of our class to whom people can look, whenever they suspect that we are not democratic. Besides, I have always fancied surgery." She told briefly of her work.

"Why, you are a famous person!" declared the athlete.

"You make me ashamed; I do nothing at all but amuse myself."

"Which is quite as well, Mr. Fort," the mother assured him. "I tried my best to keep Mona out of this; a social conquest is what I had planned for her. But she had set her mind on surgery; so—" And she left the rest to Fort's imagination.

A moment later Billie heard a flying-machine approaching. Shortly it came near enough for her to see that it was greatly like a yacht, painted white all over, and possessing exceptionally tall masts. The canvas was already unfurled and the vessel descending under the control of some unusually powerful wings.

"Mr. Powart's official boat," Mona explained to Fort.

The craft landed softly on the edge of the lawn, some distance away. The three on the terrace did not stir from their places as Powart, accompanied by eight men in uniform, stepped swiftly down a short ladder and strode rapidly to the house. The eight guards, each of whom carried a brown leather box, like a motion-picture camera, took up unobtrusive positions near at hand. These cases, however, were not used for taking photographs; Billie thought them more like some kind of condensed rapid-fire guns.

Before Powart got within ear-shot, Mona leaned toward Fort. "This is my fiancé," she said with an evident effort; and when she straightened up her hands were trembling.

Fort took it astonishingly well. He concealed any hint of his feelings as the chairman was introduced. Powart gave him a single penetrating glance, then advanced in his sure, self-confident way, and took both the girl's hands in his own. She remained in her seat.

187

"I am very glad to see you looking so well. Do you feel fully recovered, Mona?"

"Yes, thank you," coolly. "Or perhaps I should say, thanks to Mr. Fort, here."

Powart turned his keen gray eyes upon the athlete. "If there is any way I can show you how much I appreciate this—"

Fort waved his hand jauntily. "Wait till I do something that costs me a real effort!"

Something in his voice caught the chairman's ear. He scrutinized the athlete more closely; and Billie found herself comparing the two.

They were both big fellows; otherwise there was no resemblance. The one was as dark as the other was blond; moreover, he was somewhat heavier than Fort, and of the sort which must be dressed immaculately at all times. His good looks were due to the clean-cut lines of his face; for his eyes were stern and his mouth very strong.

If the one was impulsive, the other was sure. Fort loved to take a chance; the other, would not act until he was absolutely certain. Billie decided that he was the steadier, the more reliable of the two; also, the least likable, for that very reason. Infallibility is a fearsome thing.

The mother arose with some remark about going into the gardens, and Fort offered his arm. Powart took their going purely as a matter of course, and continued to stand—he seldom sat down—directly in front of Mona.

"I hope," said he in his direct fashion, "that you can see your way clear to consider wearing this," and he produced a small, blue velvet case from an inner pocket. And next moment Billie was peeking over Mona's shoulder, so to speak, to see a ring made of some milk-white metal, set with a single oval stone of a blood-red hue. The surgeon gave a tiny gasp at the sight of it.

"Bribery and corruption!" she cried, and started to slip the ring on to the middle finger of her left hand. Before it was done, however, she paused.

"I almost forgot." She gave Powart a sidelong glance. "Last night I thought it over, and—Well, you know how women are about changing their minds."

"Surely you haven't completely altered your opinion of me?" incredulously, rather than anxiously.

"No; I just want more time to think it over, that's all. It is not that I think less of you than before, but somehow, since having such a close call—I haven't quite as much confidence in my ability to meet your expectations." This as though she had worded it beforehand.

Powart showed little concern. "Of course I am sorry; but perhaps it is just as well. Beyond a doubt you will soon come to see it as clearly as you did the other day." He paused as the girl slowly extended the ring to him. "Why not wear it anyhow, Mona?"

"I'd rather not—not until I am sure. It's a dreadful temptation, though!"

And Powart had no choice other than to reflect her smile with one of his own, while he quietly slipped the little case back into his pocket.

Almost with the same motion he took out a watch. "You must excuse me. Business of state, as usual."

"Certainly," as she rose. She gave a quick glance around, then shook her head playfully as Powart took a single eager step toward her. "Next time," she said; and he bit his lip, gripped her hand tightly, and strode away. In a minute he and his guards were back in the yacht, and in three minutes out of sight.

By that time Fort and Mona's mother had returned. There was a quick exchange of glances between the two women, and then the mother excused herself and went in the house. Fort suddenly became awkwardly self-conscious.

"Well, I must be going." He paused; a gleam of mischief flashed into his eyes—a kind of final come-back. "Next time I rescue you, young lady, I shall let you get hurt ever so much worse, so that I can have an excuse to call more than I have so far!"

His face sobered swiftly.

"I nearly forgot. May I congratulate you upon your—engagement? Mr. Powart is a very fine man."

"Thank you; so he is. Really, I have lately come to wonder if I am good enough for him." Then, significantly: "The date has been postponed indefinitely. It is not impossible that I may give him up."

Fort stared incredulously for a second, then saw that she meant it. The blood rushed to his face, leaving him white and shaky with excitement. He made a sudden move toward the girl, checking himself just as suddenly.

"Well!" His usually easy speech nearly failed him. But he laughed as boldly as ever. "I am convinced that you are far from being a well woman, Miss Mona! I shall have to call—often!"

And with a short but exceedingly intense gaze of infinite meaning, he wheeled, clapped his cap to his head, dashed to his machine and was gone.

9

THE STAGNANT WORLD

Smith entered the mind of his Capellan agent at a moment when he was clearly off duty. In fact, the engineer of the Cobulus was at the time enjoying an uncommonly good photoplay.

Smith had arrived too late to see the beginning of the picture; but he found it to be a more or less conventional society drama. And for a while he was mainly interested in the remarkably clear photography, the natural colouring and stereoscopic effect that the doctor had already noted through young Ernol. Smith nearly overlooked the really fine music, all coming from a talking machine of some kind.

And then the picture came to an end, and a farce-comedy began. It was an extraordinarily ingenious thing, with little or no plot; afterward Smith could not describe it with any accuracy. However, Mrs. Kinney, down-stairs, plainly heard him laughing as though his sides would give way.

The picture over, Smith's man got up and left the place; and once outside he glanced at his watch and took up a position on the curb, much as Smith had often done when a younger man. The Capellan seemed to know a good many of the people who came out of the playhouse; and meanwhile Smith took note of something of extreme importance.

The playhouse did not have any advertising whatever in sight, except for a single bulletin-board, like the bill of fare of a cafeteria. Moreover—and this is the significant thing—there was no box-office, neither was any one at the door to take tickets.

The place was wide open to the world. It was located on a very busy street in what appeared to be a good-sized city; but, to all appearances, any one might enter who chose to.

"Free amusements," thought Smith, "to keep the boobs happy."

Shortly his agent stepped down the street, which seemed to be greatly like one in any city on the earth, except that there was remarkably little noise. Perhaps it was due to the total lack of street-cars and surface machinery in general. Certainly the space between the sidewalks was used for little else than the parking of flying-machines. The buildings housed a variety of stores, all built on a large scale. There were no small shops at all.

Smith's agent quickly reached his own flier, a small two-seater ornithopter finished in dull gray—Smith's favourite colour, incidentally—and in a minute or two he was well under way. Smith had a chance to watch, at close range, the distorted S-motion of the machine's wings. But the flight lasted only a few minutes, and presently the craft was again at rest.

This time it was parked under a tremendously long shed, which Smith afterward saw was really a balcony, one of a tier of ten. Opposite the spot was a large building, like a depot; and over its roof Smith saw the huge bulk of an airship.

It was, of course, the Cobulus; and it was when Smith's agent passed through a checking-in room that his name was heard for the first time. "All right, Reblong," was the way it came, from the official who punched his time-card. And Reblong, with Smith making eager use of his eyes, went directly through a hatch in the side of the great ship, and thence down a corridor to his engine-room.

Smith got little opportunity to study the machinery. Reblong gave the place a single sweeping glance, then strode to a short, black-bearded chap who stood near the instrument board.

"Everything as usual, my friend?" He had a pleasant voice, as Smith learned for the first time.

"Yes—as usual!" The man's voice was bitter. "That's just what's wrong! There's never any improvement; it's always—as usual! Say, Reblong; no offense, but I think we are fools to put up with what we are given!"

Smith's man complacently seated himself in front of the instruments. "Personally, I think we are mighty lucky, instead of foolish."

"Lucky!" The other man snorted. "I wish Ernol could hear you say that! He'd have a fit!"

Reblong was not at all disturbed. "By the way, what's become of the chap? I haven't seen him around for weeks?"

"Don't know, exactly," with some uneasiness. "He went back to Calastia, and that's the last I heard of him."

"Calastia? I saw an item in the paper last night, to the effect that Calastia was under quarantine. All news cut off."

The man instantly smelled a mouse. "Quarantine! Why should that cause the news to be cut off? There's something more than quarantine the matter, Reblong!" He began to pace the room excitedly. "I say it again, we're fools to believe everything the commission tells us. I think they've been hoodwinking us about long enough!"

Reblong suppressed a yawn. "I don't care if they do, old man. I'm willing to leave it up to them to run the government."

"And that's exactly what's the matter!" cried the other. "You and every other chap except those Ernol has taught, thinks that the commission is God-given and can do no wrong!"

"Yes?" politely. "Maybe so; only, you can't blame us for thinking pretty highly of a government that has done this." Reblong checked the items off on his fingers, meanwhile eying his companion steadily: "It has done away with the liquor traffic; it has fully protected women in industry; it has put an end to child labour; it has abolished poverty; it has abolished war; and"—with considerable emphasis for so quiet a man—"it has provided you and me and everybody else with a mighty fine education, free of charge!"

Reblong's manner, by its very emphasis, had the effect of making the other man suddenly quite cool. "Correct; I admit them all. And at the same time I want to show you that the commission has accomplished all this, not primarily for our benefit, but in the interests of the owners.

"They gave us prohibition because drinking was bad for business; no other reason, Reblong! And that's why the women are protected, too; a protected, contented woman brings in better dividends to the owners than one who is worked to death.

"Neither did it pay to allow child labour; it resulted in misery and reduced production, in the long run, and that meant reduced dividends. Poverty didn't pay, either; poor people do not make efficient workmen. War was abolished, Reblong, not for any humanitarian motives, but because peace brought in fatter profits and less waste.

"And as for our compulsory education"—he snapped his fingers contemptuously—"just what does it amount to? Simply this: it didn't pay the owners to allow illiteracy! An educated workman is a better dividend-producer than an ignorant one. That's all there is to it, Reblong! Don't fool yourself into thinking that the commission has done all this for your benefit! Not much!"

"Maybe you're right," conceded Reblong. "As for myself, I don't care a rap what the commission's reasons were. I'm satisfied!"

The other man looked disgusted. "Satisfied! Just because you're guaranteed your dollar an hour, and your pension at sixty! Satisfied, when half the company's profits go to the owners, not one of whom ever did a bit of work in his life! A bunch of people who do nothing but blow in the money we earn, and spend more in a day than we do in a month!"

"They're welcome," commented Reblong with much indifference. "If I got all that you have told me is coming to me, I'd probably ruin myself with high living anyhow."

"You don't mean to say that you've swallowed that old piffle!" said the black-bearded chap incredulously.

"I don't see any piffle about it. As I look at the matter, the owners are doing us a genuine favour. Not only do they take the burden of our surplus earnings off our shoulders, but they run our government for us without charge."

"Well, I'll be utterly damned!" The other fellow looked as though the words were not half strong enough. "I never thought a full-grown man could continue to believe the stuff we were taught when we were kids! Don't you ever think for yourself, Reblong? Why, look here!"

He came closer and spoke with painstaking clearness, as though he were addressing a child.

"The commission, instead of assuring us that increased wages would be our ruin, could just as well be educating us to spend wisely! Just as well, Reblong! And as for child labour—man, children ought to be kept out of industry until they're twenty, instead of sixteen! Every last one of us ought to be given a college education, instead of merely the children of the rich! And all this could be done, too. There's no earthly reason why we should permit that bunch of parasites in Hafen to graft off us any longer! Put 'em to work, like you and me, and make life easier for us all!"

"But," objected Reblong, a little upset, "there's only a few of the owners. They couldn't help much."

"But their servants could. Do you know that there's ten servants, on an average, to every family of the rich? Servants who do nothing but make life still easier for people who already hog it all!"

"Well, suppose they did all go to work; who would run our government for us, my friend?"

"Who! Why—if we can do the work, I guess we can certainly do the governing, Reblong."

Reblong turned away, plainly bewildered. "It doesn't look right to me, old man. I'd rather let things stand as they are, so far as I'm concerned."

Somewhere a warning instrument was thrumming loudly. The man with the democratic ideas automatically turned to his locker, and proceeded to change his outer clothing. Reblong meanwhile took off his suit and slipped into some full-length overalls. As he buttoned them up around the neck he stepped in front of a glass.

Smith was nearly floored. The man was almost his exact double; an ordinary, everyday sort of a chap, with a very commonplace face. Perhaps, like Smith's, his face concealed a remarkable technical knowledge; but nobody would have given him a second glance. Was he, thought Smith, a typical Capellan workman?

The other man was ready to go. He hesitated, studying the floor; then said, regretfully:

"The worst part of it is, Reblong, everybody I talk to is as bad as you are. They all admit that things are not what they should be—but nobody cares!"

He went to the door, and Reblong heard him say, under his breath, as he turned the knob:

"Great Heavens! What's come over the world anyhow? Has it gone stagnant?"

10
A Ripple in the Pool

It seemed as though he were right. The whole great pool of humanity which comprised Capellette was still, quiescent, stagnant. Was there nothing to arouse it, no ripple in the pool?

The doctor had this question uppermost in his mind when he located young Ernol. He found him getting ready to accompany his father, who seemed about to take advantage of the freedom Powart had conditionally given him. There was no doubt about it; the radical was going straight back to his revolutionary teaching.

He was saying, "Of course, my boy, I can't compel you to stay at home." The doctor delighted in the vigorous, frank manner and powerful voice of the man; they belonged perfectly with his black hair and bristling beard, his flashing eyes and aggressive nose. "I'd rather you stayed out of this; at the same time, I'd be a proud man if you didn't!"

The student calmly finished his dressing. "What time did you tell the men to come?" was all he said; and the father chuckled, then sighed.

The two took flight in a small two-seater. It was night, and the doctor took note of the planet's system of signal lights. Within five minutes, however, the flight ended with a landing in some sort of a deep depression; the doctor called it a ravine.

Climbing from the machine, the two apostles stepped a few paces in total darkness; then the elder man produced a small electric torch, which he wig-wagged above his head. There was a series of answering flashes at a distance; and next moment a door, let into the side of the ravine, opened right in front of the pair.

They stepped in and closed the door after them, then turned their light down a long corridor. Reaching the end of this the doctor noted a loophole in the wall, from which projected something suspiciously, like the muzzle of a machine gun. He had no difficulty in imagining the consequences should someone open that hidden door without first giving the signal.

Much as one might enter a lodge-room, the two radicals showed their faces at a port-hole in a door, after which they passed guards with masklike helmets. In a few seconds they found themselves in a brilliantly lighted hall, very large and commodious except for the heavy pillars which supported its low ceiling. It was half filled with men.

The elder Ernol had no use for formality. After brief greetings to some kind of a committee, he took his place on a platform; while his son unconsciously gratified the doctor by looking over the crowd. Presumably they were all workers; and in one way they were all alike; the habitual contentment in their faces had been momentarily replaced by excitement. However, they were quiet and well behaved enough.

"Comrades," began the radical without delay, "I appreciate your coming here at all, under the circumstances. The commission plainly warned me that any further teaching would be disastrous. I am not sure, but I imagine they would arrest both myself and those found with me. If there is anyone who feels that he would rather not take the risk, now is the time for him to go."

There was a moment's pause; then, in the back of the hall, two men who had been sitting together got up and hurriedly went out. Ernol waited, but there was no further exodus.

"I will lose no time then, but proceed to give you the proofs regarding the commission." He produced a small parcel of photographs. "These pictures are the most dangerous things I have ever carried on my person. I took them in the dead of night, by flashlight, in the library of the University of Calastia.

"They are"—he paused portentously—"reproductions of pages from the secret census!"

To most of the men this meant something highly significant. They craned their necks in their excitement.

"I am going to pass them around, negatives and all. You see where I have checked off the most important items. They prove to any one with reason that the commission has been lying to us; that the workers are being taxed more heavily than the owners; that the owners are being favoured in every way. I don't care whether you agree with my ideas or not; these photographs"—his voice shook the hall—"prove that the commission is not even giving you what you thought you were getting!"

He took a single step down from the platform, his hand outstretched, about to pass the parcel to the man in the nearest seat. At that instant all the lights were extinguished.

There was a moment's stunned silence; then the place broke into an uproar. Yells of fright and anger, the crashing of chairs, screams of pain; all these young Ernol heard without himself giving voice. He was sprinting down one side of the hall.

Suddenly there came a flash of light straight ahead. Ernol had reached the outer corridor. And the doctor heard a great commotion going on outside the door in the ravine; a smashing and thudding, which filled the corridor with noise.

Next second the door gave way, and simultaneously young Ernol leaped into the niche behind the thing which the doctor thought a machine gun. Another second, and he had the device in operation.

From its muzzle shot a thin stream of fire, which extended the whole length of the corridor. It lighted up everything with a bluish-white glare, revealing a mob of men at the door. They fell back, yelling with pain, some of them dropping in their tracks. And all the while the apparatus was dealing, not a shower of bullets, but a streak of liquid fire, which hissed and screamed like the blast from an oxygen blow-pipe.

But it was all over in a second or two. A noise from behind, and young Ernol started up suddenly, only to find himself in the grip of a veritable giant of a man. His struggles were simply useless. In a moment he was being carried bodily back into the hall, which the doctor saw was now lighted as before.

On one side, lined up amid a mass of wrecked chairs, stood most of the workers at bay. On the other were four men with small boxlike devices, such as Billie had already seen in the hands of Powart's guards, and which were kept trained threateningly upon the crowd. On the platform stood Ernol, now quite helpless in the grasp of two stalwart fellows.

The mob from the door poured in. Immediately they made captors of all the workers, who had precious little to say. Apparently they had been warned. The doctor also concluded that the capture was a piece of treachery, in which bribery had been employed.

Two minutes later young Ernol was placed in a large passenger flier, which the doctor labelled "Black Maria." Presumably the elder radical was taken in another; at any rate after another flight in the darkness, father and son shortly found themselves together again.

They were now in the drawing-room of some private residence, concluded the doctor. This puzzled him somewhat until, after a brief wait under the eyes of a half-dozen guards, the two radicals were taken into another room.

Here, lying on a couch, was a man whom the doctor soon identified. He was none other than Mona's patient, Eklan Norbith, the commission's deputy in Calastia. He was a burly, dark-featured fellow; and even though rigid in his plaster cast, he looked competent and formidable.

"Ernol," said he in a heavy, domineering voice, "there is no need to state the case to a man of your intelligence. You gave your word to stop your teachings; you have been caught in the act. Frankly, I rather thought you would do it; that is why I am here to-night. I want—to deal with you personally."

He paused for breath, and then went on, still ignoring the student, "Ernol, you know what I want. I want those photographs; and what is more, I am going to have them. You must have passed them to someone who escaped in the confusion; they have not been located on anyone who has been captured, nor were they hid in the hall. Now I will give you exactly ten seconds[1] to tell me what you did with them."

He eyed a clock on the wall.

The radical, whose hands were tied behind him, nevertheless managed to strike a defiant pose. "I don't intend to tell you, Norbith. It is true that I handed them to one of my comrades; but I shall not tell you which one."

"Your time is up," said the man with the silver heart evenly. "Will you tell?"

Ernol contented himself with a contemptuous shake of the head. The man of the couch, for the first time conceding young Ernol's presence, now ordered him brought forward.

"I know," he told the father, "that it would be useless to work with *you*. You are just fool enough to imagine that suffering means martyrdom.

"But I told you that I must have those photographs. I meant it. I shall have that information if I have to torture you until I get it!"

"Go right ahead!" taunted the revolutionist; but his face was white.

---

1. For the sake of clearness, the Capellan second, whose actual length is of course unknown, is used here as though it were uniform with earth standards.

Norbith turned to the boy's guards. "Strap him into this chair!"

It was done in half a minute. The doctor had no way of seeing how the boy took it, except that he studiously avoided his father's eyes, and that he made no sound.

"Now move him under that clock!"

One of the guards gave a low exclamation, instantly checked at a cold stare from Norbith. And meanwhile the boy was being placed just below, and a little to one side of the big clock.

"Remove the lower half of the clock-case!"

It was done in a few seconds. The instrument's pendulum now vibrated freely in the air, its weight swinging almost to the boy's head where he sat.

"Move him until I drop my hand," said Norbith.

A slight push, and instantly the doctor became aware that the heavy pendulum of the clock, on reaching the outward extremity of its swing, was now gently tapping at the boy's left temple. *Tap-tap-tap-tap* it went, with the peculiar quickness due to the planet's powerful gravity.

"Keep him there until I tell you to move him."

The tapping continued. To the doctor, of course, the thing was entirely devoid of pain. It made much the same noise the dentist makes with his mallet, only it went on and on, until perhaps two minutes had passed.

"Stop!"

Instantly the boy was moved away. The student said nothing; neither did the father. Yet the doctor noticed something which meant volumes to his trained senses.

The boy's gaze was no longer clear. Instead, dancing lights appeared wherever he looked; tiny flashes of violet and orange, which shimmered before his pupils even though he closed his lids.

"Will you ask your father to tell?" inquired Norbith.

"No—damn you!"

It was the first thing the boy had said. And it came through set teeth, in a voice which the doctor scarcely knew.

"Move him back; a little further this time."

The tapping began again. This time the boy's head got more

of the force of the swing; the tapping was more like a blow. *Thud-thud-thud* came the sound now; and in a few seconds the boy could see nothing for the shivering flames. He gave a faint groan.

"Ready to talk now?"

"Damn you—no!" in a voice that shook with pain.

"Move him closer!"

The thud became a pound. The doctor looked for the skull to give way at any moment; he tried his best to control the subconscious, but the boy's agony was too great. The dancing lights had become a continuous flare; the lad moaned steadily.

And then quite without warning, the boy broke down and gave out a terrible shriek. Norbith ordered the guards to move him away from the clock.

"Ready now?" he inquired calmly.

The boy's answer was a snarl. "No!"

"Once more!"

The thud-thudding began again, and now it had a sharp sound which the doctor instantly recognized. In a moment the boy was shaking the air with cries of such awful agony that the doctor—

"Stop!" cried the father convulsively, his face streaming with tears. "God—the boy doesn't—know! Don't torture him—like that!"

The man with the metal heart said:

"Will you tell now?"

"Don't do it father!" the boy whispered through palsied lips. But no Capellan heard him.

The father was saying to Norbith, "I gave the whole outfit to—"

And then that crashing and smashing came to an end. The boy had fainted.

11

THE DOUBLE WORLD

The four felt that they understood the situation quite well, indeed. It was really simple, this far-off world with its standardized life, this petrified civilization in which everything was guaranteed except the one real essential—progress.

But what was Fort going to do about it? Billie was not the only one who was interested; Van Emmon was equally curious, and Smith privately believed that the geologist was slightly jealous of the distant athlete. Certainly he was as eager as anyone to continue the investigation, and stoutly defended Powart against any criticism.

"He's the right man in the right place!" he insisted. "Lord, I wish I was in his boots!"

"Well, I'm rather thankful you're not, dear," commented Billie with a look which quickly brought an answering light to his eyes. Yet, behind her remark there was a certain wistfulness which the doctor did not overlook.

Yes, the four felt that they were very well acquainted with Capellette.

But the most amazing part of the whole proposition was yet to be discovered. It was not until after nearly two weeks of daily investigation, in fact, that the whole astonishing truth of the matter was uncovered.

It came through Billie. Fort was now calling regularly at Mona's house, evidently trying his best to understand the girl and make himself understood; for he said not a word about his suit. And one day he suggested that they make a much longer flight than any they had so far taken together.

"I haven't been down into the contact for a long while. Have you?"

And the two set out, Billie wondering mightily what "the contact" might be. They flew for several hours in a direction which would have been called "westerly" on the earth; and during the time they were above land, Billie saw no sign of factories, farms, or other forms of industry. In fact, hill and valley alike were laid out with handsome residences, beautifully kept grounds, vast parks and extensive greens, suggesting golf. That was all.

Then she noticed something that made her marvel. The sun,

which had stood directly overhead when they left the house, within less than three hours began to descend with increasing rapidity; so that in half the length of an ordinary afternoon it had approached to within an hour of setting. Its motion was so rapid that it could almost be seen.

Soon Billie concluded that the two fliers were bound for the bottom of some unusually wide and exceptionally deep canon. She tried to remember what she had read of the earth's greatest chasms; was it possible for the sun to disappear in mid-afternoon in such? And yet the flight went on and on, until Billie began to wonder if a chasm could be a hundred miles deep.

Soon she could dimly discern the dark mass of the opposite side. The fliers were steadily approaching this, and all the time going deeper and deeper. Once Mona turned her eyes searching to the right and left; whereupon Billie was still further mystified to see that, although the cleft was fifty or sixty miles in length, yet its extreme ends seemed entirely open to the world. Nothing but a deep "V" of blue sky was to be seen in either direction.

The sun disappeared altogether. Always the two walls grew closer and closer together, until at last Billie could see, despite the semidarkness, a heavy growth of vegetation on the opposite wall. Beneath her, as well, the surface was densely wooded.

Still they descended! It was unbelievable; surely the chasm did not extend right into the heart of the globe. They had been flying for hours!

At last came a time when the far wall of the cleft was so near that Billie could have shot a deer upon it. She estimated the distance at two hundred yards; and then, and not until then, did she realize that Mona, in order to inspect this bank, was now *looking* up. The wall which had seemed right ahead, all along, was now actually overhead!

Were they entering some sort of a cave? If so, it had dimensions that staggered the imagination. What was more, if it were a cave, how could the mind of man account for vegetation on its roof?

Within a few minutes Fort called from his machine; whereupon Mona located a landing-place, a small clearing dimly visible in the distance. The opposite wall of the chasm—or the roof of the cave, whichever it was—now approached to within five yards of the tops of the two machines. Mona and the athlete stepped out, and looked around.

Billie's senses swam. This clearing, as has been said, was only a few yards away from the tops of the bushes on the roof. Moreover, all this vegetation, instead of growing at right angles from the surface in the usual way, was all lying flat against the soil, and all pointing in one direction—back, the way they had come!

The sky was not overhead any longer; it was a mere strip of very dark blue, lying far off on the horizon. That is, to the right; on the left, the cave-like cleft extended still further, its limits shrouded in darkness.

"Queer, isn't it?" laughed Fort. "Shall we walk around?"

Whereupon the two young people set out on a narrow, but much worn trail. Keeping the sky always at their right, they passed through the thicket, Mona's eyes telling Billie that the queer horizontal vegetation grew always toward the light.

It was much like the growth at the bottom of any gulch; only the two were walking in the normal way, upright, at right angles to the surface, quite as though it were level ground!

Overhead the thicket grew in the same fashion; Billie thought the foliage much like ferns. Here and there, however, was a small flowering shrub; and it was to one of these that a tiny, orange-coloured bird came flying.

And Billie wondered why Mona did not gasp in astonishment. For the bird, when it alighted upon the shrub, was not over eight feet above Mona's eyes; and unless there was something decidedly wrong with the girl's vision, the bird had alighted upside down!

There it clung, chirping flatly, moving its head from side to side and watching the two with bright, unfrightened eyes. But Mona was not much interested; she and Fort moved on. And shortly Billie was gazing at a fresh wonder.

Directly opposite them, on what Billie was now calling the

roof, instead of the wall, there appeared a deep furrow in the ferns. She saw that it was a path, much like the one Mona was treading; it meandered in and out of sight from time to time. What was the meaning of it? Billie began to wonder if "the contact" was the name of some mechanical illusion, like a distorted mirror.

The two had been walking for nearly an hour when, right ahead of them, the thicket opened up, and another clearing presented itself. That is, Billie called it another clearing, until she looked more closely and made out two flying-machines in it. They were the ones the pair had come in!

Now Billie was positive that they had not turned around in their walk; they had kept the sky on their right all the while. In fact, the sky was still on that side. They were approaching the clearing from the side opposite the one they had gone out from!

Yet, neither the athlete nor the surgeon seemed to see anything peculiar in the fact. Instead, they looked at one another as much as to say, "Well, time to go, isn't it?"

Then Fort stared up at the mysterious roof. There was another clearing there, a little to one side; which accounted for Billie's overlooking it at first. Fort led the way over opposite.

"Shall we try it?" he dared Mona.

"You first," she replied, indifferently.

Whereupon the athlete, without another word, pulled his cap down tight, made sure his pockets were buttoned, cleared the shrubbery away from his feet and—leaped! Leaped straight into the air, and as he went up, he flipped his body as only an acrobat can, so that he turned a mid air somersault.

But he did not come back to where he jumped from. Instead, his jump took him five yards, which separated the ground from the roof; and when he landed *his feet were resting on the roof, and his head was pointing downward, toward Mona.*

"It's easy," he remarked, craning his neck so that he could look at the girl. "Come on; I'll catch you!"

And then Billie's senses whirled as the surgeon duplicated the feat. Next second Mona was standing beside Fort, five yards above the spot she had just left; and in that second everything had become precisely reversed; the two were now looking up! Looking up, to behold their machines, apparently upside down, just over their heads!

As though this were not enough, Mona picked a leaf from a shrub and threw it some seven or eight feet up. It remained motionless in mid air!

It was too much for Billie. She felt that she could not contemplate the thing any longer with safety to her sanity. She exerted her will, and broke the connection with Mona; so that a few minutes later her three friends on the earth were listening to her account.

The doctor waited until she was all through; then, "While you were having that experience I was in touch with young Ernol again. The boy has recovered and is still in jail, but they let him have his books now. And I've been helping him study geography."

"Well?" eagerly.

"Very simple. Capellete is a double world!"

"Double!"

"Yes! There are two globes, instead of one. They're twins, and Siamese twins at that!" He drew a figure on his knee, thus:

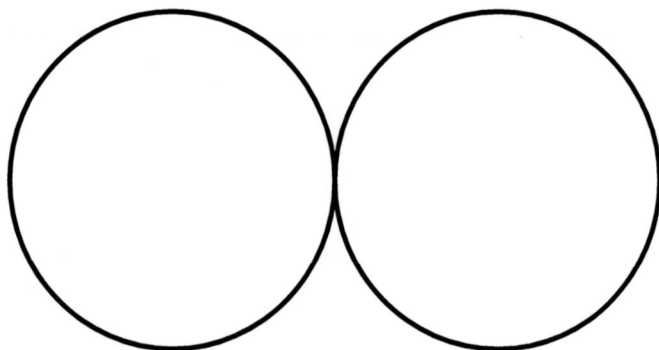

"Just imagine the earth and Venus of the same size, and so near to one another that their combined gravity has brought them together! That's Capellette! And the contact is the place where they touch!"

They considered this in wondering silence for a while. Then the doctor continued:

"It's just as we had deduced; each of the planets is larger than the earth. I saw the figures in that geography.

"But astronomically they are one. They revolve around Capella together; the rotate about a common centre daily, just as the earth rotates on its axis. This common centre is, of course, in the contact."

"Are both globes inhabited?" Billie was greatly interested.

"Yes. All parts of both planets are developed to the same extent, and evenly settled. They are just one great nation, with a common language. This, of course, is traceable to the great density of the air, enabling the people to fly wherever they wanted to go. There never has been such a thing as an 'Old World' and a 'New World' with them.

"The really remarkable fact, however, Billie has already hinted at. The country near Mona's home shows no sign of industry; there's nothing but parks and magnificent estates. And the geography explains it all. One of the planets is devoted entirely to industry and the homes of those who are engaged therein; the workers inhabit that globe exclusively. There are about ten billion of them.

"The other globe is exclusively a residence tract, set aside for the homes of the rich; what they call the owners. There is no industry of any kind. No workers live there, excepting the army of servants and park attendants which the owners need for their own comfort. The population is about a hundred million, of which only one in ten is a capitalist. The rest are serving people."

Van Emmon seemed to feel that it was his place to comment. "In other words, Newport on a grand scale!"

"Is that the way Powart seems to regard it?" from Billie.

"Apparently. There were a lot of things in his talk which I couldn't understand until now; but it's clear enough—the doctor's right."

"Then," pursed the girl deliberately, "the Capellans have divided the world between them, so that the working classes in-habit one-half, and the capitalists the other?"

The doctor explained that the dividing was all done by the owners. "Every bit of the land on the residence planet is pri-vately owned, with the exception of certain small amusement tracts. Theoretically, the planet is open to one and all; practically no worker is welcome there for more than a few hours, and then only in one of those parks. There is no hotel."

Van Emmon was straining his memory. "Let's see—I heard Powart name the place. He called it—called it—Hafen!"

"Yes. And the other—the world which is the home of the working people, but which they do not own; the world whose factories and farms provide a standard living for the workers and lives of luxury for the owners—this world is known as Holl. But if I read young Ernol's mind aright, these words mean nothing more or less than—Heaven and hell!"

12

Cause and Effect

From that time on the four did not hold any more formal discussions of what they learned. This was due to a most ex-traordinary discovery.

They found that they could keep in touch with each other while they were "visiting"! It was a tremendous help; it enabled them to communicate and compare notes as they went along. The doctor declared that the Venusians themselves had not been able to do more.

Thus, when Powart called on Mona a few days after she had declined his ring, Billie was able to tell the other three all that took place, as fast as it happened. As usual, Powart's stay was a brief one.

"I hope you have recovered your former self-confidence," said he, consciously repressing the masterful note in his voice. "Not that I am unwilling to wait, Mona."

"You are very patient," she assured him. "I am glad to say that I am no longer troubled with any doubts of myself. Something else worries me now."

He frowned at the implication. "What is it?" coldly.

"Frankly, it is your record." She knew she was jarring him terribly, but she went on with evident relish, "You are the most important man in the world. Odd, isn't it, that I should find fault with that? But it is a serious objection. You are still a very young man; you have become one of the commission; for a year, you are its head. The point is, what's before you?" She paused to let this take effect. "You've already accomplished all that any man can possible accomplish in the political field. You haven't any future!"

Powart grasped the thought with his usual instant decision. "I understand. You are right, too. I had not thought of it before." A slight pause. "You fear that you may come to tire of me; is that it?"

She nodded emphatically. "If you had asked me a few years ago, before you had reached the top—it would have been different."

He remained standing, frowning hard. Presently he glanced at his watch, and said he would have to be going.

"I will see what can be done about it," he stated. "I have a plan which should get results."

"Are you going to take up a hobby?" eagerly.

"Not a new one; but a hobby I have always had." And with this enigmatic reply he was off.

Van Emmon kept track of his further movements, and reported everything to the other three. Powart had not been in flight long before he sent off a wireless despatch, to which he received a most extraordinary reply. It was from the expedition which he had sent to Alma a week before:

People of Alma give us warm welcome. Invite us to stay. We propose to do so. The planet infinitely preferable to either Hafen or Holl. Accept our resignations or not, as you please, and be damned to you!

Powart made no comment upon this, which he read in privacy after carefully decoding it. Van Emmon had no idea what he was thinking, of course, but wondered mightily how the chairman was going to deal with the situation. He could scarcely read that aerogram to the commission. For some time he paced the cabin of his yacht, and at the end he behaved like a man whose mind had been pretty strongly made up.

The commission met, it seems, in a central part of Hafen. Powart reached the place some hours after leaving Mona. He arrived to find the other nine members waiting for him; and without the least delay he took his place at the head of the table.

"We will postpone the usual routine until the next session if you like," said he. There was no objection; whereupon Powart produced a message from his pocket.

"You will recall the expedition to Alma. I have just received their first report since reaching the planet." And then, to the vast amazement of the people on the earth, he read—not what Van Emmon had seen him receive, but this, in his strong, matter-of-fact voice:

"People of Alma facing starvation, due to overpopulation and land-exhaustion. Have disabled our boat and will not permit us to return, although allowing us to use wireless, which they do not understand.

"They are constructing a fleet of huge space-boats, all heavily armed, intending to cross over to Hafen and Holl, and conquer the Capellans."

Powart glanced keenly around the table. "This is all that has been received. Evidently our men were prevented from sending any more. I expect nothing further. It remains for us to decide, at once, what we should do."

The silence of the next few minutes was largely due to consternation. To most of the commissioners the problem was staggering. They looked up in eager relief as the shock-headed man broke the silence.

"It seems to me that war is not inevitable. Apparently the thing that Alma needs is food. We still have a good deal of underdeveloped land on Holl; why not make a bargain with them?"

"You mean present them with enough land to raise the food they need?" from the former chairman.

"Yes, in exchange for whatever manufactured goods they can supply, and which we need. I see no reason for an invasion."

Powart coughed slightly. "I do. We must not think that Alma is the same sort of a world as ours. It is a much older planet, and somewhat smaller. Yet it is more than eight times as densely populated as Holl. What land we could spare would be only a fraction of what they need. They intend not merely to invade and conquer us, but to destroy us just as we destroyed the Ammians!"[1]

The nine sat for an instant in stunned silence at this amazing fabrication. Then the big man with the aggressive face leaped to his feet, brought his fist down upon the table with a thump, and shouted:

"Well, then, if it's war, it's war!"

"Aye!" cried Powart's uncle; and in a flash the whole council was on its feet. "War be it!" they shouted.

In another moment the excitement had abated as suddenly as it had arisen. They got back into their seats, looking slightly abashed. Powart still remained standing.

"Then the only question is, shall we make preparations at once, or wait until we have thought the matter over further?" His tone was one of scientific indifference; and the discussion of the next few minutes was all in favour of his scheme. It ended in a motion to resolve the commission into a ways and means committee for the purpose of common defence.

"Second the motion!" cried the aggressive man; and the response was unanimous. Powart directed that a memorandum be made of the vote; then pressed one of a row of pushbuttons at his hand. An attendant immediately entered.

"Bring File 6, Folio 1,164, Sheet 10," ordered Powart with his usual decisive exactness. The attendant disappeared, and in less than a minute returned with a large sheet of parchment. Powart immediately located the passage he desired.

---

1. Doubtless referring to some aboriginal tribe or race, such as the Indians of America.

"The action you have just taken," he stated, "amounts to a declaration that a state of war exists. Under such circumstances, the law explicitly states the function of the chair. Read!" and he handed the parchment to the nearest commissioner. Within ten minutes the law had been read by every man present. Powart instantly continued with his statement:

"This commission is hereby automatically converted into a general staff, with myself, the chairman, as supreme commander. Your functions, while this state of war endures, will consist partly in proposing what steps I shall take, partly, in advising me regarding my decisions, and partly in carrying out whatever orders I may give."

He pressed another button, and when the attendant responded, Powart made a signal with his hand. The attendant turned on his heel, saluting, faced the door he had left open behind him, and ordered:

"In single file—march!"

A company of guards trooped straight into the hall, and formed a hollow square about the table. The nine men stared at Powart in astonishment and perplexity. He did not keep them waiting.

"Pursuant to the authority vested in me by these acts, I hereby declare that a state of war exists between us and the people of Alma. I also declare the International Commission dissolved as such; the same is now my general staff, and will remain where it now is—indefinitely!"

The nine looked at each other blankly. Were they under arrest?

"And further, I hereby declare that martial law now exists throughout all the domain formerly under the rule of the commission! Until peace is declared, my word"—he paused ominously— "is the sole and only law!"

13

THE REBEL

Meanwhile Billie was still "haunting" Mona, and shortly was able to tell the other three that Fort had called, taking the surgeon out in a machine large enough to hold them both.

They proceeded to a near-by park, where a game of aerial punt-ball was already in progress.[1]

Billie took great interest in the darting play of the little fly-like machines, the action of the mechanical catapults, and the ease with which the twelve-inch ball was usually caught in the baskets on the machines' prows. She reported the score from time to time in a manner which would have made a telegrapher jealous.

Returning from the game, Mona and Fort became pretty confidential, the natural result of a common enthusiasm; for their side won. But Fort was content for a while to merely watch Mona, who was driving.

Finally the conversation made an opening for him to say, "I asked your mother, Mona, what she thought of me as a prospective son-in-law."

The girl was in no way rattled. "I suppose she told you that it wouldn't make any difference what she might say; I'd do as I pleased anyhow. Didn't she?"

Fort nodded, slightly taken back. Then his boldness returned. "Well, I had to bring up the subject somehow. And now that I've done it—do you love me well enough to marry me, Mona?"

She pretended to be very busy with the driving; so that Billie never knew whether Fort looked anxious or not. Presently Mona said:

"I think—I rather think I like you too well to marry you. What I mean is, I'm afraid it would spoil you, my dear boy. You're too well satisfied with yourself. I don't want to marry a man who is content to fly around half the time and admire me the other half; although," she added, "I like to be admired as well as anyone."

Fort looked as though he would, with an ounce more provocation, take her in his arms and say something to get quick results. But he didn't. "I see," pretty soberly, for him. "You want me to get in and do something important. Like Powart?" suddenly.

---

1. The game is described more or less completely in various sporting publications.

213

But Mona would not answer him directly. "It's only fair to say that I've given him an ultimatum, too." She hinted at what she had told the chairman. "I said nothing about—you."

Fort took a deep breath. Mona gave him a glance or two, and Billie could see a startling change come over him. It was amazing; Fort, for the first time in his life had made a serious resolve!

"This makes everything very different!" he declared; and even his voice was altered. There was a determined, purposeful ring about it which was altogether unlike his usual reckless tones.

"Thanks for not telling Mr. Powart," Fort went on in the same quiet way. "Clearly, I should tell him myself. And I shall. After that it is up to me!"

Next instant he had thrown off his seriousness, and for the remainder of the flight was his former jovial self. He seemed a trifle ashamed, however, of his old lightheartedness; so much so that Mona warned him not to tamper too much with his disposition. "I like it too well, boy."

He went straight home after a hurried leave-taking, and Mona did not see him again until after the declaration of war. The next the four heard of him was through Van Emmon; Fort called upon the self-made commander-in-chief as quickly as he could.

"I have the honour to inform you," said Fort, coming straight to the point, "that Miss Mona has seen fit to encourage my suit. In short, sir," with the strange new note of resolution in his voice, "I am your rival for her hand! I thought it only right that you should know."

Powart took this as he took everything, standing. And Van Emmon could see no sign that the announcement had disturbed his poise.

"You are considerate," he stated with the faintest trace of sarcasm. "Let me call your attention to the fact that, because of the position which recent events have forced upon me, it is quite within my power to dispose of your opposition"—significantly.

"Quite so! I shall appreciate your consideration also." Then the athlete permitted himself a slight smile. "On second thoughts, however, you can't afford to be other than considerate. If anything happens to me now, Miss Mona will naturally think of you; for she knows I have come here!"

A single exclamation escaped Powart, and from the light in Fort's eyes, Van Emmon knew that the chief was sorely provoked. However, he spoke with his usual coolness and certainty.

"Under the circumstances, you will be exempt, Mr. Fort, from the conscription which is now under way. I shall do nothing that might hinder your activities in any way? I take it"—evenly—"that you hope to accomplish something—big?"

Fort bowed. "It is my intention to set a mark even further than your own, sir!"

For the first time Powart laughed. It was a really hearty laugh, as though Fort's preposterous boast was so utterly ridiculous that sarcasm was out of place.

"Mr. Fort"—when his mirth had subsided—"I only wish your judgment was as sound as your optimism! Tell me—do you intend to make yourself ruler of a bigger world than this?"

Fort dropped his seriousness for an instant. "To tell the truth, Powart, I haven't any plan at all—yet. Thanks for the exemption. In return, I assure you that whatever I do will be as truly in the interests of the people as what you have done."

Powart eyed him keenly. For a moment Van Emmon thought he would try to learn if Fort had any suspicions. But he said nothing further than a curt, "The audience is ended."

A few minutes later Billie, through Mona, knew that Fort was reporting progress. He did it by telephone.

"Thought you'd like to know," he finished. "Hope I didn't rouse you out of bed."

It was night in Mona's part of the world, and Billie had come upon the girl just as she was preparing for bed.

"Thank you," she said, through a tremendous yawn. "I was just about to retire. Good luck"—another yawn—"and good—"

Her voice changed. "Mr. Fort!" sharply. "Powart's declaration of war on Alma is a frame-up! Never mind how I happen to know; it is true; they are not planning to invade us at all! He trumped up this affair in order to make himself dictator!"

"What!" The athlete was astounded. "Are you sure of this, Mona?"

The girl's manner had changed again. "I beg your pardon?" she inquired, vastly confused. "Did I say something that—why, I am not aware, Mr. Fort, that I had said anything more than 'good night'!"

"You *aren't*!" His voice was strained and excited. "Mona—you just now said something of the most extraordinary—surely—incredulously—you recall saying something, don't you?"

She was still bewildered. "I do not!" Then gathering her poise again, "What did I say?"

"You said—" He stopped and waited a long while before going on. Then he stated with a soberness that was almost stern:

"Mona, you told me something which could have come only through a supernatural agency. I am sure of it, from your manner. You were temporarily possessed." He paused again.

She sensed his earnestness, and spoke just as seriously. "It is not impossible. I have heard of such things before. I was sleepy, and—the point is, what did I say?" she demanded.

"I do not intend to tell—you. What I learned gives me a great advantage over Powart; that's all I can say. More would be dishonourable. Will you take my word for that, Mona?"

"Certainly," with swift decision, and a grace that Billie envied. Whereupon she went to bed, but not to sleep until after many an hour of wide-eyed wondering.

Fort next showed himself to Smith, through Reblong. He had secured a pass to the engine-room of the Cobulus; and shortly his breezy manner completely broke down the engineer's usual reserve.

"Always glad to show the machinery," said Reblong, denying that the visitor was making any trouble. Fort's technical knowledge had delighted him. "Come again any time you like."

Which Fort did, the very next day. And this time he brought a package of sweetmeats, during the eating of which the two men became pretty friendly.

"You're different from most of the folks of your—station," Reblong finally made bold to remark. "Any harm in my saying so?"

"On the contrary," laughed the athlete. "I rather pride myself on my democracy.

"The fact is, I want you to tell me a few things about your fellow-workers. I understand you're one of the officers of your guild?"

"Secretary," replied Reblong, a little dubiously. Was Fort a secret investigator?

"Then you can tell me. Is there any dissatisfaction? Are the men entirely content with their treatment?"

Reblong hesitated about replying, and Fort assured him, "This is a purely personal matter with me, old man. I am really anxious to know whether the working world is as well satisfied, as happy as I am."

And thus Fort discovered, just as another man had already discovered, that the average Capellan workman was entirely satisfied with what he knew to be unjust treatment. Even when Fort told Reblong what he had learned about Powart's trickery—leaving out all details about Mona, of course—the engineer would not listen to any hint of revolution.

"I don't like to question your word, Mr. Fort"—Reblong was very uncomfortable—"but I have such confidence in the commission that—well, you understand."

And Fort said, just as the other fellow had said after talking with Reblong—Reblong, the representative Capellan workman; Reblong, who voiced the opinions of his billions of fellow-workmen when he refused to consider a rebellion—Fort said:

"Well, I'll be utterly damned!"

14

UNDER MARTIAL LAW

Van Emmon was pretty cross because Billie, through Mona, had told Fort about Powart's game. More than once he protested hotly, "You shouldn't have done that! It's all their affair, not ours!"

And Billie usually returned, just as warmly, "I don't care! I think Powart is a scoundrel!" And it was in the midst of one of these tiffs that the doctor interrupted, exactly as though the telepathy was telephony:

"Quiet, you two. Fort has called at the prison, and is being introduced to young Ernol. He—"

"I've been talking with your father," Fort was saying to the son. The guard had left them alone in the cell. "But he isn't interested in my ideas. He seems to think he's done all that needs to be done in getting himself imprisoned."

The boy nodded.

"He considers himself a martyr, Mr. Fort; and I guess he's satisfied like everybody else." He spoke bitterly.

All Fort's own youthful enthusiasm returned with a rush. "You're just the chap I'm looking for! If you're genuinely ambitious to do the people a great service, now's your chance!"

And he went on to tell the boy about Powart's frame-up. He gave every detail of Mona's strange disclosure, and the boy believed him absolutely.

"I might have known there was some trick about it!" cried the lad. "Alma isn't that kind of a planet! By Heaven, Powart deserves to be assassinated!"

"Nothing doing," replied the athlete promptly, his eyes sparkling with the old light. "The first thing is to get you out of here; you, and the other hundred and fifty who were put in at the same time."

Whereupon he proceeded to outline a scheme such as would look utterly incredible in the mere planning. Perhaps it is best to relate the thing as it happened, instead.

Two nights after Fort's call on Ernol, Fort again presented himself to Reblong. This time it was at the engineer's apartments.

"I was hoping to find you about to go on duty. I've been wondering how your engines control the steering." He was eying Reblong steadily. "Some time when it is convenient I wish you would show me all over the ship, and explain everything." He turned as though to leave.

"Oh, that's all right, Mr. Fort," Reblong hurried to assure him. "I'd just as soon accommodate you right now as at any time. The ship is always open to me."

Reblong had said exactly what Fort had hoped and planned that he would say. Fifteen minutes later the two men were inside the big air-cruiser, alone except for a few cleaners, who were finishing the usual work of preparing the ship for its next cruise. But Reblong could not know that Fort had carefully made sure of this fact beforehand.

The engineer took the athlete from one end of the cruiser to the other, showing him how the pilot was able to control its motions with the utmost delicacy, thanks to automatic mechanism in the engine-room, electrically connected with the bridge.

"Suppose I was the pilot now," commented Fort, standing on the bridge and looking up at the stars. "All I need to do is to set these dials"—indicating the pilot's instruments—"to 'ascend,' and the engine-room would do the rest automatically. Is that it?"

Reblong said this was practically true, and led the way back to the engine-room. The place was full of a gurgling sound, now, due to the fuel being run into the tanks. Reblong glanced at the indicating tube. "We've already got enough," he estimated, "to take the ship a thousand miles."

And next instant Fort had leaped upon him. Reblong staggered back in his surprise, stumbled against a chair, and sat down heavily, helpless as a child in the athlete's iron grip.

"Sorry, old man," remarked Fort, meanwhile pushing him, chair and all, toward the instrument-table. "But it's simply got to be done." Like a flash he let go the engineer and snatched a strap from the table—where he had of course previously placed it—and again threw himself upon his man before Reblong recovered from his surprise. In a second he was strapped tight in his chair; and not until then did he think to use his feet. Another strap put an end to his kicking.

"Surprised you, didn't I?" The athlete was enjoying himself hugely. "Now—I must remind you that I'm taking a big chance in doing this. If you make a noise, I shall treat you as any desperate man would treat you!" There was a look in his eyes which clinched the matter.

Immediately he disappeared in the direction of the nearest cleaners. Reblong heard sounds of struggling from time to time; and evidently he implicitly believed that Fort would take vengeance upon him if he called for help; for he kept perfectly quiet. After perhaps twenty minutes the athlete returned, breathing heavily, but happy.

"The last one almost spilled my beans," said he—to use the expression Smith employed. "He happened to see me shutting another one into a closet, and jumped me from behind. I had to lay him out." Reblong must have looked alarmed. "Oh, no harm done. They'll all live to tell about it for the next twenty years."

Next he made certain adjustments in the engine-room mechanism. Then he went to the telephone, and located the man in charge of the depot. "Hello—Mr. Fort speaking; Reblong isn't able to come to the phone." He winked at the man in the chair. "There's something wrong with the fuel indicator. Shut off the supply for a while, will you?"

The gurgling soon stopped. Reblong watched in continued silence as Fort disappeared again, this time taking the elevator to the bridge. He was back again in a couple of minutes.

"Now, old man," addressing the engineer, "you can guess what I'm up to. I'm going to navigate this cruiser alone!"

"I've set everything for the ascent. You see what I've done; if I've made any mistakes, it means good-by for the Cobulus, for me, and—for you!

"I leave it to your good sense to tell me if there's anything I've overlooked." And he laid his hands on the starting-levers.

Reblong said nothing so far, such was his chagrin and wonder. But now he evidently considered seriously what Fort had said.

"I see you mean it, Mr. Fort. And—you ought to know that once you've cleared the landing-dock, you'll have a hard time to keep her level unless you're up on the bridge. That is, while you're shifting the wing-angle. But you ought to be down here to do that; and, meanwhile, she might nose down and slam into something, and—" Reblong shuddered.

"I see." The athlete pondered for a moment. Then he lifted the engineer bodily, chair and all, and moved him over nearer the instrument. Next he loosened one of Reblong's hands, just enough to permit him to reach certain of the levers. He also did some more tying of knots and shifting of buckles, roped the chair to a stanchion, and made sure that Reblong could not undo himself.

"It's up to you," said Fort with the new light in his eyes. "You run this thing as it ought to be run, and you're safe. Trick me in any way, and I'll get you!"

Reblong took a single look at those eyes. "I understand," said he, in a low voice; and without further ado the athlete went to the elevator.

In less than a minute the order came to "cast off." The engineer did not hesitate, but threw the levers and turned the wheels which Fort had expected to operate himself. Another second and the great craft was rising from its seat.

Shouts, muffled and faint because of the ship's double windows, sounded from outside. Reblong saw the sheds sinking rapidly below him. In thirty seconds the vessel was free of the dock.

"First gear ahead," came the signal; and again Reblong obeyed. Practically he had no choice. Another man, of nobler training, might have preferred to be loyal at all costs. But Reblong, the representative Capellan workman, saw the lights of the sheds shift slowly to the rear, then go out of sight as the speed increased. He saw one or two fliers preparing to pursue, but he knew that the cruiser would easily outstrip the best of them.

The Cobulus had got clear away!

It was an hour later that the four, this time through the doctor and young Ernol, learned the sequel to Fort's daring feat. The boy was alone in his cell, awake in the darkness, when one of the guards marched up to his door and unlocked it.

"Come out," he ordered; and Ernol preceded him down the corridor, up a flight of stairs, through another corridor and thence into the exercise grounds. On the other side of this was a small building, with no opening save one door, now bright with light. Inside, Ernol found the other men who had been arrested with him, closely watched by a dozen of the prison guards. His father was not there; apparently they were waiting for him to be brought.

"It worked all right," whispered the man at Ernol's right, as the boy was lined up. Ernol only nodded slightly, keeping his eyes fixed upon the door. A moment later, the elder Ernol arrived, accompanied by a man whom the doctor instantly recognized.

It was Eklan Norbith, the man whose infernally ingenious use of the clock's pendulum had wrung the truth about the secret photographs from the boy's father. He looked even more cruel and repellent now, than he had that night on the couch. Apparently quite recovered, he made a truly forbidding figure.

He had evidently been sent for by the warden; for, with a slow, malignant stare at the row of prisoners, he stated the case in his heavy, ominous tones:

"You are all supposed to know the rules. One of you has been smuggling drugs into the prison; we have found specimens in each cell. It only remains to learn which of you is the guilty party; and that, I propose to uncover within one minute!"

He paused, and glared around again. The stillness was unbroken for a moment; then one prisoner coughed nervously. This started half the rest to doing the same; and under cover of the noise, Ernol whispered to the man on his right:

"No sight of him yet! I'm afraid you showed the drug too soon."

"I waited until I heard the clock strike," protested the other; and then both stood on their guard as the commission's deputy went on with his arraignment:

"It is my duty to inform you, although you probably already know it, that this building is made of iron. Floor, walls, and ceiling are the same." The doctor saw that the prisoners' feet were all bare. "And the whole place is heavily wired with high-power electricity!

"The guards and I will now leave you to yourselves." His teeth showed in an evil smile. "We will give you a few kilowatts as a starter, and shut it off after ten seconds. If you are not ready by that time to tell me which of you is guilty, I will then let you have the current twice as strong!"

The prisoners looked at each other anxiously. Ernol threw back his head defiantly.

"Don't weaken!" he exclaimed. "The juice can't hurt you!"

Immediately the guards backed out, keeping their weapons trained on the crowd. Norbith was the last to go. He left the door open; and from where the boy stood he could plainly watch the man as he worked the switches, just outside.

Instantly the place was in an uproar. Of course, the doctor felt nothing of the prickling, nerve-shaking pain that gripped every one of those barefoot men. They leaped and darted here and there, bluish sparks flashing wherever they touched the iron; or they fell after a step or two and writhed on the floor, shrieking and cursing with the exquisite torture of that awful current. Ernol alone kept from shouting; he stood and took it, trembling like a leaf.

But it lasted only a moment or two. The uproar ceased. Norbith stepped back into the room.

"Well?" The slow smile again. "Want to tell now?"

For answer the boy clapped his hand to his mouth and blew a shrill whistle. Norbith stared in astonishment. Then, all of a sudden, a tremendous thing happened.

A veritable hurricane swooped down upon the place. There was a vast rush of wind, accompanied by a thunderous noise, like breakers. Then two huge masses of metal clanged against the sides of the building; there was a grinding crash, and the whole structure rocked and swayed as though in the grasp of some supernatural monster. Next second the lights went out; the wires had snapped.

"All aboard; look out, below!" sang out a voice. It was Fort, calling from far overhead.

And then, slowly at first but with quickening speed, the iron building rose into the air; arose, and floated away like a toy balloon. It was fast in the grip of the Cobulus's grappling-irons!

Norbith was the only officer left in the room. He regained his senses with lightning speed. Out came his electric torch; he trained it on the prisoners.

"By God!" he cursed. "You'll not get away, you—" And he fumbled with the weapon in his belt.

It was one of the boxlike machine guns. Young Ernol hesitated only an instant. Then he dashed forward.

The box spat fire. The boy threw his weight against the deputy, so that the man lost his balance and toppled out the door into the arms of the guards below.

And the doctor brought his own mind back to his body not one second before the lad, burnt through and through by the flame of the man's weapon, fell back into the room—dead.

15

Powart Strikes

From then on until the end the doctor was out of it. Try as he might, he could find no other mind with which to connect, no other view-point like his own. He had to content himself with what the others learned.

Their knowledge of the rescue stopped short soon after the Cobulus, with its living freight, quitted the prison grounds. Reblong, as Smith watched, continued to operate the engines during about two hundred miles of flight; then Fort, having shown one of his new comrades how to steer, came down to the instruments, leading the force of cleaners whom he had kidnapped.

"Thanks very much," to Reblong, in the voice of a man who was having the time of his life. "I dare say you feel a little sour about this; but later on you can have the satisfaction of having helped, even though against your will."

"What are you going to do now?" Reblong wanted to know as the athlete released him from his chair. The other Capellans were content to stare and listen.

The strange glint came back into Fort's eyes. "It's up to you, folks!" And he explained the situation, making it clear that they, the cruiser's workmen, would not dare return and tell the truth, for fear of punishment for disloyalty. In the end the Cobulus was halted, and Reblong and the rest were set down in an unsettled mountain country, with enough supplies to last a year.

Thus the engineer became a fugitive. Smith learned nothing further from him. For all practical purposes, the investigation was narrowed down to what Billie, through Mona, and her husband, through Powart, were able to uncover. But it was enough; enough to strain their imaginations to the snapping point, and make all four doubt their new-found senses.

Van Emmon declared that he intended to warn Powart that his plan was suspected. "It's only fair," stoutly, "after what you told Fort, through Mona." And Billie had no answer to that.

So the geologist watched the chief closely, finding it decidedly hard to catch him in the required state of semi-consciousness. Apparently Powart was always alert, even up to the exact moment of going to sleep; after which he invariably slept like a log, but awakening with a start, bolt upright in bed. But Van Emmon continued to watch his chance.

Meanwhile another message had been received from the Alma expedition. It ran as follows, after decoding:

People here are planning to construct a great fleet to visit Hafen and Holl about the middle of next year. To carry a regular army of missionaries, to preach the gospel of social democracy.

Better make the most of your reign while it lasts, Mr. Powart. Married yet?

The chairman was glad to get this, rather than otherwise. Somehow the thing strengthened his whole plan. From his standpoint the proposed invasion of missionaries "to preach the gospel of social democracy," was far more to be feared than a military invasion.

So, although he made certain changes in the message, he did not have to counterfeit his earnestness when he presented the matter to his staff, the former commission. Perhaps the expedition's last remark, "Married yet?" had something to do with the vigour of his tones.

"They are planning," he told the nine, "to undo all that our civilization has accomplished. Unless we can circumvent them, Hafen and Holl will be turned into bedlam."

He lost no time about what he had next to say. "Knowing what we do about Alma's designs upon us, I believe that it would be folly to wait until we are attacked. They doubtless possess inventions against which we would be powerless; they are such highly advanced people in such matters. So what I propose is to prevent them from attacking us at all!"

He paused portentously, finding in each face before him an anxious excitement which was exactly what he wanted. They were hanging breathlessly upon his words.

"Let me remind you that Alma is not only our nearest neighbour in the solar system, but that, at present, only a few million miles separate us. She is within a few weeks of the nearest point. Furthermore"—speaking with care—"we must remember that Alma is not only nearer the sun than we are, but it is a much older planet. Were it not for the glass with which she is completely roofed in, the people would suffer from lack of air. In short, this roof of theirs is vitality itself to them. Now, my campaign—subject to your suggestions and advices—shall be to puncture that roof!"

The sensation was tremendous. None of the nine had ever heard the like before. And yet, such was the dominating energy of their commander, it bridged the gap for them all; instantly they saw that his idea was the best possible.

"The only question, of course—sir—is the matter of means." The shock-headed man spoke with immense respect. The others looked as though they envied him his nerve.

226

Powart was ready with his reply. "I have already considered this. Briefly we shall construct a piece of artillery of such dimensions that we can bombard the planet directly!"

He explained that it meant operations on a scale never before attempted. It meant a cannon as much beyond what had ever been made before, as that roof had exceeded anything of the kind. "And so far as I have figured the matter, the total resources of Holl will have to be pressed into service for the purpose. There will be no opportunity for insurrection while this work is in progress."

And he went on to elaborate. The nine made some suggestions, a few of which were adopted. The thing was worked out, then and there, with such completeness that the plan was publicly announced the very next day.

Powart himself carried a copy of the manifesto to Mona. He found her superintending the work of her gardeners. She did suggest going into the house, but offered him a seat on the grass beside her. He stood instead.

"It seems to be the only thing to do," commented the surgeon, after reading the document in silence. She had not the remotest idea, of course, that the whole thing was based upon pure fraud. "Are you sure that this bombardment will not cost a good many lives?"

"I doubt if there will be any loss at all," he replied. "It is my intention to communicate with Alma just before the first shot is fired, and warn them what to expect; so that they can keep away from the spot we shall aim at, and get supplies ready for repairing the break."

"I see. Your plan is to keep them so busy mending breaks that they will lose all interest in their proposed invasion." She laughed a little. "Really, it is a rather comical sort of warfare. But you certainly deserve a great deal of credit for finding such a humane way out of the difficulty. You will go down in history as the world's greatest man!"

Powart drew a deep breath. But he said quietly enough, "Don't you think that I have done enough to—dispose of that objection of yours?"

She was momentarily at a loss for words. "Really—the thing is so immense—I can hardly believe that you did all this entirely on my account. Did you?"

He was taken off his guard. "Yes—I mean, no. Your objection was what set me to thinking; but the opportunity of doing our people a service—that, Mona, is what—" He hesitated; it was not easy, with the girl staring innocently at him, declare that he had not deliberately formed his opportunity out of thin air.

But she had no suspicions. Billie had not been able to reach her again.

The four on the earth knew little of Fort. He called up Powart two days after the Cobulus's sensational flight, reporting that he had been kidnapped "by some masked men" along with Reblong and the others, but that he alone had escaped. The ship, was found, abandoned, in an undeveloped part of Holl; and all signs indicated that the former prisoners had separated at this point. Prolonged search failed to locate them, or the missing employees.

Fort continued to go and come quite as before. He called frequently upon Mona, with whom he was exceedingly careful to avoid all reference to Powart, for fear he might blurt out the truth. The girl told him that he still had a lot of time to make good; she would not marry, she said, until after all danger from Alma was past. He was satisfied.

"I have a little scheme up my sleeve," casually, "such as may amount to something, and may not. I need just about that much time to finish it, anyhow."

"Is it anything you can talk about now?"

"Not yet."

And the subject was dropped.

Thus matters stood when half the industrial army of Holl, taken from their regular tasks, were set to the making of the giant gun and its equally giant projectiles. Monstrous though they were to be, however, they were no less prodigious than Powart. Could Fort, wondered Mona, possibly equal him?

And so the weeks passed into months, and finally the great day came.

16
The Blast

"I am glad to see so many moving-picture men," said Mona thoughtfully. "If it were not for photographs, I doubt if coming generations would believe this."

And she turned her glasses again upon the scene. From the cockpit of Fort's newest ornithopter, about three hundred yards from the ground and less than that distance from the spot, she could watch operations with exceptional ease. Fort agreed with her comment.

"Yes; to merely state that the mouth of that cannon is a hundred feet in diameter, and that it is set a mile and a half into the ground, at an angle of thirty degrees—it's too much of a strain on the imagination. However, I understand they've taken flash-light pictures from the interior, such as will make it easier to believe."

A huge compound crane was slowly swinging the first projectile into place over the muzzle of that colossal gun. Mona eyed the immense shell with curiosity.

"As I understand it," she said, "the projectile is really a number of shells, telescoping, one within another. I've forgotten how many there are."

"Fifty. The idea, of course, is that the original charge of powder within the cannon will send the projectile at something like two miles a second. Upon reaching a certain point in space another charge will be automatically fired in the base of the outermost shell. Thus it will act as another cannon, from which the remaining shells will be shot. And so on, until the forty-ninth shell has been blown to the rear. The remaining one will, by that time, have travelled far enough to get out of our gravitation into Alma's."

"What is the size of the fiftieth shell?"

"Only two feet in diameter;[1] but of such length that it will hold five tons of explosive. It is expected to demolish a square mile of their roof."

---

1. All dimensions are necessarily a matter of judgment; but they represent the opinion of an architect, whose sense of proportion is presumably better than average.

The great projectile was carefully lowered until its tip was flush with the volcano-like mouth of the cannon. The proceeding took a long time; and it was well toward the end of the work that Powart's handsome yacht swept into the space provided for it in the circle of spectators.

By prearrangement this space was next to that occupied by Mona and Fort.

As soon as the yacht had come to a stop its thrumming wings keeping it as steadily suspended in mid air as any of the lighter craft roundabout, Powart himself stepped out upon the tiny bridge. It was the signal for a great outburst of applause, in which Fort joined as heartily as anyone.

"You don't seem at all envious of Mr. Powart," commented Mona, watching the athlete curiously.

He looked around as though surprised, and protested:

"On the contrary, I am really proud of his success. You see, it's this way, Mona: If he fails, then I fail too!"

And before she could ask what he meant he raised his voice enough for the dictator to hear:

"Congratulations, Powart! Everything coming along all right?"

Powart gave Fort one of his piercing looks, but showed no sign of irritation as he replied: "All reports satisfactory. We shall have our little fireworks promptly on the second." Then to Mona: "Sorry I cannot invite you aboard my ship; but I shall be so occupied with the ceremonial end of this, you know, that—"

"Of course," instantly. "I would really be in the way; and I shouldn't care to be that, to-day of all days."

And Van Emmon, through Powart's eyes, judged that the dictator stood mountain-high in her respect at that instant.

Fort listened with the utmost indifference, seeming to take a boy's rapt interest in the spectacle below him rather than in the affair at his elbow.

He glanced at his watch and remarked: "Less than half an hour now. I can hardly wait!"

Mona eyed him speculatively. "What did you mean, just now, about your success depending upon Mr. Powart's?"

"Just that," he returned lightly. "Why, if he fails, my little scheme is a miserable fiasco! I shan't be able to marry you at all; that is, unless you grant an extension!"

Mona did not respond to his levity.

"I wish you'd be serious!" she rebuked him. "Just think what this affair means!"

He pretended to be thoughtful. "Oh, to Alma, you mean! Yes, indeed; the folks will be badly upset, I imagine, if the projectile actually reaches their roof."

"Why, do you think it may not?" surprised.

"It's barely possible. The whole thing has been very scientifically calculated, of course; but the slightest flaw in the mathematics could cause a miss. Yes, the projectile may never reach its mark; it's something to be considered."

"In which case," returned Mona, evidently convinced that he was teasing, "in which case, your own scheme falls through!"

"Oh, no," with the utmost calm. "My scheme depends upon the cannon, not upon the projectile."

Mona nearly lost her temper. "I wish you wouldn't talk in riddles!" But Fort was plainly unwilling to say anything further just then; he changed the subject, directing Mona's glasses toward a point far to the rear, where the blue wall of the contact loomed, some twenty miles away. The spot had been chosen, of course, because there were fewer inhabitants in that locality than any other; the discharge of the gun would mean an immense volume of smoke and gas, likely to prove disagreeable for days. Nobody cared to live near the contact, because of its queer, sunless conditions.

"Almost time we were getting out of here," said Fort, after another look at his watch. As he spoke a warning whistle on Powart's yacht sounded shrilly; and with one accord the surrounding horde of sightseers—all belonging to the leisure class, of course—began to back away from the spot. The workmen, down below, were already taking flight. A moment later Powart, speaking for the benefit of a recording phonograph, began as follows:

231

"Precisely at the hour, minute and second determined by the commission's mathematicians the projectile will be slid into the cannon. The concussion will explode the powder in the breech. This final act is to take place"—he glanced at his watch—"within two minutes.

"By so doing, the people of Hafen and Holl, through me, their commander-in-chief, do hereby deliberately take the offensive against Alma." He hesitated, then went on with fresh determination: "Rather than permit them to prepare for the threatened invasion, then, we thus proceed to bombard their roof, in order to so harass them that they shall be made helpless against us."

Mona turned her gaze from the dictator, and took up her glasses. The great cannon was nearly a mile away from them now; not a single aircraft was closer than Fort's and Powart's, which were still backing away. The blast was not a thing to be sneered at. Mona's hands shook with excitement.

Powart's eyes were on his watch. "The thing is beyond all human power to prevent now. The projectile will be released by clockwork. In fact"—his voice rose, his excitement finally getting the better of him—"it is even now sliding! It is only a matter of seconds; the projectile is lubricated so as to slide easily."

A breathless pause; another look at the watch, then:

"By this time, my friends, the projectile has reached—"

And even as the words quit his mouth, the cannon belched forth.

17

THE DEVOLUTION

Mona removed from her ears two tiny devices like collar-buttons. She noted Fort and the others doing the same. Without this protection their eardrums would have been burst. And while the girl was doing this she heard the athlete hailing the dictator:

"Good for you, Powart! It's a fine job, and I'm ever so much obliged to you."

The dictator stared in amazement. Mona looked from the one to the other, perplexed.

Fort was laughing shakily.

"You may as well make your apologies now, Powart; you're out of it! I've won, and you've lost! I've done a bigger thing than you have!"

Mona gave an exclamation of impatience. "What do you mean?" she cried shrilly. "Are you out of your head?"

"Not a bit of it! I mean just what I say! Powart hasn't succeeded; he's failed. And because he has failed, I've outdone him."

He was gazing impudently at the dictator as he said this; Powart was leaning over the railing of the bridge, a short distance away, too indignant to speak. Next instant, however, Fort glanced at his watch.

"Have to be leaving you now," he called. He turned his machine around. "You'll learn soon enough, Powart, exactly what I mean. And you'll know that I'm right. Good-by!"

Within a minute he and Mona were two miles away. Fort kept silent all the while. He seemed to be intent upon getting the most out of his machine, and kept looking anxiously at his watch. Finally Mona could hold in no longer.

"Boy, I've simply got to know what your game is. You've kept me waiting long enough."

He immediately began to explain. First, he told her frankly and fully, just what she had said to him over the telephone, when she was under Billie's "influence."

"I was so sure it was genuine I went right ahead on that lead, Mona."

"You are positive you heard me say that?" from the girl thoughtfully.

"Absolutely. And somehow I knew it was the truth."

"Powart had tricked us; not merely the workers, whom he has been hoodwinking all along, but you and me and all the rest! So I looked into the matter and discovered that the poor devils on Holl have been treated all wrong. All wrong, Mona! I never realized it before, until I investigated; but they've been enduring rank injustice for generations, and we've encouraged them to be satisfied with it."

"I know it," she interrupted softly. "I've known it for years, boy. What could we do to help them?"

"Exactly!" cried Fort, looking ahead and down, toward the chasm of the contact, then at his watch once more. "Exactly what I found out, Mona! There was no use telling them the truth; they wouldn't believe it! They were too well satisfied.

"And so, when I heard of Powart's scheme to bombard Alma, I saw a way to free the poor idiots on Holl! A way to release them from their bondage—*our* bonds, Mona—and defeat Powart's trickery, and win you—all at one move!"

The girl was plainly thrilled. Yet she kept her voice comparatively cool as she asked:

"So far, so good. But I don't see that you've done anything at all except to kidnap me."

He made an impatient gesture. "Look at the ground!" he ordered curtly; and Mona wonderingly obeyed.

They were nearly to the contact. This time, however, they were not flying down into the cleft, but over it. The curious, canon-like chasm where the two worlds touched was perhaps ten miles below them.

"Look closely!" shouted Fort excitedly. He was glancing at his watch again, and changing the angle of his wings. "By heavens, we are just in time!" The craft dove perilously; he straightened its course. "Look closely, I tell you! It's something you've never seen before, and will never see again!"

And Mona, staring down at the point where Hafen and Holl came together—the curious region of balanced gravitations, like nothing else anywhere in the universe—saw, as she passed over, something that made her senses whirl.

Hafen and Holl were no longer one!

The two globes were now a quarter of a mile apart, and the distance was steadily growing.

Even as Mona watched the gap increased until almost a mile separated the two great worlds.

"Do you see?" cried Fort, fairly squirming in his seat. "Do you see what I've done, Mona?"

"I've taken Ernol and his friends—the bunch I rescued from the prison—and put them to work. Put them to work digging a tunnel! We've been flying above that tunnel just now. It runs—from the contact to the cannon—the bottom of the cannon, Mona!

"When Powart's shot was fired, the recoil—the kick—broke the contact! Understand? Do you see it?"

Mona stared in dull wonder. When she found voice it was strangely flat and commonplace.

"Yes, but—I don't see how the recoil could separate two worlds as large as Hafen and Holl!"

Fort chuckled breathlessly. "Your forget something. You're thinking only of the gravitation; you're forgetting the centrifugal force."

Hafen and Holl, by their daily rotation—around the contact as a centre—were always tending to separate. That recoil was just enough to turn the balance; they'll never touch again.

"And what's more," he rushed on, "Powart's shot is sure to miss! The recoil threw the cannon out of line. Hafen had already moved before the projectile left the gun. Powart—has failed!"

Suddenly the surgeon wheeled upon the athlete. "Boy, we're headed in the wrong way! We'll land in Holl, not in Hafen!"

"Who wants to live in Hafen now?" he shouted, clinging desperately to his controls. The craft was tossing in the newly created air-currents. "Don't you see?

"I've cut Hafen from Holl forever! The workers aren't to be slaves any longer; they're to have their world to themselves, to use entirely for their own benefit; not for the owners!

"And the owners—back there—they're going to have their own world, too, just as they've always insisted! But from now on it's to be their farm, too, and their factory; they've got to get along without Holl from now on.

"Mona—the commission wouldn't allow evolution, and the workers wouldn't listen to revolution! So I've given them—devolution!"

"What?" she cried.

"I've given them devolution. I've given the race of man—a fresh start."

But Mona was scarcely listening.

"Turn back!" she screamed. "I want to go back to my home! I don't want to live in Holl. Turn back, I tell you!"

Fort's face went white. He looked up at her appealingly. "You don't mean that, Mona! Say you don't!"

"I do! I want to go back!" She glanced down at the ever-widening gap. "Hurry! Turn back, or I'll do it myself!"

Fort gazed straight into her eyes for an instant; then, his face whiter than ever, he brought the craft to an abrupt halt in mid air. He looked at his watch for the last time, and said, in a strangely hollow voice:

"Just as you wish, Mona. There's plenty of time to get back before the air gets too thin in the gap.

"The point is, though, that if you go, you go alone!" They looked at one another unwaveringly. "So far as I'm concerned, I shall spend the rest of my life on Holl! No Hafen for mine! From now on I live with the workers. Come—what do you say, Mona?"

She answered instantly and stubbornly: "I go back. What about you?"

He took a parachute from a locker. "Holl is below." He buckled the thing across his chest and stepped up on the edge of the cockpit.

"Do you mean it, dear?" said he softly.

She stared at him stonily. He turned away, his mouth shaking slightly, then held out his hand.

"Good-by, then, for the last time!"

Mona suddenly grasped his hand. For an instant hope flared in Fort's eyes, then faded, leaving his face gray and drawn. He poised himself, letting go her hand reluctantly. Then he turned resolutely.

"It's the only thing for a man to do, Mona! As for you—turn about and go as fast as you can! You've got just time enough. Goodbye!"

And with Mona unable to utter a single word, able only to watch and to feel, the athlete leaned to one side so as to clear the wing, pulled his cap down tightly, and jumped into space.

18

THE SILVER HEART

Mona leaped to the controls. She turned the craft about automatically and started toward Hafen. Then she glanced over the side. What she saw brought her heart to her throat.

About a mile below, and under Fort as he sank through the air, was another flying machine which neither had noticed before. In it was the figure of a man standing; he was manoeuvring his craft so as to intercept the falling aviator. And the clear air of the high altitudes carried the sound of his voice faintly but surely to Mona's ears.

"Thought you'd get away, did you, Fort?" in heavy, insolent tones. "Well, you get—left, my boy!"

"Eklan Norbith!" cried Fort at the same instant. Next second he had landed on the deputy's machine.

"Norbith!" thought Mona, immediately recalling her patient at the hospital. She hesitated only an instant, then dived in a steep spiral down toward the two.

Fort had fouled his parachute on a stanchion, in landing. Breathless, he lay in a tangle heap, looking up at the towering bulk of the deputy.

"You're not going to get clear this time, Fort, like you did that night with the Cobulus and Ernol's gang!" Norbith was saying savagely, gloating over the man at his feet. "Thought the lad killed me, I suppose. I was barely stunned. And I've been on your tail—ever since."

His eyes glowed with anger. Mona watched him in silence as she circled nearer. Norbith! The commission's deputy in Calastia; he represented all that was evil and cruel in the government. It was he who did the nasty work, the things which Powart himself was too much of a gentleman to do. Norbith—the strong, cruel right arm on an unjust law!

237

"Well"—Fort had regained his breath somewhat—"now that you've got me, Norbith, what do you intend to do about it?"

"Do!"The man's voice fairly boomed. "I'm going to tear that parachute off your back and pitch you overboard, you infernal outlaw! And I'm going to claim that you resisted arrest!"

At that instant he noted Mona for the first time. He started as he recognized her. "The surgeon!"

Then his rage came on him again. "You hold your tongue, young woman, or I shall have it—pulled out! Do you understand?" he demanded, thrusting his face up toward hers.

And then Fort was upon him. All he cared for now was to get his fingers in Norbith's throat. And next moment Mona was desperately steering his machine clear of the other as it swayed and thrashed about under the struggling of the two men.

The advantage was with the deputy. Powerful man that he was, he was more than a match for even Fort's great strength, while the athlete's agility did him no good in the restricted space of the cockpit. The parachute hindered him, too. Down on the ground, on a clear spot, it would have been different. As it was, Fort was quickly thrust to his knees, and, despite all that he could do, he could not fight off the deputy's grip. In a moment it had shifted to the athlete's throat.

"You would, would you!" roared the deputy. "By—you'll be dead even before you reach the ground!"

Fort struggled wildly. In a moment he was strangling; Mona could see his protruding eyes and lolling tongue. She could not help. She was not athlete enough to leap to his aid. But all of a sudden, just as Fort had once come to her own rescue, her tongue came to his.

"Boy! Boy! Tear open his shirt! Tear open his shirt!"

Fort heard. For a second he hesitated, dull wonder in his starting eyes; then he reached up, and with a spasmodic jerk of his hands, ripped Norbith's shirt wide open. The man's bare chest was exposed.

"Don't you see?" shrieked Mona hysterically. "Look, boy! Look!"

And Fort saw. Saw the two silver tubes leading from the brown scar in the breast of this man—the man whose heart had been replaced by a silver instrument. Saw the tubes, leading to a belt around the man's middle, where the pumping mechanism was concealed. And as Fort saw, he understood.

With a final burst of strength he raised his quivering fingers and clutched one of the little pipes. A jerk, an exclamation from Norbith; and then, even as Fort's head fell back insensate, his hand snapped the little tube in two.

"Good God!" swore the deputy. "You—you've—" He gasped and spluttered; he let go of Fort. The athlete dropped like a log into the bottom of the craft.

But Eklan Norbith stood upright, his hands thrashing wildly, his mouth twitching horribly. One end of the broken tube hissed with escaping air; the other end spouted blood. The deputy swayed; his head dropped to his shoulders.

And then the air rushed into his lungs for the last time; he gave a single piercing shriek, tottered, and fell backward out of the machine.

Fort opened his eyes to see Mona bending over him, bathing his head. He looked around dully, blinked once or twice, frowned as though trying to remember, and then said:

"How—did I get here?"

"I waited until Norbith's machine steadied," said she in a wonderfully soft voice, "and then flew down close enough to pick you up."

He remembered. Suddenly he grasped at her arm and tried to get up. "Hurry!" he cried. "You've only got time enough to make it! The gap—don't take any chances!"

But the girl was paying no attention to where the machine was going. She was looking at the man and seeming to be perfectly satisfied.

"I don't care," she declared a little shakily. "Holl looks good enough to me, dear—if you're going to be living on it!"

The craft rocked perilously.

Back on the earth, three of the four stirred in their chairs.

The doctor was the first to arouse. He sounded the gong to warn his wife, and the action helped to awaken the others; Billie first, then Smith. But Van Emmon did not rouse. Still connected with the dictator, Billie's husband was twisting and turning in his chair, moaning slightly under his breath. In his subconscious mind some terrible scene was being enacted. Suddenly his mouth flew open, and the words fairly tumbled forth:

"Ernol—at the contact—he's telephoned! Everybody knows now!" Next:"Billie:Why didn't you tell me? I could have warned Powart!" And then, in a voice of agony:

"God, what a mob! They'll kill him!"

But he was still unconscious. The doctor exclaimed in fear.

"Quick!" he ordered. "Into the connection again!" And he threw himself back into his chair.

In a minute the three were still. Except for two great tears from Billie's eyes, there were no signs of life. Two minutes passed, then three. Finally all four roused together.

"Well!" Van Emmon was the first to speak. His voice was harsh and strained. "By George, that was a narrow squeak! I thought sure I was a goner! They threw Powart—out of his yacht!"

Billie caught his hand and patted it. Her lips were trembling; she could not trust herself to speak. Her husband stared at her with eyes that were still bewildered and tried hard to understand.

Smith could say nothing. The doctor, however, got to his feet and stretched.

"Phew!" taking off the brass bracelets and reaching for a handful of the Venusian books. "That was—going some!"

He located a passage in one of the books. "I guess we've had enough of people like ourselves. What do you say," eagerly, "to visiting a place where they're not even the same sort of animals as we are?"

He looked around enthusiastically. Smith made a brief sound of agreement, and remained in his chair. Both he and the doctor looked to Billie and Van Emmon for comment.

But the man and the woman were content to look at one another. Their minds had room for only one problem; their eyes saw nothing, cared to see nothing, save that which love seeks and, having found, is satisfied with.

Did it make any difference to Billie that her husband had sympathized with Capellette's greatest despot and worst failure? Did it make any difference to Van that Billie approved when the woman she was allied with discarded the despot for the devolutionist?

Or was Billie still his chief reason for existing, and was Van hers?

That was the real question! Small matters like life in other worlds—they could wait!

The Emancipatrix

The Emancipatrix

1

THE MENTAL EXPEDITION

The doctor closed the door behind him, crossed to the table, silently offered the geologist a cigar, and waited until smoke was issuing from it. Then he said:

"Well," bluntly, "what's come between you and your wife, Van?"

The geologist showed no surprise. Instead, he frowned severely at the end of his cigar, and carefully seated himself on the corner of the table. When he spoke there was a certain rigor in his voice, which told the doctor that his friend was holding himself tightly in rein.

"It really began when the four of us got together to investigate Capellette, two months ago." Van Emmon was a thorough man in important matters. "Maybe I ought to say that both Billie and I were as much interested as either you or Smith; she often says that even the tour of Mercury and Venus was less wonderful.

"What is more, we are both just as eager to continue the investigations. We still have all kinds of faith in the Venusian formula; we want to 'visit' as many more worlds as the science of telepathy will permit. It isn't that either of us has lost interest."

The doctor rather liked the geologist's scientific way of stating the case, even though it meant hearing things he already knew. Kinney watched and waited and listened intently.

"You remember, of course, what sort of a man I got in touch with. Powart was easily the greatest Capellan of them all; a mag-

245

nificent intellect, which I still think was intended to have ruled the rest. I haven't backed down from my original position."

"Van! You still believe," incredulously, "in a government of the sort he contemplated?"

Van Emmon nodded aggressively. "All that we learned merely strengthens my conviction. Remember what sort of people the working classes of Capellette were? Smith's 'agent' was typical—a helpless nincompoop, not fit to govern himself!" The geologist strove to keep his patience.

"However," remarked Kinney, "the chap whose mind I used was no fool."

"Nor was Billie's agent, the woman surgeon," agreed Van Emmon, "even if she did prefer 'the Devolutionist' to Powart. But you'll have to admit, doc, that the vast majority of the Capellans were incompetents; the rest were exceptions."

The doctor spoke after a brief pause. "And—that's what is wrong, Van?"

"Yes," grimly. "Billie can't help but rejoice that things turned out the way they did. She is sure that the workers, now that they've been separated from the ruling class, will proceed to make a perfect paradise out of their land." He could not repress a certain amount of sarcasm. "As well expect a bunch of monkeys to build a steam engine!

"Well," after a little hesitation, "as I said before, doc, I've no reason to change my mind. You may talk all you like about it—I can't agree to such ideas. The only way to get results on that planet is for the upper classes to continue to govern."

"And this is what you two have—quarrelled about?"

Van Emmon nodded sorrowfully. He lit another cigar absent-mindedly and cleared his throat twice before going on:

"My fault, I guess. I've been so darned positive about everything I've said, I've probably caused Billie to sympathize with her friends more solidly than she would otherwise."

"But just because you've championed the autocrats so heartily—"

"I'm afraid so!" The geologist was plainly relieved to have

246

stated the case in full. He leaned forward in his eagerness to be understood. He told the doctor things that were altogether too personal to be included in this account.

Meanwhile, out in the doctor's study, Smith had made no move whatever to interrogate the geologist's young wife. Instead, the engineer simply remained standing after Billie had sat down, and gave her only an occasional hurried glance. Shortly the silence got on her nerves; and—such was her nature, as contrasted with Van Emmon's—whereas he had stated causes first, she went straight to effects.

"Well," explosively, "Van and I have split!"

Smith was seldom surprised at anything. This time was no exception. He merely murmured "Sorry" under his breath; and Billie rushed on, her pent-up feelings eager to escape.

"We haven't mentioned Capellette for weeks, Smith! We don't dare! If we did, there'd be such a rumpus that we—we'd separate!" Something came up into her throat which had to be choked back before she could go on. Then—

"I don't know why it is, but every time the subject is brought up Van makes me so *wild*!" She controlled herself with a tremendous effort. "He blames me, of course, because of what I did to help the Devolutionist. But I can't be blamed for sympathizing with the underdog, can I? I've always preferred justice to policy, any time. Justice first, I say! And I think we've seen—there on Capellette—how utterly impossible it is for any such system as theirs to last indefinitely."

But before she could follow up her point the door opened and the doctor returned with her husband. Kinney did not allow any tension to develop; instead, he said briskly:

"There's only a couple of hours remaining between now and dinner time; I move we get busy." He glanced about the room, to see if all was in place. The four chairs, each with its legs tipped with glass; the four footstools, similarly insulated from the floor; the electrical circuit running from the odd group of machinery in the corner, and connecting four pair of brass bracelets—all were ready for use. He motioned the others to the chairs in which they had already accomplished marvels in the way of mental travelling.

"Now," he remarked, as he began to fit the bracelets to his wrists, an example which the rest straightway followed; "now, we want to make sure that we all have the same purpose in mind. Last time, we were simply looking for four people, such as had view-points similar to our own. To-day, our object is to locate, somewhere among the planets attached to one of the innumerable sun-stars of the universe, one on which the conditions are decidedly different from anything we have known before."

Billie and Van Emmon, their affair temporarily forgotten, listened eagerly.

"As I recall it," Smith calmly observed, "we agreed that this attempt would be to locate a new kind of—well, near-human. Isn't that right?"

The doctor nodded. "Nothing more or less"—speaking very distinctly—"than a creature as superior as we are, but *not in human form.*"

Smith tried hard not to share the thrill. He had been reading biology the previous week. "I may as well protest, first as last, that I don't see how human intelligence can ever be developed outside the human form. Not—possibly!"

Van Emmon also was sceptical, but his wife declared the idea merely unusual, not impossible. "Is there any particular reason against it?" she demanded of the doctor.

"I will say this much," cautiously. "Given certain conditions, and inevitably the human form will most certainly become the supreme creature, superior to all the others.

"However, suppose the planetary conditions are entirely different. I conceive it entirely possible for one of the other animals to forge ahead of the man-ape; quite possible, Smith," as the engineer started to object, "if only the conditions are different *enough.*

"At any rate, we shall soon find out. I have been reading further in the library the Venusians gave us, and I assure you that I've found some astonishing things." He fingered one of the diminutive volumes. "There is one planet in particular, whose name I have forgotten, where all animal life has disappeared entirely. There are none but vegetable forms on the land, and all of them are the rankest sort of weeds. They have literally choked off everything else!

"And the highest form of life there is a weed; a hideous monstrosity, shaped something like an octopus, and capable of the most horrible—" He stopped abruptly, remembering that one of his hearers was a woman. "Never mind about that now."

He indicated another of the little books. "I think we will do well to investigate a planet which the Venusians call 'Sanus.' It belongs to the tremendous planetary family of the giant star Arcturus. I haven't read any details at all; I didn't want to know more than you. We can proceed with our discoveries on an equal footing."

"But," objected Smith, recalling the previous methods, "how are we to put our minds in touch with any of theirs, unless we know enough about them to imagine their viewpoints?"

"Our knowledge of their planet's name and location," replied the doctor, "makes it easier for us. All we have to do is to go into the telepathic state, via the Venusian formula; then, at the same time, each must concentrate upon some definite mental quality, some particular characteristic of his own mind, which he or she wishes to find on Sanus. It makes no difference what it may be; all you have to do is, exert your imaginations a little."

There was a pause, broken by Smith: "We ought to tell each other what we have in mind, so that we don't conflict."

"Yes. For my part," said the doctor, "I'd like to get in touch with a being who is mildly rebellious; not a violent radical, but a philosophical revolutionist. I don't care what sort of a creature he, she, or it may be, so long as the mind is in revolt against whatever injustice may exist."

"Then I," stated Smith, "will stick to the idea of service." Nobody was surprised that the engineer should make such a choice; he was, first, last, and all the time, essentially a useful man.

Van Emmon was not ready with his choice. Instead: "You say, doc, that you know nothing further about Sanus than what you've already told us?"

"I was about to mention that. The Venusians say that conditions are reversed from what we found on Capellette. Instead of Sanus being ruled by a small body of autocrats, it is—ruled by the working class!"

"Under the circumstances," said Van, "I'll take something different from what I got last time. No imperiousness this trip." He smiled grimly. "There was a time when I used to take orders. Suppose you call my choice 'subordinacy.'"

"How very noble of you!" gibed Billie. "My idea is supremacy, and plenty of it! I want to get in touch with the man higher up—the worker who is boss of the whole works!" She flashed a single glance at her husband, then threw herself back in her chair. "Go ahead!"

And before two minutes were up, the power of concerted thought, aided by a common objective and the special electrical circuit which joined them, had projected the minds of the four across the infinite depths of space. The vast distance which separated their bodies from Sanus was annihilated, literally as quick as thought.

Neither of the four stirred. To all appearances they were fast asleep. The room was quite still; only the clock ticked dully on the wall. Down-stairs, the doctor's wife kept watch over the house.

The greatest marvel in creation, the human mind, was exploring the unknown.

2

ALMOST HUMAN

Of course, the four still had the ability to communicate with each other while in the trance state; they had developed this power to a fair degree while investigating Capellette. However, each was so deeply interested in what he or she was seeing during the first hour of their Sanusian experiences that neither thought to discuss the matter until afterward.

When the doctor first made connection with the eyes of his agent, he instinctively concluded that he, at least, had got in touch with a being more or less like himself. The whole thing was so natural; he was surveying a sunny, brush-covered landscape from eyes whose height from the ground, and other details, were decidedly those of a human.

For a moment there was comparative silence. Then his unknown agent swiftly raised something—a hand, presumably—to a mouth, and gave out a piercing cry. Whereupon the doctor learned something that jarred him a trifle. His agent was—a woman!

He had time to congratulate himself upon the fact that he was (1) a doctor, (2) a married man, (3) the father of a daughter or two, before his agent repeated her cry. Almost immediately it was answered by another exactly like it, from an unseen point not far away. The Sanusian plainly chuckled to herself with satisfaction.

A moment later there came, rather faintly, two more calls, each from a different direction in the dun-coloured brush. Still without moving from the spot, the doctor's agent replied two or three times, meanwhile watching her surroundings very closely. Within half a minute the first of her friends came in sight.

It was a young woman. At a distance of about twenty yards she appeared to be about five feet tall and sturdily built. She was dressed in a single garment, made of the skin of some yellow, short-haired animal. It may have been a lion cub. Around her waist was a strip of hide, which served as a belt, and held a small, stone-headed tomahawk. One shoulder and both legs were left quite bare, revealing a complexion so deeply tanned that the doctor instantly thought: "Spanish!"

In a way, the girl's face gave the same impression. Large, dark-brown eyes, full lips and a healthy glow beneath her tan, all made it possible for her to pass as a Spaniard. However, there was nothing in the least coquettish about her; she had a remarkably independent manner, and a gaze as frank and direct as it was pure and untroubled.

In one hand she carried a branch from some large-leafed shrub. The eyes which Kinney was using became fixed upon this branch; and even as the newcomer cried out in joyous response to the other's greeting, her expression changed and she turned and fled, laughing, as the doctor's agent darted toward her. She did not get away, and immediately the two were struggling over the possession of the branch.

In the midst of the tussle another figure made its appearance.

"Look out! Here comes Dulnop!"[1] cried Kinney's agent; at the same time she made a special effort, and succeeded in breaking off a good half of the branch.

Instantly she darted to one side, where she calmly began to pluck some small, hard-shelled nuts from the branch, and proceeded to crack them, with entire ease, using a set of teeth which must have been absolutely perfect.

She gave the latest comer only a glance or two. He—for it certainly was a man—was nearly a half a foot taller than the girl already described; but he was plainly not much older or younger, and in build and colour much the same. He was clothed neither more nor less than she, the only difference being that some leopard-like animal had contributed the material. In his belt was tucked a primitive stone hammer, also a stone knife. His face was longer than hers, his eyes darker; but he was manifestly still very boyish. Dulnop, they had called him.

"Hail, Cunora!" he called to the girl who had brought the nuts; then, to her who was watching: "Rolla! Where got ye the nuts?"

Rolla didn't answer; she couldn't use her mouth just then; it was too full of nuts. She merely nodded in the direction of Cunora.

"Give me some, Cunora!"

The younger girl gave no reply, but backed away from him

1. It made no difference whatever as to what language was used. The telepathic process employed enabled the investigators to know all that their agents' subconscious minds took in. The brains of the four automatically translated these thought-images into their own language. However, this method did not enable them to learn what their agents were thinking, but only what they said, heard, and saw.

as he approached; her eyes sparkled mischievously and, the doctor thought, somewhat affectionately. Dulnop made a sudden darting move toward her branch, and she as swiftly whirled in her tracks, so that he missed. However, he instantly changed his mind and grasped the girl instead. Like a flash he drew her to him and kissed her noisily.

Next second he was staggering backward under the weight of her hard brown fist. "Do that again, and I'll have the hair out of thy head!" the girl screamed, her face flaming. Yet Kinney saw that the man was laughing joyously even as he rubbed the spot where her blow had landed, while the expression of her eyes quite belied what she had said.

Not until then did the doctor's agent say anything. When she spoke it was in a deep, contralto voice which gave the impression of riper years than either of the other two. Afterward Kinney learned that Rolla was nearly ten years their senior, a somewhat more lithe specimen of the same type, clad in the skin of what was once a magnificent goat. She carried only a single small knife in her belt. As seen reflected in pools of water, her complexion was slightly paler and her whole expression a little less self-assertive and distinctively philosophical. To those who admire serious, thoughtful women of regular feature and different manner, Rolla would have seemed downright beautiful.

"Dulnop," said she, with a laugh in her voice, "ye will do well to seek the nut tree, first as last." She nonchalantly crushed another shell in her mouth. "Neither Cunora nor I can spare good food to a kiss-hungry lout like thee!"

He only laughed again and made as though to come toward her. She stood ready to dodge, chuckling excitedly, and he evidently gave it up as a bad job. "Tell me whence cameth the nuts, Cunora!" he begged; but the girl pretended to be cross, and shut her mouth as firmly as its contents would allow.

Next moment there was a shout from the thicket, together with a crashing sound; and shortly the fourth Sanusian appeared. He was by far the larger; but his size was a matter of width rather than of height. An artist would have picked him as a model for Ajax himself. His muscles fairly strained the huge lion's skin in which he was clad, and he had twice the weight of Dulnop within the same height. Also, to the doctor's eye, he was nearer Rolla's age.

His face was strong and handsome in a somewhat fierce, relentless way; his complexion darker than the rest. He carried a huge club, such as must have weighed all of forty pounds, while his belt was jammed full of stone weapons. The doctor classed him and the younger girl together because of their vigour and independence, while Dulnop and Rolla seemed to have dispositions very similar in their comparative gentleness and restraint.

"Hail, all of ye!" shouted this latest arrival in a booming baritone. He strode forward with scarcely a glance at the two younger people; his gaze was fixed upon Rolla, his expression unmistakable. The woman quietly turned upon Dulnop and Cunora.

"Look!" she exclaimed, pointing to a spot back of them. "See the curious bird!" They wheeled instantly, with the unquestioning faith of two children; and before they had brought their gazes back again, the big man had seized Rolla, crushed her to his breast and kissed her passionately. She responded just as warmly, pushing him away only in order to avoid being seen by the others. They showed only an innocent disappointment at having missed seeing the "curious bird."

"A simple-minded people, basically good-humoured," was the way the doctor summed the matter up when reporting what he had seen. However, it was not so easy to analyze certain things that were said during the time the four Sanusians spent in each other's company. For one thing—

"Did They give thee permission to go?" Rolla was asked by the big man. His name, it seemed, was Corrus.

"Yes, Corrus. They seemed to think it a good idea for us to take a little recreation to-day. I suppose ye left thy herd with thy brother?"

He nodded; and the doctor was left to wonder whom "They" might be. Were They a small group of humans, whose function was to superintend? Or were They, as the books from Venus seemed to indicate, another type of creature, entirely different from the humans, and yet, because of the peculiar Sanusian conditions, superior to the humans?

"They have decided to move their city a little farther away from the forest," Rolla overheard Dulnop telling Cunora; which was the first indication that the planet boasted such a thing as a city. Otherwise, things appeared to be in a primitive, rather than a civilized condition.

These four skin-clad savages seemed to be enjoying an aboriginal picnic. For lunch, they munched on various fruits and nuts picked up en route, together with handfuls of some wheat-like cereal which the big man had brought in a goatskin. From time to time they scared out various animals from the brush, chasing the creatures after the fashion of dogs and children. Whenever they came to a stream, invariably all four splashed through it, shouting and laughing with delight.

However, there were but two of these streams, and both of them quite small. Their banks indicated that either the season was very far advanced, or else that the streams were at one time vastly larger.

"A rather significant fact," the doctor afterward commented.

Nevertheless, the most impressive thing about all that the doctor learned that day was the strange mariner in which the excursion came to an end. The quartet was at that moment climbing a small hill, apparently on the edge of an extensive range of mountains. An occasional tree, something like an oak, broke the monotony of the brush at this point, and yet it was not until Rolla was quite at the top of the knoll that Kinney could see surrounding country with any degree of clearness. Even then he learned little.

The hill was placed on one edge of a valley about forty miles in width. A good part of it was covered with dusty vegetation, presumably wild; but the rest was plainly under cultivation. There were large green areas, such as argued grain fields; elsewhere were what looked like orchards and vineyards, some of which were in full bloom—refuting the notion that the season was a late one. Nowhere was there a spot of land which might be called barren.

Rolla and her three friends stood taking this in, keeping a rather curious silence meanwhile. At length Cunora gave a deep sigh, which was almost instantly reproduced by all the rest. Corrus followed his own sigh with a frank curse.

"By the great god Mownoth!" he swore fiercely. "It be a shame that we cannot come hence a great deal oftener! Methinks They could allow it!"

"They care not for our longings," spoke Cunora, her eyes flashing as angrily as his. "They give us enough freedom to make us work the better—no more! All They care for is thy herd and my crops!"

"And for the labour," reminded the big man, "of such brains as Rolla's and Dulnop's. It be not right that They should drive us so!"

"Aye," agreed the younger man, with much less enthusiasm. "However, what can ye do about it, Corrus?"

The big man's face flushed, and he all but snarled. "I tell ye what I can do I, and ye as well, if ye but will! I can—"

He stopped, one hand upraised in mighty emphasis, and a sudden and startling change came over him. Downright fear drove the anger from his face; his massive body suddenly relaxed, and all his power and vigour seemed to crumble and wilt. His hands shook; his mouth trembled. At the same time the two women shrank from him, each giving an inarticulate cry of alarm and distress. Dulnop gave no sound, but the anger which had left the herdsman seemed to have come to him; the youngster's eyes flared and his breast heaved. His gaze was fixed upon Corrus's neck, where the sweat of fear already glistened.

Suddenly the big man dropped his head, as though in surrender. He gasped and found voice; this time a voice as shaky and docile as it had been strong and dominant a moment before.

"Very well," he spoke abjectly. "Very well. I—shall do as you wish." He seemed to be talking to thin air. "We—will go home at once."

And instantly all four turned about, and in perfect silence took the back trail.

3

WORLD OF MAMMOTHS

Immediately upon going into teleconsciousness Smith became aware of a decided change in his surroundings. The interior of the study had been darkened with drawn shades; now he was using eyes that were exposed to the most intense sunlight. The first sight that he got, in fact, was directed toward the sky; and he noted with an engineer's keen interest that the colour of the sky was blue, slightly tinged with orange. This, he knew, meant that the atmosphere of Sanus contained at least one chemical element which is lacking on the earth.

For a minute or two the sky remained entirely clear. There were no clouds whatever; neither did any form of winged life make its appearance. So Smith took note of sounds.

Presumably his agent—whoever or whatever it might be— was located in some sort of aircraft; for an extremely loud and steady buzzing, suggesting a powerful engine, filled the engineer's borrowed ears. Try as he might, however, he could not identify the sound exactly. It was more like an engine than anything else, except that the separate sounds which comprised the buzz occurred infinitely close together. Smith concluded that the machine was some highly developed rotary affair, working at perhaps six or eight thousand revolutions a minute—three or four times as fast as an ordinary engine.

Meanwhile his agent continued to stare into the sky. Shortly something arrived in the field of vision; a blurred speck, far to one side. It approached leisurely, with the unknown agent watching steadfastly. It still remained blurred, however; for a long time the engineer knew as little about its actual form as he knew about his mysterious agent.

Then, like a flash, the vision cleared. All the blurring disappeared instantly, and the form of a buzzard was disclosed. It was almost directly overhead, about a quarter of a mile distant, and soaring in a wide spiral. No sound whatever came from it. Smith's agent made no move of any kind, but continued to watch.

Shortly the buzzard "banked" for a sharper turn; and the engineer saw, by the perspective of its apparent speed, that the aircraft whose use he was enjoying was likewise on the move. Apparently it was flying in a straight line, keeping the sun—an object vastly too brilliant to examine—on the right.

The buzzard went out of sight. Once more the clear sky was all that could be seen; that, and the continual roar of the engine, were all that Smith actually knew. He became impatient for his agent to look elsewhere; it might be that the craft contained other specimens of the unknown creatures. But there was no change in the vigilant watch which was being kept upon the sky.

Suddenly the engineer became exceedingly alert. He had noticed something new—something so highly different from anything he had expected to learn that it was some minutes before he could believe it true.

His borrowed eyes had no eyelids! At least, if they did, they were never used. Not once did they flicker in the slightest; not once did they blink or wink, much less close themselves for a momentary rest from the sun's glare. They remained as stonily staring as the eyes of a marble statue.

Then something startling happened. With the most sickening suddenness the aircraft came to an abrupt halt. Smith's senses swam with the jolt of it. All about him was a confused jumble of blurred figures and forms; it was infinitely worse than his first ride in a hoist. In a moment, however, he was able to examine things fairly well.

The aircraft had come to a stop in the middle of what looked like a cane brake. On all sides rose yellowish-green shafts, bearing leaves characteristic of the maize family. Smith knew little about cane, yet felt sure that these specimens were a trifle large. "Possibly due to difference in gravitation," he thought.

However, he could not tell much about the spot on which the machine had landed. For a moment it was motionless; the engine had been stopped, and all was silent except for the gentle rustling of the cane in the field. The unknown operator did not change his position in the slightest.

Then the craft began to move over the surface, in a jerky, lurching fashion which indicated a very rough piece of ground. At the same time a queer, leathery squeaking came to the engineer's borrowed ears; he concluded that the machine was being sorely strained by the motion. At the time he was puzzled to account for the motion itself. Either there was another occupant of the craft, who had climbed out and was now pushing the thing along the ground, or else some form of silent mechanism was operating the wheels upon which, presumably, the craft was mounted. Shortly the motion stopped altogether.

It was then that Smith noticed something he had so far ignored because he knew his own dinner hour was approaching. His agent was hungry, like himself. He noticed it because, just then, he received a very definite impression of the opposite feeling; the agent was eating lunch of some sort, and enjoying it. There was no doubt about this. All that Smith could do was to wish, for the hundredth time, that he could look around a little and see what was being eaten, and how.

The meal occupied several minutes. Not once did the strange occupant of that machine relax his stony stare at the sky, and Smith tried to forget how hungry he was by estimating the extent of his vision. He decided that the angle subtended about a hundred and sixty degrees, or almost half a circle; and he further concluded that if his agent possessed a nose, it was a pretty trifling affair, too small to be noticed. It was obvious, too, that the fellow's mouth was located much lower in the face than normal. He ate without showing a single particle of food, and did it very quietly.

At length hunger was satisfied. There was complete stillness and silence for a moment, then another short lurching journey through the cane; and next, with an abruptness that made the

259

engineer's senses swim again, the fellow once more took to the air. The speed with which he "got away" was enough to make a motorcyclist, doing his best, seem to stand still.

It took time for Smith to regain his balance. When he did, the same unbroken expanse of sky once more met his gaze; but it was not long until, out of the corners of those unblinking eyes, he could make out bleary forms which shortly resolved themselves into mountain tops. It was odd, the way things suddenly flashed into full view. One second they would be blurred and unrecognizable; the next, sharply outlined and distinct as anything the engineer had ever seen. Yet, there seemed to be no change in the focus of those eyes. It wasn't as though they were telescopic, either. Not until long afterward did Smith understand the meaning of this.

The mountains grew higher and nearer. Before long it seemed as though the aircraft was entering some sort of a canon. Its sides were only sparsely covered with vegetation, and all of it was quite brown, as though the season were autumn. For the most part the surface was of broken rock and boulders.

Within a space of three or four minutes the engineer counted not less than ten buzzards. The unknown operator of the machine, however, paid no attention to them, but continued his extraordinary watch of the heavens. Smith began to wonder if the chap were not seated in an air-tight, sound-proof chamber, deep in the hull of some great aerial cruiser, with his eyes glued fast to a periscope. "Maybe a sky patrol," thought the man of the earth; "a cop on the lookout for aerial smugglers, like as not."

And then came another of those terrifying stops. This time, as soon as he could collect his senses, the engineer saw that the machine had landed approximately in the middle of the canon, and presumably among the boulders in its bottom. For all about it were the tops of gigantic rocks, most of them worn smooth from water action. And, as soon as the engine stopped, Smith plainly heard the roar of water right at hand. He could not see it, however. Why in the name of wonder didn't the fellow look down, for a change?

The craft began to move. This time its motion was smoother arguing an even surface. However, it had not gone far before, to the engineer's astonishment, it began to move straight down a slope so steep that no mechanism with which Smith was familiar could possibly have clung to it. As this happened, his adopted eyes told him that the craft was located upon one of those enormous boulders, in the centre of a stream of such absolute immensity that he fairly gasped. The thing was—colossal!

And yet it was true. The unseen machine deliberately moved along until it was actually clinging, not to the top, but to the side of the rock. The water appeared to be about five yards beneath, to the right. To the left was the sky, while the centre of that strange vision was now upon a similar boulder seemingly a quarter of a mile distant, farther out in the stream. But the fellow at the periscope didn't change position one whit!

It was so unreal. Smith deliberately ignored everything else and watched again for indications of eyelids. He saw not one flicker, but noticed a certain tiny come-and-go, the merest sort of vibration, which indicated the agent's heart-action. Apparently it beat more than twice as fast as Smith's.

But it relieved him to know that his agent was at least a genuine living being. For a moment he had fancied something utterly repellent to him. Suppose this Sanusian were not any form of natural creature at all, but some sort of super-machine, capable of functioning like an organism? The thought made the engineer shudder as no morgue could.

Presently the queer craft approached the water closely enough, and at such an angle, that Smith looked eagerly for a reflection. However, the water was exceedingly rough, and only a confused brownish blur could be made out. Once he caught a queer sound above the noise of the water; a shrill hiss, with a harsh whine at the end. "Just like some kind of suction apparatus," as he later described it.

And then, with that peculiar sound fresh in his ears, came the crowning shock of the whole experience. Floating toward the boulder, but some distance away, was what looked like a black seed. Next moment the vision flashed clear, as usual, and the engineer saw that the object was really a beetle; and in a second it was so near that Smith's own body, back on the earth, involuntarily shrank back into the recesses of his chair.

For that beetle was an enormity in the most unlimited sense of the word. It was infinitely larger than any beetle the engineer had ever seen—infinitely! It was as large as a good-sized horse!

But before Smith could get over his amazement there was a rush and a swirl in the water behind the insect. Spray was dashed over the rock, a huge form showed itself indistinctly beneath the waves, and next instant the borrowed eyes were showing the engineer, so clearly as to be undeniable, the most astounding sight he had ever seen.

A fish of mountainous size leaped from the water, snapped the beetle into its mouth, and disappeared from sight. In a flash it had come and gone, leaving the engineer fairly gasping and likewise wondering how he could possibly expect anybody to believe him if he told the bald truth of what he had seen.

For he simply could not have invented anything half as incredible. The fish simply could not be described with ordinary language. *It was as large as the largest locomotive.*

4

THE GOLD-MINER

As for Van Emmon, his experience will have to be classed with Smith's. That is to say, he soon came to feel that his agent was not what is commonly called human. It was all too different. However, he found himself enjoying a field of view which was a decided improvement upon Smith's. Instead of a range which began and ended just above the horizon, his agent possessed the power of looking almost straight ahead.

This told the geologist that his unsuspecting Sanusian was located in an aircraft much like the other. The same tremendous noise of the engine, the same inexplicable wing action, together with the same total lack of the usual indications of human occupancy, all argued that the two men had hit upon

262

the same type of agent. In Van Emmon's case, however, he could occasionally glimpse two loose parts of the machine, flapping and swaying oddly from time to time within the range of the observer, and at the front. Nothing was done about it. Van Emmon came to the same conclusion as Smith; the operator was looking into something like a periscope. Perhaps he himself did not do the driving.

From what the geologist could see of the country below, it was quite certainly cultivated. In no other way could the even rows and uniform growth be explained; even though Van Emmon could not say whether the vegetation were tree, shrub, or plant, it was certainly the work of man-or some-thing mightily like man.

Shortly he experienced an abrupt downward dive, such as upset his senses somewhat. When he recovered, he had time for only the swiftest glance at what, he thought rather vaguely, was a great green-clad mountain. Then his agent brought the craft to one of those nerve-racking stops; once more came a swimming of the brain, and then the geologist saw something that challenged his understanding.

The craft had landed on the rim of a deep pit, or what would have been called a pit if it had not been so extraordinary. Mainly the strangeness was a matter of colour; the slope was of a brilliant orange, and seemingly covered with frost, for it sparkled so brightly in the sun as to actually hurt the eyes. In fact, the geologist's first thought was "A glacier," although he could not conceive of ice or snow of that tint.

Running down the sides of the pit were a number of dark-brown streaks, about a yard wide; Van Emmon could make them out, more or less clearly, on the other side of the pit as well. From the irregular way in which the walls were formed, he quickly decided that the pit was a natural one. The streaks, he thought, might have been due to lava flow.

His agent proceeded to drive straight over the rim and down the slope into the pit. His engine was quite stopped; like Smith, the geologist wondered just how the craft's wheels were operated. Next he was holding his breath as the machine reached so steep a point in the slope that, most surely, no brakes could hold it. Simultaneously he heard the hiss and whine which seemed to indicate the suction device.

"It was a whole lot like going down into a placer mine," the geologist afterward said; and in view of what next met his eyes, he was justified in his guess.

Down crept the machine until it was "standing on its nose." The sun was shining almost straight down into the slope, and Van Emmon forgot his uneasiness about the craft in his interest in what he saw.

The bottom of the pit was perhaps twenty feet in diameter, and roughly hemispherical. Standing up from its bottom were half a dozen slim formations, like idealized stalagmites; they were made of some semitransparent rock, apparently, the tint being a reddish yellow. Finally, perched on the top of each of these was a stone; and surrounding these six "landmarks," 'as Van Emmon called them, was the most prodigious display of wealth imaginable. For the whole queer place was simply sprinkled with gold. Gold—gold everywhere; large nuggets of it, as big as one's fist! Not embedded in rock, not scattered through sand, but lying loose upon the surface of that unbelievable orange snow! It was overwhelming.

The mysterious Sanusian lost no time. Operating some unseen machinery, he caused three shovel-like devices to project from the front of his machine; and these instantly proceeded, so swiftly that Van Emmon could not possibly watch their action, to pick up nuggets and stow them away out of sight in what must have been compartments in the hull. All this was done without any sound beyond the occasional thud of a nugget dropped in the scramble. Suddenly the Sanusian wheeled his machine about and started hurriedly up the slope. Van Emmon judged that the chap had been frightened by something, for he took flight as soon as he reached the top of the pit. And—he left half a million in gold behind him!

This new flight had not lasted two minutes before the geologist began to note other objects in the air. There were birds, so distant that he could not identify them; one came near enough, however, for him to conclude that it was a hawk. But he did not hold to this conclusion very long.

The thing that changed his mind was another aircraft. It approached from behind, making even more noise than the other, and proceeded to draw abreast of it. From time to time Van Emmon's agent turned his mysterious periscope so as to take it all in, and the geologist was able to watch his fill. Whereupon he became converted to a new idea: The birds that Smith and he had seen had not been birds at all, but aircraft built in imitation of them. For this new arrival had been made in almost perfect imitation of a bee! It was very close to an exact reproduction. For one exception, it did not have the hairy appearance so characteristic of bees; the body and "legs" were smooth and shiny. (Later, Van Emmon saw machines which went so far as even to imitate the hairs.) Also, instead of trying to duplicate the two compound eyes which are found, one on each side of a bee's head, a perfectly round representation of a single eye was built, like a conning tower, toward the front of the bow. Presumably, the observer sat or stood within this "head."

But otherwise it was wonderfully like a drone bee. Van Emmon was strongly reminded of what he had once viewed under a powerful lens. The fragile semitransparent wings, the misshapen legs, and even the jointed body with its scale-like segments, all were carefully duplicated on a large scale. Imagine a bee thirty feet long!

At first the geologist was puzzled to find that it carried a pair of many-jointed antennae. He could not see how any intelligent being would make use of them; they were continually waving about, much as bees wave theirs. Evidently these were the loose objects he had already noted. "Now," he wondered, "why in thunder did the builders go to so much trouble for the sake of mere realism?"

Then he saw that the antennae served a very real purpose. There was no doubt about it; they were wireless antennae!

For presently the newcomer, who so far had not shown himself at any point on his machine, sent out a message which was read as quickly as it was received by Van Emmon's agent, and as unconsciously translated:

"Number Eight Hundred Four, you are wanted on Plot Seventeen."

Whereupon Van Emmon's unknown assistant replied at once: "Very well, Superior."

It was done by means of an extremely faint humming device, reminding the geologist of certain wireless apparata he had heard. Not a word was actually spoken by either Sanusian.

Van Emmon kept a close watch upon the conning tower on the other machine. The sun was shining upon it in such a fashion that its gleam made inspection very difficult. Once he fancied that he could make out a short, compact figure within the "eye"; but he could not be sure. The glass, or whatever it was, reflected everything within range.

Was the airman a quadruped? Did he sit or stand upright, like a man? Or did he use all four limbs, animal-fashion? Van Emmon had to admit that he could not tell; no wonder he didn't guess the truth.

Shortly after receiving the summons, the geologist's agent changed his direction slightly; and within ten minutes the machine was passing over a large grain field. On the far edge was a row of trees, and it was toward this that the Sanusian proceeded to volplane, presently coming to another nausea-producing stop. Once more Van Emmon was temporarily helpless.

When he could look again, he saw that the machine had landed upon a steep slope, this time with its nose pointing upward. Far above was what looked like a cave, with a growth of some queer, black grass on its upper rim. The craft commenced to move upward, over a smooth, dark tan surface.

In half a minute the machine had reached the top of the slope, and the geologist looked eagerly for what might lie within the cave. He was disappointed; it was not a cave at all. Instead, another brown slope, or rather a bulging precipice, occupied this depression.

Van Emmon looked closer. At the bottom of this bulge was a queer fringe of the same kind of grass that showed on top of it. Van Emmon looked from one to the other, and all of a sudden the thing dawned upon him.

This stupendous affair was no mountainside; it was neither more nor less than the head of a colossal statue! A mammoth edition of the Goddess of Liberty; and the aircraft had presumed to alight upon its cheek!

The machine clung there, motionless, for some time, quite as though the airman knew that Van Emmon would like to look a long while. He gazed from side to side as far as he could see, making out a small section of the nose, also the huge curves of a dust-covered ear. It was wonderfully life-like.

Next second came the earthquake. The whole statue rocked and swayed; Van Emmon looked to see the machine thrown off. From the base of the monument came a single terrific sound, a veritable roar, as though the thing was being wrenched from the heart of the earth. From somewhere on top came a spurt of water that splashed just beside the craft.

Then came the most terrible thing. Without the slightest warning the statue's great eye opened! Opened wide, revealing a prodigious pupil which simply blazed with wrath!

The statue was alive!

Next second the Sanusian shot into the air. A moment and Van Emmon was able to look again, and as it happened, the craft was now circling the amazing thing it had just quit, so that the geologist could truthfully say that he was dead sure of what he saw.

He was justified in wanting to be absolutely sure. Resting on the solid earth was a human head, about fifty yards wide and proportionately as tall. It was alive; but *it was only the head, nothing more.*

5

THE SUPER-RACE

It will be remembered that Billie wanted to get in touch with a creature having the characteristic which she had said she admired: supremacy"—A worker who is the boss!" Bearing this in mind, her experience will explain itself, dumfounding though it was.

Her first sight of the Sanusian world was from the front of a large building. The former architect was not able to inspect it minutely; but she afterwards said that it impressed her as being entirely plain, and almost a perfect cube. Its walls were white and quite without ornament; there was only one entrance, an extremely low and broad, flat archway, extending across one whole side. The structure was about a hundred yards each way. In front was a terrace, seemingly paved with enormous slabs of stone; it covered a good many acres.

Presumably Billie's agent had just brought her machine from the building, for, within a few seconds, she took flight in the same abrupt fashion which had so badly upset Smith and Van Emmon. When Billie was able to look closely, she found herself gazing down upon a Sanusian city.

It was a tremendous affair. As the flying-machine mounted higher, Billie continually revised her guesses; finally she concluded that London itself was not as large. Nevertheless her astonishment was mainly directed at the character, not the number of the buildings.

They were all alike! Everyone was a duplicate of that she had first seen: cube-shaped, plain finished, flat of wall and roof. Even in colour they were alike; in time the four came to call the place the "White City." However, the buildings were arranged quite without any visible system. And they were vastly puzzled, later on in their studies, to find every other Sanusian city precisely the same as this one.

However, there was one thing which distinguished each building from the rest. It was located on the roof; a large black hieroglyphic, set in a square black border, which Billie first thought to be all alike. Whether it meant a name or a number, there was no way to tell.[1]

Billie turned her attention to her agent. She seemed to be-

---

1. Since writing the above, further investigations have proved that these Sanusian house-labels are all numbers.

long to the same type as Smith's and Van Emmon's; otherwise she was certainly much more active, much more interested in her surroundings, and possessed of a far more powerful machine. She was continually changing her direction; and Billie soon congratulated herself upon her luck. Beyond a doubt, this party was no mere slave to orders; it was she who gave the orders.

Before one minute had passed she was approached by a Sanusian in a big, clumsy looking machine. Although built on the bee plan, it possessed an observation tower right on top of its "head." (The four afterward established that this was the sort of a machine that Smith's agent had operated.) The occupant approached to within a respectful distance from Billie's borrowed eyes, and proceeded to hum the following through his antennae:

"Supreme, I have been ordered to report for Number Four."

"Proceed."

"The case of insubordinancy which occurred in Section Eighty-five has been disposed of."

"Number Four made an example of her?"

"Yes, Supreme."

Whereupon the operator flew away, having not only kept his body totally out of sight all the while, but having failed by the slightest token to indicate, by his manner of communicating that he had the slightest particle of personal interest in his report. For that matter, neither did Supreme.

Scarcely had this colloquy ended than another subordinate approached. This one used a large and very fine machine. She reported:

"If Supreme will come with me to the spot, it will be easier to decide upon this case."

Immediately the two set off without another word; and after perhaps four minutes of the speediest travel Billie had known outside the doctor's sky-car, they descended to within a somewhat short distance from the ground. Here they hovered, and Billie saw that they were stopped above some hills at the foot of a low mountain range.

Next moment she made out the figures of four humans on top of a knoll just below. A little nearer, and the architect was looking, from the air, down upon the same scene which the doctor was then witnessing through the eyes of Rolla, the older of the two Sanusian women. Billie could make out the powerful physique of Corrus, the slighter figure of Dulnop, the small but vigorous form of Cunora, and Rolla's slender, graceful, capable body. But at that moment the other flier began to say to Supreme:

"The big man is a tender of cattle, Supreme; and he owes his peculiar aptitude to the fact that his parents, for twenty generations back, were engaged in similar work. The same may be said for the younger of the two women; she is small, but we owe much of the excellence of our crops to her energy and skill.

"As for the other woman," indicating Rolla, "she is a soil-tester, and very expert. Her studies and experiments have greatly improved our product. The same may be said in lesser degree of the youth, who is engaged in similar work."

"Then," coolly commented the Sanusian whose eyes and ears Billie enjoyed; "then your line of action is clear enough. You will see to it that the big man marries the sturdy young girl, of course; their offspring should give us a generation of rare outdoor ability. Similarly the young man and the older woman, despite their difference in ages, shall marry for the sake of improving the breed of soil-testers."

"Quite so, Supreme. There is one slight difficulty, however, such as caused me to summon you."

"Name the difficulty."

The Sanusian hesitated only a trifle with her reply: "It is, Supreme, that the big man and the older woman have seen fit to fall in love with one another, while the same is true of the youth and the girl."

"This should not have been allowed!"

"I admit it, Supreme; my force has somehow overlooked their case, heretofore. What is your will?"

The commandant answered instantly: "Put an immediate end to their desires!"

"It shall be done!"

At that moment there was a stir on the ground. In fact, this was the instant when Corrus began his vehement outcry against the tyranny of "They." The two in the air came closer; whereupon Billie discovered that Supreme did not understand the language of the humans below.[2]

Yet the herdsman's tones were unmistakably angry.

"You will descend," commented Supreme evenly, "and warn the big man not to repeat such outbreaks."

Immediately Supreme's lieutenant darted down, and was lost to view. The commandant glanced interestedly here and there about the landscape, returning her gaze to Corrus just as the man stopped in mid-speech. Billie was no less astonished than the doctor to see the herdsman's expression change as it did; one second it was that of righteous indignation, the next, of the most abject subservience.

Nevertheless, Billie could see no cause whatever for it; neither did she hear anything. The other flier remained out of sight. All that the architect could guess was that the operator had "got the drop" on Corrus in some manner which was clear only to those involved. Badly puzzled, Billie watched the four humans hurry away, their manner all but slinking.

A moment later still another aircraft came up, and its operator reported. As before, Billie could make out not a single detail of the occupant herself. She, too, wanted the commandant's personal attention; and shortly Billie was looking down upon a scene which she had good reason to remember all the rest of her life.

In the middle of a large field, where some light green plant was just beginning to sprout, a group of about a dozen humans was at work cultivating. Billie had time to note that they were doing the work in the most primitive fashion, employing the rudest of tools, all quite in keeping with their bare heads and limbs and their skin-clad bodies. About half were women.

---

2. The humans did not realize this fact, however; they assumed that "They" always understood.

Slightly at one side, however, stood a man who was not so busy. To put it plainly, he was loafing, with the handle of his improvised mattock supporting his weight. Clearly the two up in the air were concerned only with him.

"He has been warned three times, Supreme," said the one who had reported the case.

"Three? Then make an example of him!"

"It shall be done, Supreme!"

The lieutenant disappeared. Again the commandant glanced at this, that, and the other thing before concentrating upon what happened below. Then Billie saw the man straighten up suddenly in his tracks, and with remarkable speed, considering his former laziness, he whirled about, dodged, and clapped a hand upon his thigh.

Next second he raised an exultant cry. Billie could not understand what he said; but she noted that the others in the group echoed the man's exultation, and started to crowd toward him, shouting and gesticulating in savage delight.

Then something else happened so sudden and so dreadful that the woman who was watching from the earth was turned almost sick.

Like a flash Supreme dropped, headlong, toward the group of humans. In two seconds the distance was covered, and in the last fifth of a second Billie saw the key to the whole mystery.

In that last instant the man who before had seemed of ordinary size, was magnified to the dimensions of a colossus. Instead of being under six feet, he appeared to be near a hundred yards in height; but Billie scarcely realized this till later, it all happened so quickly.

There was an outcry from the group, and then the commandant's aircraft crashed into the man's *hand*; a hand so huge that the very wrinkles in its skin were like so many gullies; even in that final flash Billie saw all this.

Simultaneously with the landing there was a loud pop, while Billie's senses reeled with the stunning suddenness of the impact. Next second the machine had darted to a safe distance, and Billie could see the man gnawing frantically at the back of his hand. Too late; his hand went stiff, and his arm twitched spasmodically. The fellow made a step or two forward, then swayed where he stood, his whole body rigid and strained. An expression of the utmost terror was upon his face; he could not utter a sound, although his companions shrieked in horror. Another second and the man fell flat, twitching convulsively; and in a moment or two it was all over. He was dead!

And then the truth burst upon the watcher. In fact, it seemed to come to all four at the same time, probably by reason of their mental connections. Neither of them could claim that he or she had previously guessed a tenth of its whole, ghastly nature.

The "cane" which Smith had seen had not been cane at all; it had been grass. The "beetle" in the stream had not been the giant thing he had visualized it; neither had that fish been the size he had thought.

Van Emmon's "gold mine" had not been a pit in any sense of the word; it had been the inside of the blossom of a very simple, poppy-like flower. The "nuggets" had been not mineral, but pollen.

As for the incredible thing which Van Emmon had seen on the ground; that living statue; that head without a body—the body had been buried out of sight beneath the soil; and the man had been an ordinary human, being punished in this manner for misconduct.

Instead of being aircraft built in imitation of insects, the machines had been constructed by nature herself, and there had been nothing unusual in their size. No; they were the real thing, differing only slightly from what might have been found anywhere upon the earth.

In short, it had all been simply a matter of view-point. The supreme creature of Sanus was, not the human, but the bee. A poisonous bee, superior to every other form of Sanusian life! What was more—

"The damned things are not only supreme; *the humans are their slaves!*"

6

Impossible, But—

The four looked at each other blankly. Not that either was at a loss for words; each was ready to burst. But the thing was so utterly beyond their wildest conceptions, so tremendously different in every way, it left them all a little unwilling to commit themselves.

"Well," said Smith finally, "as I said in the first place, I can't see how any other than the human form became supreme. As I understand biology—"

"What gets me," interrupted Van Emmon; "what gets me is, *why* the humans have allowed such an infernal thing to happen!"

Billie smiled somewhat sardonically. "I thought," she remarked, cuttingly, "that you were always in sympathy with the upper dog, Mr. Van Emmon!"

"I am!" hotly. Then, with the memory of what he had just seen rushing back upon him: "I mean, I was until I saw—saw that—" He stopped, flushing deeply; and before he could collect himself Smith had broken in again:

"I just happened to remember, doc; didn't you say that the Venusians, in those books of yours, say that Sanus is ruled by the workers?"

"Just what I was wondering about," from Van Emmon. "The humans seem to do all the work, and the bees the bossing!"

The doctor expected this. "The Venusians had our viewpoint—the viewpoint of people on the earth, when they said that the workers rule. We consider the bee as a great worker, don't we? 'As busy as a bee,' you know. None of the so-called lower animals show greater industry."

"You don't mean to say," demanded Smith, "that these Sanusian bees owe their position to the fact that they are, or were, such great workers?"

Before the doctor could reply, Van Emmon broke in. It seemed as though his mind refused to get past this particular point. "Now, why the dickens have the humans allowed the bees to dominate them? Why?"

"We'll have to go at this a little more systematically," remarked Kinney, "if we want to understand the situation."

"In the first place, suppose we note a thing or two about conditions as we find them here on the earth. We, the humans, are accustomed to rank ourselves far above the rest. It is taken for granted.

"Now, note this: the human supremacy was not always taken for granted." He paused to let it sink in. "Not always. There was a time in prehistoric days when man ranked no higher than others. I feel sure of this," he insisted, seeing that Smith was opposed to the idea; "and I think I know just what occurred to make man supreme."

"What?" from Billie.

"Never mind now. I rather imagine we shall learn more on this score as we go on with our work.

"At any rate, we may be sure of this: whatever it was that caused man to become supreme on the earth, that condition is lacking on Sanus!"

Van Emmon did not agree to this. "The condition may be there, doc, but there is some other factor which overbalances it; a factor such as is—well, more favourable to the bees."

The doctor looked around the circle. "What do you think? 'A factor more favourable to the bees.' Shall we let it go at that?" There was no remark, even from Smith; and the doctor went on:

"Coming back to the bees, then, we note that they are remarkable for several points of great value. First, as we have seen, they are very industrious by nature. Second, all bees possess wings and on that count alone they are far superior to humans.

"Third—and to me, the most important—the bees possess a remarkable combination of community life and specialization. Of course, when you come to analyze these two points, you see that they really belong to one another. The bees we know, for instance, are either queens, whose only function is to fertilize the eggs; or workers, who are unsexed females, and whose sole occupations are the collecting of honey, the building of hives, and the care of the young.

"Now," speaking carefully, "apparently these Sanusian bees have developed something that is not unknown to certain forms of earth's insect life. I mean, a soldier type. A kind of bee which specializes on fighting!"

Van Emmon was listening closely, yet he had got another idea: "Perhaps this soldier type is simply the plain worker bee, all gone to sting! It may be that these bees have given up labour altogether!"

"Still," muttered Smith, under his breath, "all this doesn't solve the real problem. Why aren't the *humans* supreme?" For once he became emphatic. "That's what gets me! Why aren't the humans the rulers, doc?" Kinney waited until he felt sure the others were depending upon him. "Smith, the humans on Sanus are not supreme now because they were *never* supreme."

Smith looked blank. "I don't get that."

"Don't you? Look here: you'll admit that success begets success, won't you?"

"Success begets success? Sure! 'Nothing succeeds like success.'"

"Well, isn't that merely another way of saying that the consciousness of superiority will lead to further conquests? We humans are thoroughly conscious of our supremacy; if we weren't we'd never attempt the things we do!"

Van Emmon saw the point. "In other words, the humans on the earth never began to show their superiority until something—something big, happened to demonstrate their ability!"

"Exactly!" cried Kinney. "Our prehistoric ancestors would never have handed down such a tremendous ambition to you and me if they, at that time, had not been able to point to some definite feat and say, 'That proves I'm a bigger man than a horse,' for example."

"Of course," reflected Billie, aloud; "of course, there were other factors."

"Yes; but they don't alter the case. Originally the human was only slightly different from the apes he associated with. There was perhaps only one slight point of superiority; today there are millions of such points. Man is infinitely superior, now, and it's all because he was slightly superior, then."

"Suppose we grant that," remarked the geologist. "What then? Does that explain why the bees have made good on Sanus?"

"To a large degree. Sometime in the past the Sanusian bee discovered that he possessed a certain power which enabled him to force his will upon other creatures. This power was his poisonous sting. He found that, when he got his fellows together and formed a swarm, they could attack any animal in such large numbers as to make it helpless."

"Any creature?"

"Yes; even reptiles, scales or no scales. They'd attack the eyes."

"But that doesn't explain how the bees ever began to make humans work for them," objected Van Emmon.

The doctor thought for a few minutes.

"Let's see. Suppose we assume that a certain human once happened to be in the neighbourhood of a hive, just when it was attacked by a drove of ants. Ants are great lovers of honey, you know. Suppose the man stepped among the ants and was bitten. Naturally he would trample them to death, and smash with his hands all that he couldn't trample.

"Now, what's to prevent the bees from seeing how easily the man had dealt with the ants? A man would be far more efficient, destroying ants, than a bee; just as a horse is more efficient, dragging a load, than a man. And yet we know that the horse was domesticated, here on the earth, simply because the humans saw his possibilities; the horse could do a certain thing more efficiently than a human.

"You notice," the doctor went on, with great care, "that everything I've assumed is natural enough: the combination of an ant attack and the man's approach, occurring at the same time. Suppose we add a third factor: that the bees, even while fighting the ants, also started to attack the man; but that he chanced to turn his attention to the ants *first*. So that the bees let him alone!

"We know what remarkable things bees are, when it comes

to telling one another what they know. Is there any reason why such an experience—all natural enough—shouldn't demonstrate to them that they, by merely threatening a man, could compel him to kill ants for them?"

Billie was dubious for a moment; then agreed that the man, also, might notice that the bees failed to sting him as long as he continued to destroy their other enemies. If so, it was quite conceivable that, bit by bit, the bees had found other and more positive ways of securing the aid of men through threatening to sting. "Even to cultivating flowers for their benefit," she conceded. "It's quite possible."

Smith had been thinking of something else. "I always understood that a bee's stinging apparatus is good for only one attack. Doesn't it always remain behind after stinging?"

"Yes," from the doctor, quietly. "That is true. The sting has tiny barbs on its tip, and these cause it to remain in the wound. The sting is actually torn away from the bee when it flies away. It never grows another. That is why, in fact, the bee never stings except as a last resort, when it thinks it's a question of self-defence."

"Just what I thought!" chuckled Smith. "A bee is helpless without its sting! If so, how can you account for anything like a soldier bee?"

The doctor returned his gaze with perfect equanimity. He looked at Van Emmon and Billie; they, too, seemed to think that the engineer had found a real flaw in Kinney's reasoning. The doctor dropped his eyes, and searched his mind thoroughly for the best words. He removed his bracelets while he was thinking; the others did the same. All four got to their feet and stretched, silently but thoroughly. Not until they were ready to quit the study did the doctor make reply.

"Smith, I don't need to remind you that it's the little things that count. It's too old a saying. In this case it happens to be the greatest truth we have found today.

"Smith"—speaking with the utmost care—"what we have just said about the bee's sting is all true; but only with regard to the bees on the earth. It is only on the earth, so far as we know positively, that the bee is averse to stinging, for fear of losing his sting.

"There is only one way to account for the soldier bee. Its sting has no barbs!"

"No barbs?"

"Why not? If the poison is virulent enough, the barbs wouldn't be necessary, would they? Friends, the Sanusian bee is the supreme creature on its planet; it is superior to all the other insects, all the birds, all the animals; and its supremacy is due solely and entirely to the fact that there are no barbs on its sting!"

7

THE MISSING FACTOR

By the time the four once more got together in the doctor's study, each had had a chance to consider the Sanusian situation pretty thoroughly. All but Billie were convinced that the humans were deserving people, whose position was all the more regrettable because due, so far as could be seen, the insignificant little detail of the barbless sting.

Were these people doomed forever to live their lives for the sake of insects? Were they always to remain, primitive and uncultured, in ignorance of the things that civilization is built upon, obeying the orders of creatures who were content to eat, reproduce, and die? For that is all that bees know!

Perhaps it was for the best. Possibly Rolla and her friends were better off as they were. It might have been that a wise Providence, seeing how woefully the human animal had missed its privileges on other worlds, had decided to make man secondary on Sanus. Was that the reason for it all?

All but Billie scouted the idea. To them the affair was a ghastly perversion of what Nature intended. Van Emmon stated the case in a manner which showed how strongly he felt about it.

"Those folks will never get anywhere if the bees can help it!" he charged." We've got to lend a hand, here, and see that they get a chance!"

Smith said that, so far as he was concerned, the bees might all be consigned to hell. "I'm not going to have anything to do with the agent I had, any more!" he declared. "I'm going to get in touch with that chap, Dulnop. What is he like, doc?"

Kinney told him, and then Van Emmon asked for details of the herdsman, Corrus. "No more bees in my young life, either. From now on it's up to us. What do you think?" turning to his wife, and carefully avoiding any use of her name.

The architect knew well enough that the rest were wondering how she would decide. She answered with deliberation:

"I'm going to stay in touch with Supreme!"

"You are!" incredulously, from her husband.

"Yes! I've got a darned sight more sympathy for those bees than for the humans! The 'fraid-cats!'" disgustedly.

"But listen," protested Van Emmon. "We can't stand by and let those cold-blooded prisoners keep human beings, like ourselves, in rank slavery! Not much!"

Evidently he thought he needed to explain. "A human is a human, no matter where we find him! Why, how can those poor devils show what they're good for if we don't give 'em a chance? That's the only way to develop people—give 'em a chance to show what's in 'em! Let the best man win!"

Billie only closed her mouth tighter; and Smith decided to say, "Billie, you don't need to stand by your guns just because the Sanusian working class happens to be insects. Besides, we're three to one in favour of the humans!"

"Oh, well," she condescended, "if you put it that way I'll agree not to interfere. Only, don't expect me to help you any with your schemes; I'll just keep an eye on Supreme, that's all."

"Then we're agreed." The doctor put on his bracelets. "Suppose we go into the trance state for about three minutes—long enough to learn what's going on today."

Shortly Billie again using the eyes and ears of the extraordinarily capable bee who ruled the rest, once more looked down upon Sanus. She saw the big "city," which she now knew to be a vast collection of hives, built by the humans at the command of the bees. At the moment the air was thick with workers, returning with their loads of honey from the fields which the humans had been compelled to cultivate. What a diabolical reversal of the accepted order of things!

The architect had time to note something very typical of the case. On the outskirts of the city two humans were at work, erecting a new hive. Having put it together, they proceeded to lift the big box and place it near those already inhabited. They set it down in what looked like a good location, but almost immediately took it up again and shifted it a foot to one side. This was not satisfactory, either; they moved it a few inches in another direction.

All told, it took a full minute to place that simple affair where it was wanted; and all the while those two humans behaved as though someone were shouting directions to them—silent directions, as it were. Billie knew that a half-dozen soldier bees, surrounding their two heads, were coolly and unfeelingly driving them where they willed. And when, the work done, they left the spot, two soldiers went along behind them to see that they did not loiter.

As for the doctor, he came upon Rolla when the woman was deep in an experiment. She stood in front of a rude trough, one of perhaps twenty located within a large, high-walled enclosure. In the trough was a quantity of earth, through the surface of which some tiny green shoots were beginning to show.

Rolla inspected the shoots, and then, with her stone knife, she made a final notch in the wood on the edge of the trough. There were twenty-odd of these notches; whereas, on other troughs which the doctor had a chance to see, there were over thirty in many cases, and still no shoots.

The place, then, was an experimental station. This was proven by Rolla's next move. She went outside the yard and studied five heaps of soil, each of a different appearance, also three smaller piles of pulverized mineral—nitrates, for all that the doctor knew. And before Kinney severed his connection with the Sanusian, she had begun the task of mixing up a fresh combination of these ingredients in a new trough. In the midst of this she heard a sound; and turning about, waved a hand excitedly toward a distant figure on the far side of a nearby field.

Meanwhile Smith had managed to get in touch with Dulnop. He found the young man engaged in work which did not, at first, become clear to the engineer. Then he saw that the chap was simply sorting over big piles of broken rock, selecting certain fragments which he placed in separate heaps. Not far away two assistants were pounding these fragments to powder, using rude pestles, in great, nature-made mortars—"pot-holes," from some river-bed.

It was this powder, beyond a doubt, that Rolla was using in her work. To Smith, Dulnop's task seemed like a ridiculously simple occupation for a nearly grown man, until he reflected that these aborigines were exactly like toddling children in intellects.

Van Emmon had no trouble in making connections with Corrus. The herdsman was in charge of a dozen cows, wild looking creatures which would have been far too much for the man had they been horned, which they were not. He handled them by sheer force, using the great club he always carried. Once while Van Emmon was watching, a cow tried to break away from the group; but Corrus, with an agility amazing in so short and heavy a man, dashed after the creature and tapped her lightly on the top of her head. Dazed and contrite, she followed him meekly back into the herd.

The place was on the edge of a meadow, at the beginning of what looked like a grain field. Stopping here, Corrus threw a hand to his mouth and gave a ringing shout. Immediately it was answered, faintly, by another at a distance; and then Van Emmon made out the form of Rolla among some huts on the other side of the grain. She beckoned toward the herdsman, and he took a half-dozen steps toward her.

Just as abruptly he stopped, almost in mid-stride. Simultaneously Van Emmon heard a loud buzzing in either ear. Corrus was being warned. Like a flash he dropped his head and muttered:

"Very well. I will remember—next time." And trembling violently he turned back to his cows.

"Well," remarked the geologist, when the four "came out" of their séance, "the bees seem to have everything their own way. How can we help the humans best? Hurry up with your idea; I'm getting sick of these damned poisoners."

The doctor asked if the others had any suggestions. Smith offered this: why couldn't the humans retire to some cave, or build tight-walled huts, and thus bar out the bees?

No sooner had he made the remark, however, than the engineer declared his own plan no good. "These people aren't like us; they couldn't stand such imprisonment long enough to make their 'strike' worthwhile."

"Is there any reason," suggested Billie, indifferently, "why they couldn't weave face nets from some kind of grass, and protect themselves in that way?"

Smith saw the objection to that, too. "They'd have to protect themselves all over as well; every inch would have to be covered tightly. From what I've seen of them I'd say that the arrangement would drive them frantic. It would be worse than putting clothes on a cat."

"It's a man-sized job we've tackled," commented the doctor. "What Smith says is true; such people would never stand for any measures which would restrict their physical freedom. They are simply animals with human possibilities, nothing more."

He paused, and then added quietly, "By the way, did either of you notice any mountains just now?"

Smith and Van Emmon both said they had. "Why?"

"Of course, it isn't likely, but—did you see anything like a volcano anywhere?"

"No," both replied.

"Another thing," Kinney went on. "So far, I've seen nothing that would indicate lightning, much less the thing itself. Did either of you," explicitly, "run across such a thing as a blasted tree?"

They said they had not. Billie hesitated a little with her reply, then stated that she had noted a tree or two in a state of disintegration, but none that showed the unmistakable scars due to being struck by lightning.

"Then we've got the key to the mystery!" declared the doctor. "Remember how brown and barren everything looks excepting only where there's artificial vegetation? Well, putting two and two together, I come to the conclusion that Sanus differs radically from the earth in this respect:

"The humans have arrived rather late in the planet's history. Or—and this is more likely—Sanus is somewhat smaller than the earth, and therefore has cooled off sooner. At any rate, the relationship between the age of the planet and the age of its human occupancy differs from what it is on the earth."

"I don't quite see," from Smith, "what that's got to do with it."

"No? Well, go back to the first point: the dried-up appearance of things. That means, their air and water are both less extensive than with us, and for that reason there are far fewer clouds; therefore, it is quite possible that there has been no lightning within the memory of the humans."

"How so?" demanded the geologist.

"Why, simply because lightning depends upon clouds. Lightning is merely the etheric electricity, drawn to the earth whenever there is enough water in the air to promote conductivity."

"Yes," agreed Smith; "but—what of it?"

Kinney went on unheeding. "As for volcanoes—probably the same explanation accounts for the lack of these also. You know how the earth, even, is rapidly coming to the end of her Volcanic period. Time was when there were volcanoes almost everywhere on the earth.

"The same is likely true of Sanus as well. The point is," and the doctor paused significantly, "there have been no volcanic eruptions, and no lightning discharges within the memory of Sanusian man!"

What was he getting at? The others eyed him closely. Neither Van Emmon nor Smith could guess what he meant; but Billie, her intuition wide awake, gave a great jump in her chair.

"I know!" she cried. A flood of light came to her face.

"The Sanusians—no wonder they let the bees put it over on them!"

"They haven't got *fire*! They've never had it!"

8

FIRE!

From the corner of his eyes Kinney saw Van Emmon turn a gaze of frank admiration at his wife. It lasted only a second, however; the geologist remembered, and masked the expression before Billie could detect it.

Smith had been electrified by the idea.

"By George!" he exclaimed two or three times. "Why didn't I think of that? It's simple as A, B, C now!"

"Why," Van Emmon exulted, "all we've got to do is put the idea of fire into their heads, and the job is done!" He jumped around in his chair. "Darn those bees, anyhow!"

"And yet," observed the doctor, "it's not quite as simple as we may think. Of course it's true that once they have fire, the humans ought to assert themselves. We'll let that stand without argument."

"Will we?" Smith didn't propose to back down that easy. "Do you mean to say that fire, and nothing more than fire, can bring about human ascendency?"

The doctor felt sure. "All the other animals are afraid of fire. Such exceptions as the moth are really not exceptions at all; the moth is simply driven so mad by the sight of flame that it commits suicide in it. Horses sometimes do the same.

"Humans are the only creatures that do not fear fire! Even a tiny baby will show no fear at the sight of it."

"Which ought to prove," Van Emmon cut in to silence Smith, "that superiority is due to fire, rather than fire due to superiority, for the simple reason that a newborn child is very low in the scale of evolution." Smith decided not to say what he intended to say. Van Emmon concluded:

"We've just got to give 'em fire! What's the first step?"

"I propose," from the doctor, "that when we get in touch this time we concentrate on the idea of fire. We've got to give them the notion first."

"Would you rather," inquired Billie, "that I kept the idea from Supreme?"

"Thanks," returned her husband, icily, "but you might just as well tell her, too. It'll make her afraid in advance, all the better!"

The engineer threw himself back in his seat. "I'm with you," said he, laying aside his argument. The rest followed his example, and presently were looking upon Sanus again.

All told, this particular session covered a good many hours. The four kept up a more or less connected mental conversation with each other as they went along, except, of course, when the events became too exciting. Mainly they were trying to catch their agents in the proper mood for receiving telepathic communications, and it proved no easy matter. It required a state of semi-consciousness, a condition of being neither awake nor asleep. It was necessary to wait until night had fallen on that particular part of the planet.[1]

Van Emmon was the first to get results. Corrus had driven his herd back from the brook at which they had got their evening drink, and after seeing them all quietly settled for the night, he lay down on the dried grass slope of a small hill, and stared up at the sky. Van Emmon had plenty of time to study the stars as seen from Sanus, and certainly the case demanded plenty of time.

For he saw a broad band of sky, as broad as the widest part of the Milky Way, which was neither black nor sparkling with stars, but glowing as brightly as the full moon! From the eastern horizon to the zenith it stretched, a great "Silvery Way," as Van Emmon labelled it; and as the darkness deepened and the night lengthened, the illumination crept on until the band of light stretched all the way across. Van Emmon racked his brains to account for the thing.

Then Corrus became drowsy. Van Emmon concentrated

1. It should be mentioned that all parts of Sanus showed the same condition of bee supremacy and human servitude. The spot in question was quite typical of all the colonies.

with all his might. At first he overdid the thing; Corrus was not quite drowsy enough, and the attempt only made him wakeful. Shortly, however, he became exceedingly sleepy, and the geologist's chance came.

At the end of a few minutes the herdsman sat up, blinking. He looked around at the dark forms of the cattle, then up at the stars; he was plainly both puzzled and excited. He remained awake for hours, in fact, thinking over the strange thing he had seen "in a dream."

Meanwhile Smith was having a similar experience with Dulnop. The young fellow was, like Corrus, alone at the time; and he, too, was made very excited and restless by what he saw.

Billie was unable to work upon her bee. Supreme retired to a hive just before dusk, but remained wide awake and more or less active, feeding voraciously, for hours upon hours. When she finally did nap, she fell asleep on such short notice that the architect was taken off her guard. The bee seemed to all but jump into slumberland.

The doctor also had to wait for Rolla. The woman sat for a long time in the growing dusk, looming out pensively over the valley. Corrus was somewhere within a mile or two, and so Kinney was not surprised to see the herdsman's image dancing, tantalizingly, before Rolla's eyes. She was thinking of him with all her might.

Presently she shivered with the growing coolness, and went into a rough hut, which she shared with Cunora. The girl was already asleep on a heap of freshly gathered brush. Rolla, delightfully free of any need to prepare for her night's rest—such as locking any doors or cleaning her teeth—made herself comfortable beside her friend. Two or three yawns, and the doctor's chance came.

Two minutes later Rolla sat bolt upright, at the same time giving out a sharp cry of amazement and alarm. Instantly Cunora awoke.

"What is it, Rolla?" terror-stricken.

"Hush!" The older woman got up and went to the opening

which served as a door. There she hung a couple of skins, arranging them carefully so that no bee might enter. Coming back to Cunora, she brought her voice nearly to a whisper:

"Cunora, I have had a wonderful dream! Ye must believe me when I say that it were more than a mere dream; 'twere a message from the great god, Mownoth, or I be mad!"

"Rolla!" The girl was more anxious than frightened now. "Ye speak wildly! Quiet thyself, and tell what thou didst see!

"It were not easy to describe," said Rolla, getting herself under control. "I dreamed that a man, very pale of face and most curiously clad, did approach me while I was at work. He smiled and spake kindly, in a language I could not understand; but I know he meant full well.

"This be the curious thing, Cunora: He picked up a handful of leaves from the ground and laid them on the trough at my side. Then, from some place in his garments he produced a tiny stick of white wood, with a tip made of some dark-red material. This he held before mine eyes, in the dream; and then spake very reassuringly, as though bidding me not to be afraid.

"Well he might! Cunora, he took that tiny stick in his hand and moved the tip along the surface of the trough; and, behold, a miracle!"

"What happened?" breathlessly.

"In the twinkling of an eye, the stick blossomed! Blossomed, Cunora, before mine eyes! And such a blossom no eye ever beheld before. Its colour was the colour of the poppy, but its shape—most amazing! Its shape continually changed, Cunora; it danced about, and rose and fell; it flowed, even as water floweth in a stream, but always upward!"

"Rolla!" incredulously. "Ye would not awaken me to tell such nonsense!"

"But it were not nonsense!" insisted Rolla. "This blossom was even as I say: a living thing, as live as a kitten! And as it bloomed, behold, the stick was consumed! In a moment or two the man dropped what was left of it; I stooped—so it seemed—to pick it up; but he stopped me, and set his foot upon the beautiful thing!"

She sighed, and then hurried on. "Saying something further, also reassuring, this angel brought forth another of the strange sticks; and when he had made this one bloom, he touched it to the little pile of leaves. Behold, a greater miracle, Cunora! The blossoms spread to the leaves, and caused them to bloom, too!"

Cunora was eying her companion pretty sharply. "Ye must take me for a simple one, to believe such imagining."

Rolla became even more earnest. "Yet it were more than imagining, Cunora; 'twere too vivid and impressive for only that. As for the leaves, the blossoming swiftly spread until it covered every bit of the pile; and I tell thee that the bloom flowed as high as thy hand! Moreover, after a moment or so, the thing faded and died out, just as flowers do at the end of the season; all that was left of the leaves was some black fragments, from which arose a bluish dust, like unto the cloud that ye and I saw in the sky one day.

"Then the stranger smiled again, and said something of which I cannot tell the meaning. Once more he performed the miracle, and this time he contrived to spread the blossom from some leaves to the tip of a large piece of wood which he took from the ground. 'Twas a wonderful sight!

"Nay, hear me further," as Cunora threw herself, with a grunt of impatience, back on her bed; "there is a greater wonder to tell.

"Holding this big blooming stick in one hand, he gave me his other; and it seemed as though I floated through the air by his side. Presently we came to the place where Corrus's herd lay sleeping. The angel smote one of the cows with the flat of his hand, so that it got upon its feet; and straightway the stranger thrust the flowing blossom into its face.

"The cow shrank back, Cunora! 'Twas deadly afraid of that beautiful flower!"

"That is odd," admitted Cunora. She was getting interested.

"Then he took me by the hand again, and we floated once more through the air. In a short time we arrived at the city of the masters.[2] Before I knew it, he had me standing before the

---

2. Having no microscopes, the Sanusians could not know that the soldier bees were unsexed females; hence, "masters."

door of one of their palaces. I hung back, afraid lest we be discovered and punished; but he smiled again and spoke so reassuringly that I fled not, but watched until the end.

"With his finger he tapped lightly on the front of the palace. None of the masters heard him at first; so he tapped harder. Presently one of them appeared, and flew at once before our faces. Had it not been for the stranger's firm grasp I should have fled.

"The master saw that the stranger was the offender, and buzzed angrily. Another moment, and the master would surely have returned to the palace to inform the others; and then the stranger would have been punished with the Head Out punishment. But instead the angel very deliberately moved the blooming stick near unto the master; and behold, it was helpless! Down it fell to the ground, dazed; I could have picked it up, or killed it, without the slightest danger!

"Another master came out, and another, and another; and for each and all the flowing blossom was too much! None would come near it wittingly; and such as the angel approached with it were stricken almost to death.

"When they were all made helpless the angel bade me hold my hand near the bloom; and I was vastly surprised to feel a great warmth. 'Twas like the heat of a stone which has stood all day in the sun, only much greater. Once my finger touched the bloom, and it gave me a sharp pain."

Cunora was studying her friend very closely. "Ye could not have devised this tale, Rolla. 'Tis too unlikely. Is there more of it?"

"A little. The angel once more took me by the hand, and shortly set me down again in this hut. Then he said something which seemed to mean, 'With this magic bloom thou shalt be freed from the masters. They fear it; but ye, and all like ye, do not. Be ye ready to find the blossom when I bid thee.' With that he disappeared, and I awoke.

"Tell me; do I look mad, to thine eyes?" Rolla was beginning to feel a little anxious herself.

Cunora got up and led Rolla to the entrance. The glow of

"the Silvery Way" was all the help that the girl's catlike eyesight needed; she seemed reassured.

"Ye look very strange and excited, Rolla, but not mad. Tell me again what thou didst see and hear, that I may compare it with what ye have already told."

Rolla began again; and meanwhile, on the earth, the doctor's companions telepathically congratulated him on his success. He had put the great idea into a fertile mind.

Presently they began to look for other minds. It seemed wise to get the notion into as many Sanusian heads as possible. For some hours this search proceeded; but in the end, after getting in touch with some forty or fifty individuals in as many different parts of the planet, they concluded that they had first hit upon the most advanced specimens that Sanus afforded; the only ones, in fact, whose intellect were strong enough to appreciate the value of what they were told. The investigators were obliged to work with Rolla, Dulnop, and Corrus only; upon these three depended the success of their unprecedented scheme.

Rolla continued to keep watch upon Supreme; and toward morning—that is, morning in that particular part of Sanus— the architect was rewarded by catching the bee in a still drowsy condition. Using the same method Kinney had chosen, Billie succeeded in giving the soldier bee a very vivid idea of fire. And judging by the very human way in which the half-asleep insect tossed about, thrashing her wings and legs and making incoherent sounds, Billie succeeded admirably. The other bees in the hive came crowding around, and Supreme had some difficulty in maintaining her dignity and authority. In the end she confided in the subordinate next in command:

"I have had a terrible dream. One of our slaves, or a woman much like one, assaulted me with a new and fearful weapon." She described it more or less as Rolla had told Cunora. "It was a deadly thing; but how I know this, I cannot say, except that it was exceedingly hot. So long as the woman held it in her hand, I dared not go near her.

291

"See to it that the others know; and if such a thing actually comes into existence, let me know immediately."

"Very well, Supreme." And the soldier straightway took the tale to another bee. This told, both proceeded to spread the news, bee-fashion; so that the entire hive knew of the terror within a few minutes. Inside an hour every hive in the whole "city" had been informed.

"Give them time now," said the doctor, "and they will tell every bee on the planet. Suppose we want a couple of weeks before doing anything further? The more afraid the bees are in advance, the easier for Rolla and her friends."

Meanwhile Corrus, after a sleepless night with his cattle, had driven them hurriedly back to the huts surrounding the "experimental station." Here the herdsman turned his herd over to another man, and then strode over among the huts. Outside one of them—probably Rolla's—he paused and gazed longingly, then gave a deep sigh and went on. Shortly he reached another hut in which he found Dulnop.

"I was just going to seek ye!" exclaimed the younger man. "I have seen a wondrous sight, Corrus!"

Thus the two men came to compare notes, finding that each had learned practically the same thing. Corrus being denied the right to visit any woman save Cunora, Dulnop hurried to Rolla and told her what he and the herdsman had learned. The three testimonies made an unshakable case.

"By the great god Mownoth!" swore Corrus in vast delight when Dulnop had reported. "We have learned a way to make ourselves free! As free as the squirrels!"

"Aye," agreed the younger. "We know the method. But—how shall we secure the means?"

Corrus gave an impatient gesture. "'Twill come in time, Dulnop, just as the dream came! Meanwhile we must tell every one of our kind, so that all shall be ready when the day comes to strike!

"Then"—his voice lost its savagery, and became soft and tender—"then, Dulnop, lad, ye shall have thy Cunora; and as for Rolla and I—"

Corrus turned and walked away, that his friend might not see what was in his eyes.

9

FOUND!

It was two weeks to a day when the four on the earth, after having seen very little of each other in the meanwhile, got together for the purpose of finishing their "revelation" to the Sanusians.

"Mr. Van Emmon and I," stated Billie coolly, as they put on their bracelets, "have been trying to decide upon the best way of telling them how to obtain fire."

Neither Smith nor the doctor showed that he noticed her "Mr. Van Emmon." Evidently the two were still unreconciled.

"I argue," remarked the geologist, "that the simplest method will be a chemical one. There's lots of ways to produce fire spontaneously, with chemicals; and this woman Rolla could do it easily."

Billie indulged in a small, superior smile. "He forgets that all these chemical methods require pure chemicals. And you don't find them pure in the natural state. You've got to have fire to reduce them with."

"What's your proposition, then?" from the doctor.

"Optics!" enthusiastically. She produced a large magnifying-glass from her pocket. "All we have to do is to show Dulnop—he's something of a mineralogist—how to grind and polish a piece of crystal into this shape!"

Van Emmon groaned. "Marvellous! Say, if you knew how infernally hard it is to find even a small piece of crystal, you'd never propose such a thing! Why, it would take years—Mrs. Van Emmon!"

Smith also shook his head. "Neither of you has the right idea. The easiest way, under the circumstances, would be an electrical one."

He paused, frowning hard; then vetoed his own plan. "Thunder; I'm always speaking first and thinking afterward. I never used to do it," accusingly, "until I got in with you folks. Anyhow, electricity won't do; you've got to have practically pure elements for that, too."

"Guess it's up to you, doc," said Billie. And they all looked respectfully toward their host.

He laughed. "You three will never learn anything. You'll continue to think that I'm a regular wonder about these things, but you never notice that I merely stay still and let you commit yourselves first before I say anything. All I have to do is select the one idea remaining after you've disproved the rest. Nothing to it!"

He paused. "I'm afraid we're reduced to the spark method. It would take too long to procure materials pure enough for any other plan. Friction is out of the question for such people; they haven't the patience. Suppose we go ahead on the flint-and-spark basis."

They went at once into the familiar trance state. Nightfall was approaching on the part of Sanus in which they were interested. Smith and Van Emmon came upon Dulnop and Corrus as they were talking together. The herdsman was saying:

"Lad, my heart is heavy this night." Much of his usual vigour was absent. "When I were passing Cunora's field this day, some of the masters came and drove me over to her side. I tried to get away, and one threatened to kill. I fear me, lad, they intend to force us to marry!"

"What!" fiercely, from the younger.

Corrus laid a hand upon his arm. "Nay, Dulnop; fear not. I have no feeling for thy Cunora; I may marry her, but as for fathering her children—no!"

"Suppose," through set teeth, "suppose They should threaten to kill thee?"

"I should rather die, Dulnop, than be untrue to Rolla!"

The younger man bounded to his feet. "Spoken like a man! And I tell thee, neither shall I have ought to do with Rolla! Rather death than dishonour!"

Next moment silence fell between them; and then Van Em-

294

mon and Smith noted that both men had been bluffing in what they had said. For, sitting apart in the growing darkness, each was plainly in terror of the morrow. Presently Corrus spoke in a low tone:

"All the same, Dulnop, it were well for me and thee if the secret of the flowing blossom were given us this night. I"—he paused, abashed—"I am not so sure of myself, Dulnop, when I hear Their accursed buzzing. I fear—I am afraid I might give in!"

At this Dulnop broke down, and fell to sobbing. Nothing could have told the investigators so well just how childlike the Sanusians really were. Corrus had all he could do to hold in himself.

"Mownoth!" he exclaimed, his eyes raised fervently. "If it be thy will to deliver us, give us the secret this night!"

Meanwhile, in Rolla's hut, a similar scene was going on under the doctor's projected eye. Cunora lost her nerve, and Rolla came near to doing the same in her efforts to comfort the other.

"They are heartless things!" Rolla exclaimed with such bitterness as her nature would permit. "They know not what love is: They with their drones and their egg-babes! What is family life to Them? Nothing!

"Somehow I feel that Their reign is nearly at an end, Cunora. Perhaps the great secret shall be given us to-night!"

The girl dried her tears. "Why say ye that, Rolla?"

"Because the time be ripe for it. Are not all our kind looking forward to it? Are we not all expecting and longing for it? Know we not that we shall, must, have what we all so earnestly desire?" It was striking, to hear this bit of modern psychology uttered by this primitive woman. "Let me hear no more of thy weeping! Ye shall not be made to wed Corrus!"

Nevertheless, at the speaking of her lover's name, the older woman's lips trembled despite themselves; and she said nothing further beyond a brief "Sleep well." After which the two women turned in, and shortly reached the drowsy point.

Thus it happened that Rolla, after a minute or two, once more aroused Cunora in great excitement, and after securely closing the entrance to the hut against all comers, proceeded to relate what she had seen. She finished:

"The seed of the flower can be grown in the heart of rotting wood!" And for hours afterward the two whispered excitedly in the darkness. It was hard to have to wait till dawn.

As for Corrus and Dulnop, they even went so far as to search the heaps of stone in the mineral yards, although neither really expected to find what they sought.

But the four on the earth, not being able to do anything further until morning, proceeded to make themselves at home in the doctor's house. Smith and the doctor slept together, likewise Billie and Mrs. Kinney; Van Emmon occupied the guest-room in lonely grandeur. When he came down to breakfast he said he had dreamed that he was Corrus, and that he had burned himself on a blazing cow.

Again in the trance state, the four found that Rolla and Cunora, after reaching an understanding with Corrus and Dulnop, had already left their huts in search of the required stone. Five bees accompanied them. Within a few minutes however, Corrus and Dulnop set out together in the opposite direction, as agreed upon; and shortly the guards were withdrawn. This meant that the holiday was officially sanctioned, so long as the two couples kept apart; but if they were to join forces afterward, and be caught in the act, they would be severely punished. Such was bee efficiency—and sentiment.

The doctor had impressed Rolla with the fact that she would find the desired stone in a mountainous country. Cunora, however, was for examining every rock she came to; Rolla was continually passing judgment upon some specimen.

"Nay," said she, for the hundredth time. "'Tis a very bright stone we seek, very small and very shiny, like sunlight on the water. I shall know it when I see it, and I shall see it not until we reach the mountains." Soon Cunora's impatience wore off, and the two concentrated upon making time. By midday they were well into the hills, following the course of a very dry creek; and now they kept a sharp lookout at every step.

Van Emmon and Smith had similarly impressed Corrus and Dulnop with the result that there was no loss of time in the beginning. The two men reached the hills on their side of the valley an hour before the women reached theirs.

And thus the search began, the strangest search, beyond a doubt, within the history of the universe. It was not like the work of some of earth's prehistoric men, who already knew fire and were merely looking up fresh materials; it was a quest in which an idea, an idea given in a vision, was the sole driving force. The most curious part of the matter was that these people were mentally incapable of conceiving that there was intelligence at work upon them from another world, or even that there was another world.

"Ye saw the stars last night?" Corrus spoke to Dulnop. "Well, 'tis just such stars as shall awaken the seed of the flower. Ye shall see!"

Both knew exactly what to look for: the brassy, regularly cut crystals with the black stripings, such as has led countless men to go through untold hardships in the belief that they had found gold. In fact, iron pyrites is often called "fools gold," so deceptive is its glitter.

Yet, it was just the thing for the purpose. Flint they already had, large quantities of it; practically all their tools, such as axes and knives, were made of it. Struck against iron pyrites, a larger, fatter, hotter spark could be obtained than with any other natural combination.

It was Dulnop's luck to see the outcropping. He found the mineral exposed to plain view, a few feet above the bottom of the ravine the two were ascending. With a shout of triumph he leaped upon the rock.

"Here, Corrus!" he yelled, dancing like mad. "Here is the gift of the gods!"

The older man didn't attempt to hide his delight. He grabbed his companion and hugged him until his ribs began to crack. Then, with a single blow from his huge club, the herdsman knocked the specimen clear of the slate in which it was set. Such was their excitement, neither dreamed of marking the place in any way.

First satisfying themselves that the pyrites really could produce "stars" from the flint, the two hurried down-stream, in search of the right kind of wood. In half an hour Corrus came across a dead, worm-eaten tree, from which he nonchalantly broke off a limb as big as his leg. The interior was filled with a dry, stringy rot, just the right thing for making a spark "live."

Then came a real difficulty. It will be better appreciated when the men's childish nature is borne in mind. Their patience was terribly strained in their attempts to make the sparks fly into the tinder. Again and again one of them would throw the rocks angrily to the ground, fairly snarling with exasperation.

However, the other would immediately take them up and try again. Neither man had a tenth the deftness that is common to adults on the earth. In size and strength alone they were men; otherwise—it cannot too often be repeated—they were mere children. All told, it was over two hours before the punk began to smoulder.

"By Mownoth!" swore the herdsman, staring reverently at the smoke. "We have done a miracle, Dulnop—ye and I! Be ye sure this is no dream?"

Quite in human fashion, Dulnop seriously reached out and pinched the herdsman's tremendous arm. Corrus winced, but was too well pleased with the result to take revenge, although the nature of these men was such as to call for it.

"It be no dream!" he declared, still awestruck.

"Nay," agreed Dulnop. "And now—to make the flower grow!"

It was Corrus's lungs which really did the work. His prodigious chest was better than a small pair of bellows, and he blew just as he had been told in the vision. Presently a small flame appeared in the tinder, and leaped eagerly upward. Both men jumped back, and for lack of enough air the flame went out.

"Never mind!" exclaimed Dulnop at Corrus's crestfallen look. "I remember that we must be ready with leaves, and the like, as soon as the blossom appears. Blow, ye great wind-maker, and I shall feed the flower!"

And thus it came about that two men of Sanus, for the first time in the history of the planet, looked upon fire itself. And when they had got it to burning well, each of them stared at his hands, and from his hands to the little heap of "flowers"; from hands to fire they looked, again and again; and then gazed at one another in awe.

10

AT HALF COCK

Rolla and Cunora searched for hours. They followed one creek almost to its very beginning, and then crossed a ridge on the left and came down another stream. Again and again Cunora found bits of mineral such as would have deceived anyone who had been less accurately impressed than Rolla. As it afterward turned out, the very accuracy of this impression was a great error, strange though that may seem. Finally Rolla glanced up at the sun and sighed. "We will have to give it up for this day," she told Cunora. "There be just time enough to return before night." Neither said anything about the half-rations upon which they would be fed in punishment for running away.

So the two started back, making their way in gloomy silence through the woods and fields of the valley. Cunora was greatly disappointed, and soon began to show it as any child would, by maintaining a sullenness which she broke only when some trifling obstacle, such as a branch, got in her way. Then she would tear the branch from the tree and fling it as far as she could, meanwhile screaming with anger. Rolla showed more control.

It was nearing nightfall when they came within sight of the huts. At a distance of perhaps half a mile they stopped and stared hard at the scene ahead of them.

"Hear ye anything, Cunora?" asked the older woman.

The girl's keen ears had caught a sound. "Methinks something hath aroused our people. I wonder—"

"Cunora!" gasped Rolla excitedly. "Think ye that Corrus and Dulnop have succeeded in growing the flower?"

They ran nearer. In a moment it was clear that something most certainly was arousing the people. The village was in an uproar. "Stay!" cautioned Rolla, catching her friend's arm. "Let us use cunning! Mayhap there be danger!"

They were quite alone in the fields, which were always deserted at that hour. Crouching behind a row of bushes, they quickly drew near to the village, all without being seen. Otherwise, this tale would never be told.

For Corrus and Dulnop, after having satisfied themselves that the wondrous flowering flower would live as long as they continued to feed it, had immediately decided to carry it home. To do so they first tried building the fire on a large piece of bark. Of course it burned through, and there had been more delay. Finally Corrus located a piece of slate, so large that a small fire could be kept up without danger of spilling.

The two men had hurried straight for the village. Not once did either of them dream what a magnificent spectacle they made; the two skin-clad aborigines, bearing the thing which was to change them from slaves into free beings, with all the wonders of civilization to come in its train. Behind them as they marched, if they but knew it, stalked the principles of the steam engine, of the printing-press, of scientific agriculture and mechanical industry in general. Look about the room in which you sit as you read this; even to the door-knobs every single item depends upon fire, directly or indirectly! But Corrus and Dulnop were as ignorant of this as their teeth were devoid of fillings.

Not until then did it occur to the four watchers on the earth that there was anything premature about the affair. It was Smith who first observed:

"Say, Van, I never thought to impress Dulnop with any plan for using the fire. How about you and Corrus?"

"By George!" seriously, from the geologist. And immediately the two set to work trying to reach their agents' minds.

They failed! Dulnop and Corrus were both too excited, far too wide awake, to feel even the united efforts of all four on the earth. And the two Sanusians marched straight into the village without the remotest idea of how they should act.

"It is a flower!" he shrieked, frantic with joy. "The flower has come!" the shout was passed along. "Corrus and Dulnop have found the flowering blossom!"

Within a single minute the two men were surrounded by the whole human population of the place. For the most part the natives were too awestruck to come very near; they were content to stand off and stare at the marvel, or fall upon their knees and worship it. It was now so dark that the flames fairly illumined their faces.

Shortly one or two got up courage enough to imitate Dulnop as he "fed the flower;" and presently there were several little fires burning merrily upon the ground. As for the aborigines, they let themselves loose; never before did they shout and dance as they shouted and danced that night. It was this Rolla and Cunora heard.

Before five minutes had passed, however, a scout awakened Supreme. Billie could see that the bee was angry at having been disturbed, but swiftly collected herself as she realized the significance of the scout's report.

"So they have found the terror," she reflected aloud. "Very well. Arouse all except the egg-layers and the drones. We can make use of the food-gatherers as well as the fighters."

The hive was soon awake. Billie was sure that every last bee was greatly afraid; their agitation was almost pitiful. But such was their organization and their automatic obedience to orders, there was infinitely less confusion than might be supposed. Another five minutes had not passed before not only that hive, but all within the "city" were emptied; and millions upon millions of desperate bees were under way toward the village.

Rolla and Cunora knew of it first. They heard the buzzing of that winged cloud as it passed through the air above their heads; but such was the bees' intent interest in the village ahead, the two women were not spied as they hid among the bushes. By this time twilight was half gone. The firelight lit up the crowd

301

of humans as they surged and danced about their new deity. For, henceforth, fire would replace Mownoth as their chief god; it was easy to see that.

Moreover, both Corrus and Dulnop, as primitive people will, had been irresistibly seized by the spirit of the mob. They threw their burden down and joined in the frenzy of the dance. Louder and louder they shouted; faster and faster they capered. Already one or two of their fellow villagers had dropped, exhausted, to the ground. Never had they had so good an excuse for dancing themselves to death!

And into this scene came the bees. Not one of them dared go within ten yards of the flames; for a while, all they did was to watch the humans. Such was the racket no one noticed the sound of the wings.

"Shall we attack those on the edge of the crowd?" one of Supreme's lieutenants wanted to know. The commandant considered this with all the force of what mental experience she had had.

"No," she decided. "We shall wait a little longer. Just now, they are too jubilant to be frightened; we would have to kill them all, and that would not be good policy." Of course, the bee had the pollen crop, nothing more, in mind when she made her decision; yet it was further justified. There was no let-up in the rejoicing; if anything, it became more frantic than before. Darkness fell upon a crowd which was reeling in self-induced mental intoxication.

Rolla and Cunora came a little nearer; and still remaining hidden, saw that more than half their friends had succumbed. One by one the remainder dropped out; their forms lay all about what was left of the fire. The two women could easily see what their friends were blind to: the bees were simply biding their time.

"Ought we not to rush in and warn them?" whispered Cunora to Rolla. "Surely the flower hath driven them mad!"

"Hush!" warned the older woman. "Be quiet! Everything depends upon our silence!"

It was true. Only two of the villagers remained upon their feet, and shortly one of these staggered and fell in his tracks. The one who was left was Corrus himself, his immense vitality keeping him going. Then he, too, after a final whoop of triumph and defiance, absolutely unconscious of the poison-laden horde that surrounded him, fell senseless to the earth. Another minute, and the whole crowd was still.

And the fire had gone out.

The bees came closer. Several thousands of them were stricken by smoke from the embers, and the rest of the swarm took good care to avoid it. They hovered over the prostrate forms of the aborigines and made sure that they were unconscious.

"Is there nothing we can do?" whispered Cunora, straining her eyes to see.

"Nothing, save to watch and wait," returned Rolla, her gaze fixed upon the dark heap which marked her lover's form. And thus an hour passed, with the four on the earth quite unable to take a hand in any way.

Then one of the villagers—the first, in fact, who had dropped out of the dance—stirred and presently awakened. He sat up and looked about him, dazed and dizzy, for all the world like a drunken man. After a while he managed to get to his feet.

No sooner had he done this than a dozen bees were upon him. Terror-stricken, he stood awaiting their commands. They were not long in coming.

By means of their fearful buzzing, the deadly insects guided him into the nearest hut, where they indicated that he should pick up one of the rude hoe-like tools which was used in the fields. With this in hand, he was driven to the little piles of smouldering ashes, where the fires had flickered an hour before.

Hardly knowing what he was doing, but not daring to disobey, the man proceeded to heap dirt over the embers. Shortly he had every spark of the fire smothered beneath a mound as high as his knees. Not till then did any of the others begin to revive.

As fast as they recovered the bees took charge of them. Not a human had courage enough to make a move of offense; it meant certain death, and they all knew it only too well. As soon as they were wide awake enough to know what they were doing, they were forced to search the bodies of those still asleep.

"We must find the means for growing the flower," said Supreme, evidently convinced that a seed was a seed, under any circumstances. And presently they found, tucked away in Corrus's lion-skin, a large chunk of the pyrites, and a similar piece on Dulnop.

"So these were the discoverers," commented Supreme.

"What is your will in their case?" the subordinate asked.

The commanding bee considered for a long time. Finally she got an idea, such as bees are known to get once in a great while. It was simply a new combination—as all ideas are merely new combinations—of two punishments which were commonly employed by the bees.

As a result, eight of the villagers were compelled to carry the two fire-finders to a certain spot on the bank of a nearby stream. Here the two fragments of pyrites were thrown, under orders, into the water; so that the eight villagers might know just why the whole thing was being done. Next the two men, still unconscious, were buried up to their necks. Their heads, lolling helplessly, were all that was exposed. So it was to be the Head Out punishment—imprisonment of one day with their bodies rigidly held by the soil: acute torture to an aborigine. But was this all?

One of the villagers was driven to the nearest hut, where he was forced to secure two large stone axes. Bringing these back to the "torture-place," as the spot was called, the man was compelled to wield one of the clumsy tools while a companion used the other; and between them they cut down the tree whose branches had been waving over the prisoners' heads. Then the villagers were forced to drag the tree away.

All of which occurred in the darkness, and out of sight of Rolla and Cunora. They could only guess what was going on. Hours passed, and dawn approached. Not till then did they learn just what had been done.

The villagers, now all awake, were driven by the bees to the place on the bank of the stream. There, the eight men who had imprisoned the two discoverers told what had been done with the "magic stones." Each villager stared at the offenders, and at something which lay on the ground before them, and in sober silence went straight to his or her work in the fields.

Presently the huts were deserted. All the people were on duty elsewhere. Such bees as were not guarding the fields had returned to the hives. Rolla and Cunora cautiously ventured forth, taking great care to avoid being seen. They hurried fearfully to the stream.

Before they reached the spot Rolla gave an exclamation and stared curiously to one side, where the tree had been dragged. Suddenly she gave a terrible cry and rushed forward, only to drop on her knees and cover her face with hands that shook as with the palsy. At the same instant Cunora saw what had been done; and uttering a single piercing scream, fell fainting to the ground.

Heaped in front of the two prisoners was a large pile of pebbles. There were thousands upon thousands in the heap. Before each man, at a distance of a foot, was a large gourdful of water. To the savages, these told the whole story; these, together with the tree dragged to one side.

Corrus and Dulnop were to be buried in that spot every day for as many days as there were pebbles in the heap; in other words, until they died. Every night they would be dug up, and every morning buried afresh. And to keep them from telling any of the villagers where they had found the pyrites, they were to be deprived of water all day long. By night their tongues would be too swollen for speech. For they had been sentenced to the No Shade torture, as well; their heads would be exposed all day long to the burning sun itself.

11

THE EDGE OF THE WORLD

It is significant that Billie, because of her connection with the bee, Supreme, was spared the sight that the doctor saw from Rolla's point of view. Otherwise, the geologist's wife might have had a different opinion of the matter. As it was—

"Corrus and Dulnop," said she as coolly as Supreme herself might have spoken, "are not the first to suffer because they have discovered something big."

Whereupon her husband's wrath got beyond his grip. "Not the first! Is that all you can say?" he demanded hotly. "Why, of all the damnably cruel, cold-blooded creatures I ever heard of, those infernal bees—"

Van Emmon stopped, unable to go on without blasphemy.

The doctor had got over the horror of what he had seen. "We want to be fair, Van. Look at this matter from the bees' viewpoint for awhile. What were they to do? They had to make sure, as far as possible, that their supremacy would never be threatened again. Didn't they?"

"Oh, but—damn it all!" cried Van Emmon. "There's a limit somewhere! Such cruelty as that—no one could conceive of it!"

"As for the bees," flared Billie, "I don't blame 'em! And unless I'm very much mistaken, the ruling class anywhere, here on the earth or wherever you investigate, will go the limit to hold the reins, once they get them!"

The expression on Van Emmon's face was curious to see. There was no fear there, only a puzzled astonishment. Strange as it may seem, Billie had told him something that had never occurred to him before. And he recognized it as truth, as soon as she had said it.

"Just a minute," remarked Smith in his ordinary voice; "just a minute. You're forgetting that we don't really know whether Rolla and Cunora are safe. Everything depends upon them now, you know."

In silence the four went back into telepathic connection. Now, of course, Smith and Van Emmon were practically without agents. The prisoners could tell them nothing whatever except the tale of increasing agony as their torture went on. All that Van Emmon and Smith could do was lend the aid of their mentality to the efforts of the other two, and for a while had to be content with what Billie, through Supreme, and the doctor, through Rolla, were able to learn. However, Kinney did suggest that one of the other two men get in touch with Cunora.

"Good idea," said Smith. "Go to it, Van Emmon."

The geologist stirred uneasily, and avoided his wife's eyes. "I—I'm afraid not, Smith. Rather think I'd prefer to rest a while. You do it!"

Smith laughed and reddened. "Nothing doing for an old *bach* like me. Cunora might—well, you know—go in bathing, for instance. It's all right for the doctor, of course; but—let me out!"

Meanwhile the two women on Sanus, taking the utmost care, managed to retreat from the river bank without being discovered. Keeping their eyes very wide open and their ears strained for the slightest buzz, the two contrived to pass through the village, out into the fields, and thence, from cover to cover, into the foothills on that side of the valley where their lovers had found the pyrites.

"If only we knew which stream they ascended!" lamented Cunora, as they stood in indecision before a fork in the river.

"But we don't!" Rolla pointed out philosophically. "We must trust to luck and Mownoth, ye and I."

And despite all the effort the doctor could put forth to the contrary, the two women picked out the wrong branch. They searched as diligently as two people possibly could; but somehow the doctor knew, just because of the wrong choice that had been made, that their search would be unsuccessful. He thought the matter over for a few moments, and finally admitted to his three friends:

"I wonder if I haven't been a little silly? Why should I have been so precious specific in impressing Rolla about the pyrites? Pshaw! Almost any hard rock will strike sparks from flint!"

"Why, of course!" exploded Van Emmon. "Here—let's get busy and tell Rolla!"

But it proved astonishingly difficult. The two women were in an extraordinary condition now. They were continually on the alert. In fact, the word "alert" scarcely described the state of mind, the keen, desperate watchfulness which filled every one of their waking hours, and caused each to remain awake as long as possible; so that they invariably fell to sleep without warning. They could not be caught in the drowsy state!

For they knew something about the bees which the four on the earth did not learn until Billie had overheard Supreme giving some orders.

"Set a guard on that river bank," she told her subordinate, "and maintain it night and day. If any inferior attempts to recover the magic stone, deal with him or her in the same manner in which we punished the finders of the deadly flower."

"It shall be done, Supreme. Is there anything further?"

"Yes. Make quite sure that none of the inferiors are missing."

Shortly afterward the lieutenant reported that one of the huts was empty.

"Rolla, the soil-tester, and Cunora, the vineyardist, are gone."

"Seek them!" Supreme almost became excited. "They are the lovers of the men we punished! They would not absent themselves unless they knew something! Find them, and torture them into revealing the secret! We must weed out this flowing blossom forever!"

"It shall be done!"

Such methods were well known to Rolla and Cunora. Had not their fellow villagers, many of them, tried time after time to escape from bondage? And had they not inevitably been apprehended and driven back, to be tortured as an example to the rest? It would never do to be caught!

So they made it a practice to travel only during twilight and dawn, remaining hidden through the day. Invariably one stood watch while the other slept. The bees were—everywhere!

Upon crossing the range of mountains going down the other side, Cunora and Rolla began to feel hopeful of two things—first, that their luck would change, and the wonderful stone be found; and second, that they would be in no danger from the bees in this new country, which seemed to be a valley much like the one they had quit. It was all quite new and strange to them, and in their interest they almost forgot at times that each had a terrible score to settle when her chance finally came.

Twice they had exceedingly narrow escapes. Always they kept

carefully hid, but on the third day Cunora, advancing cautiously through some brush, came suddenly upon two bees feeding. She stopped short and held her breath. Neither saw her, so intent were they upon their honey; yet Cunora felt certain that each had been warned to watch out for her. This was true; Billie learned that every bee on the planet had been told. And so Cunora silently backed away, an inch at a time, until it was safe to turn and run.

On another occasion Rolla surprised a big drone bee, just as she bent to take a drink of water from a stream. The insect had been out of her sight, on the other side of a boulder. It rose with an angry buzz as she bent down; a few feet away from her it hung in the air, apparently scrutinizing her to make sure that she was one of the runaways. Her heart leaped to her mouth. Suppose they were reported!

She made a lightning-like grab at the thing, and very nearly caught it. Straight up it shot, taken by surprise, and dashed blindly into a ledge of rock which hung overhead. For a second it floundered, dazed; and that second was its last. Cunora gave a single bound forward, and with a vicious swing of a palm-leaf, which she always carried, smashed the bee flat.

Before they had been free five days they came to an exceedingly serious conclusion: that it was only a question of time until they were caught. Sooner or later they must be forced to return; they could not hope to dodge bees much longer. When Rolla fully realized this she turned gravely to the younger girl.

"Methinks the time has come for us to make a choice, Cunora. Which shall it be: live as we have been living for the past four days, with the certainty of being caught in time or—face the unknown perils on the edge of the world?"

Cunora dropped the piece of stone she had been inspecting and shivered with fear. "A dreadful choice ye offer, Rolla! Think of the horrible beasts we must encounter!"

"Ye mean"—corrected the philosophical one—"ye mean, the beasts which men *say* they have seen. Tell me; hast ever seen such thyself? Many times hast thou been near the edge, I know."

The girl shook her head. "Nay; not I. Yet these beasts must be, Rolla; else why should all men tell of them?"

"I note," remarked Rolla thoughtfully, "that each man tells of seeing a different sort of beast. Perchance they were all but lies."

However, it was Cunora's fear of capture, rather than her faith in Rolla's reasoning, which drove the girl to the north. For to the north they travelled, a matter of some two weeks; and not once did they dare relax their vigilance. Wherever they went, there was vegetation of some sort, and wherever there was vegetation bees were likely to be found. By the time the two weeks were over, the women were in a state of near-hysteria, from the nervous strain of it all. Moreover, both suffered keenly for want of cereals, to which they were accustomed; they were heartily tired of such fruits and nuts as they were able to pick up without exposing themselves.

One morning before daybreak they came to the upper end of a long, narrow valley—one which paralleled their own, by the way—and as they emerged from the plain into the foothills it was clear that they had reached a new type of country. There was comparatively little brush; and with every step the rockiness increased. By dawn they were on the edge of a plateau; back of them stretched the inhabited country; ahead, a haze-covered expanse. Nothing but rocks was about them.

"Ye are sure that we had best keep on?" asked Cunora uneasily.

Rolla nodded, slowly but positively. "It is best. Back of us lies certain capture. Ahead—we know not what; but at least there is a chance!"

Nevertheless, both hesitated before starting over the plateau. Each gazed back longingly over the home of their kind; and for a moment Holla's resolution plainly faltered. She hesitated; Cunora made a move as though to return. And at that instant their problem was decided for them.

A large drone passed within six feet of them. Both heard the buzz, and whirled about to see the bee darting frantically out of reach. At a safe distance it paused, as though to make sure of its find, then disappeared down the valley. They had been located!

"We have no choice now!" cried Rolla, speaking above a whisper for the first time in weeks. "On, as fast as ye can, Cunora!"

The two sped over the rocks, making pretty good time considering the loads they carried. Each had a good-sized goatskin full of various dried fruits and nuts, also a gourd not so full. In fact, it had been some while since they had had fresh water. Cunora was further weighed down by some six pounds of dried rabbit meat; the animals had been caught in snares. Both, however, discarded their palm leaves; they would be of no further use now.

And thus they fled, knowing that they had, at most, less than a day before the drone would return with enough soldiers to compel obedience. For the most part, the surface was rough granite, with very little sign of erosion. There was almost no water; both women showed intense joy when they found a tiny pool of it standing in a crevasse. They filled their gourds as well as their stomachs.

A few steps farther on, and the pair stepped out of the shallow gully in which they had been walking. Immediately they were exposed to a very strong and exceedingly cold wind, such as seemed to surprise them in no way, but compelled both to actually lean against its force. Moreover, although this pressure was all from the left, it proved exceedingly difficult to go on. Their legs seemed made of lead, and their breathing was strangely laboured. This, also, appeared to be just what they had expected.

Presently, however, they found another slight depression in the rocks; and sheltered from the wind, made a little better progress ahead. It was bitter cold, however; only the violence of their exercise could make them warm enough to stand it. All in all, the two were considerably over three hours in making the last mile; they had to stop frequently to rest. The only compensating thing was their freedom from worry; the bees would not bother them where the wind was so strong. So long as they could keep on the move they were safe.

But what made it worse was the steadily increasing difficulty of moving their legs. For, although the surface continued level, they seemed to be *climbing* now, where before they had simply walked. It was just as though the plateau had changed into a mountain, and they were ascending it; only, upon looking back, nothing but comparatively flat rock met the gaze. What made them lean forward so steeply anyhow?

Rolla seemed to think it all very ordinary. She was more concerned about the wind, to which they had become once more exposed as they reached the end of the rift. On they pressed, five or six steps at each attempt, stopping to rest twice the length of time they actually travelled. It was necessary now to cling to the rock with both hands, and once Cunora lost her grip, so that she would have been blown to one side, or else have slipped backward, had not Rolla grasped her heel and held her until she could get another hand-hold.

"Courage!" gasped Rolla. Perspiration was streaming down her face, despite the bitter cold of the wind; her hands trembled from the strain she was undergoing. "Courage, Cunora! It be not much farther!"

On they strove. Always it seemed as though they were working upward as well as onward, although the continued flatness of the surface argued obstinately against this. Also, the sun remained in the same position relative to the rocks; if they were climbing, it should have appeared overhead. What did it mean?

Finally Rolla saw, about a hundred yards farther on, something which caused her to shout: "Almost there, Cunora!"

The younger girl could not spare breath enough to reply. They struggled on in silence.

Now they were down on their hands and knees. Before half the hundred yards was covered, they were flat on their faces, literally clawing their way upward and onward. Had the wind increased in violence in proportion as the way grew harder, they could never have made it, physical marvels though they were. Only the absolute knowledge that they dared not return drove them on; that, and the possibility of finding the precious stone, and of ultimately saving the two men they had left behind.

The last twenty feet was the most extraordinary effort that any human had ever been subjected to. They had to take turns in negotiating the rock; one would creep a few inches on, get a good hold, and brace herself against the wind, while the other, crawling alongside, used her as a sort of a crutch. Their fingers were bleeding and their finger-nails cracked from the rock and cold; the same is equally true of their toes. Had it been forty feet instead of twenty—

The rocks ended there. Beyond was nothing but sky; even this was not like what they were used to, but was very nearly black. Two more spurts, and Rolla threw one hand ahead and caught the edge of the rock. Cunora dragged herself alongside. The effort brought blood to her nostrils.

They rested a minute or two, then looked at one another in mute inquiry. Cunora nodded; Rolla took great breath; and they drew themselves to the edge and looked over.

12

OUTSIDE INFORMATION

The two women gazed in extreme darkness. The other side of the ridge of rock was black as night. From side to side the ridge extended, like a jagged knife edge on a prodigious scale; it seemed infinite in extent. Behind them—that is, at their feet— lay the stone-covered expanse they had just traversed; ahead of them there was—nothingness itself.

Cunora shook with fear and cold. "Let us not go on, Rolla!" she whimpered. "I like not the looks of this void; it may contain all sorts of beasts. I—I am afraid!" She began to sob convulsively.

Rolla peered into the darkness. Nothing whatever was to be seen. It was as easy to imagine enemies as friends; easier in fact. What might not the unknown hold for them?

"We cannot stay here," spoke Rolla, with what energy her condition would permit. "We could not—hold on. Nor can we return now; They would surely find us!"

But Cunora's courage, which had never faltered in the face of familiar dangers, was not equal to the unknown. She wailed:

"Rolla! A little way back—a hollow in the rock! 'Tis big enough to shelter me! I would—rather stay there than—go on!"

"Ye would rather die there, alone!"

Cunora hid her face. "Let me have half the food! I can go back to the pool—for water! And maybe," hopefully—"maybe They will give up the search in time."

"Aye," from Rolla, bitterly. "And in time Dulnop will die, if we do nothing for him—and for Corrus!"

Cunora fell to sobbing again. "I cannot help it! I am—afraid!"

Rolla scarcely heard. An enormous idea had just occurred to her. She had told the girl to think of Dulnop and Corrus; but was it not equally true that they should think of all the other humans, their fellow slaves, each of whom had suffered nearly as much? Was not the fire equally precious to them all?

She started to explain this to the girl, then abruptly gave it up. It was no use; Cunora's mind was not strong enough to take the step. Rolla fairly gasped as she realized, as no Sanusian had realized before, that she had been given the responsibility of rescuing *a whole race*.

Fire she must have! And since she could not, dared not, seek it here, she must try the other side of the world. And she would have to do it—alone!

"So be it!" she said loudly in a strange voice. "Ye stay here and wait, Cunora! I go on!"

And for fear her resolution would break down, she immediately crept over the edge. She clung to the rock as though expecting to be dragged from it. Instead, as she let her feet down into the blackness, she could feel solid rock beneath her body, quite the same as she had lain upon a moment before. It was like descending the opposite side of an incredibly steep mountain, a mountain made of blackness itself.

The women gave one another a last look. For all they knew, neither would gaze upon the other again. Next moment, with Cunora's despairing cry ringing in her ears, Holla began to crawl backward and downward.

She could plainly see the sun's level rays above her head,

irregular beams of yellowish light; it served slightly to illuminate her surroundings. Shortly, however, her eyes became accustomed to the darkness; the stars helped just as they had always helped; and soon she was moving almost as freely as on the other side.

Once she slipped, and slid down and to one side, for perhaps ten feet. When she finally grabbed a sharp projecting ledge and stopped, her vision almost failed from the terrible effort she had put forth. She could scarcely feel the deep gash that the ledge had made in her finger-tips.

After perhaps half an hour of hard work among bare rocks exactly like those she had quit, she stopped for a prolonged rest. As a matter of course, she stared at the sky; and then came her first discovery.

Once more let it be understood that her view was totally different from anything that has ever been seen on the earth. To be sure, "up" was over her head, and "down" was under her feet; nevertheless, she was stretched full length, face down, on the rock. In other words, it was precisely as though she were clinging to a cliff. Sky above, sky behind and all sides; there were stars even under her feet!

But all her life she had been accustomed, at night, to see that broad band of silver light across the heavens. She had taken it for granted that, except at two seasons of the year, for short periods, she would always see "the Silvery Way." But tonight—there was no band! The whole sky was full of—stars, nothing else!

It will be easier to picture her wonder and uneasiness if she is compared mentally with a girl of five or six. Easier, too, to appreciate the fact that she determined to go on anyhow.

Mile after mile was covered in the darkness. Rolla was on the point of absolute exhaustion; but she dared not sleep until she reached a spot where there was no danger of falling. It was only after braving the gale for over four hours in the starlight that Rolla reached a point where she was no longer half crawling, half creeping, but moved nearly erect. Shortly she was able to face the way she was going; and by leaning backward was

315

able to make swift progress. In another half-hour she was walking upright. Still no explanation of the mystery!

Finding a sheltered spot, she proceeded to make herself comparatively comfortable on the rock. Automatically, from habit, she proceeded to keep watch; then she must have remembered that there was now no need for vigilance. For she lay herself down in the darkness and instantly fell asleep.

Three hours later—according to the time kept by the watchers on the earth—Rolla awoke and sat up in great alarm. And small wonder.

It was broad daylight! The sun was well above the horizon; and not only the Sanusian but the people on the earth were vastly puzzled to note that it was the western horizon! To all appearances, Rolla had slept a whole day in that brief three hours.

Shortly her nerves were steady enough for her to look about, uncomprehendingly, but interestedly, as a child will. There was nothing but rock to be seen; a more or less level surface, such as she had toiled over the day before. The day before! She glanced at the sun once more, and her heart gave a great leap.

The sun was rising—in the west!

"'Tis a world of contraries," observed Rolla sagely to herself. "Mayhap I shall find all else upside down."

She ate heartily, and drank deep from her gourd. There was not a cupful remaining. She eyed it seriously as she got to her feet.

Another look back at that flat expanse of granite, which had so gradually and so mysteriously changed from precipice to plain, and Rolla strode on with renewed vigour and interest. Presently she was able to make out something of a different colour in the distance, and soon was near enough to see some bona-fide bushes; a low, flowerless shrub, it is true, but at least it was a living thing.

Shortly the undergrowth became dense enough to make it somewhat of an effort to get through. And before long she was noticing all manner of small creatures, from bugs to an occasional wandering bird. These last, especially, uttered an abrupt but cheerful chirp which helped considerably to raise her spirits.

It was all too easy to see, in her fancy, her lover helpless and suffering in the power of those cold-blooded, merciless insects.

In an hour or two she reached the head of a small stream. Hurrying down its banks as rapidly as its undergrowth would permit, Rolla followed its course as it bent, winding and twisting, in the direction which had always been north to her, but which the sun plainly labelled "south." Certainly the sun mounted steadily toward the zenith, passing successively through the positions corresponding to four, three and two o'clock, in a manner absolutely baffling.

About noon she came out of the canon into the foothills. Another brief rest, and from the top of a knoll she found herself looking upon a valley about the size of the one she called "home." Otherwise, it was very different. For one thing, it was far better watered; nowhere could she see the half-dried brownishness so characteristic of her own land. The whole surface was heavily grown with all manner of vegetation; and so far as she could see it was all absolutely wild. There was not a sign of cultivation.

Keeping to the left bank of the river, a much broader affair than any she had seen before, Rolla made her way for several miles with little difficulty. Twice she made wide detours through the thicket, and once it was necessary to swim a short distance; the stream was too deep to wade. The doctor watched the whole affair, purely as a matter of professional interest.

"She is a magnificent specimen physically," he said in his impersonal way, "and she shows none of the defects of the African savages."

And such was his manner, in speaking of his distant "patient," that Billie took it entirely as a matter of course, without the slightest self-consciousness because of Van Emmon and Smith.

All this while Rolla had been intent, as before, upon finding some of the coveted crystals. She had no luck; but presently she discovered something decidedly worthwhile—a fallen tree trunk, not too large, and near enough to the bank to be handled without help. A few minutes later she was floating at ease, and making decidedly better time.

317

A half-hour of this-during which she caught glimpses of many animals, large and small, all of which fled precipitately—and she rounded a sharp bend in the stream, to be confronted with a sight which must have been strange indeed to her. Stretching across the river was—a network of rusty wire, *the remains of a reinforced concrete bridge.*

There was no doubt of this. On each bank was a large, moss-grown block of stone, which the doctor knew could be nothing else than the old abutments. Seemingly there had been only a single span.

The woman brought the log to the shore, and examined the bridge closely. Instinctively she felt that the structure argued a high degree of intelligence, very likely human. A little hesitation, and then she beached her log, ascended the bank, and looked upon the bridge from above.

A narrow road met her eyes. Once it might have been twice as wide, but now the thicket encroached until there was barely room enough, judged the doctor, for a single vehicle to pass. Its surface was badly broken up—apparently it had been con-crete—and grass grew in every crack. Nevertheless, it was a *bona-fide* road.

For the first time in a long while, Rolla was temporarily off her guard. The doctor was able to impress her with the idea of "Follow this road!" and to his intense gratification the woman started away from the river at once.

Soon the novelty of the thing wore off enough for her to concern herself with fresh food. She discovered plenty of ber-ries, also three kinds of nuts; all were strange to her, yet she ate them without question, and suffered nothing as a result, so far as the doctor could see.

The sun was less than an hour from the horizon when the road, after passing over a slight rise, swung in a wide arc through the woods and thus unveiled a most extraordinary landscape. It was all the more incredible because so utterly out of keeping with what Rolla had just passed through. She had been in the wilderness; now—

A vast city lay before her. Not a hundred yards away stood a low, square building of some plain, gray stone. Beyond this stretched block upon block—mile upon mile, rather—of *bona-fide* residences, stores and much larger buildings. It is true that the whole place was badly overgrown with all sorts of vegetation; yet, from that slight elevation, there was no doubt that this place was, or had been, a great metropolis.

Presently it became clear that "had been" was the correct term. Nothing but wild life appeared. Rolla looked closely for any signs of human occupancy, but saw none. To all appearances the place was deserted; and it was just as easy to say that it had been so for ten centuries as for one.

"There seems no good reason why I should not go farther," commented Rolla aloud, to boost her courage. "Perchance I shall find the magic stone in this queer place."

It speaks well for her self-confidence that, despite the total strangeness of the whole affair—a city was as far out of her line as aviation to a miner—she went forward with very little hesitation. None of the wild creatures that scuttled from her sight alarmed her at all; the only things she looked at closely were such bees as she met. The insects ignored her altogether, except to keep a respectful distance.

"These masters," observed Rolla with satisfaction, "know nothing of me. I shall not obey them till they threaten me." But there was no threatening.

For the most part the buildings were in ruins. Here and there a structure showed very little damage by the elements. In more than one case the roof was quite intact. Clearly the materials used were exceptional, or else the place had not been deserted very long. The doctor held to the latter opinion, especially after seeing a certain brown-haired dog running to hide behind a heap of stones.

"It was a dog!" the doctor felt sure. To Rolla, however, the animal was even more significant. She exclaimed about it in a way which confirmed the doctor's guess. On she went at a faster rate, plainly excited and hopeful of seeing something further that she could recognize.

She found it in a hurry. Reaching the end of one block of the ruins, she turned the corner and started to follow the cross street. Whereupon she stopped short, to gaze in consternation at a line of something whitish which stretched from one side of the "street" to the other.

It was a line of human skeletons.

There were perhaps two hundred in the lot, piled one on top of the other, and forming a low barrier across the pavement. To Rolla the thing was simply terrible, and totally without explanation. To the people on the earth, it suggested a formation of troops, shot down in their tracks and left where they had fallen. The doctor would have given a year of his life if only Rolla had had the courage to examine the bones; there might have been bullet holes, or other evidence of how they had met their death.

The Sanusian chose rather to back carefully away from the spot. She walked hurriedly up the street she had just left, and before going another block came across two skeletons lying right in the middle of the street. A little farther on, and she began to find skeletons on every hand. Moreover—and this is especially significant—the buildings in this locality showed a great many gaps and holes in their walls, such as might have been made by shell-fire.

This made it easier to understand something else. Every few yards or so the explorer found a large heap of rust in the gutter, or what had once been the gutter. These heaps had little or no shape; yet the doctor fancied he could detect certain resemblances to things he had seen before, and shortly declared that they were the remains of motors.

"Can't say whether they were aircraft or autos, of course," he added, "but those things were certainly machines." Later, Rolla paid more attention to them, and the doctor positively identified them as former motor-cars.

The sun had gone down. It was still quite light, of course; darkness would not come for a couple of hours. Rolla munched on what food she had, and pressed on through the ruins. She saw skeletons and rusted engines everywhere, and once passed a rounded heap of rust which looked like nothing so much as a large cannon shell. Had the place been the scene of a battle?

Just when she had got rather accustomed to the place and was feeling more or less at her ease, she stopped short. At the same time the doctor himself fairly jumped in his chair. Somewhere, right near at hand, on one of the larger structures, a bell began to ring!

It clanged loudly and confidently, giving out perhaps thirty strokes before it stopped. The stillness which followed was pretty painful. In a moment, however, it was broken as effectively as any silence can be broken.

A man's voice sounded within the building.

Immediately it was replied to, more faintly, by several others. Then came the clatter of some sort of utensils, and sundry other noises which spoke loudly of humans. Rolla froze in her tracks, and her teeth began to chatter.

Next moment she got a grip on herself. "What difference doth it make, whether they be friend or enemy?" she argued severely, for the benefit of her shaking nerves. "They will give thee food, anyhow. And perchance they know where liveth the magic stone!"

In the end Rolla's high purpose prevailed over her weak knees, and she began to look for the entrance to the place. It was partly in ruins-that is, the upper stories-but the two lower floors seemed, so far as their interior could be seen through the high, unglazed windows, to be in good condition. There were no doors on that street.

Going around the corner, however, Rolla saw a high archway at the far corner of the structure. Approaching near enough to peek in, she saw that this arch provided an opening into a long corridor, such as might once have served as a wagon or auto entrance. After a little hesitation she went in.

She passed a door, a massive thing of solid brassy metal, such as interested the doctor immensely but only served to confuse the explorer. A little farther on, and the corridor became pretty dark. She passed another brass door, and approached the end of the pavement. There was one more door there; and she noted with excitement that it was open.

She came closer and peered in. The room was fairly well lighted, and what she saw was clear-cut and unmistakable. In the middle of the room was a long table, and seated about it, in perfect silence, sat an even dozen men.

13

THE TWELVE

For a minute or two Rolla was not observed. She simply stood and stared, being neither confident enough to go forward nor scared enough to retreat. Childlike, she scrutinized the group with great thoroughness.

Their comparatively white faces and hands puzzled her most. Also, she could not understand the heavy black robes in which all were dressed. Falling to the floor and reaching far above their necks, such garments would have been intolerable to the free-limbed Sanusians. To the watchers on the earth, however, the robes made the group look marvellously like a company of monks.

Not that there was anything particularly religious about the place or in their behaviour. All twelve seemed to be silent only because they were voraciously hungry. A meal was spread on the table.

Except for the garments, the twelve might have been so many harvest hands, gathered for the evening meal in the cook-house. From the white-bearded man who sat at the head of the table and passed out large helpings of something from a big pot, to the fair-haired young fellow at the foot, who could scarcely wait for his share, there was only one thing about them which might have been labelled pious; and that was their attitude, which could have been interpreted: "Give us this day our daily bread—and hurry up about it!"

Apparently Rolla was convinced that these men were thoroughly human, and as such fairly safe to approach. For she allowed her curiosity to govern her caution, and proceeded to sidle through the doorway. Half-way through she caught a whiff of the food, and her sidling changed to something faster.

At that instant she was seen. A tall, dark-haired chap on the far side of the table glanced up and gave a sharp, startled exclamation. Instantly the whole dozen whirled around and with one accord shot to their feet.

Rolla stopped short.

There was a second's silence; then the white-bearded man, who seemed to be the leader of the group, said something peremptory in a deep, compelling voice. Rolla did not understand.

He repeated it, this time a little less commandingly; and Rolla, after swallowing desperately, inclined her head in the diffident way she had, and said:

"Are ye friends or enemies?"

Eleven of the twelve looked puzzled. The dark-haired man, who had been the first to see her, however, gave a muttered exclamation; then he cogitated a moment, wet his lips and said something that sounded like: "What did you say? Say it again!"

Rolla repeated.

The dark-haired man listened intently. Immediately he fell to nodding with great vigour, and thought deeply again before making another try: "We are your friends. Whence came ye, and what seek ye?"

Rolla had to listen closely to what he said. The language was substantially the same as hers; but the verbs were misplaced in the sentences, the accenting was different, and certain of the vowels were flatted. After a little, however, the man caught her way of talking and was able to approximate it quite well, so that she understood him readily.

"I seek," Rolla replied, "food and rest. I have travelled far and am weary."

"Ye look it," commented the man. His name, Rolla found out later, was Somat. "Ye shall have both food and rest. However, whence came ye?"

"From the other side of the world," answered Rolla calmly.

Instantly she noted that the twelve became greatly excited when Somat translated her statement. She decided to add to the scene.

"I have been away from my people for many days," and she held up one hand with the five fingers spread out, opening and closing them four times, to indicate twenty.

"Ye came over the edge of the world!" marvelled Somat. "It were a dangerous thing to do, stranger!"

"Aye," agreed Rolla, "but less dangerous than that from which I fled. However," impatiently, "give me the food ye promised; I can talk after my stomach be filled."

"Of a surety," replied Somat apologetically. "I were too interested to remember thy hunger." He spoke a word or two, and one of his companions brought another stool, also dishes and table utensils.

Whereupon the watchers on the earth got a first-class surprise. Here they had been looking upon twelve men, living in almost barbaric fashion amid the ruins of a great city; but the men had been eating from hand-painted china of the finest quality, and using silverware that was simply elegant, nothing less! Luxury in the midst of desolation!

Rolla, however, paid little attention to these details. She was scarcely curious as to the food, which consisted of some sort of vegetable and meat stew, together with butterless bread, a kind of small-grained corn on the cob, a yellowish root-vegetable not unlike turnips, and large quantities of berries. She was too hungry to be particular, and ate heartily of all that was offered, whether cooked or uncooked. The twelve almost forgot their own hunger in their interest in the stranger.

It was now pretty dark in the big room. The white-bearded man said something to the young fellow at the foot of the table, whereupon the chap got up and stepped to the nearest wall, where he pressed something with the tip of his finger. Instantly the room was flooded with white light—from two incandescent bulbs!

Rolla leaped to her feet in amazement, bunking painfully in the unaccustomed glare.

"What is this?" she demanded, all the more furiously to hide her fear. "Ye would not trick me with magic; ye, who call yourselves friends!"

Somat interpreted this to the others. Some laughed; others looked pityingly at her. Somat explained:

"It is nothing, stranger. Be not afraid. We forgot that ye might know nothing of this 'magic.'" He considered deeply, apparently trying to put himself in her place. "Know ye not fire?" Of course, she did not know what he meant. "Then," with an inspiration, "perchance ye have see the flower, the red flower, ye might call—"

"Aye!" eagerly. "Doth it grow here?"

Somat smiled with satisfaction, and beckoned for her to follow him. He led the way through a small door into another room, evidently used as a kitchen. There he pointed to a large range, remarkably like the up-to-date article known on the earth.

"The flower 'groweth' here," said he, and lifted a lid from the stove. Up shot the flame.

"Great Mownoth!" shouted Holla, forgetting all about her hunger. "I have found it—the precious flower itself!"

Somat humoured her childlike view-point. "We have the seed of the flower, too," said he. He secured a box of matches from a shelf, and showed her the "little sticks."

"Exactly what the angel showed me!" jubilated Holla. "I have come to the right place!"

Back she went to her food, her face radiant, and all her lurking suspicion of the twelve completely gone. From that time on she had absolute and unquestioning confidence in all that was told her. In her eyes, the twelve were simply angels or gods who had seen fit to clothe themselves queerly and act human.

Supper over, she felt immensely tired. All the strain of the past three weeks had to have its reaction. Like a very tired, sleepy child, she was led to a room in another part of the building, where she was shown an ordinary sleeping-cot. She promptly pulled the mattress onto the floor, where she considered it belonged, and fell fast asleep.

Meanwhile, back on the earth, Van Emmon and Smith had lost no time in making use of the doctor's description of the twelve. Within a few minutes they had new agents; Van Emmon used Somat's eyes and ears, while Smith got in touch with the elderly bearded man at the head of the table. His name was Deltos.

"A very striking confirmation of the old legends," he was saying through a big yawn, as Smith made connection. He used a colloquial type of language, quite different from the lofty, dignified speech of the Sanusians. "That is, of course, if the woman is telling the truth."

"And I think she is," declared the young fellow at the foot of the table. "It makes me feel pretty small, to think that none of us ever had the nerve to make the trip; while she, ignorant as she is, dared it all and succeeded!"

"You forget, Sorplee," reminded Somat, "that such people are far hardier than we. The feat is one that requires apelike ability. The only thing that puzzled me is—why did she do it at all?"

"It will have to remain a puzzle until she awakens," said Deltos, rising from the table. "Lucky for us, Somat, that you saw fit to study the root tongues. Otherwise we'd have to converse by signs."

Neither Smith nor Van Emmon learned anything further that night. The twelve were all very tired, apparently, and went right to bed; a procedure which was straightway seconded by the four watchers on the earth. Which brings us in the most ordinary manner to the events of the next day.

After breakfast all but Somat left the place and disappeared in various directions; and Rolla noted that the robes were, evidently, worn only at meal time. Most of the men were now dressed in rough working garments, similar to what one sees in modern factories. Whimsical sort of gods, Rolla told herself, but gods just the same.

"Tell me," began Somat, as the woman sat on the floor before him—he could not get her to use a chair"—tell me, what caused thee to leave thy side of the world? Did ye arouse the wrath of thy fellow creatures?"

"Nay," answered Rolla, and proceeded to explain, in the wrong order, as a child might, by relating first the crossing of the ridge, the flight from the bees, the "masters'" cruel method of dealing with Corrus and Dulnop, and finally the matter of the fire itself, the real cause of the whole affair. Somat was intelligent enough to fill in such details as Rolla omitted.

"Ye did right, and acted like the brave girl ye are!" he exclaimed, when Rolla had finished. However, he did not fully appreciate what she had meant by "the winged masters," and not until she pointed out some bees and asked if, on this part of the planet, such were the rulers of the humans, that the man grasped the bitter irony of it all.

"What! Those tiny insects rule thy lives!" It took him some time to comprehend the deadly nature of their stings, and the irresistible power of concerted effort; but in the end he commented: "'Tis not so strange, now that I think on it. Mayhap life is only a matter of chance, anyway."

Presently he felt that he understood the Sanusian situation. He fell silent; and Rolla, after waiting as long as her patience would allow, finally put the question temporarily uppermost in her mind:

"It is true that I have crossed the edge of the world. And yet, I understand it not at all. Can ye explain the nature of this strange world we live upon, Somat?" There was infinite respect in the way Rolla used his name; had she known a word to indicate human infallibility, such as "your majesty," she would have used it. "There is a saying among our people that the world be round. How can this be so?"

"Yet it is true," answered Somat, "although ye must know that it be not round like a fruit or a pebble. No more is it flat, like this," indicating the lid of the stove, near which they sat. "Instead, 'tis shaped thus"—and he took from his finger a plain gold band, like an ordinary wedding ring—"the world is shaped like that!"

Rolla examined the ring with vast curiosity. She had never seen the like before, and was quite as much interested in the

327

metal as in the thing it illustrated. Fortunately the band was so worn that both edges were nearly sharp, thus corresponding with the knifelike ridge over which she had crawled.

"Now," Somat went on, "ye and your people live on the inner face of the world," indicating the surface next his skin, "while I and my kind live on the outer face. Were it not for the difficulties of making the trip, we should have found you out ere this."

Rolla sat for a long time with the ring in her hand, pondering the great fact she had just learned. And meanwhile, back on the earth, four excited citizens were discussing this latest discovery.

"An annular world!" exclaimed the doctor, his eyes sparkling delightedly. "It confirms the nebular hypothesis!"

"How so?" Smith wanted to know.

"Because it proves that the process of condensation and concentration, which produces planets out of the original gases can take place at uneven speeds! Instead of concentrating to the globular form, Sanus cooled too quickly; she concentrated while she was still a ring!"

Smith was struck with another phase of the matter. "Must have a queer sort of gravitation," he pointed out. "Seems to be the same, inside the ring or outside. Surely, doc it can't be as powerful as it is here on the earth?"

"No; not likely."

"Then, why hasn't it made a difference in the inhabitants? Seems to me the humans would have different structure."

"Not necessarily. Look at it the other way around; consider what an enormous variety of animal forms we have here, all developed under the same conditions. The humming-bird and the python, for instance. Gravitation needn't have anything to do with it."

Billie was thinking mainly of the question of day and night. "The ring must be inclined at an angle with the sun's rays," she observed. "That being the case, Sanus has two periods each year when there is continuous darkness on the inner face; might last a week or two. Do you suppose the people all hibernate during those seasons?" But no one had an answer to that.

Van Emmon said he would give all he was worth to explore the Sanusian mountains long enough to learn their geology. He said that the rocks ought to produce some new mineral forms, due to the peculiar condition of strain they would be subjected to.

"I'm not sure," said he thoughtfully, "but I shouldn't be surprised if there's an enormous amount of carbon there. Maybe diamonds are as plentiful as coal is here."

At the word "diamonds" Smith glanced covertly at Billie's left hand. But she had hidden it in the folds of her skirt. Next moment the doctor warned them to be quiet; Somat and Rolla were talking again.

He was telling her about his world. She learned that his people, who had never concerned themselves with her side of the planet, had progressed enormously beyond the Sanusians. Rolla did not understand all that he told her; but the people on the earth gathered, in one way or another, that civilization had proceeded about as far as that of the year 1915 in Europe. All this, while fellow humans only a few thousand miles away, not only failed to make any progress at all, but lived on, century after century, the absolute slave of a race of bees!

But it was a fact. The ancient city in which Rolla found herself had been, only a generation before, a flourishing metropolis, the capital of a powerful nation. There had been two such nations on that side of the planet, and the most violent rivalry had existed between them.

"However," Somat told Rolla, "'twas not this rivalry which wrought their downfall, except indirectly. The last great war between them was terrible, but not disastrous. Either could have survived that.

"But know you that the ruler of one of the nations, in order to carry on this war—which was a war of commerce (never mind what that means)—in order to carry it on was obliged to make great concessions to his people. In the other nation, the ruler oppressed the workers, instead, and drove them mad with his cruelty. So that, not long after the end of the war, there was a great rebellion among the people who had been so long oppressed, and their government was overthrown."

Back on the earth the four investigators reflected on this in amazement. The case was wonderfully like that of Russia after the great war. Perhaps—

"Immediately the other nation forced its soldiers to fight the victorious rebels. But at home the workers had tasted of power. Many refused to work at all; and one day, behold, there were two rebellions instead of one! And within a very short time the whole world was governed by—the working class!"

So this was what the Venusians had meant when they wrote that Sanus was ruled by the workers!

"What became of these rebellions?" Rolla asked, little understanding what it meant, but curious anyhow.

"Devastation!" stated Somat solemnly. He waved a hand, to include all that lay within the ruined city. "Not altogether because of the workers, although they were scarcely fit for ruling but because the former rulers and others of that kind, who liked to oppose their wills upon others, saw fit to start a fresh rebellion. Conflict followed conflict; sometimes workers were in power, and sometimes aristocrats. But the fighting ended not until"—he drew a deep breath—"until there were none left to fight!"

"Ye mean," demanded Rolla incredulously, "that your people killed themselves off in this fashion?"

"Aye," sorrowfully. "There were a few of us—they called us 'the middle class'—who urged equality. We wanted a government in which all classes were represented fairly; what we called a democracy. Once the experiment was started, but it failed.

"Saw ye the skeletons in the streets?" he went on. "'Twas a dreadful sight, those last few days. I were but a lad, yet I remember it all too well." He paused, then broke out fiercely: "I tell ye that I saw brother slay brother, father slay son, son slay mother, in those last days!

"Lucky am I that I fled, I and my parents! They took me to a mountainous country, but even there the madness spread, and one day a soldier of the army killed my father and my mother.

He sought me, also, that he might slay me; but I hid from him beneath a heap of manure. Aye," he gritted savagely, "I owe my life to a pile of manure!

"These other eleven men all have like tales to tell. Only one woman survived those awful days. Young Sorplee is her son; his father was a soldier, whom she herself slew with her own hands. Even she is now dead.

"Well," he finished, after a long pause, "when the madness had spent itself, we who remained came from our hiding-places to find our world laid waste. 'Tis now thirty years since Sorplee's mother died, since we first looked upon these ruins, and we have made barely a beginning. We have little heart for the work. Of what use is it, with no women to start the race afresh?"

Rolla started despite herself. Was this the reason why she, despite her savagery, had been made so welcome?

"Ye have not told me," said she hurriedly, "why ye and the others all wear such curious garments when ye eat."

Somat was taken off his guard. He had been chuckling to himself at the woman's childlike mind. Now he had to look apologetic and not a little sheepish as he made reply:

"The robes are a mere custom. It were started a great many years ago, by the founders of a—a—" He tried to think of a simpler expression than "college fraternity." "A clan," he decided. "All of we men were members of that clan."

"And," pursued Rolla, "will ye give me the magic stone, that I may take the flowing blossoms back to my people, and release my loved one from the masters' cruelty?" The great question was put! Rolla waited in tremulous anxiety for the answer.

"Aye, stranger!" replied Somat vigorously. "More; ye shall have some of the little sticks!"

Whereupon Rolla leaped to her feet and danced in sheer delight. Somat looked on and marvelled. Then, abruptly, he got up and marched away. He had not seen a woman in thirty years; and he was a man of principle.

That night, when the twelve were again seated at the table, Somat related this conversation with Rolla. Since he used his own language, of course she did not understand what was said. "And I told her," he concluded, "how we came to be here; also the reason for the condition of things. But I doubt if she understood half what I said. We have quite a problem before us," he added. "What shall we do about it?"

"You mean this woman?" Deltos asked. Rolla was busy with her food. "It seems to me, brothers, that Providence has miraculously come to our aid. If we can handle her people rightly the future of the race is assured."

Somat thought it was simple enough. "All we need to do is send this woman back with a supply of matches, and implicit instructions as to how best to proceed against the bees. Once released, their friends can make their way over the edge and settle among us. Let the bees keep their country."

The two who had seconded him before again showed agreement. Sorplee and Deltos, however, together with the other seven, were distinctly opposed to the method. "Somat," protested Deltos, as though surprised, "you forget that there's an enormous population over there. Let them come in of their own free will? Why, they would overrun our country! What would become of us?"

"We'd have to take our chances, replied Somat energetically, "like good sports! If we can't demonstrate our worth to them, enough to hold their respect, we'd deserve to be snowed under!"

"Not while I'm alive!" snarled Sorplee. "If they come here, they've got to give up their wilderness ways, right off! We can't stand savagery! The safest thing for us, and the best for them, is to make an industrial army of 'em and set 'em to work!" His enthusiasm was boundless.

"I must say," admitted Deltos, with his usual dignity, "that you have the right idea, Sorplee. If I had stated it, however, I should have been more frank about it. The arrangements you propose simply means that we are to take possession of them!"

"What!" shouted Somat, horrified.

"Why, of course! Make slaves of them! What else?"

14

THE SLAVE RAID

Despite all that Somat and his two backers could say, the other nine men swiftly agreed upon the thing Deltos had proposed. Somat went so far as to declare that he would warn Rolla; but he was instantly given to understand that any such move would be disastrous to himself. In the end he was made to agree not to tell her.

"We aren't going to let you and your idealism spoil our only chance to save the race!" Sorplee told him pugnaciously; and Somat gave his word. At first he hoped that the nine might fall out among themselves when it came to actually enslaving the Sanusians; but he soon concluded that, if there was any difference of opinion, the aristocratic element would take charge of half the captives, while Sorplee's friends commandeered the rest. The outlook was pretty black for Rolla's friends; yet there was nothing whatever to do about it.

Among the four people on the earth, however, the thing was being discussed even more hotly. Van Emmon found himself enthusiastically backing Somat, the liberal-minded one.

"He's got the right idea," declared the geologist. "Let the Sanusians come over of their own free will! Let the law of competition show what it can do! Dandy experiment!"

Smith could not help but put in: "Perhaps it's Deltas and Sorplee who are right, Van. These Sanusians are mere aborigines. They wouldn't understand democratic methods."

"No?" politely, from the doctor. "Now, from what I've seen of Rolla, I'll say she's a perfect example of 'live-and-let-live.' Nothing either subservient or autocratic in her relations with other people. Genuinely democratic, Smith."

"Meanwhile," remarked Billie, with exaggerated nonchalance, "meanwhile, what about the bees? Are they going to be permitted to show their superiority or not?" Van Emmon took this to be aimed at him. "Of course not! We can't allow a race of human beings to be dominated forever by insects!

"I say, let's get together and put Rolla wise to what Deltos and Sorplee are framing up! We can do it, if we concentrate upon the same thought at the right time!"

Smith did not commit himself. "I don't care much either way," he decided. "Go ahead if you want to"—meaning Van Emmon and the doctor—"I don't want to butt in."

"Don't need you," growled the geologist. "Two of us is enough."

"Is that so?" sarcastically, from Billie. "Well, it'll take more than two of you to get it over to Rolla!"

"What do you mean?" hotly.

"I mean," with deliberation,—"that if you and the doctor try to interfere I'll break up our circle here!" They stared at her incredulously. "I sure will! I'm not going to lend my mental influence for any such purpose!"

"My dear," protested the doctor gently, "you know how it is: the combined efforts of the four of us is required in order to keep in touch with Sanus. Surely you would not—"

"Oh, yes, I would!" Billie was earnestness itself. "Mr. Van Emmon was so good as to blame me for what I did in that Capellette mix-up; now, if you please, I'm going to see to it that this one, anyhow, works itself out without our interference!"

"Well, I'll be darned!" The geologist looked again, to make sure it was really his wife who had been talking thus. "I'm mighty glad to know that you're not intending to warn Supreme, anyhow!"

"Maybe I shall! snapped Billie.

"If you do," stated the doctor quietly, "then I'll break the circle myself." They looked at him with a renewal of their former respect as he concluded emphatically: "If you won't help us stop this slave raid, Billie, then, by George, you'll at least let the bees fight it out on their own!"

And so the matter stood, so far as the investigators were concerned. They were to be lookers-on, nothing more.

Meanwhile the survivors of a once great civilization prepared to move in person against the bees. They did this after Deltos had pointed out the advantages of such a step.

"If we rout the bees ourselves," said he, "the natives will regard us as their saviours, and we shall have no trouble with them afterward."

This was sound policy; even Somat had to admit it. He had decided to be a member of the expedition, for the reason that Rolla flatly refused to accompany the other men unless he, her special god, went along. His two liberal-minded friends stayed behind to take care of their belongings in the ruined city.

The expedition was a simple one. It consisted of a single large auto truck and trailer, the only items of automotive machinery that the twelve had been able to reconstruct from the ruins. However, these served the purpose; they carried large supplies of food, also means for protection against the bees, together with abundant material for routing them. A large quantity of crude explosives also was included. The trailer was large enough to seat everybody; and the ten men of the party had a good deal of amusement watching Rolla as she tried to get accustomed to that land of travel. She was glad enough when the end of the road was reached and the truck began to push its way into the wilderness, giving her an excuse to walk.

No need to describe the trip in detail. Within three days the truck was as far as it could go up the rock wall of the "edge." The point selected was about twenty miles west of where Cunora was hid, and directly opposite the upper end of her home valley. No attempt was made to go over the top as Rolla had done; instead, about two miles below the ridge a crevasse was located in the granite; and by means of some two tons of powder a narrow opening was made through to the other side. Through it the men carried their supplies on their backs, transferring everything to improvised sleds, a hundred pounds to a man.

While this was being done, Rolla hurried east and located Cunora. The girl was in a pitiful condition from lack of proper food, and comparative confinement and constant strain. But during Rolla's absence she had seen none of the bees.

"What are you going to do now?" she asked Rolla, after the explorer had told her story.

Rolla shrugged her shoulders indifferently. "These gods," she declared with sublime confidence, "can do no wrong! Whatever they propose must be for the best! I have done my part; now it is all in the hands of the Flowing Blossom!"

Not until they reached the head of the valley which had been her home did Rolla ask Somat as to the plan. He answered:

"Ye and the other woman shall stay here with me, on this hill." He produced a telescope. "We will watch with this eye-tube. The other nine men will go ahead and do the work."

"And will they separate?"

"Nay. They intend to conquer this colony first; then, after your people are freed and safely on the way to my country, the conquerors will proceed to the next valley, and so on until all are released." He kept his word not to warn Rolla of the proposed captivity. "In that way the fear of them will go ahead and make their way easy."

Meanwhile the nine were getting ready for their unprecedented conquest. They put on heavy leather clothes, also leather caps, gloves and boots. Around their faces were stiff wire nets, such as annoyed them all exceedingly and would have maddened Cunora or Rolla. But it meant safety.

As for weapons, they relied entirely upon fire. Each man carried a little wood alcohol in a flask, in case it was necessary to burn wet or green wood. Otherwise, their equipment was matches, with an emergency set of flint and steel as well. There could be no resisting them.

"We'll wait here till we've seen that you've succeeded," Somat told Deltos and Sorplee. "Then we'll follow."

The nine left the hills. The hours passed with Rolla and Cunora amusing themselves at the "eye-tube." They could see the very spot where their lovers were being punished; but some intervening bushes prevented seeing the men themselves. The other villagers were at work quite as usual; so it was plain that, although the bees were invisible, yet they were still the masters.

Hardly had the nine reached the first low-growing brush before they encountered some of the bees. None attempted to attack, but turned about and flew back to report. It was not long before Supreme, and therefore Billie, knew of the approaching raiders.

"They are doubtless provided with the magic flower," Supreme told her lieutenants. "You will watch the blossom as it sways in the wind, and keep always on the windward side of it. In this way you can attack the inferiors."

The word was passed, bee-fashion, until every soldier and worker in the colony knew her duty. The stingers were to keep back and watch their chance, while the workers harassed the attackers. Moreover, with the hives always uppermost in her mind, Supreme planned to keep the actual conflict always at a distance from the "city."

It was late in the day when the nine reached the stream in whose bed rested the pyrites taken from Corrus and Dulnop. This stream, it will be remembered, flowed not far from the torture-place. Deltos's plan was to rescue these two men before doing anything else; this, because it would strengthen the villagers' regard for the conquerors.

The bees seemed to sense this. They met the invaders about three miles above the village, in an open spot easily seen by the people with the telescope. And the encounter took place during twilight, just early enough to be visible from a distance, yet late enough to make the fire very impressive.

"Remember, it's the smoke as much as the flame," Deltos shouted to the others. "Just keep your torches on the move, and make as much fuss as you can!"

Next moment the swarm was upon them. It was like a vast cloud of soot; only, the buzzing of those millions of wings fairly drowned out every other sound. The nine had to signal to one another; shouting was useless.

Within a single minute the ground was covered with bees, either dead or insensible from the smoke. Yet the others never faltered. At times the insects battered against the wire netting with such force, and in such numbers, that the men had to fight them away in order to get enough air.

Supreme watched from above, and kept sending her lieutenants with fresh divisions to first one man and then another, as he became separated from the rest. Of course, nobody suffered but the bees. Never before had they swarmed a creature which did not succumb; but these inferiors with the queer things over their faces, and the cows' hides over their bodies and hands, seemed to care not at all. Supreme was puzzled.

"Keep it up," she ordered. "They surely cannot stand it much longer."

"It shall be done!"

And the bees were driven in upon the men, again and again. Always the torches were kept waving, so that the insects never could tell just where to attack. Always the men kept moving steadily down-stream; and as they marched they left in their wake a black path of dead and dying bees. Half of them had been soldier bees, carrying enough poison in their stings to destroy a nation. Yet, nine little matches were too much for them!

Presently the invaders had approached to within a half-mile of the torture-place. One of Supreme's lieutenants made a suggestion:

"Had we not better destroy the men, rather than let them be rescued?"

The commandant considered this fully. "No," she decided. "To kill them would merely enrage the other villagers, and perhaps anger them so much as to make them unmanageable." More than once a human had been driven so frantic as to utterly disregard orders. "We cannot slay them all."

The bees attacked with unabated fury. Not once did the insects falter; orders were orders, and always had been. What mattered it if death came to them, so long as the Hive lived? For that is bee philosophy.

And then, just when it seemed that the wisest thing would be to withdraw, Supreme got the greatest idea she had ever had. For once she felt positively enthusiastic. Had she been a human she would have yelled aloud for sheer joy.

"Attention!" to her subordinates. "We attack no more! Instead, go into the huts and drive all the inferiors here! Compel them to bring their tools! Kill all that refuse!"

The lieutenants only dimly grasped the idea. "What shall we do when we get them here?"

"Do? Drive them against the invaders, of course!"

It was a daring thought. None but a super bee could have conceived it. Off flew the lieutenants, with Supreme's inspired order humming after them:

"Call out every bee! And drive every last one of the inferiors to this spot!"

And thus it came about that, a minute later, the nine looked around to see the bees making off at top speed. Sorplee raised a cheer.

"Hurrah!" he shouted, and the rest took it up. Neither admitted that he was vastly relieved; it had been a little nerve-shaking to know that a single thickness of leather had been all that stood, for an hour, between him and certain death. The buzzing, too, was demoralizing.

"Now, to release the two men!" reminded Deltos, and led the way to the torture-place. They found Corrus and Dulnop exactly as the two women had left them six weeks before, except that their faces were drawn with the agony of what they had endured. Below the surface of the ground their bodies had shrivelled and whitened with their daily imprisonment. Only their spirits remained unchanged; they, of all the natives, had known what it was to feel superior.

For the last time they were dug out and helped to their feet. They could not stand by themselves, much less run; but it is not likely they would have fled. Somehow they knew that the strange head-coverings had human faces behind them. And scarcely had they been freed before Sorplee, glancing about, gave an exclamation of delight as he saw a group of natives running toward them.

"Just what we want!" he exclaimed. "They've seen the scrap, and realize that we've won!"

Looking around, the nine could see the other groups likewise hurrying their way. All told, there were a couple of hundred of the villagers, and all were armed with tools they knew how to use very well.

"Who shall do the honours?" asked Sorplee. "Wish Somat was here, to explain for us."

"Don't need him," reminded Deltos. "All we've got to do is to show these two fellows we dug up."

And it was not until the first of the villagers was within twenty yards that the nine suspected anything. Then they heard the buzzing. Looking closer, they saw that it was—an attack!

"Stop!" cried Deltos, in swift panic. "We are friends, not enemies!"

It was like talking to the wind. The villagers had their choice of two fears: either fight the strangers with the magic flower, or—be stung to death. And no one can blame them for what they chose.

The nine had time enough to snatch knives or hatchets from their belts, or clubs from the ground. Then, with wild cries of fear, the natives closed in. They fought as only desperate people can fight, caught between two fires. And they were two hundred to nine!

In half a minute the first of the invaders was down, his head crushed by a mattock in the hands of a bee-tormented native. In a single minute all were gone but two; and a moment later, Deltos alone, because he had chanced to secure a long club, was alive of all that crew.

For a minute he kept them off by sheer strength. He swung the stick with such vigour that he fairly cleared a circle for himself. The natives paused, howling and shrieking, before the final rush.

An inspiration came to Deltos. He tore his cap from his head and his net from his face.

"Look!" he screamed, above the uproar. "I am a man, like yourselves! Do not kill!"

Next second he froze in his tracks. The next he was writhing in the death agony, and the bees were supreme once more.

Supreme herself had stung Deltos.

340

15

OVERLOOKED

Of the four on the earth, Smith was the first to make any comment. He had considerable difficulty in throwing his thought to the others; somehow he felt slightly dazed.

"This is—unbelievable!" he said, and repeated it twice. "To think that those insects are still the masters!"

"I wish"—Billie's voice shook somewhat—"I wish almost that I had let you warn Rolla. It might have helped—" She broke off suddenly, intent upon something Supreme was hearing. "Just listen!"

"Quick!" a lieutenant was humming excitedly to the commandant. "Back to the hives; give the order, Supreme!"

It was done, and immediately the bees quit the throng of natives and their victims, rushing at top speed for their precious city. As they went, Supreme demanded an explanation.

"What is the meaning of this?"

For answer the lieutenant pointed her antennae straight ahead. At first Supreme could see nothing in the growing darkness; then she saw that some of the sky was blacker than the rest. Next she caught a faint glow.

"Supreme, the deadly flower has come to the hives!"

It was true! In ten minutes the city was near enough for the commandant to see it all very clearly. The fire had started on the windward side, and already had swept through half the hives!

"Quick!" the order was snapped out. "Into the remaining houses, and save the young!"

She herself led the horde. Straight into the face of the flames they flew, unquestioningly, unhesitantly. What was self, compared with the Hive?

Next moment, like a mammoth billow, the smoke rolled down upon them all. And thus it came about that the villagers, making their cautious way toward the bee city, shouted for joy and danced as they had never danced before, when they saw what had happened.

Not a bee was left alive. Every egg and larva was destroyed;

341

every queen was burned. And every last soldier and worker had lost her life in the vain attempt at rescue. Suddenly one of the villagers, who had been helping to carry Corrus and Dulnop to the spot, pointed out something on the other side of the fire! It was Rolla!

"Hail!" she shouted, hysterical with happiness as she ran toward her people. Cunora was close upon her heels. "Hail to the flowing flower!"

She held up a torch. Down fell the villagers to their knees. Holla strode forward and found Corrus, even as Cunora located her Dulnop.

"Hail to the flowing flower!" shouted Rolla again. "And hail to the free people of this world! A new day cometh for us all! The masters—are no more!"

The four on the earth looked at each other inquiringly. There was a heavy silence. The doctor stood it as long as he could, and then said:

"So far as I'm concerned, this ends our investigations." They stared at him uncomprehendingly; he went on: "I don't see anything to be gained by this type of study. Here we've investigated the conditions on two planets pretty thoroughly, and yet we can't agree upon what we've learned!

"Van still thinks that the upper classes should rule, despite all the misery we saw on Capellette! And Billie is still convinced that the working classes, and no others, should govern! This, in the face of what we've just—seen! Sanus is absolute proof of what must happen when one class tries to rule; conflict, bloodshed, misery—little else! Besides"—remembering something, and glancing at his watch—"besides, it's time for dinner."

Billie and Smith got to their feet, and in silence quit the room Billie and Van Emmon were still fumbling with their bracelets. The two young people rose from the chairs at the same time and started across the room to put flip bracelets away. The wire which connected them trailed in between and caught on the doctor's chair. It brought the two of them up short.

342

Van Emmon stared at the wire. He gave it a little tug. The chair did not move. Billie gave an answering jerk, with similar lack of results. Then they glanced swiftly at one another, and each stepped back enough to permit lifting the wire over the chair.

"In other words," Van Emmon stammered, with an effort to keep his voice steady—"in other words, Billie, we both had to give in a little, in order to get past that chair!"

Then he paused slightly, his heart pounding furiously.

"Yes Van." She dropped the bracelets. "And—as for me—Van, I didn't really want to see the bees win! I only pretended to—I wanted to make you—think!"

"Billie! I'll say 'cooperate' if you will!"

"Cooperate!"

He swept her into his arms, and held her so close that she could not see what had rushed to his eyes. "Speaking of cooperation," he remarked unsteadily, "reminds me—it takes two to make a kiss!"

They proceeded to experiment.

Printed in the United Kingdom
by Lightning Source UK Ltd.
135517UK00002B/66/P

9 781846 775581